Ancient
✳Nikopolis

AMVRAKIKOS
GULF

Preveza

Fort Aktion
(Actium)

PREVEZA
STRAIT

Roadstead

SAND
BANK

Levkas
Port

Ayios
Giorgios (Fortress)
Dredged channel
buoys

PORT
DREPANO

I S L A N D   o f   L E V K A S

Mara Point

SPARTI

SKROPIO

Port Vathy
Dessimo
Bay
Port Spiglia
TIGLIA
Spartokori
Mt. Porro
MEGANISI

Vatahori
Port Atheni
Elia Poir

1st Cave-shelter
2nd Cave-shelter
(painted caves)

Meganisi Channel

C. Dukato

ARKUDI

FORMICULA

D1327036

LEVKAS MAN

After eight years at sea and now a fugitive from Interpol, young Paul Van der Voort seeks temporary refuge in the house in Amsterdam where he had spent a strange childhood with his adoptive father, a dedicated anthropologist, with whom he has developed a peculiar love-hate relationship. He learns from Sonia, the attractive but concerned young neighbour, that his now ageing father is in Greece, doggedly pursuing his lone anthropological explorations. Fate, and an almost morbid fascination, seems to draw them both to the bare coastal region where Paul eventually finds the emaciated old man being hounded by security police and harassed by predatory colleagues. Against a background of tense Greek nationalism and the threat of war, Paul gradually uncovers the mystery of his father's past and realizes what it is that drives the old man on so relentlessly in trying to prove his own theories about man's origins. An unusual mingling of the academic and the violent, this absorbing story shows dramatically that the passage of time has not changed the primitive violent instincts inherent in man.

LEVKAS MAN

★

HAMMOND INNES

THE
COMPANION BOOK CLUB
LONDON

This edition, published in 1972 by
The Hamlyn Publishing Group Ltd,
is issued by arrangement with
William Collins, Sons & Co. Ltd.

THE COMPANION BOOK CLUB

The Club is not a library; all books are the
property of members. There is no entrance fee
or any payment beyond the low Club price of
each book. Details of membership will gladly
be sent on request.

Write to:

The Companion Book Club,
Borough Green, Sevenoaks, Kent

*Made and printed in Great Britain
for the Companion Book Club
by Odhams (Watford) Ltd.*
600871452

For
Brenda, Sarah and Theo,
and in memory of
Leonard

He carved the red deer and the bull
Upon the smooth cave rock . . .

And from the dead white eyes of them
The wind springs up anew,
It blows upon the trembling heart,
And bull and deer renew
Their flitting life in the dim past
When that dead Hunter drew.

W. J. TURNER

I: The House in Amsterdam

I

IT WAS SUNDAY, the street empty, the canal black under a louring sky. My footsteps sounded solitary on the cobbles and the years rolled back to childhood, every detail clear-etched on the retina of memory—the house barges moored by the bridge, flowers set out in pots on the pavement, the newsvendor on the corner. And then the house itself, shabbier than when I had seen it last. That had been two years ago when my ship had put into Rotterdam and some strange urge—a desire for reconciliation—had brought me here. The front door and all the windows had been freshly painted then, green like the linden trees. It had been summer; now it was March and the trees were bare.

My footsteps slowed as I neared the door, a reluctance, a sense of dread almost. Last time I had had a shipboard world behind me, a job and the companionship of men I knew. Now it was different. I could feel myself beginning to tremble as I felt once again the pull of the old man's personality. There had been no reconciliation, no renewal of our strange relationship. He had been away on one of his periodic bouts of travelling, rootling for old bones. And now, when I came seeking a temporary refuge . . . a fit of trembling reached down the muscles of my arm and into my hands. I paused, hesitating, summoning up the courage to face him again.

A small wind from the north blew cold down the gut of the canal between the old houses. The narrow gable, four storeys above me, had the date on it—1694—just below the jutting beam hooked for a pulley to hoist furniture in at the windows. I shivered, wondering why the hell I had come. The trembling reached into the pit of my stomach. It was nerves and quite uncontrollable. It had been like that in moments of stress since I was ten. I knew it would pass. It always did. But still I hesitated, unwilling to commit myself and step again into that

7

lonely, embittered world from which I had escaped eight years ago.

A car drove past me, its tyres drumming on the cobbles. A girl was driving it and the quick glance of her eyes broke the spell. I went up to the door and rang the bell, remembered that it had never worked and slammed the knocker twice. The sound of it was loud enough to wake the street, but nothing stirred within the house. I stood back then, looking up at the façade; the windows were all shut, and as I tried the knocker once again, a sense almost of relief flooded through me at the thought that he might be away and I would have the place to myself.

A gust of wind blew down the canal and a branch swayed above my head to the dry rattle of twigs. A leaf left over from the autumn fell at my feet, withered and browned by frost. I thought of all the times I had walked the streets with him. He had suffered from insomnia and sometimes he had woken me in the middle of the night to go out with him into the sleeping city; walking the streets and the banks of the canals had been a sort of sedative, a means of dulling the restless energy that drove his mind. In summer he had always worn sandals and an open-necked shirt. In winter his wiry body had been bulked out by an old goat-skin jacket, and always he had gone bare-headed, the stooped, white-maned figure with its shambling walk a familiar sight in Amsterdam. But as I had grown older he had been away more often.

The ring of keys was in my hand, still burnished bright from the years it had jostled in my pocket. Had he missed them, I wondered, remembering the loneliness, my sudden decision to go. The sun glimmered momentarily, the clouds black as ink. It looked like rain and the house stood silent, waiting. I pulled myself together then, found the key I wanted and inserted it into the Yale-type lock. The door slid open and I hesitated, the stillness of the house yawning before me. Then I picked up the suitcase I had bought the night I had abandoned the car in London and went into the house.

He was away. I could sense it the moment the door clicked shut behind me, the silence of the old house closing in. I thought of all the times I had been frightened here, frightened by his extraordinary magnetism, his unpredictable nature.

8

I hesitated, listening to the stillness that had closed about me. The wind sighed in the eaves and a board moved. As in all these old Amsterdam houses, the stairs were narrow and almost vertical, like a ladder leading to a loft, and the stair carpet showed thin and worn in the pale glimmer from the fanlight.

I forced myself to think why I was here, and gradually the trembling ceased, and my throat relaxed. I wasn't a child any longer and the house was empty, the old man no more than a ghostly presence. I had what I wanted—a refuge in which to lie low and time to sort myself out. That was all that mattered. I humped my suitcase up the stairs and went into the study on the first floor.

It was just as I remembered it, nothing changed; the big desk with the Anglepoise lamp, the heavy swivel chair padded in black leather, the bookshelves ranged along the wall opposite the windows, even the sombre velvet curtains and the marble clock on the mantelpiece. Though it was almost mid-day—a quarter to twelve, in fact—the room was shadowed and dark. The sun had gone, rain gusted against the windows. I switched the light on, put my suitcase down, and took off my raincoat. What I needed was money, Dutch money. And then a round of the dockside taverns to see what I could pick up.

I went over to the desk, where a pile of letters and journals lay as though awaiting his return. I tried the drawers, but with no success. They were crammed with old bills, bank statements, cheque stubs, correspondence dating back for years; in one I found my old school reports under a litter of broken pipes, birds' feathers and old tobacco tins. And in the bottom right-hand drawer, in an old cigar box full of letters I had written him from school, I came across a short note from my mother, written from Kenya, announcing my birth and asking him to be my godfather. Pinned to it was my birth certificate and the adoption papers that changed my name from Scott to Van der Voort. In another drawer was some correspondence about a mortgage, with the deed attached, and a bundle of letters relating to his mother's estate in South Africa, faded now and held together by a thick rubber band. And below these were the details of the sale of the boat. He had only had it just over a year and the sale had been within a few months of my leaving him.

As I straightened up, the clock on the mantelpiece struck twelve. Its beautiful, clear tinkling chime was so much a part of my memory of the room that I took it for granted. My eye was caught by the top letter on the pile of correspondence. It was from a Dr Gilmore in Cambridge, something about carbon-14 and a dating of 35-30,000 BP. Bones, of course, and the journals were all scientific. There were unpaid bills too, and right at the bottom a note from somebody who signed himself Alec Cartwright, confirming that he would be arriving in Belgrade with the Land-Rover on February 26.

So the old man had been gone at least three weeks.

I turned to the bureau then. That was where I'd found the cash I had needed as a kid. It stood in the corner opposite the door, a tall piece with glass-fronted shelves for books and a curved let-down flap, the walnut surface of it gleaming with the rich patina of the years. The glass case held the same collection of antique-bound books on the top shelf, the rest of it full of old bones and bits of worked flint—artefacts, he had called them. The word Mousterian came back to me, for the bones and the primitive flint axe-heads had had a certain fascination for me when I was about twelve years old. The picture my young mind had conjured up was of wild, hairy men emerging from caves to attack each other with blunt-bladed axes. I had even produced axes of my own, made with flint found at the bottom of a derelict barge, and he had shown me how to work them and how to bind the 'blade' to the wooden haft with leather thongs. But it was only a passing phase and I had lost interest after he had given me a hiding for gashing another boy's head open.

The contents of the top three shelves were exactly as I had last seen them, the skull in the same place, in the centre of the third shelf, a lower jaw and a few pieces of bone, the rest built up of a smooth, ivory-like composition. The bottom shelf was empty except for some small fragments of bone in the right-hand corner; there were some teeth amongst them that looked as though they were human teeth. It was on this shelf that he had kept the books he valued most—a first edition Darwin and several old-fashioned tomes, some in French, some in German. Breuil—that name came back to me—the Abbé Breuil, and Chardin. They were gone now, all except the worn leather-covered Bible. A slip of paper caught my eye and I opened the glass front and took it out. It was gummed paper and on it he had written: *skull-cap fragments and 2 teeth, Kyzyl Kum No. 3.*

Seeing his writing again after all these years, I stood there for a moment, the faded slip in my hand, remembering in detail the night I had surprised him sitting at the bureau with a pen in his hand and a leather-covered book in front of him. I had come down in my pyjamas, startled out of my sleep by a cry like that of a wounded animal. He was just sitting there, his head bowed in his hand and the book open in front of him. Something, the draught from the open door perhaps, had made him turn. I had never forgotten the strange look in his eyes, the shock my presence seemed to give him. For a moment he had been unable to speak, his whole body shaking as though the effort of control was almost beyond him.

And then, suddenly, he was himself again and he had quietly ordered me back to bed. But that was the last time I ever dared enter his study at night, and even in the daytime I always knocked first. And though it had happened at least fifteen years ago, the terror of that moment when he had turned and discovered me in the doorway, the blank look in his eyes, was so vivid that my hands were trembling again as I found the key that unlocked the flap below the glass-cased shelves.

But there was nothing in the satinwood drawers, only sheaves of paper covered with notes in his minute, spidery writing, and when I slid back the writing-top to reveal the secret cavity below, there was nothing there but letters; the leather-covered book he had always kept there—his journal, a diary, or whatever it was—had gone. The letters were in two bundles, each tied with string, the larger from somebody in Cambridge who signed himself Adrian. But it was the other bundle that caught and held my attention, for the writing was the same as in the letter I had found announcing my birth. They were signed Ruth, which was my mother's name, and they were love letters, each beginning *My Darling* or *Darling Peter*.

I sat there for a long time, staring at that bundle of letters—not reading them through, not wishing to pry, but disturbed, almost appalled, by the thought that they had once loved each other. I had never understood why, following the death of my parents, I had been sent half across the world to live with a man whose whole life was devoted to dusty digs and anthropology. He had never told me and I had never dared to ask. Now at last I knew, and the knowledge shocked me in a way I did not quite understand—as though a door, previously barred to me, had suddenly swung partly open.

I could only just remember her—tall and serious, full of warmth and a dark-eyed vitality, at moments very emotional. My father had been the complete opposite, a broad, sunburned man with a moustache and a voice that carried through the bush like the roar of a lion. It was the country I remembered mostly, and those last moments when the Mau-Mau had come to the farm.

I put the letters back unread, slid the writing-top over the cavity and unlocked the cupboard under the flap. But all I found there was an album of snapshots, myself mostly at various ages between ten and nineteen, though the first few pages were taken up with faded pictures of an old stone farmhouse, of himself as a boy with his parents—Edwardian figures against a background of overhanging cliffs and a winding river. A cutting from a French newspaper had been pasted in and a letter signed 'H. Breuil'. His boyhood, I remembered, had been spent in France. Also in the cupboard were some models of boats I had made and a chess set; he had tried to teach me chess once. At the back were old copies of the *American Journal of Anthropology*, but nothing of value, and I got to my feet, looking round for something I could raise some money on.

The two Greek statues on the mantelpiece were no longer there and the clock was too heavy. The wind outside had dropped and in the stillness I could hear it ticking. It was an eight-day clock and he had always wound it first thing Sunday morning. The sound of it, so faint, yet so persistent, held me rooted to the spot for a moment. Somebody had been in this room, somebody who knew his routine.

The key was where he had always kept it, in the old clay tobacco jar to the right of the mantelpiece, and when I fitted it into one of the holes in the clock's white face, it only turned twice before the spring was fully wound. Whoever it was had been in the study within the last two days. I wiped my fingers across the clock's marble top, down the whole length of the mantelpiece, but no dust showed. The bureau was the same, the desk, too. I couldn't understand it. He had never had a housekeeper or even a woman in to clean. He had always looked after the place himself, and we had made our own beds, got our own meals—a bachelor existence.

In the tiny dining room opposite the study, everything was clean. But the bits of silver, the salvers and the rather ornate candlesticks, were gone, put away perhaps for safe keeping. I went upstairs. In the spare room I found blankets and an eiderdown neatly stacked at the foot of the bed, and in the drawer of the dressing table there were hairpins and a dusting of powder. The room had a faintly alien smell, quite different from the rest of the house.

I crossed the landing to my own room. The bed was completely stripped and nothing had been altered since my abrupt departure. I stood for a moment in the open door, a world of memories flooding back. My first chart, stolen from a vessel in the docks, had been studied at that table by the window. The window was closed now, but on summer nights . . . it looked out on to the backs of houses, each window, as the lights went up, revealing glimpses of other boxed-in worlds, and of that girl; my eyes switched involuntarily to the second-floor window of the old grey house opposite, where she had undressed so slowly through the hot nights of that last summer.

I closed the door quietly, shutting out the tawdry memories of adolescence, and was standing at the head of the stairs, considering what to do next, when I heard the click of the front door closing, and then the creak of the stairboards, the sound of somebody climbing, slowly, hesitantly.

I thought at first it was the old man and my body froze. But then a woman's voice called out, 'Who is it? Who's there?'

I shrank back into the shadows and the house was suddenly still.

'Is anybody there?' Her voice sounded scared. I thought I could hear her breathing. The footsteps started to climb again.

There was no point in staying where I was. The light was on in the study and she would see my suitcase. I went down the stairs and I could feel her waiting, breathless, on the landing. We met outside the study door and she said, 'Who are you?

What are you doing here?' Her voice was pitched high, barely controlled. I could almost smell her fear as she stood very still, peering up at me in the half-light that filtered through from the fanlight at the bottom of the stairs. Then she gave a little gasp. 'You're Paul Van der Voort, aren't you?'

'Yes.'

Her face was no more than a pale oval, her head, outlined in silhouette, was bare.

'What are you doing here? How did you get in? I saw the light. . . .' And then: 'You had your keys, of course.' And she added, the whole timbre of her voice changed, 'There's nothing for you here, no money—nothing that would interest you.' The nervousness was gone, cold anger in its place: 'And if it's his Journal you're after, you won't find it. There's nothing for you here—nothing at all. They shouldn't have sent you.'

'What the hell are you talking about?' I stepped past her and thrust open the study door. 'Come in here where we can talk.' I wanted to see who she was, what she looked like.

'No. I'll go now.' The nervousness was back in her voice. 'I'd no idea it was you. I thought . . .' But by then I had her by the arm and had pushed her through into the light. She was younger than I had expected, a plain-looking girl with large eyes and wet, straw-coloured hair cut like a boy's. She wore a plastic mac that dripped water.

'Now then,' I said, closing the study door. 'Let's start with your name.'

She hesitated, then said 'Sonia Winters.'

'English?'

'Half-English.'

'How did you recognize me?'

'The photograph in his bedroom. Another in your old room.'

'You don't look like a housekeeper.'

She shook her head.

'Then why have you got the keys to the house?'

She didn't say anything, but just stood there, staring at me with hostile eyes, her breath coming quickly as though she had been running.

I was certain she wasn't a relative. I don't think he had any relatives—either he had alienated them or else they were all dead. And then I remembered the pile of opened letters on the desk. 'You were acting as his secretary, is that it?'

'I did some typing for him. I live just across the canal. And then when he became ill I looked after him.'

'When was that?'

'About three months ago.'

'And you lived here?'

'For a week or two. It was pleurisy. He had to have someone to look after him.'

'And where is he now?'

She hesitated. 'Somewhere in Macedonia. I'm not sure where. He wouldn't think of writing to me. But my brother's with him and I had a card from Hans recently, posted at Skopje, which is in the south of Yugoslavia.' She stared at me. 'Why are you here? What have you come back for after all these years?'

'I need some money and a roof over my head.'

'Well, there's no money here,' she snapped. 'The house is mortgaged, even the furniture, everything's sold that could be sold.'

'You mean he's pawned the house to go looking for bones in Macedonia?'

That seemed to get her on the raw. 'You don't understand him, do you?' she blazed. 'You never did. He's one of the world's most brilliant palæontologists and it means nothing to you. No wonder he spoke of you with contempt. You owed him everything—education, your upbringing, a roof over your head, even the food you ate, everything. And what did you do? Got yourself expelled, mixed with the riff-raff of the docks, stole, lied, beat people up, landed in jail. . . .'

'You seem to know quite a lot about me.'

'Yes, I do—and everything I've heard about you sickens me. You left him like a thief in the night, and now you come back——'

'It wasn't all my fault,' I said quietly. 'He's a very strange man and he expected too much.'

'You took everything—gave nothing. Of all the heartless, selfish people . . . you didn't even answer his letters.'

'I came to see him two years ago. But he was away. He always seemed to be away.'

She sighed. 'You could still have answered his letters. He was lonely. Didn't you realize that? No, I suppose not. You wouldn't understand what it's like to be alone in the world. But you could have written. That was the least you could have done.' She gave a little shiver and drew her dripping mac tight to her body. 'I'll go now. I can't stop you staying here, but I warn you, if I find anything missing, I'll call the police.'

She was halfway through the doorway when I stopped her. 'Have you any Dutch money on you?'

She turned, her eyes wide. And then after a moment she felt in the pocket of her slacks and produced a 20-guilder note from a purse. She seemed surprised when I offered her two pound notes in exchange. 'No,' she said quickly. 'No, it's all right. I expect you need it.' She looked at me speculatively for a moment, and then she was gone. I listened to her footsteps on the stairs, the sound of the front door closing, and from the window I watched as she crossed the bridge by the house barges and walked quickly down the other side of the canal, head bent against the rain and the lash of the wind. The house she entered was almost directly opposite.

It was unfortunate. She'd probably talk and I wondered what her father did. It would take time for them to trace me to Amsterdam, but it was dangerous and I'd need to move that bit faster. I switched out the light, put my raincoat on and went quickly down the stairs, cursing myself again for having involved myself in somebody else's troubles. I could still see the look on the man's face, the heavy jowls, the small eyes wide with sudden fear—bastards like that shouldn't be allowed to do their dirty political work in a free country.

I could have shipped out in a tanker that night. Stolk tipped me off in the Prins Hendrik by the Oosterdok. But it was bound for Libya, a quick turn-round and back to Amsterdam again. And anyway I was tired of ship routine. I had a feeling that this was a sort of crossroads in my life, that what I had done must lead me on to some new road. The sea was all I knew, but the sea is wide—Australia or South America, I thought. I wanted a new world, a new life. I was twenty-seven.

Dusk was falling, the night sky darkening over the Amstel river, when I finally found my way to Wilhelm Borg's shop on Amsteldijk. I hadn't seen him since the days when I'd been mixed up with his gang of dockside toughs. Quite a few Dutchmen had crossed my path in the five years that I had been at sea and Borg was reputed to handle anything from fake antiques to a lorry-load of Scotch. He had put on weight since I had seen him last. He looked prosperous now and the old oak furniture and brasswork in his shop were certainly not fakes.

He took me through into an office at the back, gave me a drink and listened while I talked. His round face was as innocent-looking as ever, but his eyes were colder. 'You want a change, eh—something different. Why come to me?' He spoke Dutch with a Friesland accent. His family, I remembered, had been barge people from Delfzijl.

'Why does any man come to you?' I left it at that, not telling him I was on the run, but I think he guessed it.

I was talking to him for about half an hour before he said, 'There are some things I want out of Turkey, collectors' pieces. You could be just the man.'

'Smuggling?' I asked.

He smiled. 'For you it would be just a pleasant little holiday. The sort of break I think perhaps you are needing. You charter a boat—out of Malta, I think—for a cruise in the Aegean. You go to Crete and Rhodes, behaving all the time like a tourist—eating in the tavernas, visiting the ruins of Knossos, the fortress of the Knights of St John. And then you go north to Kos, possibly to Samos. Both these islands are very close to Turkey. It's not organized yet, but you will almost certainly be making delivery to my clients somewhere off the Tunisian coast.' He lumbered to his feet. 'Think about it, eh?'

It was something, the escape door opening. Dangerous probably, but I didn't care. The Eastern Mediterranean, full of islands—you could lose yourself there, change jobs, change a name. 'How much?' I asked.

He laughed and patted my shoulder. 'You make up your mind, then we talk business.'

I got him to change one of the two fivers I had with me, and that was that. It wouldn't get me to Australia or South America, but it was something to fall back on if things went wrong. I went to the *Bali* and stuffed myself full of Indonesian food.

It was about ten before I got back to the house, and when I switched the light on in the study, I found the curtains drawn and a note placed carefully on top of my suitcase. It said: *Dr Gilmore is in Amsterdam. He is another 'bone' man and he would like to see you. I will bring him to the house at 11 a.m. tomorrow. Please be in.* The writing was round and feminine. She hadn't bothered to sign it.

I crossed to the desk and read the letter I had glanced at before. Dr Gilmore's world and the world of Wilhelm Borg were poles apart. I found it difficult to adjust my mind to the fact that here was a doctor of something or other at Cambridge University who seemed greatly excited over a piece of bone the old man had sent him. *If you are right and this belongs to Cro-Magnon Man, then I don't need to tell you how important it is. The dating puts it earlier than Les Eyzies or subsequent finds. I respect and understand your secrecy, but in view of the importance of this discovery I feel you have no right to keep the location to yourself. I have agreed to attend a conference at the Hague and will be arriving in Amsterdam on Sunday, March 16 . . .*

Now, I was being asked to see him instead, and I wondered what the point was as I carried my suitcase up to my old room. There I found the bed had been made up ready for me. It seemed an odd gesture in view of the things she had said. The water heater had been switched on, too, so that I was able to have a bath, which I badly needed. Lying there, naked and relaxed, I was amused by the girl's clumsy attempts to involve me. I was also mildly curious, so that after my bath I went back down to the bureau in the study and got the bundle of Cambridge letters from the secret cavity.

The signature was the same untidy scrawl, but they told me little about Dr Gilmore. They were chiefly answers to scientific queries, all typewritten and highly technical, except one, which was in the Doctor's untidy hand and might almost have been referring to some criminal activity. *Whilst I sympathize with you, I cannot, of course, condone. What you have done places you beyond the pale. Whatever you write, whatever you discover from now on, will be suspect. You have affronted the moral rectitude of a world that, whilst often confusing truth, believes in it absolutely. However, whilst I cannot obviously defend your conduct in public, I want you to know that I understand and wish that it will make no difference to our long-*

standing friendship. That was all. Nothing stated, only implied. The notepaper was headed Trinity College, Cambridge, and dated April 21, 1935.

It was a long time ago now, but like the love letters from my mother, it had obviously been put there for greater secrecy. I found some Fuckink geneva in the usual place in the dining room sideboard, and as I sipped the old familiar liquor and browsed through his bookshelves, I wondered what he had done that had brought such a severe reprimand from a man who seemed to have been both tutor and a life-long friend.

The books ranged over everything associated with anthropology, and words and dates, sometimes whole passages, had been underlined; most of them had notes scribbled in the margin. A passage about the behaviour of an unusual insect caught my eye, chiefly because I had actually seen the coral-coloured flower take wing and it took me back to the dim-remembered life in Kenya.

The oblong blossom of this artificial flower is formed by the clustering of moths on a dead twig. An example of insect camouflage—yes, but it is something much more. Shake the twig and the moths rise in flight, then after a while they settle again on the twig and for a moment they are just moths of different colours crawling over each other with no apparent purpose. But purpose there is, for in another moment order has replaced chaos and, suddenly, there is the flower again, the full flower, all coral—so perfect a blaze, so natural a form that humans are fooled into leaning down for the scent and birds ignore it in their flighting search for food. But there is more to this wonder yet, for the flattids have not assumed a natural camouflage; there is, in fact, no real blossom that approximates to the form they take instinctively. They have thought this form up for themselves, creating it in the same way that an abstract painter creates a picture. And if you breed these little insects, you will find that each batch of eggs produces at least one with all-green wings, whose place will always be at the tip, several with shades of green tinged with coral, and the rest pure coral. In other words, the whole fantastic hoax is self-perpetuating from the egg to the twig.

For some reason insects and birds had meant more to me in those early years in Kenya than all the big game. Even the long journeys through the bush in the battered old Plymouth were remembered chiefly for the birds around Lake Victoria. The passage was heavily underlined with a date scribbled in the margin. And on the second shelf I found an album of photographs with pictures of caves and digs. One of them, heavily ringed in red, was of a scattering of bones, including the lower jaw and part of a cranium that looked human, laid out in the dirt at the bottom of some pit. Against the picture he had written: *Only a hundred miles from Olduvai!* The picture was not a very clear one, but further on in the album they became sharper and less faded, as though he had been able to switch to a better camera, and the captions ranged from Africa to Turkey, even Russia.

It seemed strange that he had never been able to communicate his own enthusiasm to me. I could remember his voice, dry and detached, talking about bones and flints and ape-men with long, impossible names, and it had all meant nothing to me, nothing at all. No doubt I was a great disappointment to him, but I couldn't help being the boy I was, and beating me hadn't helped. I could remember those beatings more distinctly than anything he had ever told me—his impatience, that barely concealed sadistic streak.

The books, and the geneva perhaps, made me feel suddenly sad. If he had gone about it differently, our relationship might have been changed. My life, my outlook, my whole behaviour pattern, too. I had finished my drink and was just on the point of going to bed, when my eye was caught by a group of foreign books on the bottom shelf, the dust wrappers still on and the titles curiously anonymous in an unknown alphabet. They contained no marked passages, no notes, but some of the pictures had been reproduced from the photographs in the album. They were, in fact, duplicate copies of two titles published in Russian. And on the same shelf, I found other copies published in Berlin, Prague and Warsaw. The East German edition carried his name in recognizable print—Dr P. H. Van der Voort. I could find no sign of an English, or even a Dutch edition. He had always disliked the English, but that did not explain why his work only seemed to be recognized by the Iron Curtain countries.

I went to bed then. The wind had died, the rain had stopped. The house was very still as I lay thinking of the last time I had slept in that room, the urgent desire I had had to get away, the wild plans I had made. Now, once again, I had plans to make and it was a long time before I could get to sleep.

The sun was shining when I woke next morning. It was late and by the time I had been out for coffee it was almost eleven. I got back to the house only a few minutes before they arrived. Dr Gilmore was small, neat and very alert for his age. 'So you're Pieter Van der Voort's son.' His hand was dry and barely touched mine, but his eyes and his smile had extraordinary warmth.

'Dr Gilmore is a palæontologist also,' the girl said.

'Which means what exactly?' It was a word I had never really understood.

Dr Gilmore smiled. 'Put crudely, I'm a bone man—an expert on all types of fossils. It derives from the Greek: palaios—old; ontologia—the study of being. I like to think it was because he studied under me that your father specialized in palæontology.'

'I always thought of him as an anthropologist.'

'Anthropology is a broad term covering the whole study of man.'

'Dr Gilmore is a leading authority on Stone Age Man,' the girl said. 'He is the author of *Neolithic Settlements of Eastern Europe.*'

I took them up to the study and the old man paused in the doorway, his eyes travelling over the room. 'I take it that this is where Pieter worked. I often wondered . . .' His gaze went unerringly to the bureau and he walked over to it and stood for a moment, peering closely at the skull and the artefacts. He was like a bird, his eyes bright, his movements quick. But age showed in the stoop of his shoulders and in the dry, parchment texture of his skin, which was slightly chapped with the winter's cold. 'There you are, Miss Winters,' he said, turning to the girl. 'That's what all the trouble was about.' His voice, his whole manner, was extraordinarily boyish. He shook his head. 'Too clever. Too clever by half, you see.'

I sat him down at the desk and offered him a cigarette. He hesitated, smiling quietly to himself. 'I have been told to cut down smoking.' But he took one all the same and I lit it for him.

'You wanted to see me,' I said.

21

He nodded and leaned back in the swivel chair, holding the cigarette between thumb and forefinger, puffing at it quickly, drawing the smoke into his lungs. 'But I don't know whether it will help. I was hoping to find you—' he hesitated—'a more academic type. Now I'm not certain that it will do any good, particularly as I gather you haven't seen your father for some time.'

'Not for eight years,' I said.

'It's as long as that, is it?'

'We didn't get on very well. . . .'

'No, no—I understand. Miss Winters has told me something of your relationship. A very difficult man. Very brilliant. Too brilliant in some ways. I would go further—a genius. Men of that calibre are never easy to live with.' He waved his hand at me. 'Sit down, my dear fellow, sit down.'

I hesitated. As long as I was standing I felt I could cut the interview short. I didn't see what he wanted, why the girl had brought him here. And I didn't want to get involved. 'I know nothing about his world——'

'Of course. I understand. And that makes it very difficult for me—to explain my sense of uneasiness.' He looked at me, a long, appraising stare, his eyes grey like pebbles as they caught the light from the windows. 'But perhaps that's an advantage —that you know nothing about his world.' And then he surprised me by saying, 'I met your mother once. In London during the last war—1942, I think; I was up for a meeting of the Royal Society and he brought her to see me at my hotel. A charming woman, very good for him. Gave him confidence. They should have married.' He was smiling to himself, a gentle, quiet smile. 'Companionship of that sort would have made all the difference. She had a strong, unselfish personality.'

'He has a strong personality, too,' I said, wondering at his reference to a sense of uneasiness.

'Yes, but not unselfish.' And then abruptly he said, 'He kept a journal. Has done for many years. Did you know that?'

'A leather-covered book?'

He nodded.

'Yes,' I said. 'There's a secret cavity in the bureau over there. That's where he kept it.' And without thinking I told him how I had once surprised him writing in it.

He nodded. 'Yes, that would be it. A very personal document.'

'Well, it's not in the usual place,' I said, thinking that that was what he had come for. 'I imagine he's taken it with him.'

But he shook his head. 'No, I have it. And there are altogether three volumes of it now. I've just read them. That's why I wanted to see him. It's a very strange, very disturbing record—not a diary exactly, something much deeper, more personal. It covers about twenty years of his life—intermittent entries, about himself, his thoughts, his inmost fears and hopes. And then suddenly, when he was ill . . .' He stopped there and turned to the girl. 'You tell him, Miss Winters. It will have more immediacy coming from you.'

She nodded. 'He was going to burn it. That was the night I telephoned for a doctor. He had me light a fire here in the study. He was in bed at the time. I thought perhaps he was feeling better, and then he sent me out for something. When I came back, I found him down here, half-collapsed in his chair, and the Journals were lying on the floor. Several pages had already been ripped out and their charred remains were lying in the grate. When I asked him why he had done it, he said, "I don't want him to have it. I don't want anybody to have it." And he asked me to put it on the fire for him. "That's the best place for it".'

She was sitting very tense, her hands clasped tight in her lap. And when I asked her who it was he wanted to conceal the journal from, she looked at me, her eyes wide. 'Why, from you, of course.' And she added, 'But I wouldn't do it. I refused. And when he began to recover, I think he was glad. In the end he sent it to Dr Gilmore. I posted it for him just before he left. He was up half the night writing a letter of explanation.'

Gilmore nodded. 'It needed explanation. In toto it amounts to an indictment of Man based on a self portrait as it were.' He hesitated. 'This is something it may be difficult for you to understand. A practical man, you're naturally impatient of the sort of introspective self-analysis on which Pieter Van der Voort was engaged. "Probing the ultimate depths of Man's aggressive instincts," he called it, and he talked of the Devil and a spiritual struggle. It's all there, all his instinctual urges—

23

the good and the bad. It goes back to his original thesis.' And he added a little wistfully, 'I should have come here before—as soon as I had read it. A man like that—alone, delving into the fundamental problems of mankind. . . . I should have come at once.'

'Then why didn't you?' I asked.

'My dear fellow, if one did everything one ought to . . . But I did come here once. When was it? In 1954, I think, for a conference rather like the one that has brought me to Holland now. But there was nobody here, the house empty. He was in Russia, and of course his reputation . . .' He gave a little sigh. 'You must realize I had an official position.'

'But since you retired,' I said. 'Surely you could have——'

'My dear boy.' He held up his hand, smiling. 'That is just the point. Until last vac I was still teaching, still Reader in Physical Anthropology. Then all the business of handing over. I had the money to travel—a stroke of extraordinary luck—but never the time. Students are very demanding and to teach well . . .' He drew a last puff from his cigarette and stubbed it out in the onyx bowl on the desk that had come from Turkey. 'How I envy men like Teilhard de Chardin—Java Man, Pekin Man, off to Africa to check on Leakey's discoveries. As a Jesuit he had his problems, but he wasn't tied to generations of students. And your father—I even envy him, too, in a way. You know he was brought up in France? His family had a house at St Leon-sur-Vézère and he had the priceless advantage of coming under the influence of the Abbé Breuil at the precocious age of eleven. This was when Breuil and other French savants were digging into the limestone caves of the Vézère to reveal more and more engravings and paintings done by men fifteen to sixty thousand years ago. It was a remarkable experience for a young boy and it set him on his way at a very early age, marked him for life, you might say.'

He leaned back, his eyes half-closed. 'Breuil, Peyrony, Capitan, Rivière—he met them all at the most impressionable age, squirming down limestone cracks, exploring caves that no man had been in for thousands of years. It was not only the savants, you see, it was the fact that he was living and breathing the prehistory of a long dead age of Man's evolution.' He nodded his head slowly, opening his eyes to gaze out of the window. 'A boy with that background . . .' He sighed, I think in envy. 'Hardly surprising that he was the most dedicated student I ever had through my hands. But the thesis he elected to work on . . . it was on the Weapon as the basis of Man's development.' He shook his head, smiling a little sadly. 'They didn't like it, of course. It was just after the first war and he was ahead of his time. He only just scraped through, and that annoyed him. He went off to South Africa, where his family still had relations. In fact, I think they returned there just before the Germans invaded France in 1940.'

He looked down at his hands, frowning. 'Pieter's sensitivity was always his greatest weakness.' He made a little movement of his hands, a gesture almost of helplessness. 'And to choose a thesis like that. . . .' He shook his head, reaching for the packet of cigarettes I'd left on the desk, and when he had taken one, he sat staring out over the canal, his eyes half-closed, tapping it against the edge of the desk. 'It was flying in the face of accepted thinking, and of the Church, of course. Man the Tool-maker was one thing. Man the Weapon-maker . . .' He smiled and lit the cigarette. 'Now, after a second world war, after Korea, Vietnam, Nigeria, the Middle East, the pendulum has swung—from optimism we have switched to pessimism, forgetting Man the Thinker—that we have within us the power of good as well as of evil.' The grey eyes, turned inwards, suddenly stared directly at me. 'Eight years—that's a long time. Do you know what he looks like now?'

'He can't have changed all that much,' I said.

'Perhaps not.' He reached into his pocket and pulled out an envelope. 'To me, of course, he has aged a great deal—beyond his years. And that in itself is disturbing. But it is the loneliness, the absorption. . . .' He pulled two photographs from the envelope and passed them across to me. 'They were taken in Greece last year by John Cassellis, a young American who studied under me. Pieter had written to me that, after investigating a possible site in the Jannina area, he had worked his way down to the coast and found nothing, but that he was now engaged on a dig that might prove of considerable importance. He didn't say where it was, but his letter was postmarked *Levkas*. It's one of the Ionian islands on the west coast of Greece and I suggested to Cassellis, who was doing a tour of the Aegean and Asia Minor, that he try and locate him. I thought he might be of some use to Pieter since the boy had time to spare.'

They were colour prints enlarged to postcard size. The first showed the curve of a cliff overhang, dark in shadow, with a glimpse of blue sea beyond. A figure was seated cross-legged in the foreground, bare to the waist, his thin body burned almost black by the sun. He had a piece of stone in his hand and he was examining it, his head bent, his face in shadow and half obscured by his white hair.

'Now look at the second,' Gilmore said. 'Cassellis was using a ciné-camera and it's a frame from a shot taken at the moment Pieter looked up to find a stranger intruding on his territory.'

He had zoomed in on the figure itself. The old man was staring straight at the camera, his hands hovering protectively over the stone. 'What is it?' I asked. 'He's trying to conceal it.'

'A stone lamp, I think.'

But I barely heard him. I was staring at the face, so lined and aged, and the expression secretive, almost hostile, like a dog guarding a bone. 'Is that stone important?' I asked.

'Perhaps—I don't know. And Cassellis didn't comment, or even say where he'd found him—only that he was on his own. *A very lonely figure* was the way he put it in the letter he wrote me, and that's not good. Not at his age and with his background.'

I handed the photographs back to him. 'What are you suggesting—that he's in danger of going mad?' It seemed the only conclusion to be drawn from what he was saying, and it didn't altogether surprise me.

'Mad?' His eyes flicked open, staring at me, grey and direct. 'You tell me what madness is. A man who is mad is only somebody who has moved on to a different mental plane. However . . .' He gave a little shrug. 'My thoughts are of no concern to you. You're young, full of life, and I'm old enough to dwell, a little unhealthily perhaps, on the final frontiers of the mind.' He paused, still staring at me. 'You're different. I can see that. You will be very good for him.' He cocked an eyebrow at me, waiting.

I didn't say anything, and after a moment he went on, 'Miss Winters has told me about a book he is writing. The self-analysis of his Journal forms the basis, and this has so coloured his view of world events, of the urges that produce mob violence in a world where man has proliferated to the limits of natural tolerance, that it is leading him inevitably to the conclusion that modern man is a rogue species and doomed. This gloomy view ignores the fact that man's aggressive instincts are the mainspring of all his achievements.'

I thought of my own aggressive instincts, the way my fist, my whole body had moved, and the man going backwards over the edge of the oil pier, that last thin, high-pitched cry, and the way the other man had closed in, his features distorted by the need to attack.

'I can't help him,' I said. 'I've told you, we don't get on together. We've nothing in common.'

'He's your father.'

'By adoption.'

He looked at me for a while, not saying anything, and the directness of his gaze gave me an uneasy feeling, as though there were something he hadn't told me. 'I'm almost eighty,' he said finally. 'Too old to go out myself. Miss Winters has offered to go. But it would be difficult for a girl. Anyway, that isn't the answer. He needs your sort of strength. Particularly now, when he has made what may prove to be an important discovery. He will have great difficulty in convincing the academic world.'

'Why, if he's as brilliant as you say?' I was thinking of the books on the shelf behind me. 'He's published in Russia. If they recognize him . . .'

But he shook his head. 'The Russians backed him because his writing was helpful to the Soviet image. With their money he was able to lead expeditions to the Caucasian mountains, to Turkey and up through Georgia into Kazak, one I believe as far as Tashkent, and the books he wrote as a result both supported the view that *homo sapiens sapiens* came from the east; in other words, that civilized man stemmed from the Soviet Union. But now he certainly hasn't the support of the Russians, for he's changed his line of thinking. As a result, he's had to go it alone, using his own resources.'

'He's nothing left now,' the girl said. 'This is the third expedition he's financed. He's operating on a shoe-string and in such a hurry he's gone out into the mountains of Macedonia before the winter is over. He's killing himself.'

'To prove what?' I asked.

'That modern man came north, from Africa.'

'Does it matter?'

'Not to you,' she said tartly.

Dr Gilmore sighed. 'I appreciate that it's difficult for you to understand, but Good God! If I were your age and gifted with a brilliant father . . .'

'He's not my father,' I said curtly. 'He adopted me. That's all.'

His eyebrows lifted and then he stubbed out the half-smoked cigarette. 'Very well. But at least I have told you what I felt you should know. What you do about it is your own affair. I can only repeat that in my view he needs you very badly indeed.' He glanced at his watch and turned to the girl. 'I have to go now. Professor Hecht is expecting me at noon.' He got to his feet.

I opened the door for him and he paused momentarily, taking in the room again with that alert, bird-like glance of his. 'A pity,' he murmured. 'If I could only have talked with him myself. . . .' He gave me a long, searching look, and I thought for a moment he was going to appeal to me again. But then he turned and went down the stairs with astonishing agility.

I was lucky enough to find a taxi for him and as he stepped into it, he touched me on the arm. 'Think about what I have told you. Pieter Van der Voort is a very remarkable man, but he should not be too much alone.' He got in then and the taxi drove off, leaving me standing there with the girl. It was a perfect spring morning, the canal a bright gleam under the arches of the bridge, the sky a cloudless blue. It was an awkward moment, the silence stretching between us like a gulf.

Finally she said, 'You don't intend to do anything, do you— about your father?'

'No.'

She stared at me, her tight little face cold and hostile. Finally, she turned without a word, and walked away towards the bridge. I watched her go, and when I went back into the house it seemed more empty than ever. I sat in the chair where Dr Gilmore had sat, staring out over the canal and thinking about what he had told me. I had never thought of the old man as being important in the academic world. A genius, he had said —and difficult to live with. He had certainly been that; but now time and the emptiness of the house made it all seem different, the shadow of his personality touched with greatness. I was beginning to realize what I had been living with. And his loneliness—that was something even I could understand.

But his world was not mine and right now I had more immediate problems facing me. I got my raincoat and went out into the roar of the traffic, walking quickly towards the docks. Five hours and a lot of drinking later I got wind of a vacancy on an ore carrier completing repairs at a shipyard in the Maas. The third officer had been taken to hospital with suspected peritonitis and the ship was sailing next day for Seven Islands in the St Lawrence. I went back to the house to get my case, intending to spend the night in Rotterdam and be at the yard first thing in the morning. Drinking around the dockside taverns costs money and I had changed my last fiver by the time it was dusk.

It had been a long day and my feet seemed barely connected to my body as I stumbled back along the canal. The house barges all had their lights on, the square, hulked shapes warmed by the lit curtains. In some the curtains had been left drawn back in the manner of the Dutch country towns, and in these I glimpsed the comfort of families at home, the flicker of TV sets. It was cold, a touch of frost in the air, and mist was hanging like a grey veil over the waters of the canal.

In my stumbling haste, I nearly passed the house. I checked, and focused carefully on the traffic. It was the evening rush hour and they drive fast in Amsterdam. Standing there, waiting to cross, I gradually registered the fact that there were lights on in the house, the fanlight over the door and the tall windows above. I crossed the road, fumbled the key into the lock, and hauled myself up the stairs by the rope hand-support, impatience and anger mounting in me at the unwelcome intrusion.

I found her waiting for me in the study, sitting in the swivel chair with a book in her lap and the curves of her body picked out by the Anglepoise lamp. 'What the hell are you doing here?' My voice sounded thick in my ears. She had turned at my entrance and her face was in shadow, so that I could not see her expression. But I could guess what she was thinking, and that made me angrier still. 'There's no point in your talking to me. I've got the chance of a ship and I'm leaving for Rotterdam right away.'

'A ship?' I could almost hear her waiting for an explanation.

'I'm a ship's officer—I forgot to tell you.' I was just at the stage where sarcasm sounds clever.

'Oh—then I don't quite understand. A Mynheer Borg called while you were out. He seemed under the impression that you were going on some sort of a yachting trip in the Mediterranean.'

'Why didn't he phone?'

'He couldn't. There isn't a phone here any more. The electricity would have been cut off by now, too, if they hadn't muddled the dates.'

I leaned against the bureau, my head touching the glass. It was cool, the skull right under my nose and my eyes trying to focus on the cracks between plaster and bone. 'Borg shouldn't have come here,' I muttered. 'What did he want?'

'I've no idea,' she said coldly. 'He mentioned that he'd seen something he thought would interest you in an English newspaper.' I could feel her working herself up into a cold fury. 'I've been waiting for you all afternoon. This morning I had a letter from my brother. I'd like you to read it. Or are you too drunk?'

'You read it for me,' I said, 'while I go up and pack.' What the hell did I care about her damned brother? What was his name? Hans? Yes—Hans. Well, to hell with him, it was Borg that worried me, and I turned to go.

She must have got up from the chair very quickly, for suddenly she was there, between me and the door. 'You can read Dutch, can't you?'

I nodded automatically and she thrust the sheet of paper at me. 'Read it then.'

The light was on her face now and I could see her quite plainly. She looked pale and tired, very intense. I pushed the letter aside. 'I have to hurry.' I didn't know when the last train went and I wasn't going to miss it. Borg wouldn't have come here unless I'd killed the man.

'You're running away again.' Her eyes flashed, colour showed suddenly in her cheeks. 'You've spent your whole life running —running. . . .'

'Have it your own way,' I said wearily, and I lurched past her towards the door.

She hit me then. 'You callous bastard!' It was an open-handed slap across the face, and I picked her up and flung her back against the wall. It knocked the breath out of her.

'Now stop making a bloody nuisance of yourself,' I said. 'I've got problems enough of my own without having some-body else's troubles hung round my neck.'

'It's about your father.' She was sprawled slackly against the wall, breathing heavily.

'My father!' I almost laughed in her face. 'My father's head was sliced from his body by a gang of native boys when I was ten.' I saw her eyes widen at the shock of what I had said. It shocked me, too, for I could still see it lying there on the verandah, the moustache, the thick head of hair, the sun-burned face with the teeth bared, all bright with blood, and the trunk some feet away, inert and lifeless like a rag dummy. I was suddenly almost sober. 'Forget it,' I muttered. 'It was years ago.' I was thinking of those letters in the bureau, wishing I had never seen them. 'I'll go up and pack now.' And I went quickly up to my room.

It didn't take me long to throw the little I had into my suit-case and she was still there when I came down. She was sitting in the chair again, her body slack, the letter on the desk beside her. 'You're going now.' It was a statement, not a question, her voice flat and without expression.

I nodded, hesitating, unwilling to leave her like this. 'Better tell me what your brother says.'

She gave a little shrug, a gesture of hopelessness. 'There's no point now.' She turned her head and I saw she had been crying. 'I'm sorry for what I said.' The toneless way she spoke, I didn't know whether she meant it or not. 'I hope you get the job you want.'

I thanked her, and that was that. I left her sitting there at his desk and went downstairs, out into the streets again. The mist had thickened, the lights all blurred, and it was cold. I caught the last train and spent a miserable night in a cheap hotel in Schiedam. When I went to the yard in the morning, I found tugs standing by and the ship ready to be towed out into the stream. She was sailing as soon as she had bunkered, and the third officer was back on board. He had strained a muscle, that was all.

I took a bus down-river to the Europort. I was so short of money by then that I would have taken a job on any ship. But there was nothing immediately available, and in the end I went back to Amsterdam. There at least the roof over my head was free. But by the time I had paid the fare and had had coffee and a sandwich at the railway station, I had only a few guilders left in my pocket.

My train got in just after five. I took a Number 5 tram as far as the Ruyschstraat and walked back across the Niewe Amstel bridge to Wilhelm Borg's shop. There was nothing else for me to do now, and anyway I wanted to know what he'd seen in the English papers. This time there was a young woman in charge. She was small, dark, expensively dressed, and had a diamond on her left hand that would have kept me in idleness for at least a year. I gave her my name and she asked me to wait. 'Wilhelm is engaged at the moment.' She spoke Dutch with what I think was a Belgian accent. But at least Borg was in. I put my suitcase down and seated myself on what she assured me was a genuine sixteenth-century Italian chair. It was high-backed, ornately carved, and the colours of the leather had faded to a soft richness. A large Buddha sat facing me, cross-legged on an ornate cabinet. The oak and the brass-work were all gone.

'Quite a change since I was last here,' I said.

'Ja, ja. All this . . .' The diamond flashed in the light from the glass chandelier. 'It is new, and in a few days it will have been shipped out and more will come in.' The telephone rang and she answered it, speaking swiftly in German. She cupped her hand over the mouthpiece. 'I have remembered now,' she said, switching into English. 'I was in Dusseldorf when you came before.' She leaned down over the telephone and reached into a drawer. 'Wilhelm said to give you this if you called again.' She handed me a press-cutting from the *Daily Telegraph* and I read it whilst she got on with her call. It was just a short paragraph headed: POLISH SEAMAN DROWNED. The man hadn't looked like a Pole to me, but they gave his name as Zilowski and referred briefly to a dockside brawl. The paragraph ended: *The police are interested in discovering the whereabouts of Paul Van der Voort, second officer of the tanker* Ocean Bluebird, *who may be able to help them with their inquiries.* I knew the formula. It meant a charge of murder, or at best manslaughter. There was no mention of Mark Janovic.

The door to the inner office opened and Borg came out with a man who looked English. He went with him to the door. 'Okay, we ship it across as soon as we have made up a complete container.' A taxi had drawn up outside and Borg stood there with a big smile on his face while the other got in. He waited there until it had driven off: then he closed the door and turned to me. 'Nina showed you the cutting? Good. Then come into the office.' And he added as he led the way, 'That man who has just left—we ship stuff over to him and he puts it up for auction in London as part of an estate.' His manner was friendly, almost confidential. 'That way we get good prices and no questions asked.' And he added, 'All my arrangements are very efficient, you see.'

'What's the proposition?' I asked.

He sat himself down at the desk. 'You are broke, ja? And you need to get away until they have lost interest in you.' He smiled comfortably, knowing I was in a jam, and his offer was tailored to the situation—all expenses, including the chartering and running of the boat, but no salary, only the vague promise of a bonus on delivery. 'And if this consignment goes well, then maybe we make it a regular run, eh?'

'What's the risk?'

He smiled and reached into a drawer. 'For a man like you, very little, I think.' He produced a rolled-up chart and spread it out on the desk. 'We have now decided on Samos as the best place—about early May I think.' It was the British Admiralty Chart No. 1530 covering the eastern half of the Greek island of Samos and part of the Turkish shore. 'As you see, the straits between the island and the mainland are very narrow here, less than a mile wide. Ideal for your purpose. And there is a good port.' He pointed to Pythagorion just west of the southern entrance to the straits. 'You can lie there until you receive final instructions. Okay?' He let go of the chart and it rolled itself up. 'Now, about the boat.' He was still speaking in English, slowly and with a strong accent. 'There is a man in Malta—Barrett. I have met him. His boat is called *Coromandel* and he lives on board. He is an engineer, has very little money and is also somewhat——' He hesitated, searching for the right word. 'Unworldly, ja?' He smiled.

'And that's the boat I'm to charter?'

He nodded. 'I have cabled him already.'

'Is he a good seaman?'

He shrugged. 'You are the seaman, so what does it matter? But inshore—ja—he is good. And he knows the Aegean. He has done a lot of diving—for old wrecks and underwater cities.'

I asked him then about the nature of the consignment and he laughed. 'No drugs, nothing like that. Just antiques. And small objects at that—bracelets, drinking cups, pottery. You can easily stow it out of sight in a boat the size of *Coromandel*.'

'It's stolen, I take it?'

'Not at all.' He managed to look suitably hurt. 'My friends will have purchased it at the market price. Of course, the market price to a peasant who has been plundering the graves at Alacahüyük is not the same as the open market price in, say, London or New York. But first you have to get it there.' He sighed. 'Governments, you see. It's always the same— export restrictions, Customs dues, licences; it is the biggest headache I have in the antique business.'

'And it provides you with the fattest profits—so long as you can find fools who'll risk their necks for you.'

He raised his eyebrows slightly, the babyish face blandly innocent, and then he shrugged and said, 'What do you want me to do—inform the English police about you?' And he added, smiling, 'Come here at ten o'clock tomorrow morning. Nina will have your air ticket by then. Okay?' He was on his feet and moving towards the door. No offer of a drink this time.

'Where have I got to deliver the stuff?'

'Pantelleria. But we can discuss the details in the morning.'

I hesitated. 'This fellow Barrett—he can't be so innocent he'll agree——'

'How you fix it with him is your business.'

He had the door open and I paused, wondering how sure

he was of me. 'See you tomorrow at ten,' he said. It couldn't be easy to find the right people for his sort of business.

'Maybe,' I replied.

2

THERE WERE STARS that night as I walked back through Amsterdam and I barely noticed the traffic. My mind was already at sea. The first voyage I had ever made in a tanker had been outward in ballast from Southampton, through the Mediterranean to Kuwait. That was in 1966, and by the time we were loaded Nasser had closed the Canal. Since then all my voyages had been by way of the Cape. I had never seen the Mediterranean again and all I knew of Malta was a hazy rampart of buildings looking like cliffs in the early morning sunshine as we'd ploughed our way eastwards about three miles offshore. But it was the stars I chiefly remembered, for before then I had been in cargo ships on the North Atlantic run; the night sky was so clear we could watch sputniks and satellites wheeling across the Milky Way.

As I approached the house, I glanced up at the windows, half-expecting Sonia Winters to be waiting there for me. But they were dark, and when I went up the stairs into the study there was no message for me. I had a vague feeling of disappointment. She had seemed to haunt the place like a stray cat, and now that I had thrown her out, I was conscious of the emptiness and the past closing in again. I took my suitcase up to my room. The bed was unmade, the towel I had used still lying on the floor and the air cold from the window I had left open.

I should have gone out then and walked the city until I was tired enough to sleep. But this was my last night, the last time I should be alone in the house, and something held me there, something more powerful than myself.

I made the bed and went down into the kitchen. The fridge was empty, but in one of the cupboards I found a stale packet of biscuits that the mice had been at and two tins of sardines tucked away behind old jam jars and a litter of plastic bags. It wasn't much of a meal, but it was something, and I poured the

35

remains of the geneva into a tumbler and took it through into the study. I ate at his desk, sitting in his chair and browsing through an English book called *Frameworks for Dating Fossil Man*. It had a chapter on the changing levels of sea and land, and what had attracted me was a table giving mean height above present sea level at various stages: Sicilian showed ± 100 metres, and Calabrian ± 200 metres. But the rest of the chapter was beyond me. For example:

> One of the most important events in the history of the Mediterranean shores was the 'Great Regression' sometimes known as the Roman or Romanian regression which followed the 'Milazzian' (or as some prefer, Sicilian II) and preceded the Tyrrhenian stage of high sea-level. The fact that it co-incided with a very striking change in the composition of the marine molluscan fauna is of considerable interest because the Mindel Glaciation, with which this regression probably corresponded, was a time of equally dramatic change in the continental mammalian fauna (Zeuner, 1959a, p. 285).

That paragraph, and others, reminded me of the way the old man had talked, and I wondered why scientists had to make things so unbelievably abstruse. *There can be little doubt that the immediately preceding drop in sea level by nearly 300 feet was eustatic.* What the hell did eustatic mean? ... *and that it reflected the withdrawal of water during the Würm Glaciation.* Vaguely I remembered that the level of the oceans had varied in geological time according to the amount of water held in suspension in the form of ice.

I sat there for a time, sipping my drink, thinking of the seas I had sailed and how changed the shore line would have been with the water level lowered by 300 feet. I could not recall what the depths were in the Malta Channel, but all that area of the Mediterranean was shallow. Volcanic, too—those banks that had emerged, been reported, and had then submerged again.

Thinking about the Mediterranean I suddenly remembered my birth certificate. As proof that I had another name, that I had been born Paul Scott, it might be useful. I reached down and got the old cigar box out of the bottom drawer of the desk. I was just about to fold the papers small enough to fit into my wallet when I saw that the half-sheet of notepaper announcing my birth had something written on the back. I unpinned it and turned it over, laying it flat on the desk and smoothing it out as I read the words my mother had written twenty-eight years ago: *My husband will never know, of course, but it was wrong, wrong, wrong—of me, of you. We should never have met again. Now God knows whose child he is.* Just those three lines, nothing more, except her name—*Ruth.* She had signed it. If she hadn't signed it I could have pretended it was a lie, something added later. But it was in the same hand—the same hand as the love letters in the bureau. Christ Almighty! To discover you were born a bastard and that your mother was sleeping with a man old enough to be her father. Or was he? What age *would* the old man have been then? I didn't know. All I knew was that the last childish tie, clung to through all the years of loneliness following the tragedy, was now gone, killed by the lines my mother had added, now lying faded in the pool of light cast by the Anglepoise lamp.

My first reaction was one of anger. I was filled with a deep, instinctive sense of shame. But then, as I thought about it, my mood changed, for I had no doubt, no doubt at all. Everything suddenly made sense—the long, vividly remembered journey to Europe, his meeting me at Schipol Airport and the years in this house. No wonder Dr Gilmore had looked at me so strangely when I had insisted that he was only my father by adoption. And now that I knew the truth, the whole relationship took on a deeper significance. I understood at last the emotions of love and hate that had always existed between us.

I pinned the sheets of paper together again—my mother's note, my birth certificate and the adoption papers. It was all there, the whole story. Why hadn't I realized it before? I should have known the truth without my mother's frantic confession of guilt. And he had never told me. In all those years he had never even implied that I owed him a deeper allegiance than that of an adopted son. Why? Was it just the code of an earlier generation, their greater chivalry towards women, or had it been the fear that I might not understand a love that must have been compelling and uncontrollable?

I sat there for a long time, the papers in my hand. The conviction that he was my natural father—a certainty that was instinctive rather than logical—affected me profoundly as I went over in my mind all that Dr Gilmore had said. It gave me a sense of pride I had never had before, pride in him and in that part of me that I now recognized as belonging to him. We were so entirely different on the surface—but underneath . . . I was smiling to myself, remembering the latent hostility, my struggle to survive against the strength of his personality, when my thoughts were interrupted by the knocker banging at the front door. I slipped the papers into my wallet and went downstairs to find a man of about forty-five standing at the door.

'You're Dr Van der Voort's son, are you?' He spoke English with a North Country accent and my body suddenly froze. But then he said, 'I'm Professor Holroyd of London University. Gilmore told me I'd find you here.'

I was too relieved to say anything. I just stood there, staring at him. He had a pipe in his mouth and his face was round and smooth, his manner brisk. 'I'd like a word with you.'

I took him up to the study and he went straight over to the swivel chair and sat himself down. 'I haven't much time,' he said. 'I'm attending a conference at the Hague and I'm due shortly at the Rijksmuseum.' His overcoat was unbuttoned and his dark suit hung on him so loosely it might have been made for somebody else. 'I'm not a man who believes in beating about the bush. I've done some checking up on your father. I'll tell you why, later.'

Though he was speaking with his pipe clamped between his teeth, he still managed to arrange his mouth in a smile. The smile, and the twinkle that went with it, were both produced to order. He thrust his head forward in a way that I was sure he had found effective. 'He was a Communist. You know that, I imagine.'

'What do you want?' I asked.

'Your co-operation. That's all.' He took his pipe out of his mouth and began to fill it. 'You're not a Communist yourself, are you?'

'No.'

'You reacted against your father's ideological principles, eh?'

'How do you mean?'

38

'Well, I presume you are aware of his political activities.'

'He was helped by the Russians—I know that. But only from Dr Gilmore.'

'I see.' He lit his pipe, puffing at it quickly and watching me over the flame, his eyes narrowed. 'I'd better fill in the picture for you then. Pieter Van der Voort joined the Communist Party as a student in 1928. He resigned in 1940 following the Russian invasion of Finland. I have no information as to whether he renewed his membership following the German invasion of the Soviet Union in 1941. Probably not, since he would have been suspect as a revisionist. We can, however, regard him as a fellow-traveller. Certainly he was in Russia in 1946 and was mixing freely with their most prominent academics in the years immediately after the war. Later he returned to Amsterdam, and from 1950 onwards he was kept supplied with substantial funds. This enabled him to embark on a whole series of costly expeditions, the results of which were published in Russian scientific journals. Later, they were incorporated into books produced by the Russian State Publishing House with eulogistic forewords by Ivan Szorkowski, a very mediocre, but politically powerful, professor of Moscow University.'

'Are you suggesting the work he did during this period was purely political?'

'No, no. The articles he wrote for the scientific journals, which concerned only the *results* of his expeditions, were of universal interest. They established him as one of the most outstanding men in his field.'

'Then why are you telling me this?'

He held up his hands. 'Let me finish. Then I think you'll see. The books were undoubtedly political. They drew certain quite unwarranted conclusions. And since these were favourable to the Russian image, they were widely reviewed and acclaimed throughout the Communist world. The second of them was published in 1956, the year Russia crushed the Hungarian uprising. He was, therefore, very much in the limelight at the precise moment when he was again faced with the sort of personal political dilemma that had caused him to resign his Party membership in 1940.'

He had been talking very fast, his pipe clenched between his teeth, so that I had difficulty in following him. Now he took it out of his mouth and looked across at me. 'His father died in South Africa, I believe. Do you know when?'

'It was in 1959,' I said. 'Why?'

He nodded. 'Yes, that fits in nicely—the Hungarian rising, his political doubts and then suddenly he finds himself for the first time financially independent.'

'I don't believe it was just a question of money,' I said.

He looked at me sharply. 'Well, no—1959 and '60 were the years of the great East African discoveries at Olduvai.' The smile switched on briefly. 'But money makes a difference, even to a scientist. It meant he no longer had to concentrate his efforts in the East. Instead, he switched his attention to the Central Mediterranean—to Malta, Sicily, North Africa. He was in Cyprus in 1964, and the following year he made his first expedition to Greece.' He leaned back over the desk and tapped his pipe out in the onyx bowl. 'Four years ago he suddenly offered a book to a British publishing house. That manuscript was the first indication I had that he had changed his line of thinking. It was based on an entirely new conception; nothing revolutionary, you understand, but the theories it advanced were new as far as he was concerned. The publishers asked me to advise them. I had no hesitation in recommending rejection.'

'Why?'

'For many reasons, most of which will probably be beyond you.'

'And it was never published?'

'As far as I know he never offered it to another London publisher.'

He obviously sensed my hostility, for he added quickly, 'I'm not the only scientist in the West who has followed his career with interest, many of us envious of the advantages of State patronage while deploring the inevitable distortion of facts. But there was nothing personal about my rejection of the book. Please understand that. It was a clever piece of writing, but not definitive, and I formed the impression that he was mainly concerned to convince himself of the validity of his own arguments. He had shifted his ground, you see.' He leaned forward, his pipe clasped in both hands. 'Just over a year ago I heard he was short of funds. He was then concentrating his energies on Greece, in the area of the Ionian Sea. As a member of a Committee that advises on the allocation of certain Government grants, I persuaded the Chairman to write to him suggesting this was something that might come within the scope of our Committee. There was no reply to this. But then, in November of last year, Lord Craigallan had a letter from him. No doubt you are well aware of your father's present financial straits. He admitted he could not mount another expedition unaided. In the end, we not only gave him a grant, but, through my university, put a Land-Rover at his disposal and also provided him with a very able assistant. I had a report from Cartwright just before I left London. He had already informed me that he had found Dr Van der Voort difficult to work with. But I had no idea how bad things were between them until I read his report.'

He paused there and I knew we had at last reached the object of the interview. He put his pipe back in his mouth. 'You know, I suppose, that Van der Voort has disappeared. What you may not know is the circumstances.'

I stared at him, my mind adjusting slowly to this new information.

'Cartwright had a broken wrist, and other injuries—fortunately minor.' He shook his head. 'A clash of personalities I can understand. That's always possible in an expedition. Men get tired. The weather makes camping uncomfortable. Disappointment saps morale.' He was frowning angrily. 'But in this case the weather was fine—cold, but fine—and after more than a month of slogging it through the mountains without achieving anything, they had just made a significant discovery. There was no justification for it whatsoever.'

'You mean my father attacked him?'

'So Cartwright says. Van der Voort called him out of his tent. There was an argument and he went for him with a stick. It was night, and the attack was so unexpected Cartwright didn't have a chance to defend himself. He took to his heels and that saved him. He describes Van der Voort's behaviour as that of a maniac.'

'What happened then? You say my father disappeared?'

'He drove off in the Land-Rover.' He was looking at me curiously. 'You didn't know about this?'

'No.'

'I presumed you did—that it was the reason you were in Amsterdam.' I could see his curiosity mounting. He took his pipe out of his mouth and I said quickly:

'Where did this happen?'

'In Greece, near a village called Despotiko up by the Albanian border.'

'There can't be many Land-Rovers in Greece,' I said. 'The authorities ought to be able to trace it quite easily.'

He nodded. 'Of course. But Cartwright thought it inadvisable to contact the police. They had difficulty enough getting into the country. In any case, he found the Land-Rover himself, abandoned in the nearby town of Jannina. What is disturbing is that the expedition's funds were gone.' Apparently they had been keeping the money in the tool locker for safety and the padlock had been forced. 'We've cabled them additional funds, but the whole thing is unpleasant to say the least of it.' He leaned his head forward, his eyes narrowed. 'You haven't heard from your father at all?'

'No.'

'It's just a coincidence then that you're here?'

'Yes.'

He leaned back. 'I was hoping perhaps you could help me. What I'm concerned about, you see, is my own responsibility in the matter. I sponsored the allocation of the Government grant and I feel it my duty to see that the taxpayer's money is not wasted.' He was staring at me. 'If anything happens to him you're presumably his heir.'

I laughed. 'I shouldn't think so for a minute.' And then, because he was still staring at me, as though holding me responsible, I said, 'It's nothing to do with me. And anyway, as I understand it, he hasn't any money.'

'I wasn't thinking of money,' he said. 'But he was writing a book. That book would almost certainly give us the information we need to continue the work of this expedition. And since he hadn't got the manuscript with him, I presume it's here in this house, and if I may say so . . .' He stopped at the sound of the street door closing and at the sound of footsteps on the stairs.

It was Sonia Winters. She burst into the room and then

checked at the sight of him sitting there at the desk. 'I'm sorry. I didn't know you had anybody with you.' She had been hurrying and her voice sounded breathless.

I introduced them. She seemed to have heard of Professor Holroyd for she repeated his name and then stood there, staring at him, wide-eyed, in that infuriating way she had.

Holroyd smiled. 'There's a young man with Dr Van der Voort on his expedition——'

'My brother.' Her voice was tight and controlled. Her eyes switched from Holroyd to me, and then back to Holroyd again. 'I'd better go,' she murmured. But she didn't move and her eyes remained fastened on him as though mesmerized.

I started to tell her what had happened, but she cut me short. 'That's what I tried to tell you last night. Your father has disappeared. It's all in the letter I had from Hans—everything, if you'd only listened.' Her gaze swung back to my visitor. 'Why are you here?' She was suddenly so defensive, her tone so imperious, that even Holroyd was surprised and at a loss for words. She turned to me. 'What does he want?'

'He's convinced my father was working on a book. . . .'

'He wants to see it?'

Holroyd began to explain about the grant again, but she cut him short. 'First an East German professor trying to bribe me, then threatening. Now you. There isn't any book.'

'Come, come, Miss Winters.' Holroyd's features were still set in a smile, his whole expression moulded to charm. 'He's had two books published in Russia. He wrote a third which he offered to a London publisher. Since then he's been on a number of expeditions. Don't tell me he hasn't been committing the results of those expeditions to writing. It wouldn't be natural.'

'I was acting as his secretary,' she said. 'I should know.'

'Well, if it's not in book form, then it's in notes—nobody exhausts his personal resources on a series of expeditions without recording the result.'

She gave a little shrug. 'You can't judge Dr Van der Voort by your own or anybody else's standards. He kept everything in his head.' And she added pointedly, 'He didn't trust anybody, you see.'

'Then what was Gilmore talking about?' Professor Holroyd's voice had sharpened. Her attitude had clearly got under his skin. 'He said something about a journal.'

'Dr Van der Voort's Journal would hardly interest you.'

'Why not? A journal—a diary—call it what you like. . . .'

'His Journal was concerned with behaviourism. It was a very personal document, nothing to do with his expeditions or any discoveries. . . .'

'I don't believe it.' His tone was blunt, his accent more pronounced. 'A journal is just what I would expect him to keep; the basis for another book.' He had risen to his feet, and now he moved towards her. He was a big, flabby man, and she looked tiny as she stood facing him. 'Come on, lass. Better tell me where it is. He's disappeared, you know—with money that doesn't belong to him. I don't have to bring the authorities into it, but if the expedition is to go on, it must have all the necessary information.' He stood there, waiting, while she hesitated.

Finally she said, 'Very well then—Dr Gilmore has it.'

'Gilmore?' He didn't bother to hide his annoyance. 'But you have a copy, haven't you?'

She gave him a tight-lipped smile. 'It was in manuscript.'

'I see.' He hesitated. 'Well, I expect Dr Gilmore will be at the Rijksmuseum for tonight's lecture. I'll have a word with him.' He turned to me. 'And I'll contact you again as soon as I have any news. I take it this address will find you?'

I was about to say I was leaving next day, but Sonia Winters intervened. 'I'll see to it that any letters are forwarded.'

He smiled, his eyes twinkling. 'I'm sure you will, Miss Winters.' He was suddenly all charm as he said goodbye to her. I took him downstairs then. 'Tell me,' he said, as I opened the door for him, 'is Miss Winters a relative?'

'No.'

'Do you know her well?'

'I've met her twice.'

He grunted. 'Well, it's none of my business, but she seems to regard herself as something more than a secretary.' And he added, 'I would strongly advise you to make certain you have control of your father's writings—his notes, his journal, everything. They could be of great value—scientifically.' His manner was suddenly confidential. 'I have a great deal of

44

influence in academic circles and I know what I'm talking about.' He smiled and patted my arm in a friendly way. 'I hope when we meet again the situation will have resolved itself.'

Back in the study I found her standing in the same position. 'That man.' Her voice trembled. 'If Dr Van der Voort had known the money came from him. . . .' She stared at me. 'Have you got a cigarette, please?'

There were only three left in the crumpled packet I took from my pocket. She took one almost blindly and I lit it for her. 'He hated the academic world, all the institutional professors who sit in judgment, never dirtying their hands in the field, never getting sweaty and tired, living off the work of others and not risking a penny of their own money. The English in particular.'

'He always hated the English,' I said. 'He was a South African, remember.'

She turned on me then. 'You think that lets you out—that he hated you because you're English. Let me tell you this: It was because of what you are, not your nationality. . . . Goede Hemel!' she said. 'Can't you understand? The academic world is a terribly ruthless one. That's why he opted out. He said they were like leeches, sucking the blood of others, taking all the credit. And that man Holroyd is the worst of the lot. His whole life and reputation—it's built on the brains of others.'

'Then why did you tell him Gilmore had the Journal?'

'Because he's the only one Dr Van der Voort trusted. The Journal is safe with him. He knows the sort of man Holroyd is. And anyway, it isn't the Journal Holroyd's after—that wouldn't help him.'

She paused then and I said, 'Where's the old man now—d'you know?'

'How should I know?' She went over to the desk, drawing on the cigarette as though she had never smoked one before and staring out of the window, her back towards me. 'It would never have happened if he'd known. He'd never have accepted the money. But he was desperate, and then he remembered the letter he'd had from Lord Craigallan. It was like the answer to a prayer. Even then he delayed for months. And after he'd written to Craigallan and had been promised a Land-Rover and the help of a qualified assistant, he never suspected.'

45

'He must have realized there were strings attached.'

'Political strings, yes. He was used to that. Politics meant nothing to him any more. All he cared about was completing the work he had already started. He was like a child in some ways, and his illness had frightened him. It had made him realize that he hadn't much time. And now this.' And she added, 'I never read the Journal. But Dr Gilmore has. That's what he wanted to see him about. I think he was afraid something like this . . .' Her voice trailed away. She was silent for a moment. Finally, she stubbed out her cigarette, grinding it into the ashtray. 'I didn't expect you back here.' Her voice was hard and brittle. 'Then, when I saw the light on this evening, I came straight over. I felt I had to tell you what Hans had said in his letter.' And she added, 'But it doesn't matter now. You know it all.' She turned suddenly and faced me. 'I suppose you didn't get the job you were after?'

'No. But I've got the offer of another.'

'Oh.' Her face looked tired. 'And it makes no difference—what's happened out there?'

'No.' What the hell did she expect me to say? 'I haven't the money to go looking for him.'

'No, I suppose not.' Moving slightly her hand touched the plate I had left on the desk and she glanced down at the sordid remains of my meal. 'I should have thrown those biscuits away.' She seemed at a loss for a moment. Then she smiled, a bright, artificial smile. 'I'll make you some coffee, shall I?' She was already moving towards the kitchen and I didn't stop her. She clearly felt the need to do something actively feminine and I needed time to collect my thoughts.

Two things filled my mind—the way this house drew those who were connected with my father, as though his brooding personality were a living force within its walls, and the extraordinary pattern that was dragging me almost against my will into the area of his activities. What if that pattern continued? I sat down at the desk and lit one of my two remaining cigarettes, thinking about it, conscious of a sense of inevitability, wondering what I would do if our paths crossed.

I was still thinking about that when the girl returned with coffee on a tray. 'I'm sorry, there's no milk,' she said. 'And it's instant coffee.' I offered her my last cigarette and she took it.

46

The coffee was thin and bitter. We drank it in silence, our thoughts running on different lines. And when I tried to get her to explain what had happened, she only shook her head and said, 'It's no good. It wouldn't mean very much to you.' And she added, half to herself, 'I'm worried about Hans. He's a very serious boy and so absorbed in his studies that he wouldn't know what to make of this.' She was withdrawn and very tense, sitting there, nursing her steaming cup and puffing at her cigarette. Her fingers were long and slender, her wrists small. The boyish cut of her hair emphasized the delicacy of her features. It was the first time I had had the chance to study her face. It was like a piece of fine china, very pale, very clean-cut, the brow high, the nose straight and finely chiselled, the mouth and jaw strong.

She met my gaze and smiled uncertainly. Her eyes were the colour of aquamarine and in the gleam of the lamplight they looked brilliant against the surrounding whites. 'When are you leaving?' she asked.

'Tomorrow.'

She nodded. She wasn't really interested. 'It's that man Borg, I suppose.' And she added, 'He's a crook, isn't he?'

'He deals in antiques,' I said.

'And where's he sending you?'

'Malta. And then Turkey.' I don't know why I told her. I suppose I wanted her reaction, to share the feeling I had of a pattern forming.

Her eyes widened, but that was all. 'Well, I hope you have a good voyage.' She drank the rest of her coffee and stubbed out her cigarette. 'I must go now.' She got to her feet, her hands smoothing automatically at her woollen dress. It was very brief and close-fitting so that she looked even smaller than she really was. I, too, had risen, and she hesitated, staring up at me. 'If you're short of money . . .'

'No, I'll be all right, thank you.'

I saw her down to the door. It was cold outside, the canal a black ribbon broken by the reflection of the lighted windows opposite. We stood there for a moment, an awkward pause that held us silent. Finally she said, 'My address is No. 27B—if you need to contact me.' She turned then and was gone, walking quickly towards the bridge.

47

I watched her for a moment, feeling suddenly alone, then abruptly I went back up the steep little staircase and got my coat. It was already nine-thirty. Not much time, but there was just a chance—a last chance to break the pattern. And if I stayed in that house I knew the pull of his personality would be overwhelming. But all through the icy streets, though I was walking fast, I couldn't get away from him, my mind going over again what Holroyd had told me, the girl's behaviour, and that nice old man with his strange concern for a student he hadn't seen in thirty years.

There was no wind, and when I reached the Oosterdok a mist was hanging white over the water, the ships standing like ghosts at the quays, with only their funnels and masts visible. It was just on ten when I entered the Prins Hendrik and Stolk was there, his tousled hair standing out of the dark collar of his monkey jacket as he leaned on the bar. He was with a bunch of Norwegians, all talking bad English, and I hesitated. But then he turned and saw me. 'You!' he shouted in his deep booming voice. 'Vat you doing here? Iss the yob no good?'

I told him the man had recovered and he laughed. 'So, no yob, eh?' He called for another Bokma. 'Drink that. And now I introduce you to Kaptein Johannessen. He is bound for Durban and afterwards Auckland and his third officer has—what do you think, eh?—measles. He has measles, ja.' And they roared with laughter.

I stayed drinking with them for an hour, and all the time I was turning it over in my mind. Johannessen was a big, friendly man, his officers a decent crowd, like all Norwegians. And the ship was going to New Zealand. I had only to ask him. I had only to say I wanted the job. Stolk gave me the opening and waited. But somehow the words stuck in my throat. A ship, the sea, the uncomplicated routine life, the crude jokes, the laughter, the easy companionship—I had it in my grasp, and I let it go. 'You refuse this yob,' Stolk boomed, 'and you can buy your own Bokma.'

It was bloody stupid of me. The ship was going where I wanted to go—a new life, and all I said was, 'I've got a job already, thank you.'

It was the old man, of course. I knew that. And walking

48

back alone through the deserted streets, back again to that house and my childhood bedroom, I tried to understand what it was I had done. I'd been given the chance of escaping from the pattern and, God knows why, I had rejected it. I'm not the sort of person to suffer from a guilt complex and the discovery that he was my father didn't really make a damned bit of difference.

Lying in bed, still thinking about it, I began to be dimly aware that it wasn't so much the old man as the world he represented that was drawing me away from the old shipboard life towards an uncertain future. The things he had tried to teach me, and which I had rejected—it almost seemed as though they had lain dormant in my sub-conscious. There was no other way to account for the awakening of interest I had felt when looking at his books, particularly when talking to the girl and Dr Gilmore. And then, too, there was the feeling that I had to see him again if I were ever to understand my own behaviour pattern—a favourite phrase of his I remembered. About the only thing we had in common was the hastiness of temper that led to violence.

I was at Borg's shop just before ten with my suitcase packed. He was standing by the Buddha, waiting for me, and I could see he was relieved. 'You're all ready. Good. I have ordered a taxi.' He pulled an envelope out of the pocket of his loose-fitting tweed jacket. 'That is your air ticket, also sterling for Malta and some drachmas—you will need that in the islands.' He handed it to me, smiling. 'You see, I am trusting you.'

'You've no option,' I said, and the friendliness went out of his eyes. He stood there, waiting, knowing I had a reason for saying that. 'Have you got a big chart?' I asked. 'One that includes the whole of Greece?'

He took me through into his office and produced the Eastern Mediterranean sheet. It was folded in four, and as he opened it out, the creases showed that it had been much used. Black hairs gleamed on the back of his hand and his signet ring flashed in the sunlight from the window as he traced the line from Malta to Crete. 'About five hundred miles,' he said. 'And Heraklion is a port of entry. You can get your Greek transit papers there.'

'Is it a power boat?' I asked.

'Sail and power. It's an old boat, but she has a new engine.'

'Say four days.' My eyes were searching the long, south-thrusting peninsula of the Greek mainland. 'Another two, perhaps three days to Samos. And you don't need me there until early May. That's more than a month.'

'A month is not too long for the authorities to get used to your presence. What are you getting at?'

I had found what I wanted and I straightened up. 'No objection if I take a more northerly route, have you? We've plenty of time.'

'Why?'

'The Ionian Sea—I've always wanted to have a look at the west coast of Greece.'

He knew it wasn't the real reason, and for a moment I thought he was going to be difficult. I put the envelope with the ticket and the money down on the desk. He looked at it and then at me. 'How long will it take you?'

'A week,' I said. 'Not more.'

He hesitated. Finally he nodded. 'Ja. Well . . . okay.'

We talked over the details then, and when the taxi came he took me out to it himself.

'And when I've completed delivery?' I asked.

'Then we have another little talk, eh?'

Just over an hour later I was in the air.

II: Man the Seeker

I

IT WAS DARK when I arrived in Malta, the air soft and smelling of the sea. The airport taxi took me to the Phoenicia Hotel and from there I got a bus to the yacht marina at Ta' Xbiex. The waterfront was crowded with boats, a forest of spars standing against the night sky, and it took me some time to locate *Coromandel*. She was lying on the Manoel Island side between a chromium-plated gin palace and a big Italian ocean-racer. She appeared to be a conversion from some sort of fishing boat, and sandwiched between those two gleaming monsters, stern-on to the quay like all the rest, she looked her age. A light showed in the wheelhouse for'ard and my hail was answered immediately by a short, ruddy-faced man with greying hair. He was dressed in blue jeans and an old blue jersey and he came aft wiping his hands on a piece of cotton waste.

'Mr Van der Voort?' A wooden board served as a gangplank and he put his foot on it to hold it steady as I went on board. 'Sorry not to meet you.' He took my case. 'Is this all your gear?' He seemed pleased when I said it was.

The decks were badly worn, the bulwarks shabby, and there was paint flaking from the lockers aft. But the deckhouse itself gleamed with new varnish. 'We slapped a second coat on this afternoon, so mind out.' And he added, 'Sorry the old girl's in a bit of a mess, but as soon as I got Mr Borg's cable I had her slipped for a scrub and a coat of anti-fouling. We only got her back this morning.'

I followed him into the wheelhouse where the floorboards were up and most of the steering gear dismantled. He was installing an automatic pilot, purchased as scrap from a yacht that had been towed in badly damaged. 'Most of the equipment on this ship is my own work, as you might say,' he said. Aft of the wheelhouse was a short companionway leading down into a cubby-hole with a work bench. The light was on, illuminating a chaos of paint pots, brushes, tools and bits of machinery. But the chaos was only superficial, the after bulkhead lined with a neat array of boxes for screws and bolts, the area above the work bench fitted out for tools, and clamped to the starboard wall were pyrotechnics, log, foghorn, fire extinguishers. Below these, in special racks, were three aqualungs and a couple of outboard motors.

On the far side of the wheelhouse a second companionway led for'ard, down into a saloon which had probably once been the fish hold. The contrast was very marked. Here was order and comfort, chintz coverings to the settee berths, chintz curtains over the portholes, the brasswork gleaming and the fine Honduras mahogany polished to a rich gloss. He showed me to my cabin, which was aft, a two-berthed stateroom with a different patterned chintz. And when I complimented him on the condition of his ship below, he said, 'Ah, that's the wife. She's very particular.' And he added, 'She's gone to a movie with the people from *Fanny Two*. Had enough for one day. It's always bad after you've been on the slip—the dirt, you see.'

He showed me where the 'heads' were and then left me to sort myself out. In the lights below he had looked younger than he had seemed at first, around forty, I thought. A good solid type, not very bright, but reliable. I wondered what his wife would be like. Borg hadn't said anything about a wife.

When I returned to the saloon, he was waiting for me there, the drink locker open beside him and two glasses on the table. 'What'll you have, Mr Van der Voort—a Scotch?' He had cleaned the oil from his hands and face and was wearing a bright check shirt with the sleeves rolled up.

I said a Scotch would be fine and told him my name was Paul.

He smiled, showing me an even line of what looked like false teeth. 'Good. First names are best on a small ship. Mine's Bert and my wife's is Florence, though she answers to Florrie.' He gave a quick, cackling laugh. And as he poured the drinks he said, 'It's lucky you didn't ask for gin. They only let us have one bottle a week out of the bonded locker, and the gin's just about had it.' It was malt whisky and he gave it to me neat.

'Does your wife go with you on all your trips?' I asked.

'Oh, yes. The ship's our home, you see, and Florrie's a good sailor. Better than I am in some ways.'

I asked him when we could leave and he said he thought by the week-end. 'We've tanked up with fuel and water, and the stores are ordered for tomorrow. It's more a case of getting the ship ready. Mr Borg's cable caught us on the hop like and the Aegean is quite a long haul.'

'We'll be going to the west coast of Greece first,' I said.

'Oh? Mr Borg said Crete.' But he took the change of plan in his stride. In fact, he seemed relieved. 'Pylos is a good port of entry. We've done that before. It's 366 miles and the course is nearer the South Italian ports. Whereas Crete—it's a lonely run, you see.' And he added, 'As long as we don't get a *gregale* —a nor'-easter wouldn't be comfortable heading for Pylos. But with luck we'll have a westerly this early in the season. Not that it matters, mind you. *Corie's* a sturdy little ship. Built as a fishing boat up on the Clyde way back at the turn of the century—1906 to be exact—and sound as a bell. And she's got a brand new engine.' He said it with pride. 'Come and have a look.'

He took me up into the wheelhouse and down the companionway on the port side. Aft of the workbench he lifted a hatch. 'I spent all winter installing this myself.' He switched on the light to reveal a big Perkins diesel. There was a generator, too, and a range of Nife batteries, also a compressor, and the whole engine compartment reflected the loving care of a dedicated engineer, copper and brasswork gleaming and not a smear of oil anywhere on the bright paintwork. 'She's been test run for about six hours with extra warps out aft, and going round to Manoel Island shipyard and back she ticked over sweet as a bird. Can't wait to get to sea and give her a proper try-out.'

'What speed will it give you?'

'About eight knots I reckon.' He was staring down, his eyes bright with anticipation. 'Did Mr Borg tell you what he'd done?'

'How do you mean?' I asked, wondering what Borg had got to do with it.

'No, of course not. A nice fellow like that wouldn't go advertising the fact that he'd helped somebody.' He leaned his

53

thick hairy arms on the edge of the hatch, feasting his eyes on that gleaming lump of machinery. 'When I bought *Coromandel* she had an old Kelvin in her. One of the very early ones. I sweated blood on that bugger—everything gummed up and rusty as hell. The miracle is that it got us out here.'

And he told me how for two seasons he had kept it going, making his own replacements when anything broke. Then in August last year Borg had chartered the boat for a few days.

'I think he got a bit tired of the Hilton and wanted a breath of sea air. Then, when we got out to Gozo, he said what about making a quick passage to Pantelleria. He'd been looking at the charts, you see, and he suddenly had this urge to make a passage. He didn't seem to understand about Customs clearance, but as it was a quick trip there and back I thought I'd take a chance on it. Halfway across, that clapped-out old engine started playing up. It was a broken valve and it took me a whole day to machine and fit a replacement. We couldn't even sail. There wasn't a breath of wind.'

'Did you get to Pantelleria?'

'In the end, yes. By then I had explained to him about Customs and entry formalities—Pantelleria is Italian, you see —so we didn't go into the port of Pantelleria, just motored round the island, close in, so that he could see the extraordinary lava formation. We spent the night in a little cove, gave him a quick run ashore and then back to Malta. Well, to cut a long story short, on the way back he said he happened to know a scrap merchant in Holland who had a modern diesel engine for disposal. It had been salvaged from a small trawler sunk off the Hook. He'd enjoyed himself so much, he said, that he'd like to make me a present of it. And that's it,' he added, pointing with pride. 'Mind you, it was a bit rusty, but it was bloody generous of him all the same—must have cost a damn sight more than the charter. I waived that, of course. And all he got out of it was four days at sea, a few hours ashore on Pantelleria, and some wine.'

'Where did you pick up the wine?' I asked.

'At Pantelleria. He was very fond of wine, and some people in the cove we anchored in for the night let him have four cases.'

What about the Customs when you got back to Malta?'

'Oh, we didn't clear Customs—couldn't very well after slipping out like that. Not that they worry about wine. Anyway,' he added, 'when we put into Emerald Bay—that's on Little Comino in the straits between Malta and Gozo—some friends of Mr Borg's were there in a motor boat, so we were on our own when we got back to the marina.' He straightened himself up, still staring at the engine. 'Looks nice, doesn't it?' He switched off the light and closed the hatch with obvious reluctance. 'Mr Borg's a friend of yours, I take it,' he said as he led the way back to the saloon. 'Well, you tell him how grateful I am. That engine, and now a charter we didn't expect. It's not often you meet a rich man like that who'll do a good turn for somebody less fortunate.'

Unworldly was the way Borg had described him. But it was difficult to believe that anybody could be quite so naïve. It was only when I got him talking about himself that I began to understand. He was an East Londoner, who had spent most of his life as a fitter in the R.A.F. He had married in Cyprus and had then left the Air Force and settled at Great Yarmouth, where he had built up a small engineering business turning out specialized items for the North Sea rigs.

'But the Government changed, inflation hit us and we lost business to Dutch and Danish firms. If I'd held out until they devalued maybe I'd have been all right—at least I'd have got a better price. As it was, I sold out at about the bottom.' His broad shoulders moved, a self-deprecating shrug. 'I'm not much of a business man, but at least the boat was cheap.'

He had converted her himself in the fish port at Great Yarmouth, and then they had sold their house and sailed south into the Channel. 'It was marvellous—just ourselves and the sea and foreign ports. Nothing to worry about, only the weather.'

He was on to his second drink then and he began telling me the story of the voyage out, how they had run into a force 10 gale in the Bay of Biscay. 'Can you navigate?' he asked suddenly. 'By the stars, I mean. Mr Borg said you were an experienced sailor.' When I said I could, he nodded. 'I studied it a bit—we've got a sextant on board, Reed's Almanac and all the tables. But I haven't the patience for that sort of thing. Anyway, we didn't see the sun for three days. . . .'

55

He paused, his head on one side, listening. There was the sound of voices and then footsteps on deck. A moment later a small, bright-eyed woman in orange slacks appeared in the companionway. She stopped when she saw me. 'Oh, you've arrived.' She came forward quickly and shook my hand. 'I'm sorry I wasn't here.' She glanced at the glasses and her nose wrinkled. 'I don't suppose Bert thought of offering you anything to eat?'

'I had a meal on the plane,' I told her.

'Sure? I could knock you up an omelette very quickly.'

'Quite sure.'

She hesitated, her eyes taking me in. She was a good deal younger than her husband, a small, sturdy woman with dark eyes and a very clear olive-brown skin. Her black hair and the oval shape of her face gave her a madonna-like quality. But that was only in repose. She had a volatile personality, and this, I learned later, stemmed from her mixed parentage—her father had been English, her mother Cypriot. 'Well, I'll make some coffee, anyway.' And she disappeared into the galley, which was aft of the saloon on the port side.

It was over the coffee that she asked me a question I should have been expecting. She wanted to know why I was going to Greece so early in the season. 'Hardly anybody leaves the marina before May, most of them not until June.' She was frowning slightly and there were little lines at the corners of her eyes as she stared at me, waiting for an answer.

Her husband sensed my reluctance. 'Where he goes is his own business, Florrie. He's the charterer, after all.'

'I know that, Bert. But still . . . it *is* our boat. I think we should know.' Her voice was subdued, but quite determined.

I don't think she suspected anything. It was just that the hasty fixing of the charter made her uneasy. And rather than attempt to invent a reason, I told them about my father's expedition.

She relaxed at once. 'Oh, that explains it.'

'Is it caves he's exploring?' Bert asked. 'Or just a dig?'

'I've no idea,' I said.

He asked me where the camp was, and when I told him he went up into the wheelhouse and returned with a chart of the west coast of Greece. 'If it's caves I might be of some use,' he

56

said, spreading it out on the table. 'As a kid I belonged to a spelæological group—pot-holing, you know. We went to Spain one year—had a look at Altamira. That's the cave that's full of prehistoric paintings, on the north coast near Santander.' His stubby finger indicated Jannina. 'It looks as though Preveza would be the best port—Jannina is about sixty miles away and a good road by the look of it. We can make our entry at Pylos and then go straight up the coast, through the narrows between Meganisi and Levkas. Do you know the Levkas Canal?'

I shook my head.

'A queer place—for Greece, that is. More like Holland really. Very flat, and a bloody great fort at either end. Preveza is only about eight miles beyond the north end of the canal.'

We studied the chart for a bit, and then I said I was tired and went to bed.

I saw very little of Malta during the next two days, only Manoel Island and a few of the narrow balconied streets of Sliema. Whilst Bert finished the installation of the automatic steering gear and Florrie dealt with the stores, I completed the varnishing of the brightwork and started on re-painting the bulwarks. 'Not often I get a charterer who'll work as hard as you,' Bert said. But I didn't mind. There was something very satisfying about getting the old boat ready for sea, and the work kept my mind off my own problems.

Saturday morning we took on bonded stores, cleared Customs, and after a meal ashore, we slipped and headed out towards the entrance of Sliema Creek under engine. It was blowing hard from the south-west and we turned under the battlements of St Elmo and winched the gaff mainsail up and then the mizzen. The sun was shining on the piled-up mass of Valetta's honey-stoned buildings, and as we cleared Dragut Point a machine-gun rattle of firecrackers burst from the roof of one of the churches, little puffs of smoke against a cloudless sky to celebrate some saint's day.

Outside the entrance the sea was rough and it was cold, so that I was glad of the oilskins I had purchased. We were hoisting the jib then in flurries of spray, and when we had got it properly set at the end of the short bowsprit, Bert switched off the engine, and in the sudden quiet we sailed close under the stern of an American carrier of the Sixth Fleet and set course for Greece on a bearing just north of east.

Visibility was good and it was not until almost 1700 hours that we lost the low line of Malta below the horizon. An hour later we broke the seal on the bonded stores locker and had our first drink at sea, the boat sailing easily at about six knots with the wind on our starboard quarter. We had an early meal, and then, as darkness fell, we went into watches, Bert and I sharing the night turns, with Florrie relieving us for the dawn watch.

When I called her, at the end of the last night watch, the wind had strengthened to nearly force 7 and the helm was heavy with the ship showing a tendency to yaw. I think she was already awake, for her eyes were open when I switched on the light in their cabin. 'Do you want to shorten sail?' she asked as she slipped quickly out of her bunk, her black hair tousled and her face still flushed with sleep. 'I'll wake Bert, if you like.' He was snoring gently in the other bunk.

'Better see what you think first,' I said, and I went back to the wheelhouse. We had swung about a point off course and I brought her head back. The light of the compass was fading with the dawn. I could see the waves more clearly now. They were steep and breaking, the sea flecked with white to the horizon, the sky ahead a pale translucent green just starting to flush with the sun's hidden rays.

She didn't take long to dress, and when she entered the wheelhouse, she stood there a moment, looking at the sea and at the sails with eyes slightly narrowed, a cool, almost professional appraisal. Then she took the wheel from me and held it, getting the feel of the boat. 'No, I think she's all right,' she said. 'It always sounds worse below.' She gave a quick little laugh. 'I'm inclined to get panicky when there's a lot of noise.'

She was wearing a thick black polo-necked sweater and red oilskins. 'It's hard on Bert,' she said. 'He did want to run that new engine of his. But I like it like this—just the noise of the sea.' She was fully awake now and her eyes sparkled with the exhilaration of the speed and the movement. 'Doesn't it excite you—the sea, when it's like this?' But then she laughed. 'No, of course—you must have experienced plenty of really big seas.'

'In the North Atlantic, yes. But with a large vessel it's much more remote.'

She checked the wheel as a breaking wave rolled under us, biting her lip with concentration, and the jib emptied and filled with a bang to the roll. The green had gone from the sky ahead. Ragged wisps of cloud showed an edge of flame and right on the horizon an island of molten lava seemed to blaze up out of the sea.

'How old is your father?' she asked.

'I don't know,' I said. 'Sixty-ish, I suppose.'

She glanced at me. 'You're worried about him, aren't you?'

'Yes, I suppose so.'

'Then why didn't you fly out?'

I had no answer to that, but fortunately she took my silence as a rebuke. 'I'm sorry, I ask too many questions, don't I?' She gave me a little laugh, low and strangely musical, and then she was looking up at me, her lips slightly parted, her dark eyes gentle.

We were alone, the two of us in a wild dawn, and I put my hand on her shoulder and the next moment she was in my arms, her mouth soft, her body clumsy in her heavy weather clothing. She stayed like that for a moment, and then the ship yawed and she pushed away from me and took the wheel again. She was smiling, a quiet, secret smile. 'You're lonely, aren't you?'

'And you?' I asked.

'I'm not lonely. It's just the sea. It excites me.' And she added, 'Now go to bed. You've been up half the night.'

'I'm not tired.' I hesitated, conscious of a need, but no way of satisfying it.

'Of course not. You're too tensed-up to feel the tiredness.'

'Perhaps.'

She was looking at me, those large, dark eyes of hers suddenly offering sympathy. 'Those two days in Malta—nothing but work, and you hardly left the ship. Even Bert noticed it. And now—at sea . . .' She shook her head. 'I don't know what the trouble is, and I'm not asking, but bottling it all up inside you —that's not good.' She checked the wheel, staring ahead. 'Try to relax, why don't you?'

'Was that why you kissed me?'

She smiled. 'It helps—sometimes.'

I nodded, and we stood in silence, watching as the sun's upper rim lipped blood-red over the horizon. Then I checked the log reading and entered up the course and mileage covered during my watch. When I turned again she was a squat, almost square figure, in silhouette against the sudden flare of light that had turned the steel grey heaving surface of the sea to a shimmer of orange. She was braced against the wheel, hands holding the ship, her whole being concentrated on the lift and swoop of the movement. The sun rose clear of the horizon, a flaming ball, and the whole empty world of sea and sky was lit by blinding light, the cloud wisps swept away like a veil and the sky a brazen blue.

My limbs felt slack and I was suddenly tired as I turned without a word and went below to my cabin. But sleep came slowly. There was something of the peasant about her and I was deeply stirred, furious that my vulnerability had been so obvious.

She called me for breakfast at nine-thirty. Bert was at the wheel and we were alone. But she was cool and distant, efficiently feminine in blue slacks and white shirt. The movement was less, and by midday the wind had died away and we were under engine. We had drinks in the wheelhouse and the three of us lunched together with the automatic pilot doing the work. It was like that for the rest of the voyage, and the third day out, at dawn, Florrie and I watched the outline of Sapienza Island emerge as a dark silhouette against the sunrise straight over the bows.

'Your navigation is very exact.' The way she said it, I thought there was envy as well as admiration, for by then I had discovered that there was a basis of fear in the excitement she felt for the sea. Bert was easy-going, almost slapdash, in everything not connected with machinery. 'Last year our first sight of Greece was Cape Matapan. Bert was navigating on dead reckoning and he was miles out—we had to make our entry at Kalamata instead of Pylos.' She was laughing, her teeth white against the dark of her skin, which was already tanned by the sun and salt air. 'You don't speak Greek, do you?'

'No.'

'Well, don't forget—if you want to telephone about your father, I can do it for you.'

I stayed with her in the wheelhouse until we had closed the coast and I had identified the gap in the cliffs that marked the entrance to Navarino Bay. Then I called Bert and went into the galley to make some coffee. When I got back to the wheelhouse, we were close in, our bows headed towards a jagged stac with a hole in the middle. Just beyond it, the sea swell died and the water was glass-calm, the great expanse of the bay shimmering like a mirror in the warm sunlight. Ashore the hills were green and bright with flowers. It was suddenly spring.

'This was where Admiral Codrington caught and destroyed the Turkish fleet,' Bert said. 'There are eighty-three vessels lying sunk under the waters here.' He was grinning, an eager glint in his eyes. Bronze and copper are worth a lot of money and he had never dived in Navarino Bay. "All I've ever found in the Aegean, apart from amphoræ and sherds and bits of Roman glass, is one—just one—bronze figurine, rather battered. Plenty of marble, of course, column drums and carved seats and a couple of massive statues. But nothing that was worth the trouble of bringing up.'

I asked him what had happened to the figurine, thinking he might have sold it to Borg. But he said it was ashore with friends in Malta. 'Daren't have it on board. The Greeks are very hot on underwater looting.'

We were opening up the port now and a massive Turkish castle slung a great rampart wall over the protecting peninsula. Behind us, on hills that stood like a crater rim along the seaward side of the bay, the ruined remains of another castle perched precariously.

We dropped anchor off the end of the quay and hauled ourselves in, stern-on to the blue and yellow diagonals that marked the area reserved for visiting boats. The Port Captain came on board almost immediately, a young, very alert, very charming man, who spoke reasonably good English. Customs and police followed, also the doctor. We took them down to the saloon, offered them Scotch, which they accepted out of politeness, but barely touched, and after half an hour they left, taking our passports for stamping and the ship's certificate of registration from which the Port Captain's office would prepare the transit log. 'You may go ashore now,' the Port Captain said. And when Bert offered to collect the papers, he gave a little shrug.

'It is not necessary. We will find you.' And he added, laughing, 'Pylos is not too big a place.'

Ten minutes later we were having our first retsina in the little tree-shaded square, where Codrington's statue stood guarded by bronze cannon. All around the square small dark men in dark clothes sat over their coffee, whilst women in black went about their shopping. And over the shops the names unreadable in the Greek alphabet.

We had just finished our first bottle of the dry resined Achaian wine, and I had ordered another, when the Port Captain came hurrying towards us, accompanied by a tough-looking Greek in light khaki uniform. 'This is Kapetán Kondylakes of the Police.' He smiled disarmingly, his manner as charming and friendly as when he had visited us on the boat. The police officer also smiled, a flash of gold teeth in a pockmarked face.

My muscles were suddenly tense. This wasn't part of the routine passport check. This man looked like the senior police officer in Pylos.

'May we sit down with you, please?' the Port Captain asked. 'For one minute when we make some questions?'

They pulled up two chairs and Bert offered them a drink. More smiles and a sharp clap of the hands to summon the waiter. Extra glasses were brought, the wine poured, and I sat there, watching them and wondering what the hell I was doing here, risking my neck, when I could have been safe aboard Johannessen's boat en route for New Zealand.

'Kapetán Kondylakes is not speaking English, so I speak for him. Okay?' And then the Port Captain turned to me as I had feared he would. 'Your name is Van der Voort.'

I nodded, dumbly.

The police officer produced my passport from the side pocket of his tunic, opening it at the page with my photograph and pushing it across the table to his companion. They talked together for a moment, both of them staring down at the passport. 'Van der Voort,' the Port Captain said and he looked across at me. 'That is a Dutch name?'

'Yes.' My hands were trembling now and I kept them out of sight below the table, cursing myself for not realizing that Interpol operated in Greece.

'But you have an English passport. Why, please?'

'Both my parents were English. After their death I was adopted by Dr Van der Voort and took his name.' This took some time to explain and when I had finished he said: 'And this Dr Van der Voort of Amsterdam—what is his full name?'

I told him and he repeated it to the police officer, who nodded emphatically. 'And when do you last see him?'

'About eight years ago.'

'So long?'

And when I had explained, he said, 'Then why do you come to Greece, if you do not like this man?'

I had no ready answer to that. But at least I could relax now. It wasn't me they were interested in, but the old man. 'What's the trouble?' I asked him. 'Why all these questions?'

He conferred briefly with the police officer and then said, 'Dr Van der Voort entered Greece on March 9 with an Englishman and a Dutch student. They say they are a scientific expedition looking for prehistoric settlements. Now Dr Van der Voort is not anywhere to be found. Do you know that?'

'I knew there'd been some trouble between him and another member of the expedition.'

'And so you come to Greece. You charter a yacht and sail to Pylos because there is trouble between Dr Van der Voort and this Englishman, Cartwright.' The police officer stabbed his finger at my passport. The Port Captain nodded. 'But it says here that you are a ship's officer.' He pushed the passport across to me, indicating the entry against Occupation. 'Ship's officers do not have money to charter yachts.'

'I'm in tankers,' I said, and they nodded. Pylos was a tanker port and they knew what the pay was like.

'And you do not know where Dr Van der Voort is?'

'No.'

'Where do you expect to find him?'

'At Despotiko, a village north of Jannina.'

He conferred again with the police officer. 'Kapetán Kondylakes insists that you explain why you come to Greece.'

I did my best to satisfy him, but it was difficult to explain when I didn't really know myself. The Port Captain passed it all on to his companion, and when he had finished I again asked him what all the fuss was about, why the police were so interested. But I met with a blank wall. All he said was, 'Dr Van der Voort has disappeared. Naturally the police have to find him.'

But that did not explain why, in a little place like Pylos in the south of Greece, the local police captain had been informed about a man who was missing in quite another part of the country. And when I tried to insist on an explanation, the Port Captain rose to his feet saying that Kapetán Kondylakes would have to report back to Athens. They left us then, with many apologies for inconveniencing us and a request that we did not attempt to leave until permission had been granted.

'Well, this is a fine old mess,' Bert said.

'It's something political, I think.' Florrie was staring thoughtfully at her empty glass. 'Kapetán Kondylakes referred at one point to security arrangements. But don't worry,' she added. 'In Greece everything is twisted into a political issue. You have to have patience.'

We drank another bottle, the retsina ice-cold and pungent, the sunlight warm. Later we had lunch in the taverna opposite, picking out the things we wanted from the bubbling pots on the kitchen range—a fish soup and shish-kebab with stuffed tomatoes. The bare concrete room echoed to the rapid sound of Greek. We didn't talk much ourselves. And then, just as we were finishing, the Port Captain and Kondylakes came in, accompanied by a civilian in a light grey suit. He was taller than the other two. 'Which is Van der Voort?' he asked as he reached our table.

I got to my feet and he said, 'Kotiadis my name. Demetrios Kotiadis.'

We shook hands and he sat down, motioning the other two to pull up chairs. He had a long, rather sallow face, with a big beak of a nose and heavy-lidded eyes. He was smoking a Greek cigarette and this stayed firmly in his mouth. 'Do you speak French?'

I shook my head.

'Then excuse my English please.' He clapped his hands for the waiter and ordered coffee for all of us. 'You are arriving here in Greece to see Dr Van der Voort.'

I nodded, wondering what was coming.

64

'We also wish to see him. So we co-operate, eh?' He smiled at me thinly.

I didn't say anything. I wanted a cigarette, but my hands were trembling again.

'You know he has disappeared?'

'Yes.'

'He has been missing for two weeks now. Do you know why?'

I shook my head.

'And you don't know where he is?'

'No.'

'Then why you come? Have you some message for him, some instructions?'

'How do you mean?' And because I didn't understand what he was driving at I started to explain again why I had come to Greece. The coffee arrived, poured out of individual copper pots, and he sat staring at me through the smoke of his cigarette.

'Do you know this man Cartwright who is with him?'

'No.'

'Or the Dutch boy, Winters?'

I shook my head.

'But you know there has been some trouble?'

'I know that—yes.'

He hesitated. 'There was a question of some money taken. But that has been settled now; it is a young Greek boy who breaks open the tool locker of the Land-Rover. So it is not for that reason he disappear.' He stared at me, waiting. Finally he gave a little shrug. 'If you wish I can take you to this village where they camp.'

I muttered something about not wishing to trouble him, but he brushed it aside. 'No trouble. I like to help you. Also we can talk—privately, eh?' And he added, to make it absolutely clear that I had no alternative, 'It is fortunate for you that I am at Methoni today, otherwise Kondylakes here must take you to Athens for interrogation. If we leave after our coffee we can be at Despotiko tomorrow morning and then you can talk with this man Cartwright. Maybe you discover what I have failed to discover—where Dr Van der Voort is.' He smiled at me and left it that.

I lit a cigarette and sat there watching him, thinking of the journey ahead and the two of us alone. He was a man in his late forties, or early fifties, well educated and with a strong energetic personality. It was difficult to place him. When I asked him about his official position, all he replied was that he was with a Ministry in Athens and was here to help Kapetán Kondylakes in his enquiries. He could have been security police, of course. But there was a peculiar mixture of toughness and charm in his manner; also a certain air of secrecy. I thought he was probably Intelligence.

The coffee was strong and sweet and very hot, and as we sat there drinking it, the three Greeks talking amongst themselves, I felt a strong sense of isolation. Florrie touched my hand. 'It will be all right, Paul. I'm sure it will.' And she added, 'We can meet you in Preveza.' Bert agreed. 'We can be there in two, possibly three days—dependent on the weather. We'll wait for you there.'

When we had finished our coffee, Kondylakes returned our passports and the Port Captain handed Bert the ship's papers. They were free to sail when they wished. Back at the boat, I threw some clothes into my suitcase and by the time I was ready to leave, Kotiadis was waiting for me on the quay, his battered Renault backed up to the gangplank.

It was shortly after two when we drove out of Pylos, following the coast road that took a wide sweep round Navarino Bay, and then up into the hills, with Kotiadis talking all the time about his country's ancient history. He was a compulsive, explosive talker, his English interspersed with French and Greek words, and his enthusiasm for Greek antiquities was genuine. All the way up through the Peloponnese he was talking and driving fast, using his horn on the bends.

We crossed to the mainland of Greece by the ferry that plies the narrows separating the two gulfs of Patras and Corinth. By then the sun had set and we stopped the night at the ancient port of Navpaktos. It was here, after our meal, that I faced the questions I had been expecting.

We were sitting under the plane trees in the square and Kotiadis was talking about his early life on the island of Crete where he had been born.

His family had owned a small vineyard, growing grapes for

66

the raisin trade, but when the Germans invaded in 1941, he had left to join the guerrillas in the mountains. The air in the square was soft, and below us lay the medieval harbour, a circle of still, dark water surrounded by massive stone walls that had been built at the same time as the castle piled on the hill above us. Beyond the black curve of the harbour wall, the Gulf of Corinth lay serene and pale under the moon. The serenity of the scene was almost unreal in contrast to the story of hatred, violence and sudden death revealed by Kotiadis in staccato English.

The tide of liberation had swept him across to Athens, and the picture he drew of a young man flung into a political maelstrom made my own background seem humdrum by comparison. In Athens he had been involved in yet more killing, this time his own people. 'The Communist organization ELAS,' he said. 'I hate Communists.' We had been drinking coffee and ouzo and the tone of his voice was suddenly quite violent. 'You are lucky. You do not experience civil war. To kill Germans because they invade your country—that is good, that is natural. But war between men of the same race, that is terrible.' He sighed and tossed back the remains of his ouzo. 'We are a very political peoples—very excitable. It is the climate, the chaleur. In summer we play with our beads, we try to soothe our nerves, and then we explode like the storm cloud. That is why politics are so dangerous in Greece.' He leaned towards me. 'Have you seen a father kill his own son, deliberately and in cold blood?' He nodded, his eyes staring, bloodshot with cigarette smoke. 'I have. The boy was a Communist. And when it was done the father threw himself down on the boy's body, kissing his cheek and weeping. That is *la guerre civile*. I don't like. That is why you are here with me now. For us a man like Dr Van der Voort can be dangerous. He is a Communist and if we do not find him——'

'That's not true,' I protested. 'He hasn't been a Communist——'

'Ah, so you admit he was a Communist?'

'Yes. As a student. But not after 1940.'

'Ohi, ohi.' He made a negative movement with his fingers. '*Après la guerre*—long after, he is travelling in Russia, accepting money from the Soviet government, writing books for publication in Moscow and information for their scientific journals. Why does he do that if he is not a Communist?'

'That was years ago,' I said. 'Since about 1959 he's been working entirely on his own.'

'How do you know? You tell Kondylakes you do not see him for eight years.'

I repeated what Gilmore had said, but it made no difference. 'Once a man is a Communist, he does not change because of a little brutality in Hungary. Communism is the creed of the proletariat, and the proletariat represents man at his most brutal.'

'He wouldn't have seen it that way,' I said. 'For him Hungary would have come as a terrible shock. Anyway,' I added, 'I'm certain he isn't a Communist now.'

'That is not my information.' He summoned the boy from the kaféneion across the road and ordered more ouzo. 'Not only have the Russians financed his expeditions in the Soviet Union, but also in Turkey. You know we have been invaded by Turkey since six centuries. We do not like the Turks, and he was in Cyprus when the troubles begin.' And after that he sat, silent and morose, until the boy came running with a tray loaded with bottles and glasses. He drank half a tumbler of water and then said, 'Now, tell me about yourself. Particularly about your relations with Dr Van der Voort. I wish to understand please.'

The interrogation seemed to last endlessly, with him probing and probing as though I were trying to conceal from him some obvious truth. But in the end he gave it up, or else he just became bored. It was already past eleven, and shortly afterwards we left the square and walked back to the hotel. It had been an exhausting two hours, and even when I was in bed, his belligerent, staccato English continued drumming in my head.

Next morning I was called at six-thirty and we left early, driving back the way we had come to rejoin the main road, which ran west to the swamps of Missolonghi. 'Do you read your poet Byron in England now?' Kotiadis asked.

'No,' I said.

'Not at school?' He shook his head at me sadly. 'Here in Missolonghi he has his headquarters for the struggle to liberate Greece from the Turks. Here he dies. He never saw the liberation. But in Greece we remember Byron. Why do you not remember him?'

I had no answer to that, and Missolonghi looked a miserable place. The road swung north to Agrinion and then down to the shores of the great inland sea that I remembered from the chart—the Gulf of Amvrakikos. And all the time, slices of history mingled with questions, and the sun getting hotter. As we swung away from the gulf we came to a road junction signposted Preveza to the left, Arta and Jannina to the right. We turned right, climbing again, and there were peasants on the road and in the fields.

'Beyond Jannina we shall be very near the frontier with Albánia.' He said it with strong emphasis on the second 'a' as though he hated the place. 'Albánia, Yugoslavia, Bulgaria— all the north of our country is a border with Communist territory and it is from these Communist territories Dr Van der Voort comes with his expedition. You know the Red Army is holding manœuvres in Bulgaria, all the Warsaw Pact forces? And their fleet is in our waters, in the Aegean.' He was staring at me, his cigarette dangling from his lips. 'Don't you think it strange that he should come into our country from Macedonia at this exact moment?'

'I doubt whether he gave it a thought.'

'You think he does not know there is trouble coming again between the Arabs and the Jews?'

'Another Israeli-Egyptian war?'

'You do not read the papers—listen to the radio?'

'I don't speak Greek,' I reminded him.

'But Dr Van der Voort does.'

'He wouldn't be interested.'

'No?'

'A mind like his,' I said, 'dedicated to the work that has been his whole life——'

'Phui! He is trained by the Russians and he has been in Greece before.'

We were still climbing, the road snaking through bare hills with a great deal of rock. With every mile we were driving deeper and deeper into the heart of Greece, and further away from Preveza and the sea.

'When is he in Greece before, do you know?'

'I've no idea.'

He nodded. 'Of course, you do not see him for eight years. So how can you know he was here last year. He arrived on 4th April, in Kérkira—what you call Corfu.' He sounded his horn and thrust past a truck loaded with reeds, a blind bend just ahead. 'Last year he is alone, and for three months he is wandering by himself in the Ionian islands, particularly Levkas, and he is on Meganisi, where he lives for some days at the village of Vatahori. He has a tent with him and a rucksack, and then for almost two weeks there is no trace of him. Next I find him at limáni Levkas—the port, you understand—and afterwards he walks from Preveza towards Jannina, along the way we are driving now, talking to people, climbing to the top of the hills, wandering down dry river beds as though he is looking for gold, and all the time he is making notes and drawing little plans. Why, if he is not an agent?'

'He's a palæontologist,' I said wearily. 'He was looking for bones.'

'Bones?' He stared at me, his eyebrows lifted, and I found myself in the difficult position of trying to explain my father's work. If I had said old Greek coins, or bronze statuettes, he would probably have understood, but searching for bones and worked flints, for traces of early man, was beyond his comprehension. 'The only proper study in my country is the great civilization of Ancient Greece. Nothing else is important.' And he went on to say that he had traced Dr Van der Voort to a village called Ayios Giorgios. 'There we lose track of him again, nothing for a whole month.'

'You seem to have followed his movements very closely.'

'Of course. That is why I am at Methoni when you arrive. At Methoni he take a caique north along the coast. But it all happened a year ago, so it is difficult to follow him with exact dates. About the middle of August he take the caique—to Levkas again.' He muttered something to himself in Greek.

'Why does he go back to Levkas? And he is on that island more than a month. Why?' he demanded excitedly.

'I don't know.'

'Levkas, Kérkira, Cephalonia, all those Ionian islands—seven of them—are under a British Protectorate for fifty years. Turkey and France held them for a short time. For centuries

70

before, they are Venetian. Is that why he goes back to Levkas
—because they are more vulnerable politically?'

'He wasn't interested in politics.'

'No? Then why does he return to the islands? He is there all
last September. What is his particular interest in Levkas?' He
was staring at me again, ignoring the road, so that we touched
the verge.

'I tell you, I don't know.'

'You know nothing about him.' He hit the steering wheel
angrily. 'But all the time you say he is not any more a Communist.'

'Yes.'

'How can you be sure? He is like a stranger to you.' By then
his patience was wearing thin. 'Why did he attack this Cartwright?'

'I don't know.'

'And to draw attention to himself by disappearing—he is
either a very stupid man . . . What do you think?' And when I
didn't say anything, he turned his head, staring at me angrily.
'You are not being co-operative.'

'I can only tell you what I know. I was never interested in
his expeditions.'

'But you come to Greece. Why? Why you come now?'

He had put this question to me before. He seemed to sense
that this was the weak point, and it worried me. 'I tell you,
to find out what's happened to him.' I closed my eyes wearily.
It was hot in the car, the smell of his Greek cigarettes strong
and acrid.

The road swung away from Arta, and a few kilometres
further on we came to a reservoir with the arched remains of
an old aqueduct at the far end. He slowed the car where a dirt
track turned off to the right. 'That is the road to Ayios Giorgios
—what you call St George. See the hole in the hill up there?'
He pointed to a natural bridge spanning a rock outcrop high
on the hillside. Blue sky showed through the gap. 'Here is one
of many places in the Eastern Mediterranean where St George
is supposed to slay the dragon; that is the hole his lance makes.'
And as we gathered speed again, he said, 'Now, if last year he
comes to Ayios Giorgios to examine the Roman ruins of that
aqueduct I would understand, for it is a part of history. At the

71

entrance to the Gulf of Amvrakikos, at Aktion, close by Preveza, is where Caesar Augustus defeated Antony and Cleopatra. To celebrate his victory he built the city of Nikopolis and to provide water for Nikopolis he builds that aqueduct. It is a very long aqueduct, nearly fifty kilometres.'

We were into the valley now, a river flowing fast below us and high rocky slopes enclosing us in. The valley was cool and green, trees growing by the water, and the grass of the hills not yet seared by the sun's heat. There was peace and a time-less quality, and for a moment I forgot about Kotiadis and the future.

'Do you know when Dr Van der Voort first come to Greece?'

'Last year you said.'

'Ohi, ohi.' He shook his head violently. 'When he *first* come is what I ask.'

I tried to remember whether Gilmore had said anything about previous visits, but my mind was a blank.

'You do not know?'

'No.'

He seemed resigned to my inability to help him, for he gave a little shrug. 'My information is that he is here in 1965—you think that is possible?'

I remembered then that Holroyd had said something about a visit in 1965. 'Since his new theories involved the Central Mediterranean it's highly likely,' I said. 'But I was at sea then and we were out of touch.'

'You never write letters to your father?'

'No.'

He sighed and offered me one of his evil-smelling cigarettes. 'Perhaps when you have talked with Cartwright . . .' He flicked his lighter and after that he filled me in on what had happened after the old man had gone off in the Land-Rover, talking and driving with the cigarette in his mouth and his eyes half-closed against the smoke.

Cartwright had gone into Jannina the following morning on the village bus accompanied by Hans Winters, and in search-ing for a doctor, they had stumbled on the Land-Rover. As soon as he had had his wrist strapped up, Cartwright had air-mailed a report to Holroyd, and they had then driven round the town, questioning bus drivers, garages, hotels and tavernas without success. The next day they had stayed in camp and it was not until the morning of March 17 that they had informed the police in Jannina. They were then very short of petrol and by the time London had cabled them additional funds, the security police had taken over. 'That is when I go to Despotiko to interrogate them. Maybe it is true that they don't know where Van der Voort is. But I don't want any more archaeologists disappearing, so I confine them to the area of their camp with a guard to see that they stay there.'

'You got nothing out of Cartwright?'

'No. Nothing that interested me.' And after that he drove in silence as we passed through Jannina, still heading north. And now that we were nearing the end of our journey, I wondered whether I would do any better, whether Cartwright would give me some sort of explanation.

About twenty minutes later we turned right on to a dirt road that was signposted Despotiko. The village was on the shoulder of a hill, a huddle of nondescript buildings round a central square with the tiled roofs of older houses sloping into the valley below. We stopped beside an army truck parked outside the taverna and Kotiadis got out to have a word with two young soldiers sitting on a bench in the sun drinking Coca-Cola.

'Cartwright and Winters have gone up to the cave,' he said as he got back into the driving seat. 'It is about one kilometre beyond the camp.' And he added, 'His sister has arrived here.'

'Whose sister?' I asked, but I could guess the answer.

'The Dutch boy's,' he said, and started the engine.

We took a cobbled alleyway that ran out into bare rock as the houses thinned, the Renault in low gear and lurching on the steep slope, scattering hens from its path. The track led down to a stream and finished at a communal wash-house where women were busy slapping and kneading clothes on flat rocks at the water's edge. Two donkeys stood with dripping wooden water casks strapped to their backs, while a boy filled the last casks from a natural fountain gushing from a rock. There was a Land-Rover parked where the track narrowed to a path, and as we drew up beside it, two pigs, long and russet-coloured like wild boars, eyed us from the edge of the stream where they lay wallowing in the sun.

The chatter of the women died as we got out of the car. Kotiadis said something to them in Greek and the music of their laughter mingled with the tinkling noise of water running over stones. 'Now we walk.' And he led the way along the path, which followed the stream. Old olive trees twined gnarled branches over our heads, their trunks dark against the green of close-cropped grass, the white of cyclamens. In the distance, goat bells tinkled, and in a clearing ahead, a glint of orange marked the camp.

There were three small sleeping-tents, all orange, and one blue mess-tent. Some clothes hung on a line and smoke drifted up from a stone fireplace with a blackened iron pot on it. It was such a beautiful, peaceful place, with the sun dappling the grass through the grey leaves of the olives and the cool sound of the water, that it was difficult to imagine two men coming to blows here. I thought I saw a movement in the mess-tent, a figure standing in the shadows. But Kotiadis went straight past the camp and I followed him, wondering why she was here, what her brother would have told her.

The olive trees ceased and we could see the valley then with the hills on either side running back to a blue vista of distant peaks. We were walking on a carpet of thyme, oleanders by the water and the slope above us patched with a bright pattern of early spring flowers. The air was full of an unbelievable scent.

Kotiadis pointed to a gaping brown wound in the hillside ahead. 'That is where they dig.' He halted suddenly. I thought it was to get his breath, but then he said, 'Why does a man attack his assistant when they are already together almost one whole month? Have you thought of that? Why not the day before, or the week before?' He was staring up at the brown gash. 'I tell you why.' He turned and faced me. 'Because that night Cartwright is telephoning to Athens from the taverna.'

'What about?'

He shrugged. 'That is for you to discover. Some friend of his, an archaeologist. That is what he says. Myself, I think it is that he discovered that Dr Van der Voort is a Communist.'

If his long face hadn't looked so serious I would have thought

74

he was joking. 'You've got Communism on the brain,' I said angrily. I was thinking of all he had told me, how the old man had walked this area of Greece alone, going out to the island of Levkas again and again. And before that in the Sicilian islands, in Pantelleria and North Africa. For four years, since 1965, he had been searching, desperately searching, using up every penny he possessed, and all Kotiadis could think of was Communism. 'If he were a Communist, why the hell do you think he'd want to bury himself up here in this lonely valley?'

He turned on me then. 'What sort of a world are you living in?' He caught hold of my arm and swung me round. 'Regardez! There is Albánia.' He flung out his arm in a broad gesture. 'That one is Mao-Communist. And there is Yugoslavia.' He pointed to the north. 'Tito-Communist. A third frontier is with the Bulgars—Russian puppets.' He almost spat. 'We are ringed with Communist enemies. Their armies are on our north-eastern frontier, their fleet among our islands, and beyond the Aegean we are face-en-face with Turkey. The smell of war is in the air and you wonder we are sensitive?'

And when I reminded him again that this was just an anthropological dig, he said, 'That is good cover for a man who wishes to travel the villages of my country.'

It was no good arguing with him, and we walked on, climbing the final slope to the cave. A young corporal in olivegreen uniform came to meet us and Kotiadis talked with him for a moment. Then we had reached the dig, where Cartwright waited for us, stripped to the waist and wearing a pair of over-long khaki shorts. Behind him, Hans Winters was standing in the trench they had dug. He reminded me of Sonia, the same features, but rounder and heavier. He, too, was stripped to the waist, and his long fair hair, bleached almost white by the sun, hung over his eyes, limp with sweat.

They already knew Kotiadis. It was I who was the stranger, and their eyes fastened on me, waiting to know who I was— and Kotiadis let them wait, watching them both, a cigarette in his mouth, his sleepy-lidded eyes half closed.

My gaze had fastened on Cartwright. He was about my own age, tall and thin, his ribs showing through the tight-stretched skin of his torso, his stomach flat and hard with muscle. But

75

the shoulders were sloped, the head small. He had a little sandy moustache and high colouring; and the round steel spectacles he wore gave him a studious, rather than an athletic appearance. His left arm was in a sling.

He blinked when I told him who I was. 'I didn't expect you'd . . .' He hesitated. 'He never m-mentioned you.' He was on the defensive, his nervousness showing in a slight stutter. His eyes shifted to Kotiadis, owl-like behind the thick lenses. 'Any news of Dr Van der Voort?'

'Ohi.' Kotiadis shook his head.

He was glad. I sensed it immediately; it probably gave him a glow of importance to have the dig to himself. 'I suppose you're in charge here now?'

'Yes.'

I looked beyond him, along the line of the trench into the shadowed interior of the cave. It wasn't really a cave at all, more of a scooped-out hollow in the hillside, as though a great piece of it had been prised out and let fall into the valley below. And it was large. Even where we stood the overhang protruded above our heads. The height of it must have been a good 50 feet and the cave itself about 80 feet wide and 40 feet deep. Stones had been piled on the far side, and at the back, where they had erected a little blue Terylene shelter on an aluminium frame, the curve of the rock wall was black, and so smooth it might have been glazed. 'How old is this cave?' I asked him. He hadn't expected that, and I was thinking of the letter from Gilmore lying on the desk in the house in Amsterdam. 'Does it go back thirty-five thousand years?'

'I've no idea.'

'But it's important?' It had to be important, otherwise there was no sense in the old man's behaviour.

'It's a cave-shelter,' he said. 'But how long it's been a cave-shelter . . .' He gave a shrug. 'That we'll only know when we've dug down through the layers.'

'But you must have some idea what you're going to find. You're not digging here just for the fun of it.'

'It's worth a try. That's all one can say at the moment.'

'But what did my father think?'

'Dr Van der Voort?'

'Yes, what did he say about it?'

76

He hesitated. 'You've got to remember we'd been walking steadily, mostly in bitter cold, all the way down through Macedonia and a bit of Montenegro—about two hundred miles of territory we'd covered—and apart from a few artefacts, all quite recent, we'd found nothing.' And he added, 'Everything's relative on an expedition like this. In the end, you've got to justify it somehow. Our finances limit us to three months' work.'

'In other words, it's a shot in the dark?'

'If you like.'

I couldn't believe it. I couldn't believe that the old man would have gone out in winter with such desperate urgency to work on something he didn't believe in. 'You hadn't much confidence in him, had you?'

'I didn't disagree with him, if that's what you mean?'

'That's not what I meant at all,' I answered. 'It's just that I want to know how this fits in to the pattern of his discoveries.'

'The pattern?' He seemed puzzled.

'You must have realized that he was working to some sort of an over-all pattern—a framework if you like. You know very well he was out here last year, that he covered the whole area from here to the coast and out to the islands. Didn't he tell you? Didn't anybody tell you what he was aiming at?'

His manner, his whole attitude to the dig, annoyed me. I had expected enthusiasm, a sense of excitement, something that would enable me to understand what it was my father was searching for. Instead, he was making it all seem dull and ordinary, like those students you read about digging around in the foundations of old hill forts in Britain. 'You haven't been in charge of a dig before, have you?'

'Not in charge. But I've been on digs before.'

'Where?'

'In Suffolk—Clactonian Man. In Germany and France. Why?' He was frowning. 'Why are you so interested in this cave? You're not an anthropologist.'

'No. I'm a ship's officer.' I stared at him, trying to see into his mind, trying to understand. 'You came out here with a man who's regarded as a brilliant palæontologist and you don't seem to know what his theory is, what he's working towards. Didn't Holroyd brief you?'

'Of course. And I knew Dr Van der Voort's reputation.'

'What do you mean?'

'Well, it's common knowledge. Planting that skull in a dig in Africa. Trying to fool people, and then working for Moscow and twisting his theories to suit the Russians. He may be brilliant. I know some people think so. But it's a damn tricky sort of brilliance.'

'What was he trying to prove here in Greece? Or don't you know?'

'Yes, of course I do.'

'Well?'

'The Cro-Magnon-Mousterian gap. That's something anthropologists have been puzzling over for years. He had a theory about that. But his main interest was to prove that *homo sapiens sapiens*—modern man—came up from Africa across a mythical land-bridge. It was a complete reversal of all that he had written previously.'

'You don't agree with him then?'

He hesitated. 'Well, if you want to know, I think a man should be consistent; he shouldn't switch his ideas to suit his convenience the way Dr Van der Voort did.'

'And you didn't believe in it?' I insisted.

The question seemed to worry him. 'No,' he said finally, 'No, I didn't.' He said it reluctantly, as though I had forced the admission out of him.

'Then what's the point of this expedition?'

'To check. There's always a chance, you know.'

'An outside chance, as far as you're concerned?'

'Well, yes, if you like. It's a theory, nothing more. And a pretty wild one. If you knew anything about anthropology you'd realize that.'

I turned to Hans Winters. 'Is that what you think?'

He stared at me, not saying anything, a stubborn, mulish look on his face.

'What puzzles me,' I said, turning back to Cartwright, 'is why Holroyd got him a grant, why he sent you out to spy on him, if there's no basis for his theory.'

'I w-wasn't spying. I was here to help.' Two angry spots of colour showed in his cheeks.

'If you'd done that, he wouldn't have disappeared.'

He stared at me, his face flushed. 'You don't seem to under-stand what sort of a man Dr Van der Voort is.'

'I think I do.'

'He's mad.' He said it almost viciously.

'He's difficult, I agree. But I've no reason to believe that he's mad.'

'Then why did he attack me? Suddenly like that, and for no reason.'

'That's what I came to find out.'

'He was like a maniac.'

'I think you'd better explain.' I was keeping a tight rein on my temper. 'Suppose you tell me exactly what happened?'

He hesitated, staring at me owlishly as though I'd dug a pit for him. 'There's nothing to tell you,' he said. 'Nothing you don't know, I imagine. He called me out of my tent. He'd been for his usual walk and I came out and saw him standing there in the moonlight. And then he went for me. No warning—nothing. He just seemed to go berserk. And he had that stick with him, the one he always carries.' He moved his left arm slightly. 'It broke my wrist.'

'You wrote to Holroyd that there was an argument.'

'Did I?' He seemed surprised. 'I don't remember.' And he added, 'In fact, I don't remember much about it. I was pretty badly knocked up.'

'What time was it?'

'I've told all this to Mr Kotiadis.'

I moved a few steps nearer, staring him in the face, getting a sense of pleasure almost as I saw him shrink back. 'Well, you're telling it to me now,' I said. 'Go on. What time did it all happen?'

'Sh-shortly after eleven o'clock.'

'And there was no argument, no altercation?'

'No.'

'Do you mean to say he attacked you without a word?'

'I tell you, I don't remember.'

I couldn't decide whether that was the truth, or whether there was more to it. In the end I left it at that. If there had been a reason for the attack, then he wasn't admitting it—not yet. And with Kotiadis standing there, I felt this wasn't the moment to question him about his telephone call to Athens.

I turned to Hans Winters. 'Where were you when this happened?'

'In my tent.'

'And you didn't hear anything?'

'The first I knew about it was when Alec woke me with blood on his face and in pain from his broken wrist.' And he added, 'I sleep very heavily.' His manner was surly, and though his English was good, the accent was more pronounced than his sister's.

'And what did you do then?'

'I went out to look for Dr Van der Voort.'

'And by then he'd gone?'

'Ja. He'd gone. The Land-Rover, too.'

A small wind had sprung up and it was suddenly quite cool. Cartwright was already putting on his shirt, moving away from me. Somewhere on the hillside above us, bells were tinkling. 'Goats?' I asked.

Hans Winters nodded. 'Ja. Goats.'

The breeze was from the north, carrying the sound with it, but the wide mouth of the cave, with its beetling overhang, blocked all sight of the hillside above. I moved further into the cave, staring about me. The floor was packed hard, dry powdery earth flattened by long ages of occupation, and embedded in it were great slabs of rock fallen from the arch of the overhang. They had cut their trench a little left of centre from the back right out to the beginning of the drop down into the valley. It was about 3 feet wide and 4 feet deep at the outer edge. The parapet of it came up to Hans Winter's chest. 'So this is what you call a cave-shelter?'

He nodded.

'Does that mean occupied by men?'

'We think so.'

'How do you know?'

He smiled. 'We don't yet. In recent years it's been a winter shelter for sheep and goats. The first thing we had to do was to remove the stock fence.' He indicated the stones piled at the side. 'That was a dry-stone wall—right across the whole mouth of it, three or four feet high.'

I glanced back at Cartwright, but he was now talking to Kotiadis. Down in the valley, sheep were moving along the grass at the river's edge. It was like being on a natural balcony, the valley spread out below and a glimpse of purpled mountains across the tops of the hills opposite. 'Very different sort of country to Holland.' I wanted to get him talking.

'Ja.' And for the first time I caught a gleam of warmth in his eyes. 'Is good. I like these hills, the valley. It's very beautiful. But I miss the sea.'

'The sea's not all that far away,' I said, smiling. He couldn't be more than nineteen and he was homesick. 'Did my father talk about the islands at all?'

'Ja, ja. Often. He thought our species of man came up through the islands—the Ionian Islands. Across from Africa and through Sicily.' He glanced quickly towards Cartwright, and seeing that he was out of earshot, he added, 'Alec doesn't see it that way. He's a flat earth man.' He grinned. It was a grin that lightened the heaviness of his Dutch face, so that for a moment I glimpsed the elfin look his sister had. 'He's very practical, likes everything straightforward and simple. Dr Van der Voort was a man of ideas, of vision.'

'Did you like him?'

He stared at me, the warmth fading, the surliness returning. 'I thought him very interesting, very intelligent. That's why I came on this expedition. I like his ideas.'

'But you don't like him personally.'

'No.' He glanced at his watch. 'Time for lunch,' he said and he put his hands on the edge of the trench and heaved himself out. It was the easy, fluid movement of a man whose muscles are in perfect tune. 'You coming?' The others were moving off down the slope. He picked up his sweater and started to follow them, tying the sleeves round his neck.

'Just a moment,' I said. 'Was it my father who insisted that this cave-shelter was occupied by early man?'

He nodded, pausing. 'He said it might not prove anything beyond doubt, but for him it was confirmation.'

'Why?'

'The situation.' He was standing in silhouette against the sunlight, a thick-set powerful figure, staring down into the valley. 'The river right at their door,' he said. 'And it faces south with a good view. That's important—to watch for game and to avoid being surprised by human enemies. And the sun—those early hunters went practically naked. They needed the sun. And they needed water, for themselves and to attract the animals that provided them with food, weapons, tools, fat for their lamps, skins to lie on.'

I had moved to his side, and standing there on that high platform of beaten earth, looking down upon that flock of sheep moving slowly beside the river, I could almost imagine myself, with a skin over my shoulders and a flint axe in my hand, preparing to go down and cut the next meal out.

'It's a textbook situation, you know.' He turned, smiling at me. 'I'm still a student. I'd never seen a cave-shelter before. But as soon as I saw this place . . . it's a natural.'

'You think it's important then?'

He hesitated, his gaze switching to the two figures of Cartwright and Kotiadis moving slowly down the slope towards the river and the olives. 'I tell you, I'm only a student. But ja—ja, I do. So little work has been done in the Balkans—almost nothing in Greece. And Dr Van der Voort . . . maybe his theory is wild, as Alec says, but he had a most extraordinary eye for country. All down through Macedonia, in the mountains of Montenegro, and then after we crossed the border into Greece—I watched him, trying to learn, to understand. He seemed to know—instinctively. About the country, I mean. Sometimes he drove the Land-Rover. More often he was walking himself, a queer slouching walk, his head bent, his eyes on the ground or on the lie of the land. It was almost . . .' He hesitated. 'I don't know . . . as though he saw it all with the eyes of prehistoric man. He had that sort of *rapport* with the subject. Identification—ja, that's the word. He was involved, identified, so completely dedicated and entirely absorbed . . .' He grinned as though to cover his unwilling admiration. 'Maybe it's just because I'd never worked with a real expert before.'

'Cartwright said you didn't find anything very much.'

'Oh yes, we found traces here and there—quite a few things, chert flakes mainly. But nothing Dr Van der Voort thought worth while. Not until we came here. And it wasn't only the situation that excited him. Come and look at this.' He took me to the back of the cave, to the blackened curve of the rock. 'Alec is not convinced. He thinks it may be water seepage.

But Dr Van der Voort insisted that the discoloration was carbon deposit from the smoke of open hearths.' He put his hand on the rock face. 'Feel that. Feel how smooth it is. That's calcium. A thick layer of it overlying the fire marks and acting as a protective coating. It's caused by water seeping down from the limestone overhead, and if we knew when it had happened, how fast it had built up, we'd know how old the fire marks are. Dr Van der Voort thought ten thousand years at least.'

'Did he give any reason?'

He shook his head. 'No, he didn't say. But you can see here where he chipped a bit out with the small geological hammer he always had with him.' The calcium coating was almost an inch thick, opaque like cathedral glass. 'What he was hoping for, of course, was a hearth burial. They used to leave their dead beside their hearths and move on. At least, that's what the books say. And then wind-blown earth gradually covered the body—a natural burial. But there's a lot of work to do before we get anywhere near that level.'

We were standing on the lip of the trench and at the back here it was less than two feet deep, with rock showing at the bottom.

'We're in trouble already, you see. Big slabs fallen from the roof. They'll take a lot of shifting. And out near the edge of the platform, where the earth is softer, we are already having to widen the trench to prevent it from collapsing.' He glanced at his watch again. 'Well, let's go and eat. I don't know about you, but I'm hungry.' He picked up his shirt and we started down the slope. The breeze was stronger now and quite cool, but he didn't seem to notice it.

'I gather your sister has joined you.'

'Ja. She is come four days ago.'

'Why?'

He looked at me, his pale eyes suddenly hostile. 'Sonia can be very obstinate at times. And she has money of her own.'

'That doesn't answer my question.'

'Well, you ask her yourself.' And he muttered, 'That old devil had a sort of fascination for her.'

'You mean my father?'

'Dr Van der Voort—ja. It's not healthy for her. He may be a very clever palæontologist, but he's a damned strange old man.' And when I asked him what he meant by that, he rounded on me. 'You should know. You're his son and you haven't been near him for years.'

He closed up after that, and a few minutes later we arrived at the camp. She was standing by the stone hearth, looking more like a boy than ever in a pale shirt and very short shorts, and all she said was 'Hullo!', as though we had parted only that morning. And then she turned back to her cooking, reaching for a wooden spoon, and in doing so dislodged a packet of biscuits. She bent down to retrieve it, the curve of her buttocks stretching the flimsy shorts. I saw Cartwright staring, a sly look that was somehow unexpected in an academic. He glanced round, caught my eye—a satyr with glasses and a schoolboy flush. My feeling of dislike intensified.

'A word with you, please.' It was Kotiadis, and he took me aside, along the path through the olive trees that led back to the village. 'I have sent the corporal for your valítsa. Also I have told him you are free to come and go as you please.'

'You're leaving?'

'Yes. I do not wish to eat here. I prefer Greek food.'

'And I'm to stay?'

'It's what you want, eh?'

'Yes. Yes, of course.'

He nodded, smiling and holding out his hand. 'I will be back in two, perhaps three days.'

'And I can go where I like?'

'Of course. You can go to Preveza, meet your friends, leave Greece—if that is what you want. You are free and you have your passport.'

I shook his hand and he walked off through the olive grove, still smiling quietly to himself. Shortly afterwards the corporal arrived with my suitcase.

2

IT WAS HOT that afternoon and I was alone. The three of them had gone up to the dig. Lunch had been a hurried meal, eaten largely in silence. No doubt I was responsible for that, but I got the impression that the midday meal was always

84

hurried. The hours of daylight were precious and Cartwright seemed driven, as though he had a deadline to meet. 'If you want to sleep here,' he said, 'then you'd better use Dr Van der Voort's tent. Everything's still there, including his sleeping bag. We'll be back at dusk.' I had expected Sonia to stay in the camp, but she went with them.

I sat for a while on the gnarled trunk of a fallen olive tree, listening to the strident sound of the cicadas, the distant tinkling of sheep bells. The breeze had died and it was very still, very peaceful. An idyllic spot, except for the picture in my mind —moonlight and the old man going for Cartwright without any reason. It didn't make sense—and yet . . . I wondered why Hans hadn't liked him when his sister so obviously did.

In the end I got up and prowled around the camp site. Something—something had happened that night to drive the old man to violence. He'd been for a walk, Cartwright had said. But you don't go berserk walking on your own. Unless it had been building up inside him for a long time. . . .

My gaze switched to the tents. His was next to the mess-tent. I went across to it and pulled back the flap. His things had all been neatly stacked—a rucksack, a battered suitcase, bed roll and sleeping-bag. No camp-bed, everthing very spartan, and the whole interior suffused with a weird orange light, the sun shining through the gaily-coloured Terylene.

I went in and opened up the suitcase. But all it contained was clothes—no notes, not even any books. Whatever he had learned on the way down through Macedonia was locked away in his head.

I went down to the river then and lay for a while in the warm sun, listening to the sound of the water. It was a relief to be on my own in the quiet of the Greek countryside instead of cooped up in that car with the smell of Kotiadis's cigarettes and his explosive talk. I took my clothes off and waded into the water. It was almost knee-deep, running fast over flat, worn stones, and at the deepest part I plunged myself into it, clinging to the bottom and letting it wash over me. It was clear, sparkling water, very cold, and I came out refreshed to lie on the grass again and dry out in the sun. The bathe had relaxed me and my mind felt clearer. If I had known enough about anthropology to understand what was in the old man's mind, what this cave-shelter meant to him . . . I closed my eyes, soaking up the warmth of the sun, thinking of Cartwright and Hans. There was the girl, too. She had been here four days, and she knew the old man better than any of us. In four days she must have discovered something. Kotiadis was probably right. If I stayed here a day or two, living with them in the camp, perhaps working with them on the dig, sooner or later I would discover what had really happened.

After a while I put on my clothes again and went back to the camp. I would have gone up to the dig then, but I needed a sweater and the corporal had put my case outside the mess-tent. The flap of the tent was open and in the blue interior of it was a folding table with two canvas chairs. There was a pressure lamp on the table, and amongst a litter of books and papers, I saw a pocket mirror, comb, hairbrush and powder compact. Sonia had been using it as a dressing-table and her sleeping-bag was laid out on the grass at the back.

I ducked my head and went in. The papers were notes—notes on the books she had been reading. Two of them were open—a little British Museum booklet called *Man the Tool-Maker* and a much bigger volume, *Hundert Jahre Neanderthaler*. The other books, four of them, were also anthropological. One in particular caught my eye: *Adventures with the Missing Link* by Raymond Dart. There was also a typewritten article by E. S. Higgs dealing with A Middle Palæolithic Industry in Greece. I skimmed this through, and then, intrigued by the title, I took *Adventures with the Missing Link* and one of the canvas chairs out into the sunshine and began to read.

It was just curiosity, no more—an excuse to sit in the sun and do nothing except enjoy the stillness and the emptiness of the olive grove. It never occurred to me that I should enjoy it, that I should become so engrossed in a book on anthropology that I should lose all sense of time. But this told of the first discoveries that proved man had originated in Africa. It was a fascinating story, written in a language I could understand, and though the setting was much further south than Kenya, it brought back something of my own childhood.

In 1924 Raymond Dart had been shown the fossilized skull of a baboon. He was an Australian who had recently taken the chair of Anatomy at the little-known University of Witwatersrand. The skull, brought to him by a young girl student, had come from limeworks at a village called Buxton on the edge of the Kalahari desert, and it was the first of a whole series of discoveries that led him ultimately to the conclusion that the evolution of man from primate ancestors had begun, not in Asia, as was then generally thought, but in Africa. This first discovery was followed almost immediately by a consignment of fossil-laden rocks, two of which were complementary. From these two, Dart pieced together the skull of a six-year-old primate with a small ape-sized brain and a facial appearance that was almost human. This became known as the Taung skull, after the railway station nearest to the point where it had been blasted out of the limestone.

The man-ape child had lived in the early Pleistocene period, about a million years ago, and the form of the skull made it clear that it was a true biped and had walked upright. Moreover, the teeth, which were like human teeth, proved beyond doubt, to Dart at any rate, that it had been a carnivore. In other words, about a million years ago, in Africa, environment had developed a breed of killer apes that had branched off from their arboreal ancestors; they had taken to the ground, standing erect, and had used bone weapons instead of teeth for hunting.

A slip of paper had been inserted as a marker at chapter two and somebody, presumably Sonia, had underlined the opening paragraph: *For many years after the news of my find was presented to the world, I was to be accused of being too hasty in arriving at the definite conclusions I had formed after studying the skull, teeth and endocranial cast for a matter of only four months.*

The major part of the book concerned Dart's work on limestone breccia from the Makapansgat Valley in Northern Transvaal. In fourteen years 95 tons of bone-bearing breccia were recovered from thousands upon thousands of tons of limestone dumped by the quarries, and each of those 95 tons had yielded an average of 5,000 fossil bones. From these he had reconstructed, not only the appearance, but the whole way of life of the early man-ape, proving that his development had been associated throughout with the use of weapons.

It read like a detective story, the bones, so carefully chipped from their limestone matrix, acting as the clues, for these man-apes accumulated only those remains of their prey that were useful to them as weapons or tools. They had even inserted teeth or sharp slivers of bone into the larger bones they used as clubs to give an edge to them, and they were already essentially right-handed.

The sun had dropped below the hills and it was getting chilly when I reached the chapter entitled—*The Antiquity of Murder*. It showed the man-ape as a killer and an eater of his own, as well as other, species, and I was just considering this in relation to what Gilmore had told me about the old man's Journal when I became conscious that somebody was standing behind me. I turned. It was Sonia.

'That's mine,' she said possessively.

'I thought it probably was.'

'It never occurred to me . . .'

'What?'

'That you read—books, I mean.'

'Only the lighter ones.' I closed the book and held it up so that she could see the title. 'This man Dart—he's like a sort of anthropological private eye.'

'Raymond Dart,' she said coldly, 'is probably the most out-standing anthropologist since Darwin.'

'Well, anyway, he makes it interesting.'

'Really—to you?' She smiled. 'That's probably because it was written in collaboration.'

'Then it's a pity more anthropologists don't collaborate with somebody. Here he is, rattling his old fossil-bones, making deductions nobody believes in——'

'I suppose you mean the Taung skull—*Australopithecus africanus*.'

I stared at her and then burst out laughing. 'Is that meant to encourage me? Why the hell can't you call it a man-ape child like he does? Then we know what we're talking about.' I opened the book at the marker paper, pointing to the first paragraph of chapter two. 'Did you underline that?'

'No.' She was leaning down over my shoulder. 'It was like that when he gave it to me.'

'Who—the old man?'

'Dr Gilmore.'

'He'd marked it, had he?'

'I suppose so.'

'Why did he give it to you?'

She hesitated, frowning. 'I don't quite know. He bought it for me especially at a bookshop in Amsterdam. I knew all about Dart, of course. But I hadn't read this book. He said it might interest me. That was all. I don't know why.'

'You've read it, have you?'

'Yes, of course. I read it straight away. And then again in the plane coming over.'

'And you still don't know why?'

'No.'

'This chapter on the antiquity of murder,' I said. 'I was just reading it when you arrived. How far back do our instincts go? I mean how deep are they?'

She didn't answer that, and when I looked up at her, she seemed to have stiffened as though she were holding her breath.

'What this man seems to be saying is that as soon as the man-ape came down from the trees he was a killer. In fact, that that was the reason he was able to leave the trees. When he found he could stand upright, then he could see above the tall grass and had his hands free to use weapons to assist him in killing much larger animals than himself. He became a flesh-eater. Why does Dart use the word murder?'

'To emphasize his point—that's all.'

'About man being a killer?'

'Yes.'

'And that's a million years ago—a long time.'

I think she knew very well what I was driving at. 'There isn't much known about man's deep-buried, instinctive urges. They've only just started a proper study of the brain.'

'And the instincts may not be in the brain. They may be in our nerves, our tissues, our blood cells. Is that what my father was after in his Journal?'

'I haven't read it,' she said quickly.

'No, but Dr Gilmore has. Didn't he say anything to you about it?'

'A little. Not much.' She turned away. 'I can't stay talking. The others will be here soon and there's a meal to be got ready.' She went over to the stone fireplace, leaning down and blowing on the embers. Then she put on some more wood.

89

'Will you get some water, please? I'll need water for the tea.'
She gave me a blackened iron kettle and I took it down to the
river. I was feeling disturbed, confused. Dart's categorical
statement, my own satisfaction at seeing that man fall back
over the edge of the oil terminal pier, the old man's attack on
Cartwright—it all seemed to add up, and it worried me.

Dusk was falling fast, and by the time I got back she had lit
a pressure lamp and flames were leaping between the stones of
the fireplace. 'I should have come down earlier,' she said. 'I
had to use paraffin. But it's exciting up there. Sifting each
shovelful of soil, wondering what you're going to turn up.
I've never been on a dig before.' She went to get something
from the mess-tent and then Cartwright and her brother came
into camp. Hans went down to the river immediately, stripped
to the waist, his towel over his shoulder. Cartwright busied
himself lighting the second pressure lamp.

The meal did not take long to prepare—tinned stew,
followed by tinned pears. Only the bread and a rather acid
sheep cheese was local. We washed it down with a lot of dark,
sweet tea. Hans had found a coin that afternoon. It was of no
value, an Augustan bronze coin, but it proved that the cave-
shelter had been occupied, or at least visited, by somebody in
the first century A.D.—a shepherd probably who had taken his
sheep to the market in Nikopolis. They were speculating as to
why he had dropped it there, and I sat listening, not asking any
questions. I thought if I let them get used to my presence in the
camp . . . 'Care to see it?' Hans asked. He dredged in the
pocket of his shorts and flipped the coin across to me. 'I was
widening the trench and that was just over a metre down—112
centimetres to be exact. So that's the amount of dirt and turd
dropping that have accumulated there during two thousand
years.'

It was the only thing they had found that could be given an
exact dating. The rest had been animal bones and broken pieces
of pottery—sherds of simple country work. At the lowest point
they had reached Cartwright reckoned they were only back to
the Homeric period. 'We've a lot of digging to do before we
get down to a depth that's of any interest to us. And it's all so
slow—the soil to be sifted, everything catalogued so that we
have a complete picture of man's occupation century by cen-

tury.' He spoke slowly, staring at me all the time, the firelight reflected in his glasses, as though he were explaining something to a child. But he sounded depressed all the same, and when I asked why they didn't drive a pilot trench straight down to the depth that did interest them, he answered me quite sharply: 'That's not the way we do things. We might miss something vital. And anyway, without a steady build-up of the picture, we can't be sure what depth we are interested in. We need a complete stratified picture, all the layers of occupation. It wouldn't make sense otherwise.'

We had finished supper by then, and as soon as we had washed up, Cartwright went off to his tent to write up his notes and Hans took the other pressure lamp. 'I have some books I must study.' Sonia had disappeared with a torch and a towel to the river. I got my suitcase and moved into the old man's tent, setting my things out by the light of a candle. And then I picked up Dart's book again and re-read that chapter on the age-old instinct of man to kill, lying stretched out on the bed roll, the candle in its bottle on the ground beside me.

I had just started on the next chapter when Sonia pulled back the entrance flap. 'I feel like a drink,' she said.

I put the book down and sat up. She meant the taverna up in the village, for she had put on a skirt and was wearing an anorak against the growing chill of the evening. 'What about your brother?'

'He's working. He works most evenings. And Alec doesn't drink.'

She had a torch and as we left I saw Cartwright sitting on his camp bed, the interior of his tent bright with the light of the pressure lamp. He looked up as we passed the dying embers of the fire, staring at us, the papers on his knee momentarily forgotten. He half rose as though to say something, or perhaps to join us, but then he seemed to change his mind and a moment later we were alone together in the darkness of the olive trees. The moon had not yet risen. The only light was the stars and the pencil gleam of her torch.

She seemed to be waiting on me, for she didn't say anything and we walked for a time in silence, the only sound the growing murmur of water ahead. And then she stopped. 'Well, now that you've come, what do you intend to do?' She was facing me, suddenly very tense, the way she had been when we had first met.

'Stick around for a day or two, I suppose.' I wasn't sure myself.

'Is that all?'

'What else? You've been here four days—you tell me what I ought to be doing.'

She stared at me, biting her lip. 'Why did you come here?'

I laughed. 'If I knew that, I'd know a lot more about myself than I do at the moment.'

'But you came here with that man Kotiadis. I don't understand.'

I told her how it had happened and she said, 'Oh, that explains it. I wondered.' She seemed relieved and I realized that this was why she had been avoiding me.

As we walked on, she said, 'You know about this Congress, don't you? There's a Pan-European Prehistoric Congress being held at Cambridge at the end of May. That's why Alec is in such a hurry to get this dig opened up.' And when I asked her what that had to do with it, she said, 'I don't know whether Professor Holroyd initiated it, but he's certainly been closely involved in organizing it. All the leading academics of Western Europe will be there, possibly some from Russia and Eastern Europe as well. And he has the chance of reading one of the papers. That's why Dr Van der Voort was given a grant.'

'Who told you that? Cartwright?'

'No. Hans. Alec, as you've probably guessed, is Holroyd's protégé.' We had reached the water point and she paused, the stream close beside us, the gleam of it like steel in the starlight. 'You remember that book Holroyd read for an English publisher? It was all there, all Dr Van der Voort's thinking on the origin of our own species. In outline, that is. Nothing confirmed. Just theory. But then he sent those bones to Dr Gilmore for dating.' She seized hold of my arm, her voice suddenly raised against the sound of the water. 'Please—try to understand. If Holroyd can get supporting evidence, then he'll go to this Congress, read his paper. Dr Van der Voort's theories are unpublished. He'll present them as his own.'

'And what am I supposed to do about that?'

'Find him, you fool,' she answered stridently. 'Find him and bring him back, so that he can take credit for anything that's discovered here.'

'That's all very well,' I said. 'But Cartwright has already searched the area. Your brother was with him. And Kotiadis has been searching too—not just this area, but half the country. You realize he's a Greek Intelligence Officer?'

She nodded. 'I wasn't sure. He said he was from the Ministry of Antiquities in Athens—the General Direction of Antiquities and Restoration, he called it.'

'He's Intelligence,' I repeated. 'And he thinks the old man is a Communist agent. Not only that,' I added, 'but he's leapt to the conclusion that Cartwright knew this and that's why my father attacked him.'

'But that's ridiculous.'

'Maybe, but what's the alternative? Why did he attack him? D'you know?'

'No. I can only guess.'

'Well?'

'Can't you see it—from his point of view? Knowing Holroyd was using him. Alec, too. It must have worked on his mind—a feeling of frustration, depression. . . .'

'He was in a manic-depressive state, you mean?'

'I don't know—yes, probably.'

'But why—suddenly like that?'

She shook her head. 'I don't know. He's so complicated. I don't pretend to understand him.'

'Nor do I,' I said. 'I never did.' I took hold of her arm. 'Come on. Let's go and have that drink.'

She nodded, and as we walked on I told her about Kotiadis and the questions he had asked as we drove up through Greece. 'So you see,' I said finally, 'there's no question of my father being allowed to continue his work here.'

'Yes, I see. And that's why we have a guard on the camp.' She was silent as we turned into the steep alleyway that led up to the centre of the village. At length she murmured, 'I can't bear the thought of Holroyd getting the credit for it all, for all his years of work.'

'Not much chance of that,' I said, trying to cheer her up. 'Cartwright didn't seem at all optimistic about this dig when I questioned him this morning.'

93

'Of course not. His instructions were to locate the dig from which those dated bones had come. The cave-shelter has a virgin floor, quite undisturbed. He knows this isn't it, but since Dr Van der Voort disappeared . . . well, he's in charge now. He may not believe in your father's theories, but it's a great opportunity for him, and there's always a chance.'

We had reached the square by then. There were lights on in the taverna and the radio was blaring Greek music as I pushed open the door. The interior was not designed for comfort, bare wood tables, some forms and the walls cracked and peeling. At one of the tables four men in open-neck shirts were playing dominoes, two others were talking, and an old man with drooping moustaches and baggy Turkish trousers occupied the only chair. All eyes were turned upon us as we entered. The owner appeared behind the counter that did service as a bar. He was a short bull of a man with black eyebrows and features that suggested he had just suffered some terrible loss. Sonia smiled at him. 'Kalispéra, Andreas.'

'Spéras,' he replied, his eyes on me, watchful like all the rest.

'What would you like?' I asked her.

'Coffee,' she said. 'Just coffee. All we have at the camp is tea and I'm not used to it. We drink coffee at home.'

I nodded, remembering how it had been in Holland—coffee at all hours of the day. 'Bad for the liver,' I said, and she smiled. 'We're plain eaters and we don't suffer from le foie.'

I ordered coffee and ouzo for both of us, but she shook her head and said something to Andreas. 'I'm sorry, I don't like ouzo. Just coffee, please.'

We sat at the one vacant table, watching Andreas make the coffee on a paraffin burner. She had a few words of Greek, but though the occupants of the taverna were polite, it was not a congenial atmosphere. I talked to her about the Barretts and the voyage from Malta, but it scarcely seemed to register. She had withdrawn into herself, her small face devoid of any expression, her eyes fixed on one of the faded posters that decorated the walls, seeing nothing, only what was in her mind.

The coffee came, black and sweet in tiny cups, each with its glass of water and my ouzo smelling of aniseed. 'Tileghráfima,' Andreas said and handed Sonia a cable.

'It's for Alec,' she said, glancing at it, and then she seemed

94

to freeze, sitting very still, staring down at it. Finally she looked at me. 'Professor Holroyd is taking the night flight. He will be in Athens tomorrow morning.'

'Does he say why he's coming out here?'

'No.' She folded the cable sheet and slipped it into the pocket of her anorak. 'No, he doesn't say why. But it's obvious, isn't it?' She called to Andreas, and then she said to me, 'I'm so sorry. I don't like the stuff, but I've ordered one all the same.' And when it came she picked it up and drank half of it at a gulp as though it were geneva. 'They're like vultures,' she breathed. 'That's what he always called them—the desk-bound academics—vultures.' She looked at me suddenly, her face pale and tense. 'Can I have a cigarette please?'

I produced one of the duty-free packets I had brought from the boat, and as I lit her cigarette, she said, 'Suppose I told you where he was—what would you do?'

I stared at her. 'You know where he is?'

She shook her head. 'No—not for certain. But I think I can guess.'

'How?'

'The book—I told you I was typing his new book.'

I had forgotten that. I lit my own cigarette, watching her, waiting for her to tell me, conscious that I was nearing the end of my journey now.

'What would you do?' she repeated.

I sipped my ouzo and drank some water. The water was very good, soft as milk and yet like crystal; spring water from the mountains, uncontaminated by chemicals. I hadn't expected this and I couldn't think of an answer. I looked at her and our eyes met, and after that my hands began to tremble, for I was certain she knew, and the prospect of meeting him, wild and alone in some secret place, brought back my boyhood fears.

'Well?' she asked in a level, controlled voice.

'Why didn't you go yourself if you knew where he was?'

'I wasn't sure——' She hesitated. 'I thought perhaps he needed to be alone. But now——'

'Well, where is he?' I asked. 'Where has he holed up?'

'First answer my question.'

'All right,' I said. 'I'll go.'

'Of course you'll go,' she answered quickly. 'But what happens then?'

'That's up to him,' I told her, not relishing the prospect. 'I can only offer to help in any way I can.' It was what I had come for, after all.

I don't know whether that satisfied her or not. She drank her coffee and finished her ouzo. 'Let's go,' she said. 'I can't talk here.' I paid and we said goodnight, but it wasn't until we were clear of the village that she told me where he was—or rather, where she thought he was. 'On the main road, before you got to Jannina, did you see the remains of an aqueduct?'

It came back to me then, the hillside sloping green with that gaping hole high up in the rock, and Kotiadis saying my father had been in that village the previous year. 'Ayios Giorgios?'

'No, not Ayios Giorgios.' We had reached the water now and she stopped, her voice only just audible above the sound of it. 'On the other side of the valley. I've never been there, of course, but he describes it in great detail—two whole pages. And it was so important to him that, typing it, I could see the whole thing. The road cuts the line of the aqueduct; on one side the water was carried on great arches, on the other the Roman engineers drove a tunnel through the mountain. The entrance to that tunnel is right beside the road. The tunnel itself is blocked by a fall, but above it, on the tops of the hills, there is an area of red desert sand. It's a hangover from something that happened twenty thousand years ago.'

'And you think he's there?'

'I don't know . . . it's just a feeling.' She was no more than a shadow in the starlight, standing staring towards the steel ribbon of the water. 'That place was terribly important to him. He writes very factually, you know, not at all interestingly, except to experts. But this passage was different. It had a compelling sense of excitement.' She hesitated, and then said, 'You'd have to read it, I think, to understand. I can only give the facts—the geophysical facts and they're quite extraordinary. What he says is that during the last and most severe stage of the Würm glaciation the sea level of the Mediterranean was up to four hundred feet lower than it is at present. Violent winds from the south picked up the sand from the exposed North African coast and carried it to the Balkan peninsula.

96

Greece was buried under that sand to a depth of two or three hundred feet. It's all gone now. You can see traces of red here and there in the soil, but twenty thousand years of erosion have washed the great blanket of sand away—except in this one place.'

She looked at me and her hand touched my arm, holding it. 'Will you go there—tomorrow? Will you see if he's there?' And without waiting for me to reply, she went on, her words coming in a rush: 'If he is there . . . it scares me to think of it. Alone in that place all this time. It made such a deep impression on him—the atmosphere of it. It seemed to fascinate him. You see, ever since those great dust storms, there's been life there, human life—Bronze Age, Neolithic, the old Stone Age, right back to Mousterian Man. There's chert in the area and they knapped it like flint—chipped sharp slivers off to make their implements . . . knives, arrowheads, all their weapons, and the chippings aren't buried as they are in a cave-dwelling. Because of erosion, the evidence is lying there on the surface, so that he didn't have to dig—he could just read the whole story as he wandered about. He said it was a dead place, a sort of cemetery of continual human occupation.' And she added with sudden intensity, 'It's not healthy for him to be there alone.' Her fingers tightened on my arm. 'Will you go—please? Not in the Land-Rover. It's too conspicuous. There's a bus leaves the village about seven and you could hitch-hike on from Jannina.'

That was how I came to find myself wandering alone next day in the lunar landscape of the red dunes near Ayios Giorgios. Sonia had produced food for me, which she had stowed in his old rucksack, and by ten that morning I was in the cab of a cattle truck driving south out of Jannina. We called at two villages on the way, and it was a little after eleven-thirty that we came to the valley, the road snaking down between the hills, and that hole in the rock showing like a watchful eye above us. The aqueduct came into view, its ancient arches spanning the river, and beyond it the reservoir gleamed like a mirror in the sunshine. 'Endáksi—Ayios Giorgios.' The truck slowed to a stop where the road to the village turned off to the left. I thanked the driver and climbed out. 'Hérete.' I waved him goodbye and he drove off, leaving me standing alone in the dust of the verge, the sun warm on my face.

As soon as the truck was out of sight, I started down the road which had been blasted out of the hillside above the reservoir. There was no breeze and already it was hot, an early spring heat-wave. Patches of red earth showed on the far side, and high in the sky a bird wheeled and hovered. At the far end of the reservoir the sloping face of the dam was white with the water pouring down it. And on the other side of the road, the aqueduct tunnel was a shadowed slit in the naked rock. There was no difficulty in reaching it. You could even walk in it without stooping, for it was built to the height of a man, tapered at the top like the entrance to a catacomb. It was so narrow that my body blocked the light and I probed ahead with her torch only to find that she had been right—the cleft was blocked by a rock fall about 25 or 30 yards from the entrance.

I switched the torch off and stood in the semi-darkness, thinking for a moment of those Romans hacking their way into the mountainside nearly 2,000 years ago. It must have been quite an engineering feat in those days. I wondered what the old man had been thinking when he had stood where I stood now. Had the rock walls told him what he would find on the top of the hill inside which he stood? It seemed unlikely. I had no idea what chert looked like then, but the walls were smooth, except for the marks of Roman tools. It appeared to be a fairly soft rock, volcanic probably, and no doubt an earthquake had caused the rock fall.

I walked slowly back towards the slit of brightness that marked the entrance, and when I reached it and stood again in the sunshine, I found my mind had moved far enough back into the past for the road itself to seem an intrusion. I followed the road, moving almost automatically, and where it curved round the shoulder of a hill, I found a goat track leading steeply up. It was not a very long climb, but the track zig-zagged to a bluff, so that I had no view of what lay ahead of me until I topped the last rise and it burst upon me with all its strange unearthly beauty. Here, suddenly stretched out before me, was a world that was out of time, completely apart from the landscape in which it lay. Instead of grass and rock, and the

Greek flowers of mountains in springtime, here was nothing but desert—red, desiccated dunes, so bare of anything that a withered, stunted bush was like the prospect of an oasis.

I hesitated, shocked by the transformation. And when I finally started forward again, that red world, with its extraordinary timeless atmosphere, seemed to swallow me completely. The colour of the sand absorbed the sun's heat. The place was like an oven, and so deathly still that it seemed all life had ceased here long, long ago. I felt my nerves tingle and the hair of my neck stiffen. I glanced quickly up at the blue vault of the sky. Nothing stirred, no sign of that eagle, or whatever it had been, hovering: the sky was empty, as empty as the red dune world into which I was slowly advancing. And when I looked back, there was no sign of any other world behind me, only the scuff of my feet in the loose sand to show the way I had come.

It was a confusing place, for the dunes were a series of humps and hollows without any regular pattern. The sun was little help, for it was almost overhead, but as I topped a rise, I came upon something I could use as a guide line. At first I did not understand what it was. I was looking across a steep ravine of sand, and on the far side, the smooth red surface of the next dune was broken by a spill of stones. These stones built up like a cone to a point on the dune-top where they stood proud by at least the height of a man, as though a great cairn had been erected there. What puzzled me was where the stones had come from.

Standing there, looking around me, I saw that there were other points where stone showed through the sand. But these were all quite different, for there was no spill of stone and nothing had collapsed; here the rains and strong winds had eroded the sand overlay to expose the rock below. And since in every case the rock had been shattered as by a giant hammer, it was clear that this could only have been caused by ice. I realized then that the rock I was seeing exposed in the twentieth century A.D. was rock that had not seen the light of day since its shattering by the deadly cold of the last Ice Age.

But that did not explain the spill of stones on the far dune. I slithered down into the ravine. The floor was packed hard, but the soft sides made it difficult to claw my way up. When I finally reached the top, I found that the pile of stones had the form of a collapsed circle. There was a distinct hollow in the middle. It was like the shaft of an old well exposed by erosion of the surrounding soil until it stood like a column above the ground, finally falling in upon itself and spilling down the slope.

I was standing fairly high at this point and had a good view over the whole dune area. It was all of it red in colour, but two shades of red, as though formed by two different types of sand, and the dune formation was uneven—steeply humped in the ravines, but thin on the slopes with the underlying rock exposed in places. And then, as I turned to view the whole area, which looked as though it covered about four, possibly six square miles, I saw that there was another spill of stones several hundred yards away, and I thought I could see yet another beyond that. These spills were not so pronounced, the 'well-heads' standing less proud of the surrounding sand, but what struck me immediately was that they were more or less in a straight line running in a south-westerly direction.

I understood what they were then. These were the remains of vertical shafts connecting with the line of the aqueduct tunnel deep in the hill below me. They were either ventilation shafts, or else the Romans had used them for hauling out the rock cut from the tunnel, and where the rock ceased and they were in to the red sand, they had had to line the shafts as well-diggers have to line a well in soft ground. A geologist could probably have gauged from the amount of stone debris exposed just how much erosion had occurred in the two thousand years since those shafts had been built. My guess was that it was 20 feet, and if the rate of erosion had been constant for the whole twenty thousand years since the last Ice Age, then that would give an original depth of 200 feet for the sand overlay. This more or less confirmed the depths Sonia had given me, since obviously the rate of erosion over such a long period would not have been constant.

I have gone into this in some detail, because the sense of being in a world lost to everything but geological time was very strong, and it affected my mood. It is true that I had seen goat, possibly sheep droppings in the dune bottoms, but this evidence that animals crossed the area in search of the next grazing land did not detract in any way from the feeling that this was a world apart; rather the reverse, in fact, for it made me conscious of the struggle life must have been when all of Greece had looked like this red throwback to a long dead age. And there were the flakes of chert. At least, I presumed they were chert—between brown and ochre in colour, quite small and sharply edged, so that I was certain they had been chipped from larger stones. I had seen them everywhere, lying on the surface as Sonia had said. One, which I had put in my pocket, looked like an arrow-head.

I think I must have stood there for quite a time, my mind lost in the past, my eyes searching and searching the whole hot expanse of shimmering sand. There was a small wind blowing from the north and it gradually chilled the sweat on my body. Search as I might, I could see no sign of life. There were no birds, no cicadas even, the whole area so utterly still and lifeless it might indeed have been the moon. And when I called out in the hope of an answer, my shouts seemed deadened by the dunes, the sand acting like a damper.

It was almost two and I stopped to eat on the top of a dune where the breeze touched my damp skin. Below me the sands pulsed with the heat, and on a ridge away to my left the third of those strange shafts spilled stones into a hollow. It had the shape of an old worn-down molar, and near the crown of it a shadow cast by the sun showed black like an unstopped cavity. It was a possibility—about the only one left in this desolate stretch of country. But by then I had opened up the rucksack. Sonia had made up a package for me of bread and cheese and tinned ham. I put on my sweater and began to eat. I was facing south-west at the time, my back to the breeze and the way I had come. I don't know what made me turn—some instinct, some sixth sense. The second of those stone shafts stood like a cairn, sharp against the blue sky, and beyond it, a long way away, the purpling shape of a distant range stood humped on the horizon. And then my gaze fell to the red sand valley below and I saw something move, a shambling figure wandering with head bent intent upon the ground.

The sight of him so shocked me that for a moment I did not move. I just sat there unable to believe what my eyes recorded, for he looked so frail, so insubstantial. Partly it was the khaki shirt and trousers. They seemed to have taken on the colour of the dunes so that they merged into the sand. But the long white hair, the way he walked, head bent, searching the ground . . . those nights in Amsterdam so long ago came back to me and the certainty that it was him was overwhelming.

I got to my feet, tried to call out to him, but though I opened my mouth no sound came and I was trembling. He was moving slowly nearer all the time, coming up the floor of the valley, and he looked small, a ghost of a figure in the red immensity of that dune landscape, walking with slow uncertain steps, searching, but not stopping, not picking anything up.

I started down the dune slope then, loose sand under my feet, and even when I reached the hard-packed sand of the valley floor, he still did not hear me. It wasn't until I was within a few yards of him that he stopped suddenly, his head lifted, his body quite still, alerted to the fact that he was not alone. I had stopped, too, waiting for him to turn. And when he did so, slowly, there was no recognition in his eyes, only a secret, hunted look.

'Who are you?' he asked, the words coming falteringly as though speech were strange to him. 'What do you want?'

I didn't answer. I couldn't—I was too appalled. I had expected him to look older, of course, and those two photographs should have warned me, the observations Gilmore had made. But I was not prepared for such fragility. He seemed smaller, a shadow of his former self, withered and stooped, and so thin he looked half starved, the khaki trousers hanging loose, the rib cage staring through the torn shirt. But it was his face that really shocked me, the hunted, burning look in his eyes.

It had always been a remarkable face, the leathery features like a piece of deep-chiselled, fine-carved wood. Now there was the grey stubble of a beard, and beneath the stubble the lines had deepened. The flesh seemed to have fallen away, exposing the bone formation of the skull, accentuating the jut of the jaw and the beetling brows. It was a haggard, tortured face, and the eyes, which had always been deep-sunk, seemed to have retreated deeper into their sockets.

They were staring at me now, seeing me only as a stranger who had invaded his secret world. I said my name, and for a moment it didn't seem to register. And then suddenly there was recognition and his eyes blazed. 'Who sent you?' There was hostility, no sign of affection—I might have been an enemy out to destroy him. 'What are you doing here?' The words came in a whisper and he was trembling.

'I was worried about you,' I said.

A rasping sound came from his throat, a jeering laugh of disbelief. 'After eight years?' And then, leaning forward, he repeated his first question—'Who sent you?'

'Nobody sent me. I came of my own accord.'

'But you knew where to look.'

'Sonia thought I might find you here.'

'Sonia Winters?' His face softened, the eyes becoming less hostile.

'She's at Despotiko,' I said.

'And you came—to look for me?'

I nodded, wondering how to break through to the man I had once known.

He was silent for a long time. Finally he seemed to gather himself together. 'That was good of you.' He said it slowly as though making an effort, and then suddenly there were tears in his eyes and I stood there, staring at him stupidly, uncertain what to do or what to say. He'd been here—how long? A fortnight, nearly three weeks. The red dunes all around him, and nobody with him, nobody at all. 'What have you found to live on?'

But his gaze had wandered, searching the ground. 'You haven't seen the sole of my boot, have you? I lost it last night, and I've been searching.'

He was wearing an old pair of desert boots, tough camel skin, and the right foot had the crêpe rubber missing. 'It's no good to you,' I said. 'You couldn't repair it here.'

'Somebody may find it. . . .' His eyes were roving again, his voice irritable. He seemed obsessed by his loss and I realized he was afraid it might betray his presence here. 'Are you sure nobody sent you?' He was looking at me again, his eyes shifting and uneasy.

I did my best to reassure him, but it was only when I told him how I had come to Greece that his attention seemed to focus. 'A boat? You chartered a boat?'

I nodded.

'Where is it—at Pylos you say?'

'No, Preveza. They should have arrived at Preveza by now.'

'Preveza?' His eyes gleamed, a strange suppressed excitement. 'If they'd let me come on my own—that's what I wanted. I could have been there a month—more now. But they gave me a Land-Rover and an assistant.' His body sagged, dejected. And then, suddenly, he sank to the ground as though he couldn't support himself any more. 'I'm tired,' he murmured. 'Very tired. I haven't the strength I had once.'

I offered to get him some food, but he shook his head. 'It's only the sudden heat. And walking. . . . I thought if I searched for it now, in the middle of the day, nobody would see me.'

'But you must eat,' I said.

He shook his head again. 'I'm beyond that. And the last time it made me sick.'

He told me then how he'd killed a sheep, had beaten it to death with a stone and taken it to his lair up there on the dune ridge where that third shaft showed a cavity in the circle of fallen stones. He'd cooked it inside his burrow, gorging himself sick and sucking the marrow from the bones. He told it with his eyes closed, dwelling on all the revolting details as though to saturate himself with disgust. 'Have you ever gone for a long period without food?'

I shook my head.

'I did it once before—lost my way in the Kyzyl Kum desert. The mind floats free. Everything very clear. But it was different then. It wasn't of my own choice and I had no water.'

He had no water here either, but every night he told me he went down to the reservoir. That was how he had come to lose the sole of his boot. 'And what happens when you're too weak?' I asked. 'You can't live without water.'

'No, I'd die then.' The dusty lips behind the stubble cracked in a smile. 'That would be the easy way.' The smile had lit his face with some inner calm. 'But I shan't die. I mustn't die— not yet.' His brows dragged down, his eyes suddenly glaring at me. 'You don't know what I'm talking about, do you? It was always the same with you—like talking to somebody who's never learned—who'll never bother to learn—one's own language. We're strangers, you and I.'

There was nothing I could say and I stood there, silent. The stillness of the place, the sense of being alone with somebody who was not quite real. . . . I didn't understand him. I never had. And the way he was staring at me from under those shaggy brows. . . . 'What do you want?' he asked abruptly. 'Eight years, isn't it?'

I nodded.

'Then why are you here?' His eyes drew mine, holding them, the stare so penetrating that I had the feeling I had always had that he could read my thoughts. 'You're in trouble again. Is that it?'

I couldn't help it. I laughed, an awkward, jarring sound in the stillness. Looking down at him squatting there, weak with hunger and half out of his mind, and thinking I'd come to him for help. Yet perhaps he was right. In the end I had always come back to him. Perhaps it really was the reason. 'Yes,' I said. He might as well know. It might help him even—to know that he wasn't the only one who was on the run. 'I think I've killed a man. In fact, I'm certain I have.'

I saw the shock of that register, his eyes appalled, a look almost of horror on his face. 'You?' He bowed his head. 'You were always violent—always that same streak of violence.' And then after a while he said, 'Sit down, Paul. Sit down here and tell me about it. How did it happen?'

'It was at the end of the voyage,' I said. 'We'd come into Fawley with oil from Kuwait—the long way round the Cape.' I had seated myself cross-legged on the sand, the two of us facing each other like a couple of Arabs. 'I was first officer and we had a Czech on board, a man called Mark Janovic—a good deckhand, cheerful, hardworking. The papers said he was a Pole, but I'm damned sure he was a Czech, and they were waiting for him—two toughs from the Polish embassy. The turn-round is quick, but I'd given several of the hands shore leave and I was on the pipeline terminal when they came off the ship. Janovic was the last to leave, and as he did so these two thugs closed in on him. They had a car waiting. There was an argument and I went over to see what it was all about. It was something to do with his family. I could see Janovic was scared, and then he suddenly made a break for it. One of the bastards grabbed him and I just reacted instinctively. I smashed his face in. He was right on the edge of the pier. He went straight over into the water. It was dark and the tide was running. There wasn't a chance of anybody fishing him out alive. And then the other man started to come at me.' I felt like a child again, telling him my troubles. 'I didn't stop to think. I just hit him in the stomach, grabbed the car and drove off.'

He didn't ask me why I'd been such a fool, why I hadn't stayed to justify my actions. He just sat there, silent, lost in his own thoughts. Finally he said, 'I've been afraid of this—always.' The words seemed dragged out of him. 'Both you and I, we've the same temperament, the same predilection to violence. . . .' He was staring at me as though looking at a ghost. 'It's an odd place to tell you—but you're old enough now, a man. . . . I loved your mother once. A long time ago now.' He seemed to gather himself together, his eyes looking straight at me, very direct. 'You're my son. My own son.'

'Yes,' I said. 'I know that now.'

'You know?' It seemed to worry him, the brows dragged down, the eyes staring, bloodshot. 'How do you know? When?' And he added slowly, almost painfully, 'I tried to keep it from you. After what had happened . . . the shock of their death . . . I felt I had to. How did you find out?'

'The letters—that note pinned to my birth certificate.' And I told him how I had gone back to the house in Amsterdam. 'But I didn't come here to burden you with my own troubles.'

'You went to Amsterdam?'

'I needed money, somewhere to hide out till the heat was off.'

'Is that all?' He sighed. 'I've never refused to help you. Surely you know——'

'How the hell could you help me?'

I saw him wince. 'No, of course. You're right. And there was no money in the house.' He was peering at me, his eyes probing my face. 'Then why are you here?'

'To tell you that Professor Holroyd left London by air last night. He should be in Athens by now. Sonia thought you ought to know.'

He didn't seem surprised. 'He's in a hurry, of course. And she told you where to find me?'

'Yes.'

'But that doesn't explain why you came to Greece.'

I told him about Gilmore then, his concern after reading his Journal. But all he said was, 'It was good of Adrian to bother.' He was following quite a different train of thought. 'Now tell me the truth.' He leaned forward, his voice urgent. 'Why did you come—after eight years? And not a word from you in all that time. You're not interested in me or my work.'

I didn't know how to answer him. 'I just felt I had to.'

'Because you discovered I was your natural father?' That rasping sound again, that jeering laugh.

How I hated him! I always had—his twisted mind, his bitterness. He saw the hate in my eyes and smiled. 'You haven't changed.'

'No,' I said angrily. 'I haven't changed. And nor have you.' I got to my feet. 'I'll go now.'

I left him then, climbing the dune side hurriedly, back to where I'd left the rucksack. There was still some food left, but when I called down to him that I'd leave it there for him, I saw him staggering up the slope towards me. By the time he reached me I'd taken off my sweater and slipped it, with the remains of the food, into the rucksack. 'Here you are,' I said, handing it to him. 'The rucksack's yours, anyway.'

He had collapsed on the sand at my feet, breathing heavily. 'We shouldn't—part—like this,' he gasped. 'You and I—the same blood—and those nine years. We had nine years together.'

'You were away most of the time.' My voice sounded hard and brutal.

'Yes. So much to do—always seeking—a new location, some find reported. There was always something, beckoning me on. That's what drove me. I'm sorry.' There were tears in his eyes again. And then he was staring up at me. 'I need your help.'

'No,' I said. 'No, I'm leaving.'

'Paul.' He was gasping for breath. 'I've no time left. I'm old and ill and I need you.'

Gilmore's words almost, and our roles reversed. It was incredible. 'I'm going now.' If I didn't go now, I'd get involved. And I didn't want to get involved. 'I can't help you.'

'Yes, you can. That boat.' He was tense and urgent, his eyes over-bright. 'You said you had a boat, and it's not more than a day's run from Preveza.' He was pleading.

'You want to go to Levkas, is that it?'

'If I had the use of that boat—just for one day.'

The urgency, the absolute driving urgency, his eyes burning with excitement, his whole face lit by a desperate desire. I hated to kill it. But there was Kotiadis, and when I told him what had happened after we had landed at Pylos, the light died in his eyes, a dead look, and his hands clenched slowly. They were big hands, big in proportion to his body. 'So they've checked with the Russians now. Everything I do. . . .' His body seemed to droop. 'Ever since I was a student. Do you wonder that I'm here, hounded, alone—my ideas, my whole life wasted. Nobody believes in me—nobody except myself.'

'There's Dr Gilmore,' I reminded him.

'Yes, but Adrian's old. It's men like Holroyd rule the academic world now. And in Russia—they only helped me so long as it suited them.' And then he returned to the subject of the boat, what sort of boat and asking about the Barretts. 'The dig at Despotiko would take too long. But on Levkas—a week, a month at most, and I'd have the answer—know for certain. And the summer ahead of me—warmth. I've friends there.' Then he leaned forward, gripping hold of my hand and pulling me down on to the sand beside him. 'Listen, Paul. You're a seaman. Have you been through the Malta Channel?

'Once,' I said.

'Then you'll know the depth there.'

'I know it's shallow.'

'And further west, between Sicily and Tunisia—the islands?'

'I've seen Marettimo, once in the dawn.'

'No, not Marettimo, though there is a cave further inshore on Levanzo. But south of Sicily—Linosa and Pantelleria, both volcanic, and another island, Lampedusa, much older.' His gaze had fastened on me, his voice urgent with the effort to communicate, to engage my interest. 'Geologists have for some time believed that the Mediterranean was a hundred to two hundred feet lower during the Ice Age. Here you see the evidence of it.' He waved his hand at the dunes around us. 'This sand belongs to two distinct periods—the lighter colour has an iron ore content, the darker and later is manganese. Nobody has checked it, as far as I know. I don't know of anybody who even knows about it, and if I could get one really authoritative geologist . . .' He picked up a handful of sand and ran it through his fingers, watching it intently like a man watching an hour glass. 'But why should I help them? They don't like being taught their business any more than anthropologists. They'd take the credit for themselves . . .' He flung the remains of the sand away in a gesture of disgust. 'They don't know the water level of the Mediterranean twenty thousand years ago. They're just guessing. It's an enclosed sea and they're not even sure that the Straits of Gibraltar existed then. Suppose the level was four or five hundred feet lower. Then all the sea between Sicily and Africa would have been one vast plain, with Lampedusa a small mountain range. Have you ever seen Pantelleria?'

I shook my head, and he went on, barely pausing for breath, 'It's like a volcanic slag heap, the north of it all black lava, probably dating from the period when Knossos, the old capital of the Minoan civilization of Crete, was destroyed. There's a Greek volcanologist who believes that the destruction of Santorin was the basis of the legend of Atlantis. But the rest of Pantelleria is the product of older eruptions. I spent a month there some years back. If I could have stayed longer . . . there are some underwater caves there, but you'd need divers—aqualung equipment. In Homer's day there was a story about Odysseus descending into Hades, meeting the shades of the great men of Greek history. Why did he write that into the Odyssey? Everything he wrote was based on stories handed down by word of mouth, and if Atlantis was Santorin, remembered to this day, why not a cave some sailor had stumbled on?' He looked at me then. 'You've never seen the Vézère—those beetling limestone cliffs with caves marked by the engraved drawings of mammoths going back sixty thousand years. I was brought up in the Vézère, you remember. It's a long time ago now, but I've never forgotten. It's been my dream—that somewhere, some time before I die, I'll find others—painted caves that will prove beyond doubt the pattern of Cro-Magnon migration.'

His voice faltered and his body sagged again with weariness.

'It's just a dream,' he murmured. 'But if I had a boat, a few months . . . there was nothing in Asia Minor or Russia, nothing that proved anything—definitely. What I wrote then . . .' He was leaning forward, intent, his words coming slowly, as though by speaking his thoughts aloud he could clarify his mind. 'Theories—nothing more. And I was guilty, like the rest of them, of twisting facts to prove what I believed to be true. But there comes a point when you know the facts don't fit. Then you can only sit back and re-think your theories. I did that one whole winter in Amsterdam, arguing it out on paper. A new thesis—negative, rather than positive. If *homo sapiens*, as represented by Lartet's Cro-Magnon type, did not come from the east, via Russia, or up through Mesopotamia, then either he evolved on the spot—there is a theory that each Ice Age produced its own natural development of our species —or else he must have come north from Africa.'

'Is that the book you sent to a British publisher?'

'Yes. I knew the Russians wouldn't print it. . . .' He looked at me, suddenly puzzled. 'You know about it? How? I never told Adrian. I never told anybody.' And then he became very excited as I told him about Holroyd's visit and how the book had come to be rejected. 'I knew it. I knew he must be involved.' His eyes were blazing, his body literally trembling. 'Holroyd used it in a book of his own—published quite recently—my theories, my own words. And no acknowledgment. None.' Those hands of his, those big hands, were clenching and unclenching, as though he were going through the motions of throttling the man. He smiled to himself, his teeth bared, and his face had changed. It was wolfish and there was something in his eyes. A crafty look. The trembling had stopped and there was a stillness about him now. I was conscious suddenly of evil. I can't explain it—the dunes maybe, the heat; but something had invaded us. And yet his words were ordinary enough, his manner practical:

'You're going back—to Despotiko? You'll see Holroyd?'

I nodded, not saying anything, appalled by that unreasoning sense of evil. A cold shiver ran down my spine, for the evil stemmed from him. I was certain of that. It wasn't the dunes or the heat—it was there, deep inside him, and it scared me.

'Last year . . .' his voice was tense, the words beating into my brain with the glare of the heat refracted from sand and stone. 'I discovered something in a cave-dwelling on Meganisi. By an island called Tiglia in the channel between Meganisi and Levkas. Some bones. I sent them to Adrian. I asked him to get them dated. Human bones—pieces of a skull-cap, part of a jaw, some teeth. Also fragments of animal bone, part of a woolly rhinoceros.'

'There's a letter from him on your desk.'

'Does he give the dating?'

'About 35,000 BP.'

He nodded as though it confirmed what he already knew.

'He also made the point that you had no right to keep the location of such an important find to yourself.'

'Good!' He seemed pleased. He was smiling. 'When something like that is sent in for dating . . .' The smile had bared his teeth again, the eyes cunning, that wolfish look. 'They talk. They pass it on. Soon everybody knows, and then the vultures gather.' He laughed, but only as an emphasis to bitterness. 'You're staying at the camp, are you? You'll be there when Holroyd arrives?'

I nodded, wondering what was in his mind. His face had smoothed out again, an expression of innocence. 'Perhaps Adrian is right. The individual in the field is unimportant. What is important is the corporate knowledge of the scientific world as a whole. That's what they say, isn't it? That's their excuse.' His hands clenched again. 'But what happens if the scientific world doesn't believe you? How do you make them understand if they reject, not the truth, but the man himself?' He was speaking in a whisper, his eyes lowered as though communing with his feet. 'Then you must use other methods. I've been thinking about that, all the time I've been alone. And now you come here, young, thoughtless, full of energy and vitality . . .' He stopped suddenly, his head cocked on one side, listening. I heard it then, the faint sound of a bell. 'Sheep,' he said. 'Every few days that bell-wether leads the flock across the dunes to grazing on the far side. There's a shepherd with them.' His head had turned towards the shaft of stones that was his refuge and he began to get to his feet. The bell was jangling now and he paused, his hands still on the ground, his body crouched, and that hunted look back in his eyes. 'Something has disturbed them. They're running.'

Faint on the wind I heard the distant sound of a human voice, a man shouting. It came from the far side of the dune, from the way I had come, and I thought I heard a dog bark. I was on my feet then, running along the dune top, and where it fell into the ravine out of which I had climbed to have my lunch, I saw the sheep in a huddle, facing away from me, their eyes on the dog. It was an Alsatian, and the soldier who held it on its leash was arguing with the shepherd. Beyond them was Kotiadis, in his shirt sleeves, his jacket over his arm and his tie hanging loose.

I turned and ran back, out of sight below the crest of the dune, the sound of the shepherd's voice raised in anger fading behind me. The old man was on his feet when I reached him and I grabbed the rucksack and thrust it into his hand. 'Quick!' I said. 'Down there.' And I pointed to an area of rock exposed by erosion. There was just a chance. 'It's Kotiadis with a tracker dog. But he's following my tracks, not yours. Lie flat and keep your head down.'

I didn't wait to see whether he understood. There wasn't time. I back-tracked along the ridge, and where the dune ended, I saw the dog again pulling the soldier along on a tight leash, Kotiadis close behind them. They were circling the flock now and for a moment I was in full view of them as I slid down the side of the dune. But they were so intent on the trail, and on keeping their footing in the loose sand, that I got away into a hollow in the dunes without being seen. I was on the floor of the ravine then, the dune between me and the parallel ravine, the old shaft-head out of sight.

I kept to the floor of the ravine, following a line of old sheep droppings. It led me to the end of the dune country, and as I climbed the last slope of sand, I heard the sheep bell again, far away and sounding quietly. The dog was silent. By then I had put the better part of a mile between myself and the place where I had left him. There was no point in going on, and where the sand ended, giving way to rock and a sort of maquis scrub interspersed with patches of poor grass, I sat down to recover my breath.

About five minutes later they came into view, the dog with

his nose down, still following my trail. The soldier saw me first, standing and pointing excitedly, the dog straining at the leash. 'Are you alone?' Kotiadis called up to me. He could see I was alone and he said something to the soldier, and then came panting up the slope. 'Where is Dr Van der Voort?'

'I didn't know you were following me,' I said.

'Of course, I follow you. What do you expect?' He was hot and angry at finding me alone. 'Where is Dr Van der Voort?' he repeated. 'He is somewhere here. I am sure of it.' He was out of breath and a whiff of garlic came to me on the hot air. 'Why else do you come here?'

I began to tell him about the geological significance of the dunes. But he hadn't come here with a soldier and a tracker dog to be lectured on the last Ice Age. 'Where is your rucksack? You have a rucksack when you get on to the bus.'

'Have you been following me since seven o'clock this morning?'

'But of course.'

I was annoyed with myself for not realizing the trap he had set for me.

'Where is your rucksack?' he repeated.

'Somewhere around,' I said. 'I put it down when I had lunch, but these dunes are confusing.'

He sat down beside me. 'Now you answer my questions please. Why do you come here?'

Patiently I started in again on the strange nature of the dunes. But he refused to be side-tracked. He was still hot and angry, impatient for something to justify the time and energy he had expended. The interrogation was not a success. Finally he said, 'Okay, we look for your rucksack now.'

But of course we didn't find it. He'd given the dog the wrong briefing and only once did the animal take us anywhere near the shaft with its shadowed cavity. Finally I suggested the shepherd might have picked it up and that took us a good mile from the dune country and wasted almost an hour. In the end he gave it up and we went down to the road where the soldier had parked his army truck.

The sun had set and it was almost dark by the time we got back to Despotiko.

They were just settling down to their evening meal. 'You

will stay in the camp now,' Kotiadis said. 'You are not permitted to leave it—any of you.'

It was dark under the trees and their faces, as they listened to him, were lit by the glow of the fire. 'What about the cave?' Cartwright asked. 'I take it you're not stopping us from continuing our work?' And as Kotiadis hesitated, he added quickly, 'I think I should tell you that Professor Holroyd of London University is in Athens. I had a cable from him last night. He'll be at the General Direction of Antiquities today. That's under the Prime Minister's Office. And then he'll be coming on here to examine the cave-dwelling himself.'

'You are not permitted to leave the camp. That is all I have said.' Kotiadis moved towards Cartwright. 'And now a word with you please.'

Cartwright put his plate down and got to his feet. They went off together and Sonia said to me, 'You must be hungry. Would you like some stew?' I think she expected me to be leaving with Kotiadis, for her eyes beckoned me to the fire, and as she handed me a plate, she whispered, 'Did you find him?'

'Yes,' I said. 'He's all right—for the moment.'

'Thank God!' she breathed.

I started to tell her what had happened, but she shook her head. 'Not now.'

Cartwright was leading Kotiadis to the old man's tent. She followed them with her eyes, the ladle poised over the stew-pot. The old man's things were in there and I bent down, my head close to hers. 'They've got a tracker dog.' Her hair touched my cheek as she nodded. 'Better eat this quickly,' she said, pouring the contents of the ladle on to my plate.

But she was wrong in thinking Kotiadis would take me with him. He came out of the tent with a bundle under his arm wrapped in newspaper, and after talking a moment with Cartwright, walked over to where I sat stuffing the food hurriedly into my mouth. 'Mr Cartwright has promised that he and his companions will not leave the camp. You will give the same promise please.'

I looked up at him. 'Why should I? You've got soldiers here.'

'You are not being co-operative.'

114

'Of course not.' The plate was shaking in my hand, anger sweeping through me. Why the hell couldn't they leave him alone? 'Do you think I don't know what you've got under your arm?'

The firelight glimmered in the pupils of his eyes. 'Perhaps if we have some of Dr Van der Voort's clothes today . . .' He gave his habitual little shrug. 'But it does not matter. You have indicated where we must search and tomorrow we try again.' He was so sure of himself he was actually smiling. 'And now I will do as you suggest. I will order the soldiers to watch you. So please do not try to leave the camp. They have guns and they will shoot.'

He left then, and shortly afterwards the soldiers arrived with their tent. The corporal sited it on the path leading to the village, and after it had been erected and a guard posted, they all sat around watching us. Under surveillance like that, the atmosphere in the camp was strained and there was little conversation until the meal was over. Whilst the others were washing up, Cartwright moved over to where I was sitting. 'Mind if I join you?'

I didn't say anything. It was his camp and he could sit where he liked. He pulled out a pipe and sat down, chewing at the curved stem of it. Finally he said, 'I don't know how long you will have to stay here. But since we're forced into each other's company like this, I think I should tell you that I'm not responsible for what Kotiadis is doing. I knew, of course, that Dr Van der Voort had been in Russia, that he had had books published there and that he spoke the language. By inference, I suppose, you could say that I knew he was a Communist. But I did not inform the authorities.'

It was a categorical statement and I did not doubt for a moment that it was true. 'Then why did he attack you?'

He hesitated, his owl-like eyes staring straight at me. 'That evening'—he began to fumble for his tobacco pouch—'I had to telephone Athens—an archaeological friend, Leo Demotakis. I made the call from the taverna and was in bed shortly after nine. Dr Van der Voort had gone off on his own—he often walked alone at night. But he was in the taverna around ten o'clock and by then somebody from the Public Order Ministry had telephoned Andreas to check on the expedition and the identity of its leader. He's the village headman. The enquiry was political and he admits he warned Dr Van der Voort.' He began to fill his pipe. 'It's not easy to explain. Dr Van der Voort and I'—he hesitated—'you know Professor Holroyd sponsored this expedition. I'm his assistant and Dr Van der Voort hated Bill Holroyd—a quite unreasoned, pathological hatred. I found that out very early on, when we were still in Macedonia. Anyway, when Andreas told him I had phoned Athens earlier, I suppose he leapt to the c-c-concl-clusion . . .' He turned to me suddenly. 'I wasn't given a chance to explain. He seemed driven by a f-fury of rage, words pouring out of him——' Hans called to us that tea was ready and he got quickly to his feet as though glad of the opportunity to escape. 'I thought you ought to know. That's all.' And he added, 'I can tell you, it was a most unpleasant experience.'

He went over to the fire then, and I sat there trying to understand my father's behaviour, the violence of his reaction. Cartwright's explanation of what had happened had been quite direct. I didn't like the man, but I was certain that what he had told me was the truth.

'Here's your tea.'

Sonia stood there, holding an enamel mug out to me. It steamed in the cool night air. I took it and she hesitated, as though about to say something. I wanted to have a talk with her, but alone, not in front of the others. Our eyes met for a moment, then she turned abruptly and went back to them. The fire had died to embers, the glow of it on their faces, and behind them, and all around, the olive grove was dark in shadow. Somewhere a bird, or perhaps it was a frog, repeated and repeated its single fluting note, regular as a metronome, while I continued to sit there, withdrawn and alone, thinking of that tired old man preparing to make his nightly journey to the reservoir for water. And tomorrow Kotiadis would pick him up and that would be the end of all his dreams, all the years of wandering and searching. It would finish him. I felt that very strongly, and when eventually I went to the tent and crawled into his sleeping-bag, it was with a feeling of resentment, almost a physical sickening, at the way the pattern of both our lives was being drawn inexorably closer.

SO FAR my involvement in my father's affairs had been largely accidental, and in writing about what happened during that hot summer in the Mediterranean, I find it difficult to decide exactly when and how I stopped fighting against the inevitable and decided to let myself become engaged emotionally in his affairs. Certainly Holroyd's arrival in the camp at Despotiko was a decisive factor. It personalized the old man's struggle for recognition and made me realize for the first time the powerful forces he had to contend with.

Holroyd was a member of the academic Establishment. It was typical of him that, instead of coming straight out to the scene of operations, he had spent a whole day in Athens first. And when he did arrive, it was in an official car and accompanied by one of the directors of the General Direction of Antiquities. They had stopped the night somewhere on their way up from Athens and Holroyd had taken the trouble to telephone ahead to say he would be arriving at eleven o'clock. As a result, nobody went up to the dig that morning and Cartwright fussed around the camp, making certain that everything was in order. The folding table and the two canvas chairs were brought out from the mess-tent, mugs laid ready, a bottle of ouzo, glasses. They had even purchased some mocha coffee from the taverna. Hans dug a new latrine and then appeared, transformed in blue trousers and pale shirt, with his fair hair slicked down with water. Sonia put on a short white dress and Cartwright a tie to go with his grey flannels and elbow-patched sports jacket.

It was a little before eleven that Holroyd came into the camp. He had his pipe in his mouth and he was smiling, his round, babyish face looking pink and newly scrubbed. Cartwright went forward to meet him, holding himself very erect in an effort to conceal that slouching, gangling walk of his. I almost expected him to salute. It was all very old-fashioned and English, the two of them in grey flannels and sports jackets formally shaking hands against the exotic background of the olive grove, and the Greek official standing beside them, neat in a dark blue suit and dark glasses.

I now knew a little more about Holroyd's background, for

the night before, Sonia had settled down on the grass outside my tent and we had talked for nearly an hour. He was the son of a Bradford spinning mill operator and all through the early 'thirties, when he had been growing up, his father had been unemployed. He had been newspaper boy, errand boy, and then his father had got part-time work at another mill and they had moved out to Cleckheaton. Through voluntary work at a local library he had managed to bring himself to the notice of one of the founders, a rich mill owner, who had supplemented his scholarships and seen him through grammar school and then university. Anthropology was not a very popular subject at the time, and with the war just over, he had got himself appointed to a department of the Allied Military Government in Germany that was dealing with papers and documents of scientific interest.

'It is not too large a step,' she had said, 'from the appropriation of the discoveries of a conquered country to picking the brains of your own scientists.' He had stayed close to government, always with some official position that gave him a certain amount of power. 'If the plagiarism is not too blatant, there are few people who will openly oppose a man who has the ear of senior officials and can influence academic appointments.' She had got all this from Gilmore and I was remembering her words now as I saw Holroyd glance quickly across to where I was standing slightly apart from the others and then turn to question Cartwright. 'He's politically astute and quite ruthless. He's also a publicist.' By this she had meant he could write for a wider public than the purely academic. 'You'll see, he'll have the Greeks eating out of his hand. He's a born schemer.'

Holroyd was moving towards the table now. He shook hands with Hans, said something to Sonia which was received in stony silence, and then, after accepting a glass of ouzo, he came across to me. 'Well, young man—so you changed your mind, eh?' A smile was creasing the corners of his eyes, but the eyes themselves were without warmth. 'Dr Gilmore told me he had failed to persuade you to come out to Greece.'

'I changed my mind, as you say.'

He nodded. 'Now, come and have a drink—I want to talk to you in a moment about your father. I hope to persuade him to behave more sensibly in future. I shall expect your help.' The aroma of coffee filled the air. Cartwright brought a tray of artefacts from his tent and placed it on the table, also his notebooks. The soldiers were dismantling their tent. 'I have brought Mr Leonodipoulos with me.' Holroyd nodded towards the Greek official who was talking to the Corporal. 'I'll explain why, later.'

Coffee was served, and whilst we drank it the talk was entirely scientific as Cartwright explained the artefacts they had picked up on their trek down through Macedonia, mostly chippings of chert and obsidian, and all neatly labelled. Now and then he referred to his notes. Holroyd listened, smoking his pipe and only occasionally asking a question. At the end of it, he said, 'Well, at least you've got something to show for your efforts. But the earliest of these chert flakes is probably not more than seventeen thousand.' He leaned forward, stabbing with the stem of his pipe at the contents of the tray. 'There's nothing here, nothing that could remotely be associated with a carbon-14 dating of thirty-five thousand BP.'

'No, sir, I agree.'

'But that was the whole purpose of the expedition.'

Cartwright nodded, his face flushed. 'I understand, sir. But, as I wrote you, I have high hopes of the present location. When we've dug down——'

'That's a full season's work. You admit it yourself.' And Holroyd added with harsh emphasis, 'This expedition was not undertaken with a major dig in mind. You know that very well. If we had envisaged that, it would have meant a much bigger grant and a dozen or so students.'

'With all due respect, I think the two of us can manage to get a pilot trench cut to the Solutrean level at least.'

'Solutrean, or Aurignacian—what does it matter? You don't know what's there. Whereas this expedition was based on quite positive information—a carbon-dating of bones that had already been unearthed.'

'I think when you see the site itself——'

'In a moment, Alec. In a moment.' Holroyd smiled, his manner suddenly more conciliatory. 'What I'm trying to establish for you is the real intention of this expedition. It is purely a reconnaissance, an initial probe to test the validity of Dr Van der Voort's theories.' He turned to Sonia. 'You were right about his Journal. I had a talk with Dr Gilmore and I must accept his word for it that it is personal and deals with behaviourism. What I do not accept is that there is no record of his discoveries out here. He made three expeditions in the Central Mediterranean area, two of them entirely on his own. Last year he brought back bones for dating that would appear to be highly significant. You, as his secretary, must know——'

'I'm not his secretary,' she said quickly. 'I merely did some typing for him.'

'You also nursed him through an illness. You lived for a time in his house.' He was staring at her intently and I began to understand why he had decided to discuss the expedition publicly like this, instead of having a private talk with Cartwright. 'You could assist us greatly, and Dr Van der Voort, if you would tell us where he was last year, also perhaps the year before—the exact locations.'

She was staring back at him, very pale, very intense. 'Surely it is for Dr Van der Voort to tell you himself,' she said in a tight, controlled voice.

'That is precisely my difficulty, Miss Winters. If Dr Van der Voort were available——'

She went for him then, all the feelings that had been bottled up inside her during the days she had been in Greece bursting out of her in a torrent of words: 'You of all people—to come here and complain that Dr Van der Voort is not available. You know what is happening today—this very minute. A man called Kotiadis—Intelligence agent, Security Police—I don't know what he is—but he is hunting him down with a police dog like a—criminal. And you're responsible.'

'What do you mean by that?' Holroyd's voice was sharp.

'Don't pretend you don't know.' Her voice was wild and unrestrained. 'Do you think I'm a fool? Who set them on to him? Who tipped off the authorities that he was a Communist? You hound him. You drive him half out of his mind. And then you have the effrontery to come here asking me—*me*—to tell you where he was working these last two years. That's something you'll never——'

'Calm yourself.' He was leaning forward, his hand gripping her arm. 'I assure you I did not inform the authorities of his political background. Why should I?' he added. 'It is of no advantage to me that he has disappeared. Quite the reverse, I assure you.' He turned to Cartwright. 'Is that what he thinks —that I informed the authorities?'

Cartwright shook his head. 'No. He thought it was me.'

'And that's why he attacked you?'

'Yes.'

'I know all that,' Sonia snapped. 'He went for the wrong man.'

'You mean he should have attacked me?'

She shook her head, biting her lip. 'He shouldn't have attacked anybody, of course. But imagine how he felt—how you would have felt? He was engrossed with his work, and then suddenly this old bogey of Communism——'

But Holroyd was looking across at the Greek official. 'Tell her, will you,' he said. And then, turning back to Sonia, 'I knew this would have to be explained—if not to Van der Voort himself, certainly to you, and his son since he's here. It was one of the reasons I asked Mr Leonodipoulos to accompany me.' He nodded to the Greek, who said:

'On March 13 the Intelligence branch of the Public Order Ministry learned that a Communist agent had entered Greece under cover of leading a scientific expedition and was operating from a camp near this village. The information came from a Yugoslav source that has generally proved reliable.' He was speaking in impeccable English, smoothly and with scarcely a trace of accent. 'They checked first with our Immigration people, then with my Ministry. It was not difficult to confirm that this Dr Van der Voort had been associated with the Soviets and had published books in the Communist countries. The Security Police were informed and that evening they phoned the local headman here, Andreas Dikeli. Discreet enquiries were then made through the Russian Embassy in Athens. It all seemed to confirm the information our people had been given. However, since the expedition was British-sponsored, they sent Demetrios Kotiadis, one of their most senior men, up to interview Dr Van der Voort. When he discovered this man is disappeared in somewhat unusual circumstances——' He left it at that with a little expressive shrug.

'But—and this is the point I want to make clear to you, young lady.' Holroyd had lit his pipe and was puffing at it happily.

'While I was in Athens I was able to convince both the Ministry and the Security Police that Dr Van der Voort has broken with the Russians and that his presence here in Greece is entirely innocent.'

I don't think Sonia believed him even then. 'But why——' she said. 'Why should you do that?'

'Well, it's the truth, isn't it?'

'Yes, but——'

'You have to have a reason, do you?' He was smiling at her, perfectly relaxed now. 'Try looking at it from my point of view. Without Dr Van der Voort this expedition will achieve nothing. And I had great hopes of a break-through, something new. I've been asked to read a paper at the Pan-European Prehistoric Congress in May and this would be an ideal platform from which to launch Dr Van der Voort's new theory. And Mr Leonodipoulos here is keen, very keen, that his country should be involved in any scientific advance in our evolutionary knowledge.'

The Greek official nodded. 'That is quite correct. Despite Dr Van der Voort's political background, my Ministry is now satisfied that it is important for Greece that he continues his work here.'

Holroyd smiled and got to his feet. 'You think about that,' he told her, 'while we go up and look at this cave-dwelling. And remember, the Congress meets in less than two months. There's not much time.'

'You mean—when he's found—he's free to go on with his work?'

'You heard what Mr Leonodipoulos said.'

'But then you don't need information from me. You will be able to talk to him personally.'

'Perhaps. I hope so.' He patted her arm in a fatherly way. 'Well, we'll see, eh?' He turned to Cartwright, gave a peremptory jerk of his head, and as the party began to move off through the olive grove, he began explaining the cave to Leonodipoulos. 'I'm afraid this may not appear to you very impressive, accustomed as you are to tholos tombs and the glories of Ancient Greece. But Greek civilization stemmed from successive waves of primitive people coming down from the Black Sea coasts and the Caucasus. What Alec Cartwright hopes to unearth here, and perhaps elsewhere, is the *original* source of your civilization. This may be the first of a whole series of exciting discoveries——'

His voice faded and I looked round for Sonia. She was walking slowly down to the stream. Her long bare legs, her fair hair, the white tunic of her dress—in that setting she looked like one of the early Greeks. I started to go after her, but Hans stopped me. 'We go up to the dig now,' he said. 'She wants to be alone.' That surprised me, that he should be so considerate. 'She is concerned about Van der Voort.'

I nodded. 'She behaves as though . . .' I didn't know quite how to put it to him. 'How did they come to meet in the first place?' I asked. 'I suppose she was also studying anthropology?'

'No. Biology.'

'It was through you, then?'

'Partly.'

I continued to question him as we started up the track to the dig, but he was not very communicative. And yet her concern had been so deeply emotional. . . . 'Tell me about your own father,' I said finally.

'My father is dead. A car accident. It happened three years ago.' The tone of his voice discouraged further questions and we walked on in silence.

When we reached the cave Holroyd was standing back, sucking at his pipe and looking up at the overhang, his eyes narrowed against the glare. Cartwright was watching him anxiously. 'I think you're going to have trouble here.' Holroyd turned to Leonodipoulos. 'What we are concerned with is the fate of Neanderthal man when the oceanic climate changed to a continental one. The Neanderthalers went into a sort of decline and a new race of man—the Cro-Magnon or Aurignacian type —began to take over.'

'I do not understand.' Leonodipoulos was frowning. 'Why does this new type, this Cro-Magnon, take over?'

'Aye, well, there you've put your finger on it.' Holroyd nodded. 'That's the question we've all been asking ourselves. Mousterian man—the Neanderthalers—had been in existence a long time, sixty thousand years at least. We've found traces of him all over Europe, in Russia, in the Near East, in Africa, and with the passage of time you would expect his artefacts, his chippings of flint and chert and obsidian for use as weapons, to show a gradual improvement. And yet the reverse is the case, particularly after the emergence of Cro-Magnon man.'

'You have told me,' Leonodipoulos said, 'that this Cro-Magnon is our own species.'

'Yes. *Homo sapiens sapiens.* He's named after the Cro-Magnon cave-shelter at Les Eyzies in the Dordogne. That was where the first skeletons were unearthed, in 1868. But where he came from, that too is a mystery. The general view is that he came from Asia. Dr Van der Voort thinks from Africa.' He put a match to his pipe. 'So there you have it—two mysteries. Where did he come from? Why did Mousterian man disappear? Did this taller, more intelligent type of man—a man with a bigger brain capacity, with a head like ours, no ape-like brow ridges and a square jaw—destroy the Neanderthalers, or did Mousterian man just fade away naturally, a sort of death wish, like an African under the spell of a witch doctor?' His pipe was drawing again, his round babyish face smiling. 'Fascinating, isn't it? But whether this cave-shelter will throw any light on it——' He took his pipe out of his mouth, shaking his head, still smiling. 'Difficult to say. But perhaps Van der Voort will be able to tell us.'

His inspection of the dig took about half an hour and most of his comments were directed to Leonodipoulos. He seemed very anxious to establish the importance of the research they were doing into the prehistory of man in Greece. Several times he referred to the tourist attraction of the caves in the Dordogne region of France. But what interested me, as I stood there listening to him, was the way he managed to convey how primitive man, and the animals he hunted, could be associated, through the juxtaposition of bone remains, with definite climatic conditions and the period of their existence established in geological time by relating each new find to others of the same period. It was, in fact, a short lecture on how early man had developed along similar lines in different parts of the world, and the way he put it, in his slow, matter-of-fact North country voice, even I could understand and appreciate why, once all the correlated parts of a discovery—human bones, animal bones, artefacts and the soil in which they had been found—had been established and the date determined, then the name given to that discovery was used to describe others of a similar type.

Finally, standing once again on the slope below the cave, he pointed the stem of his pipe at the overhang and said, 'There's been a lot of water coming down this hillside. The evidence is there at the back of the cave.' He turned to Cartwright. 'I'm afraid, when you get down a little deeper, you'll find that whole layers of occupation have been washed down the slope or are interspersed with detritus from above. It looks as though Van der Voort has put you to work on a dig of extreme complexity.'

We went back to the camp then. It was pleasant under the trees and Sonia had prepared a cold lunch. Holroyd seated himself next to me. 'Now about your father . . . you will appreciate from what I've been saying that the whole success of this expedition depends on him.' His eyes were fixed on me. 'You saw him yesterday?'

I nodded. In view of what he had said earlier there seemed no point in denying it.

'Where?' And when I told him, he said, 'Good. Then they'll pick him up today. Did he talk to you about the future at all? Did he say whether he planned to concentrate on this cave site or move on to another area?'

'We were interrupted.'

'I see. Well, it doesn't matter. He'll be able to tell us that himself, I hope.' He concentrated for a moment on his food. He was a very purposeful eater, the sort of man who regards food solely as fuel for his energy, and he talked and ate at the same time. 'How did you know where to find him, eh?' He seized a glass of water and drank deeply, his little eyes watching me. 'Alec didn't know. Nor did that Greek fellow—he had to follow you. Well?'

I hadn't expected the question and I hesitated.

'You turn up here out of the blue, after the police have been searching the countryside for him without success for nearly three weeks, and the very next day you go straight to the place where he's been hiding out.' He jabbed at my arm with his forefinger. 'You found something in his house—his notes—locations where he worked last year?'

I didn't say anything, and he smiled as though my silence

was sufficient answer. 'Now, how long did you have together before you were interrupted?'

'I don't know. About fifteen or twenty minutes, I suppose.'

'And what did you talk about?'

I hesitated. 'The dunes mainly,' I said, and I began to explain to him the significance of that odd stretch of country. But he wasn't interested in that. He wanted to know whether I had been shown any excavations, any prehistoric bones or artefacts. He brushed aside my description of the ventilation shafts. 'Modern—Roman,' he said impatiently. 'I'm talking about things that are thirty-five thousand years old. Surely you realize that by now.'

The others had fallen suddenly silent and I looked up to find Kotiadis coming into the clearing. He was alone and he came straight to where I was sitting, walking fast and with purpose. 'Here's your rucksack,' he said and dumped it on the table in front of me. 'You know where I find it?'

'Where is he?' I demanded.

'That is what I come to ask you.' He was hot and tired and extremely angry. 'He has been hiding out in the top of that old shaft for a long time. The evidence is everywhere.'

I was staring at him, barely listening to what he was saying. 'He must be there,' I said.

'Not now.'

There was finality in the way he said it, and the memory of his violent anti-Communism scared me for a moment. 'Have you searched the dunes?'

'Of course I searched the dunes—the whole area. He is not there.'

The intensity of his frustration convinced me and I relaxed. The old man must have realized they would come back. He had seen the trap and escaped. But where to? Weak as he was, where could he possibly have gone? Sonia caught my eye, the same question in her mind. I shook my head. I didn't know.

I put the rucksack on the ground beside me. Kotiadis had switched his attention to Leonodipoulos now, and as the changed situation was explained to him, he became very heated. Holroyd gripped my arm. 'If you know where he is, laddie, you'd better tell me. It's for his own good. This Congress is a great opportunity. Where's he gone to ground now?'

'I'm sorry,' I said. 'I don't know.'

'You must have some idea, surely?' And when I shook my head his grip on my arm tightened. 'What else did you discover in his house? You knew he would be somewhere on those dunes. What was the next location?'

'I don't know.'

'You're lying.'

Sonia intervened then, leaning across the table. 'He's telling you the truth. He'd never have found Dr Van der Voort if I hadn't told him about the dunes near Ayios Giorgios.'

'You?' He let go of my arm and stared at her. 'He was there last year, was he?'

The corners of her lips turned up in a little secret smile. 'It was just something I typed for him, a description of the dunes. He was very interested in the geological aspect of his discovery. It confirmed, you see, the climatic conditions . . .'

'Yes, but what else? Was there something near—a cave-dwelling? What was the next passage you typed for him?'

'Nothing else.'

'Nothing? But these were his notes. He was out here two seasons——'

'I'm afraid that's all I can tell you.'

He hesitated, staring at her hard. Then he got abruptly to his feet, pulling his pipe out of his pocket, and went over to where the two Greeks were still arguing. Cartwright got up, too, nervous, ill-at-ease, fumbling with his pipe. Hans followed him.

I turned to Sonia then. 'Have you any idea where he is?'

She shook her head. 'He may have gone up to the village of Ayios Giorgios. He lived there for a time last year.'

'Kotiadis will have searched there.'

'Probably. But he could be in the hills, hiding. From what you've told me he's too weak to have gone very far.' And she added angrily, 'All Professor Holroyd cares about is where those bones came from—the ones I sent to Dr Gilmore for dating. If it wasn't for that he'd be glad to see your father dead.' Her voice shook with the intensity of her feeling.

I leaned across the table. 'And where *did* the bones come from?' I saw the muscles of her face tighten, her eyes go blank. 'Was it Levkas?' I asked, lowering my voice to a whisper.

But Levkas was an island. 'He couldn't possibly have got there.'

'You don't realize how desperate he is.' There were tears in her eyes. 'This is his last chance. You mustn't—please you mustn't tell Holroyd about Levkas.'

But Holroyd was talking to Kotiadis now. They were standing together on the edge of the clearing, away from the others, and Kotiadis already knew about Levkas. He knew all the locations.

'I think they'll decide to move camp to Ayios Giorgios now.'

'Will Holroyd stay out here?' I asked.

She nodded. 'I think so. He feels he's on to something now and he won't leave it to Alec. The time's too short if he's to read that paper. Yes,' she said with finality. 'He'll stay.' And she added, with a little jerk of her head to where Cartwright and her brother were standing alone and silent, 'They're resigned to it already, both of them. Alec is ambitious, and Hans is a dreamer. They thought this dig here——' She gave a little brittle laugh. 'The academic world is full of conceit, you know.'

Cartwright's dejection I could understand. I had seen the way he had flushed like a girl up there at the dig when Holroyd had condemned it as a site of great complexity. But Hans Winters was still a student. 'I should have thought your brother would be glad to work under a man like Holroyd.'

She gave a little shrug. 'You can't dream dreams with a man like Professor Holroyd in charge, and Hans is my father all over again.'

'Your father's dead, I believe.'

'Yes, he's dead. Did Hans tell you?'

I nodded.

'Did he tell you how?' She was looking at me very directly. 'He committed suicide.'

'I'm sorry,' I murmured.

'No need to be,' she said harshly. 'He wasn't cut out for this world. He was a Christian. A real Christian. And he thought everybody was like him. He was too bloody good to be true. And so unworldly . . . he drove his car straight off the road into the Amstel.'

'You obviously don't take after him.'

'No. I take after my mother's side of the family, thank God.

But'—her face suddenly softened—'on the surface, that is; deep down—I'm not so sure.'

'You're older than your brother.'

'Yes. Two years.'

'He says you studied biology.'

'Foreign languages. Biology was only a side line.' The habitual tenseness of her face was lit fleetingly by that quick elfin smile of hers. 'You're wondering how I came to be associated with Dr Van der Voort.'

'I presumed it was through your brother.'

'Yes. Indirectly. Dr Van der Voort's books have never been published in Holland, but Hans got hold of the East German editions, and German being one of my languages'—she gave a little shrug—'I just became fascinated, that's all. Not the writing. He writes very technically. But the ideas, the way he correlates man and his environment—the effects of the Würm Glaciation in particular—the extraordinary changes produced by the interstadials—hippopotamus, rhinoceros, reindeer, bison, mammoths, tropical animals interchanging with an almost arctic fauna, and man himself evolving all the time. And then, when I realized he was in Amsterdam, actually lived just across the canal from us——'

I had never asked her what her feelings for him were, and now, when I felt she was just about to explain of her own accord, Holroyd interrupted us. 'I've had a talk with Demetrios Kotiadis,' he said to me. He was looking pleased with himself, standing over me, puffing contentedly at his pipe. 'He's done a very thorough job tracing your father's movements last year and during his earlier visit in 1965. He's going to check up now on all the likely places, and when he finds him, he'll keep him under surveillance. But that's all. Leonodipoulos was very emphatic. I don't think he convinced him, but Kotiadis has his orders and Dr Van der Voort will be free to rejoin the expedition, if that's what he wants.' He patted my shoulder. 'So you've no cause to worry about him any more.'

I looked across at Kotiadis. He was still arguing with Leonodipoulos, the staccato sound of his voice ringing in the quiet of the glade as they walked towards the path that led to the village. 'What are you planning to do?' I asked Holroyd.

'First thing tomorrow morning we'll move camp—to

OOP/7341—E

Ayios Giorgios first, and if that doesn't produce what I'm hoping for, then we'll be going to one of the islands. Levkas. Van der Voort seems to have been particularly interested in Levkas last year.'

Kotiadis was shaking hands with Leonodipoulos. I watched him turn and hurry away up the path. 'So you've found out all you need.'

Holroyd nodded. 'Enough, I think, to ensure that our time isn't wasted.'

There was a smugness in the way he said it that had me simmering with anger. 'You've no further use for him now?'

He was quick to understand my mood. 'No man is indispensable, you know,' he said mildly. 'And from what Kotiadis told me, he's not fit to be in charge of an expedition on his own. Would you agree with that?' And when I didn't say anything, he said, 'Be honest now. He's not a fit man, is he?'

'He's been without food for some time. He's very weak, that's all.'

It seemed to satisfy him. 'In that case, he won't have gone far. He'll probably turn up at Ayios Giorgios. Kotiadis enquired there, of course, but——' He patted my shoulder in that aggravating way of his. 'Anyway, don't you worry. When he does turn up, I'm sure Miss Winters will see to it that he's properly looked after.' He wanted to know my plans then. 'Kotiadis told me you had a boat waiting for you at Preveza. Leonodipoulos will be leaving shortly for Athens. I'm quite certain he'd give you a lift—as far as Arta, at any rate.'

I looked across at Sonia, but she was already on her feet and moving away. I had a feeling then, a sudden urgent feeling, that I must visit Levkas—now, before Holroyd got there. 'Yes,' I said. 'I'd be glad of a lift.' Levkas was on our route to the Aegean, whether we took the Corinth Canal or went south round the bottom of Greece.

Holroyd nodded as though the matter had never been in doubt. 'Good. To be plain with you, I don't like people on a dig who are not a part of it. They get in the way. And as for your father, most of his life has been spent in strange countries. He's well able to look after himself.'

'I expect you're right,' I said.

'No doubt about it. And you've got your own life to live,

eh—your own problems?' And he went off to fix it with Leonodipoulos.

That night I slept in a private house in the old Roman town of Arta. Leonodipoulos arranged it at a taverna where he was known. They were kindly people who spoke a few words of English and sent me to bed full of a strong local wine after showing me endless photographs of their son, who was about my own age and serving in a tank regiment somewhere up by the Bulgarian border. They had given me their best room, all Victorian style furniture and lace—lace curtains and the sheets and pillow cases of the big double bed edged with lace and smelling of lavender. A ewer and basin in blue china stood on a marble-topped washstand and there was even a chamber pot. Probably the room was typical of countless others belonging to the *petit bourgeoisie* in the country towns of Greece, so spotlessly clean, so lovingly cared for, that to me it was almost a museum piece. A single naked light bulb hanging from its flex in the middle of the ceiling was the only indication that the world had progressed in the last fifty years.

Lying there in the faded splendour of that brass-trimmed bedstead, the camp at Despotiko already seemed remote, part of another world to which I did not belong. When we had left they had already started packing up for the move to Ayios Giorgios. In the morning the tents would be gone, the olive grove empty except for the goats. The involvement which I had begun to feel was a very tenuous one. I was on my own again now and even my concern for the old man faded as my mind began to grapple with the problems of the voyage ahead. Leonodipoulos had given me a lot of information about sea conditions in the Aegean. He had sailed there regularly in a friend's yacht out of Vouliagmeni. He not only knew Samos, but he knew the actual port I should be using and warned me against the severe down-draughts to be expected off Pytha-gorion whenever the mcltemi was blowing.

This common interest in the sea had made the drive pleasant for both of us, and it amused me that Holroyd, in his haste to be rid of me, had made me a present of such a useful contact in the Greek Establishment. In fact, during our meal together in the taverna, Leonodipoulos had assured me that he would see

131

to it that my father was all right; Kotiadis had orders to report to him as soon as he had located him.

I was woken in the morning by the daughter-in-law bringing my breakfast in on a tray. She had put in a brief appearance the night before, leaving with a giggle and flash of dark eyes. I watched her now as she stretched up to pull the curtains. Like most of the girls I had seen in Greece she was too broad in the beam, too thick in the calves—a dumpy, unattractive figure. And yet somehow she managed to imbue her movements with a sensuous sexuality. And when she leaned over me to put the tray on the bed I forgot about her figure; all I was conscious of was her eyes, big and shining and black like newly-washed grapes.

'Kafé,' she said firmly and almost filled the cup with hot milk before adding a little of the very strong black coffee. Her skin had the sheen of olives. She smiled at me, and the smile lit up her eyes, and then she gave that embarrassed little giggle and was gone in a swirl of skirt and fat little buttocks.

I drank my coffee, wondering when the boy in those photographs would get home again. Six months they had said since he last had leave. She was too ripe a plum to be left on her own that long. She reminded me a little of Florrie. Florrie had that same southern sensuality—and there'd be another dawn, or perhaps a night watch. . . .

Somewhere above me a baby cried, and then I heard the murmur of the mother's soothing voice. Sex, procreation, birth, death—it all seemed much closer, more natural down here in the Mediterranean, an inevitable part of living. And the old people worrying. That had seemed inevitable, too. Worrying about their son, about themselves, about the future—that strange mixture of fear and human warmth and happiness that seems to be a characteristic of hot countries.

I was stripped to the waist, shaving, when she returned for the tray, and she stood there, her body thrust out to take the edge of it as she tried a few words of conversation—'You—Preveza—Símera?'

She meant today, of course, and I nodded.

'Autobus—ten half hours.'

She giggled, her eyes bright and liquid with the excitement of this contact with a stranger from another country. But then the baby started crying again, and as she listened the excitement in her eyes changed to something softer. 'Stefan,' she said, smiling gently, and she was gone—no swirl of skirt, but a mother to her young, quickly and with purpose.

They saw me to the bus, the whole family, including the baby; made sure I got a seat and waved me goodbye as though I were the son of the house. It was a leisurely journey, for we stopped at every village, and the waits were sometimes long. It was afternoon before we saw the Gulf of Amvrakikos. The great expanse of water was a silken blue, arrowed by the wake of a few fishing boats, and the hills beyond were puffed up to twice their size by the clouds that hung over them.

All the way down I had been seeing traces of that same aqueduct whose ventilation shafts marked the erosion in the red dunes. Now at last I was catching glimpses of the great city it had served, the ruins overgrown with creepers, half-buried in vegetation, but still gigantic in size. The outer wall ran like a stone rampart into green grass country where sheep and goats grazed. Beyond Nikopolis, the grass gave way to agriculture, and where there was irrigation, the land was intensively cultivated. And then at last we were in Preveza itself, swinging through an area of new building centred around a petrol storage depot and out on to the waterfront, a broad promenade built on the scale of a major seaside resort with the town behind it a low huddle of nondescript buildings.

The water was absolutely still, a sheet of glass mirroring the blue of the sky. I pressed my face to the dirty window. But there were no boats. The whole length of that waterfront was absolutely empty. The emptiness of it came as a shock to me. I had been so certain the Barretts would be waiting for me there, the boat anchored stern-on. The weather had been perfect. There had been no gales. The bus came to a stop and I got out with the rest of the passengers, standing there, irresolute in the sunshine, my suitcase in my hand. A group of gypsies passed with a mule-drawn cart, two dogs slinking in the shade below the axle, the women following, free-striding and upright, their skirts and shawls bright with colour. The little band was a gay contrast to the drab black of the Greeks sitting over their coffee at the kaféneion, which was also the bus terminal; and out beyond the smooth strip of water that was the entrance to the Gulf of Amvrakikos, the further shore showed as a fringe of low-lying land. It was all flat country, the hills a long way away, and seaward I could see the buoys that marked the dredged channel. No vessels were coming in and the only thing that moved on the flat molten surface of the water was a small open fishing boat powered by an outboard.

For a moment I was at a complete loss. *Coromandel* should have arrived two days ago. Standing there, conspicuous and somewhat forlorn, I realized how urgent had been my desire to get to Levkas, how committed I was to the idea of searching for a cave-shelter there similar to the one at Despotiko.

'Say, fellow—you American?'

I turned. A broad, grizzled man was staring at me with bright dark eyes from one of the tables. 'No, English,' I said.

'Englézos, Americanós—same thing, eh? I sail many ports.' He reeled off the English ports he had been in, most of them barely recognizable the way he pronounced them. 'I was stoker, see. In the old *Mauritania* one time. Jeez! That was work. You like a kafé, sump'n to drink? What you like?'

He was a battered, garrulous old man who had knocked around the world in all sorts of ships. 'Ain't many coal burners left now. They want greasers, not stokers. Anyways, I'm too old. An' I got dollars. Anybody got dollars in Greece, they can sit in the kaféneion an' do nothin'—jus' talk. That's a good life, eh?' He gave a toothless chuckle. 'Not bad for an old man who's bin a stoker all his life. You in the war? No, too young, I guess. Torpedoed twice. Second time was on one of those P.Qs. Jeez, that was cold. We was in the goddam ice three days. . . .'

I sat and drank my coffee and listened to that Ancient Mariner going on and on about the disaster that had hit a convoy to Murmansk. It was an incredible story, but difficult to follow. Finally he ran out of steam and I asked him if he had seen an English boat in Preveza during the last two days.

'An old fishing boat with a bowsprit? Yeah. She come in Thursday evening, but she don't stay. She was lyin' right there.' He indicated a position almost opposite us with a hand that had two fingers missing. 'Woman spoke Greek. Very bad Greek. Said they gonna wait for a friend. Guess that was you, eh? Well, they was gone next morning. Yesterday morning.'

'Where did they go to?' I asked.

He shook his head. 'They jus' vamoose.' He smiled. I think he was pleased at remembering that word. And then he thrust his mutilated hand in front of my face. 'See that? That was the first time I get the torpedo. Lucky I don't lose my fukkin arm.' He was in mid-Atlantic then and it was ten minutes before I could extricate myself and visit the Port Captain's office. It was about a hundred yards further along the waterfront and there I was able to confirm *Coromandel*'s movements. The Port Captain himself showed me the entry in his book. She had arrived at 18.30 hours on Thursday evening direct from Pylos and she had left the following morning at 08.30 bound for Port Vathy on the island of Meganisi. He did not speak English so that I was unable to question him, but just as I was leaving he indicated a poste restante box on the wall. There was a note in it addressed to me, just a line from Bert to say they would be back by Saturday evening, or at the latest Sunday morning.

There was a local chart pinned to the wall beside the Port Captain's desk. 'Meganisi?' I asked him and he pointed to an island shaped like some extraordinary crayfish with a thick, pronged body and a whiplash tail. It was about ten miles south of the Levkas Canal and separated from the island of Levkas by the narrow Meganisi Channel.

There was a restaurant nearby and I left my suitcase there and walked out to a wooded promontory that looked across to the ruined fortress of Actium. By then a small breeze had come in and the sea glinted between the red boles of the pines. I sat at a table near a logwood kiosk that served coffee and soft drinks, watching the dredged channel. But though I stayed there until the last of the boys who had been running in and out of the water had gone home and the sun was slanting towards the sea, I saw only two ships come in, and both of them were caiques.

It was almost dark by the time I got back to the restaurant and there I had the best meal I had had in weeks—huge meaty prawns, fresh-caught that morning from the sands off Preveza. I was sitting over my coffee, wondering whether I would have to find myself a room for the night, when I saw the green and red of navigation lights close off the quay, heard the rattle of an anchor chain running out. By the time I was out of the restaurant the boat had turned stern-on and was coming in fast. It was *Coromandel* and I reached the edge of the quay just as Bert heaved the first warp for the waiting harbour boy to slip over a bollard. He saw me, gave a cheerful wave, and the next moment the bight of chain that carried the second warp crashed at my feet. As soon as he had made fast and the gangplank had been rigged, I went on board. Bert's hand gripped mine.

'Are you alone?' he asked.

'Yes.'

'Where's Kotiadis?'

I began to explain, but then the glimpse of a white sweater showed for'ard and Florrie was spotlighted green as she came quickly down the starboard side. 'Paul!' I suddenly found myself embraced, enveloped almost in the warmth of her emotional personality. 'You're alone?'

'Yes, of course I'm alone.' But when I started to explain what had happened so that they would understand why I wanted to visit Levkas, Bert stopped me. 'Something we've got to tell you, something important. When we arrived here—the morning after, that is——'

'Not now.' Florrie indicated the shadowy figures crowding the quay to look at the boat. 'Wait till we're down below.'

We made the warps fast, hauled in on the chain for'ard and then went down to the saloon. 'It's your father, y'see,' Bert said as he opened up the drink locker. 'There's a village called Vatahori out there on Meganisi——'

'For heaven's sake,' Florrie cut in. 'Begin at the beginning.'

'That's what I was trying to do.' He shrugged. 'Oh, well, you tell him yourself then.'

She turned eagerly towards me. 'You know we got in the evening before last? Well, yesterday morning it was—about five-thirty. There were footsteps on the deck. I'm a very light sleeper. I thought perhaps it was you. A voice called from the wheelhouse and I woke Bert and we went up to find this man sitting there slumped in the chart table seat. He looked like a scarecrow almost, his face drawn, his clothes hanging on him like rags. I thought for a moment he was some sort of beggar. And then he staggered to his feet, mumbled his name and said

136

he was your father . . . and all in the same breath he asked if we'd take him out to Meganisi.'

'He said you'd sent him.' Bert handed Florrie the brandy he had just poured for her. 'You did send him, didn't you?'

'I told him about your boat, how I'd got to Greece. But that's all.'

'Well, it doesn't matter,' she said, sipping her drink. 'There he was, and he was so ill-looking and weak—we brought him down here, and when he told me he hadn't eaten for a long time, I made him an omelette and some coffee. He had the sense to eat it slowly, but he was dreadfully tired. And he wouldn't go to bed—not until we'd promised to take him to Meganisi.'

'You're sure it was Meganisi, not Levkas, he wanted?' I asked.

'Of course. The village of Vatahori on Meganisi, that's where he wanted to go—and without anyone knowing.'

'Did he tell you why?'

She shook her head. 'Not really. He kept talking about a cave, something he had to do. He wasn't very coherent.'

'He never mentioned Levkas.' Bert handed me the bottle of Scotch and a glass. 'And he was quite straight with us—about the risk, I mean. But he seemed so desperately urgent——'

'We couldn't just leave him here to be picked up by the police or that man Kotiadis. Even if he was a Communist agent. Which I don't believe.'

'He told you about that, did he?' I asked.

'Oh yes—everything. But it was all very confused. The words just poured out of him. I don't think we understood half of it, did we, Bert? He just went on talking and talking, as though he couldn't stop. And then, when Bert said we'd take him, he just collapsed. We put him to bed in your bunk, and then Bert went ashore to clear with the Port Captain's office.'

'Where is he now?' I asked.

'I told you, at Vatahori,' Bert said. 'And that made it a little more risky. They haven't got a harbour official at Vatahori so I had to tell the Port Captain here we were going to Port Vathy.'

'Does he know you had a passenger on board?'

He shook his head. 'They didn't ask me about that, and

137

where officials are concerned, I always say what the eye doesn't see . . .' He laughed. 'But then it was dark when he'd come on board, and the truck that had brought him down to Preveza had gone straight on to a farm further along the coast. There was no way they could know we'd got an extra bod on board.' He took a quick gulp at his whisky. 'I suppose it was about eight-thirty when we cleared. A nice westerly breeze, motor-sailing all the way, right through the Levkas Canal. And no trouble at Vatahori—nobody there, just a long inlet marked on the chart as Port Atheni. You anchor in the middle and the village of Vatahori is about a mile from the end of it.'

'And you put him ashore there?'

'Yes, after breakfast this morning.' And he added, 'He wouldn't let us go with him up to the village. Said he'd be all right—he had friends there.'

'He didn't need help, anyway,' Florrie said. 'He'd slept most of the time we were sailing. And afterwards, when we'd anchored, he had the most enormous meal—bacon and eggs, the lot.' She smiled. 'I thought he'd never stop eating. And though he looked so ill, he had enough energy to walk up the hill.'

Bert nodded. 'He's tougher than he looks, that's certain.'

'He was like a kid, really. I just poured food into him, and you could see him converting it into energy. And talking all the time. To himself, mostly—for his own benefit. All technical stuff. I couldn't understand half of it.' And she added, 'I can see him now, walking away with a brief wave of his hand, up the stony track that led to the village, a bent old man, his shoulders stooped, his eyes on the ground, and still wearing those ragged clothes. It didn't seem right—to let him go like that, all alone.'

'It's what he wanted,' Bert said.

After that they had sailed round to Port Vathy, the next bay to the west, and made their number to the Customs man and then steamed straight back to Preveza. 'Dead easy.' He hesitated, looking at me a little uncertainly. 'I hope we did right—taking him out to that island and leaving him there?'

'Yes,' I said. 'Of course. It was very good of you. And you say he had friends at Vatahori?'

Bert nodded. 'That's what he said.' And Florrie added, 'We

wouldn't have left him otherwise—not like that. He didn't look at all well. Very drawn and his skin a bad colour.'

'Did he say why it was so urgent?' Only a narrow strip of water separated Meganisi from Levkas and if he had friends at Vatahori they could presumably take him across there. 'He must have given you a reason.'

'Oh, yes.' Florrie nodded. 'But as I say, it was all very confused—something he had to do—some bones. He kept talking about bones.'

'That's right,' Bert agreed. 'A collection of bones and artefacts they were keeping for him—his friends, I think. What was their name, Florrie? Pappa-something. They were Greeks.'

'Pappadimas.'

'Yes, that's right. I remember now. A collection he'd brought out with him. The previous year. But, as Florrie says, it was all a bit confused like. He kept talking about a cave. And a professor came into it. He had to get to them before this professor.'

'Professor Holroyd?'

'Yes, I think that was the name. Like I say, he seemed to have something he had to do very urgently before this professor bloke beat him to it. He kept on about time. He hadn't much time, he said. I remember that because he gave me the creeps for a moment, staring at us, his eyes shining under his shaggy brows. I thought he was ... well, you'll excuse my saying this about your father, but I thought he was a bit off his rocker.'

'He was very tired, that's all,' Florrie said. 'Tired and ill.'

'Okay.' Bert shrugged. 'Tired and ill and a bit delirious. But it comes to the same thing. A bloke in that sort of state, you have to humour him, so we took him to Meganisi.'

I nodded. I knew what he meant. I had felt the same up there in the red dunes. 'I'll have to go there,' I said. 'When can we leave?'

'For Meganisi?'

'Yes.'

He thought about ten in the morning. Florrie needed to get some fresh stores from the market and he'd have to clear again with the Port Captain's office. 'They'll think I've got a ruddy girl friend there, or something.'

Florrie laughed. 'Not with me on board, they won't.'

It was late by the time I had retrieved my suitcase and told them what had happened at Despotiko. But even so, I found it difficult to sleep. Partly it was the stuffiness of the cabin after camping out in the open air. But chiefly it was the old man. It was extraordinary the effect he had on people. When I had asked the Barretts why they had taken the risk of running him out to Meganisi—and it was a big risk, knowing that he was in trouble with the Security Police—all Florrie had said was, 'You weren't here, Paul. If you had been, you'd understand.' And Bert added, 'If he'd been pleading for us to ship him out of the country, I wouldn't have done it. But he wasn't trying to escape. He had something urgent and positive he wanted to do. I may not understand about anthropology, but a man who's dedicated to his work and his beliefs——' He had turned then and poured himself another whisky. 'You may not like him. You don't have to like him. But you respect him, even if there is something very strange about him. I felt——' His open, honest features had reflected his own puzzlement as he searched for words to express his feelings. 'He sort of made me feel I was in the presence of an enormously powerful mind. Y'see, when a man is ranging over thousands of years—it's like the stars at night when you're sailing—you feel so small and insignificant. It just didn't seem important that we were taking a risk in helping him to get where he wanted.'

When I went on deck next morning it was cloudy, a grey day with the wind from the west. It looked as though we would have a good sail and after breakfast I went with Bert to the Port Captain s office. I think they knew all about me. Anyway, we had no difficulty in clearing again for Meganisi. Then, back on board, we heard the sound of women's voices in the saloon and I went below to find Sonia there. She was on the settee berth, facing Florrie across the table, and she jumped up as I came in. 'Paul.' Her voice was urgent. 'They're packing up. They're not staying at Ayios Giorgios.'

Holroyd had spent an afternoon in the red dunes, had found nothing of real interest and had made the decision to move after supper the previous night. She had left the camp at four in the morning, walked down to the main road where she waited over an hour before getting a lift. 'I was afraid I'd miss you.'

'She wants to come with us.' Florrie's tone was controlled —not openly hostile, but it was clear she didn't want another woman on her own boat.

'Only to Meganisi,' Sonia said quickly. 'You see—last night —Kotiadis came up to the camp——' She was facing me, her voice, her whole manner, distraught. 'The Chief of Police at Levkas had been making enquiries for him and that evening he had phoned him at his hotel in Jannina. I've just been trying to explain to Mrs Barrett. They know where Dr Van der Voort is now. Kotiadis can't do anything—not at the moment. But he's passed all the information on to Professor Holroyd— where your father's staying, the locations he was working on last year, everything. And I'm scared. I'm scared of what will happen when Professor Holroyd gets there. Please——' she was leaning forward, a note of desperation in her voice. 'Mrs Barrett doesn't realize . . . please try and convince them of the urgency. They shouldn't meet—your father and Professor Holroyd—not before I've seen him, not without warning.'

So it was all coming to a head on this island of Meganisi. I sat down. 'You say Holroyd knows the location of his digs?'

She nodded. 'Kotiadis told him. That's why they're moving camp this morning.'

'And the digs are on Meganisi, not Levkas?'

'One on Meganisi—by an island called Tiglia. That's in the channel between Meganisi and Levkas. The other is across the channel, on the Levkas side—a bay. I can't remember the name now. I typed it. But it's gone for the moment.'

'What are you suggesting, then?' I asked. 'That he'll go for Holroyd the way he went for Cartwright?'

She shook her head. 'No, not that. But something. I don't know. I must get there first. Otherwise——' She hesitated. 'Oh, it's all so stupid. And to try and explain what I feel. Can't you see? Working on his own all last year, and now . . . if it isn't all to be wasted, he's got to fight this man. Not physically, I don't mean that. Not with violence. But he mustn't become another Marais. He mustn't lose out to an academic publicist, have all his work filched by a man who's never done any real basic research in his life. It's wrong, wrong—all wrong. He's got to fight back—somehow.'

She was looking anxiously at the three of us. 'Please—please take me. I don't like the thought of him there alone. Anything could happen. But if he had support, people there who believed in him . . .' She reached for her handbag. 'Something else I have to tell you. Dr Gilmore is arriving by plane this afternoon, at Corfu.' She handed me a cable. 'I got that just before we left Despotiko.' It gave Gilmore's flight number and ETA and instructed her to contact him at the Kérkira Hotel. 'I kept him informed, everything, by letter. He asked me to. And then, when I knew Professor Holroyd was coming out, I cabled him. I think Dr Gilmore is the only man who can help your father now.'

'And you want us to pick him up at Corfu?'

She nodded, her silence more pleading than words.

4

THE WHITE limestone cliffs of Paxos were on our starboard bow, Corfu dropping astern, when Bert relieved me at the helm. 'Are you going outside Levkas or through the Canal?' I asked him. 'The wind's north-westerly, increasing.' It was the prevailing wind of this coast and I thought it would be force 6 by the late afternoon.

'Oh, I think the Canal,' he said, without even glancing at the chart.

'It's a dead run and a lee shore when we make the entrance.'

He nodded. 'But once inside we'll be in quiet water.' He was thinking of our passenger. He had looked tired, almost frail when we had met him at the airport the previous day, and though we had had an early meal, he had insisted on staying up until he had all the facts of the situation clear in his mind. I had given him my cabin and he had not stirred from his bunk all morning.

'It's running it a bit fine—it'll be almost dark when we get there.' I handed over the wheel and took another look at Chart 1609. It was divided into two sections—the canal itself and the north and south entrances, including the whole of the island of Levkas. The northern entrance was a bight formed by the island and the mainland; it had a sand spit backed by shallows running away to the north-east, and the entrance itself was a 90 degree turn to starboard, close in to the shallows and flanked by sandbanks. It looked singularly unattractive for a boat running under sail before a strong north-westerly breeze. 'Well, you know what it's like.'

'Yes, I know it.'

He had altered course to port, and though the jib was still full, the staysail was beginning to slat under the lee of the main. The boat was steady, but pitching slightly now that the sea was getting up. He asked me to boom the staysail out, and up for'ard I was more conscious of the surge of the bows, could feel the weight of the wind. The sky was blue, but veiled with cirrus, the sea white with the break of wave-caps. When I'd rigged the boom and clipped it to the clew of the staysail I went aft and eased out the mainsheet. From the stern I could still see the Pindus Mountains, a white glint of snow at the far end of the Corfu Channel where the Albanian coast began.

Down in the saloon Florrie and Sonia had finished their lunch. 'Dr Gilmore all right?' I asked.

Sonia nodded. 'He's had a cup of Marmite and now he's propped up in his bunk reading some abstruse paper in the *American Journal of Anthropology*. He said he had no idea that a small boat could be so comfortable.' She smiled. 'He's really remarkably chirpy. Oh, and he asked me to give you this. He thought it might help you to understand your father.' She reached to the shelf behind her head and handed me a wadge of typewritten sheets. 'It's an article written by one of his students.' It was headed—*The Tragic Life of Eugene Marais*.

'You mentioned that name yesterday morning.'

She nodded. 'Marais was also a South African. That's why it came to my mind. And because it's a very sad, very well-known case. A brilliant man who had his work filched by somebody else.'

'And he killed himself?' It was there in the first paragraph— *'Lawyer, journalist, poet and naturalist, patriot and drug addict, and in the end—suicide; but for all that a man so in advance of his time . . .'*

'Is that what you're afraid of?' I asked. 'That he'll commit suicide?'

'No. No, I don't think so. I hadn't really thought. But you read it. You'll see then why Dr Gilmore thought it relevant.'

Florrie came in from the galley with my lunch and I put the

typescript on top of the drink locker. I was hungry. Also I was more concerned at the moment about the entrance to the Levkas Canal. I was remembering what Florrie had said about her husband's navigation, and it would be dark by the time we got there.

However, there is no point in anticipating a moment of crisis, and since I had nothing else to occupy my mind when I had finished my meal, I took the typescript up on deck and settled myself for'ard of the wheelhouse. I was sheltered from the wind there and the sun was warm. I'm not a great reader, not of biographies anyway, and I don't think the piece was particularly well written. Nevertheless, it was such an extraordinary story that I forgot for a moment about the difficult entrance we would have to make, barely noticed the increase in the wind's strength.

It was certainly a tragic story, and as I read it, I found myself comparing it all the time with my father's life. Communism had been at the root of his loneliness. In the case of Marais, it was patriotism. He came of an old Afrikaaner family and the outbreak of the Boer War had caught him in London still studying for the Bar, having abandoned medicine after four years. He was interned, but by the end of the war he was in Rhodesia, smuggling arms across the border to the Boers. All this I could understand; it was the sort of thing I would have done myself. But then he had cut himself off from the human race and in an isolated part of the Transvaal, the Waterberg, had lived with a troop of baboons.

In a sense it was not unlike my father's disappearance into the red dunes, except that while Marais had had the company of living creatures, my father had been cut off from all life, with only the dead past of human occupation for company. But only for three weeks, not three years.

In carrying out this intense study in the field Marais was half a century ahead of any other scientist. Nobody, until after the Second World War, had apparently considered it important to observe the behaviour of primates in their natural state, rather than in captivity. And since the violence of his patriotic fervour dictated that the only account of his observations should be published in an Afrikaans newspaper, his work went unrecognized. The articles were not translated into English until 1939, and by then he was dead. And it was the same with his later study of termite society.

Six years after Marais's articles on the white ant appeared in Afrikaans, a Belgian named Maeterlinck had published in a popular scientific series a little book called *La Vie des Termites.* Marais had sued him, but Maeterlinck was not only a man of letters who had been awarded the Nobel Prize for Literature, but his books on scientific subjects were widely read. The truth was confused with sour grapes. In any case, barrister though Marais was, an international legal action of this kind against an established public figure was beyond his resources. Most of his money had gone long ago in compensation to farmers for the depredations of his baboons during those three years spent alone in the Waterberg. It was not until after his death, when his articles were translated into English and published under the title *The Soul of the White Ant,* that the basis for Maeterlinck's book became apparent to the scientific world and Marais recognized for the genius he was.

But for Marais himself, the comfort of morphine and ultimate suicide had replaced justice. He remained unrecognized throughout his life. *A man who voluntarily cuts himself off from society cannot complain if that same society ignores him.* This sentence, on the last page of the typescript, had been underlined and in the margin Gilmore had written—*Pieter Van der Voort has done just this as far as the Western world is concerned and anything he may discover will be accorded an even more hostile reception than would Marais's observations. The reasons for this I will explain later.*

That was it—the strange life of another South African with a chip on his shoulder. And though my father hadn't confined his writings to Afrikaans, it had amounted to almost the same thing as far as the Western world was concerned—his two books published only in Communist countries. I sat there for a long time after I had finished reading, not feeling the sun on my face, not hearing the roar of the bow wave as we ran downwind, only thinking of my father, comparing his story with Marais's. Would my father also have to wait half a century for recognition—presuming that he, too, was a genius? And I couldn't help thinking that if some dedicated student had written an article about him, setting out his whole life story like this, and I had read it, then perhaps I would have seen him for the sort of man he was and have understood him.

I looked down again at that last page, at the passage Gilmore had underlined and the comment he had written in the margin. *I will explain later*. What more was there to explain? I was thinking of the old man alone there in the red dunes, that strange feeling I had had of something terrible and evil, and then Bert called to me from the wheelhouse. He wanted the jib lowered.

We were closing the land fast now, the wind force 7 in the gusts, and the sun slanting into cloud. By the time I had got the fores'l down single-handed, dusk was closing in. By six we were in the shallows and the sea a white mass of broken water with the high north-west of Levkas looming large on our starb'd side. To the east of it, the land dropped away to sea-level, and in the fading light it was quite impossible to make out the entrance to the Canal against the background of Levkas town.

The four of us were in the wheelhouse then, watching tensely as the boat drove towards the shallows. Florrie was at the wheel. It was at this moment that Dr Gilmore emerged from the companionway, still in his pyjamas and wearing an old fawn dressing gown. He stood for a moment looking at the land. 'Levkas?' he asked.

I nodded. I thought I could see the lighthouse on the western arm now, a small white tower, and behind it the ruined bulk of the citadel. Bert must have seen it, too, for he ordered a change of course to starb'd and started the engine. We began to roll then, spray spattering the windshield, and Gilmore grabbed my arm for support. 'You read that little paper on Marais, did you?'

'Yes.' I was preoccupied, going over in my mind the handling of main and mizzen sails which would be necessary when we made the turn inside the Canal. At least there was some daylight left.

'Tragic. Very tragic. A genius, and unknown, disregarded for years. But an intellectual, of course.' He looked at me. 'Don't confuse him with your father. The fact that they are both South Africans is only incidental.'

'Then why did you ask me to read it?'

'I thought it might help you to understand the ruthlessness of the scientific world, the loneliness of pure research.' He had found his balance now and let go my arm. 'But don't worry. Your father is a fighter. He is more like Dart, for instance, than Marais.' He looked at me, smiling. 'Sonia tells me you've been reading Dart's book. I gave it to her because I think Pieter . . .' He hesitated. 'Well, maybe not as great as Dart or Broom, but when a man conceives a theory, spends all his resources— money, time and energy—to prove it, then there's always a chance. . . .' He had turned and was leaning forward, peering at the land ahead. For a time he seemed lost in his own thoughts. 'But then Dart had the advantage of large areas of limestone, his specimens preserved by fossilization. Here there's no surface limestone. We're into volcanic country now, a continuation of the middle Mediterranean fault.' And he added, 'An interesting formation this, a promontory of the mainland rather than an island. I wonder if there is anything left of the old Roman canal. There was an earlier one, too, built by the Corinthians.'

'Bits of the Roman canal are still visible,' Bert said. 'You'll see them in the morning.' He had taken over the wheel now and was leaning slightly forward, his eyes narrowed. He seemed quite confident, and shortly afterwards he asked me to go aft and stand by the sheets. 'Harden the main right in as we turn the sandbank. The mizzen, too.'

Outside the wheelhouse the noise of the sea and the boat's movement was much louder. The lighthouse at the end of the protecting wall seemed to rush towards us out of the darkening line of the land. Bert gave it a wide berth, steering perilously close to the further shore. The piled-up yellow of a naked sandbank slid by close to starboard. The bows swung as we made the turn, the sea smoothed out under the lee, and suddenly all was quiet except for the flapping of the sails. We were inside, motoring in calm water, the boat heeling as I winched in the sheets.

The port of Levkas is no more than a bulge in the Canal, three-quarters of a mile south-south-west of the entrance. We berthed alongside the quay, handed our transit-log to the harbour official, and having stowed the sails, went below for a drink. For an old man who had never been to sea in a small boat before, Dr Gilmore seemed in remarkably good heart. 'It's only when I'm ill that I get a chance to spend the whole day in bed—and that's not very often.' He was smiling, sitting there very bright and alert in his dressing gown and drinking whisky.

It may have been the drink, or perhaps it was the excitement of the voyage, but he became very talkative. He had never been to Africa, had never met Dart or Broom, only Leakey, yet he could talk about all three of them as though they were old friends. 'They are the three giants of modern anthropology —Broom particularly. He was almost as old as I am when he turned from zoology to Dart's collection of fossils, taking up the process of man's evolution from small mammalian ancestors, rather like Smith did with that living sea creature of his, the coelocanth, which he called "Old Fourlegs".' There was a glint of laughter in his eyes. 'We're back fifty million years now.' And he added, 'It has always been my dream that a student of mine would become one of the greats. There was a moment, a long time ago now—in 1935 I think—when I thought that Pieter might. . . .' He shook his head. 'A pity. A great pity. There he was, in Africa, within a stone's throw— you might call it that in relation to the size of the continent —within a stone's throw of the world's greatest anthropological site. . . .' Again that sad shake of the head. 'Just a youngster with a bit of a chip on his shoulder. He was in too much of a hurry, too impatient. And there it was, waiting for him—the Olduvai Gorge. A stone's throw away, that's all. The chance of a lifetime. . . .'

His mention of the Olduvai Gorge reminded me of that album. I asked him where the gorge was, and he said, 'Tanganyika. I believe they call it Tanzania now.' He shook his head. 'So much has changed. When I was a young man we owned half Africa. All gone now.'

He sat looking at nothing for a moment. I thought his mind was wandering back down the long vista of the years— incredible as it might seem, he would have been alive at the time of the Boer War. I told him about the album with its faded pictures of a collection of bones at the bottom of a dry dusty pit, the words that had been written beside it. He smiled and nodded. 'Yes, yes. That's it. Only a hundred miles from

Olduvai—he wrote that, did he? A stone's throw, just as I said.'

'What was it all about?' I asked. He had closed his eyes again and I was afraid his mind would wander off on to something else. 'You wrote him a letter, in 1935. He kept all your letters, in a bundle in the bureau.'

Gilmore nodded, smiling vaguely. 'He was always writing to me, always asking my advice or for information. So he thought them worth keeping. I'm glad.'

'They were typewritten,' I said. 'All except the one written in 1935—in it you said you couldn't condone his behaviour, that it placed him beyond the pale and that thereafter everything he discovered would be suspect.'

'You saw that letter, did you?' He leaned back, his eyes half-closed. 'I see. And you don't understand it? You don't know what it's about?'

'No.'

'He never told you?' And then he nodded. 'No, no, of course not. No man likes his son to know he was caught cheating.' He sipped his drink, staring at me. 'You've read that paper on Marais. You know how a genius can be treated. And now . . . this is what I said I'd explain later.' He leaned forward quickly. 'Whether he likes it or not, you've a right to know, for it will be remembered against him. However sound his theory, they won't believe him. And all because of something that happened a long time ago.' He paused and took a cigarette from the box above the drink locker. Bert lit it for him and he leaned back, puffing at it eagerly, his eyes half closed again as though collecting his thoughts. 'He was just a kid at the time. It was after he had got his degree and had returned to South Africa. He was in an angry mood and it took him alone into the bush in search of the "dawn man". He had a theory, you see.' He hesitated. 'The theory won't interest you, of course, and since you obviously know nothing about his world it will be difficult to make you realize the enormity of what he tried to do.' His hand suddenly banged at the side of the settee berth. 'And he was right. That was the tragedy of it. Everything that has been discovered since—a great deal during the last decade or so—has proved him right.' He sighed, leaning forward so that the bulkhead light sharpened the brittle bone formation of his face, glinted on his pale grey eyes. 'But he tried to cut corners; he manufactured evidence. And that was unforgivable.'

'You mean the picture I saw in the album?'

He nodded.

'And the evidence he manufactured—it was the skull, I suppose; the one displayed in the glass top of the bureau in his study?'

Gilmore nodded again, vigorously. 'That's it. You remember I recognized it at once, as soon as I came into the study. I had never seen it before. Photographs, yes; but he never let it out of his hands. Wouldn't trust anybody to handle it.' He paused for a moment, his eyes a little wide and staring as though he were still appalled at what my father had done. And then suddenly he gave a small chuckle. 'Does the Piltdown Man mean anything to you?' He seemed to assume my ignorance for his eyes searched the faces of the others, all listening intently, as though gathering his audience together. And then he went on, barely pausing for breath, 'It was a hoax, the most fantastic, barefaced hoax in the history of anthropology.' Again that sudden, amused chuckle. 'Students love it, of course. It makes all the experts look such fools.'

He paused there, and in the silence I could hear the wind ruffling the water against the hull. 'Pieter was always fascinated by the Piltdown story. He argued that it fitted too neatly the post-Darwinian belief that *homo sapiens* was God-created, even though he did evolve from the apes.' He leaned back, drawing reflectively at his cigarette, blowing the smoke in a long streamer from his pursed lips, his eyes bright with the thought of what he was telling me. 'You have to remember that the Darwinian theory of evolution was a great shock to the religious beliefs of the period. Even now, we are still very reluctant to face up to the realities of man's evolution—we tend to describe him as a tool-maker, when, in fact, his development is based mainly on his ability to produce weapons. When Darwin died in 1882 his theory of evolution was established beyond question, but most scientists clung doggedly to the idea of man created in the image of God. The Piltdown skull fitted this theory perfectly. The bits and pieces included part of a skull that indicated a brain almost as large as modern man's, and associated with it were the bones of animal remains dating back about a million years. The size of the brain case, in association with the known date of the animal remains, indicated that man had developed through God's gift of a large brain, not that his present large brain and capacity for thought had been part of the normal processes of evolution. Some of the more progressive scientists had reservations about the "dawn-man" as they called it, chiefly because there was half a jaw that clearly belonged to the chimpanzee family and the skull fragments could be reconstructed in various ways to give different sizes of brain.'

He went on to describe its discovery by some workmen in the gravels of the Sussex Ouse in 1912, how it had been accepted as genuine for forty years, and then he was explaining the way in which the whole thing had been bust wide open by a backroom anthropologist in the basement of the British Museum. His voice, his whole manner of telling it, had a sort of boyish enthusiasm that was infectious. Like Dart on the Taung skull, he made the Piltdown mystery sound like a detective story. First, the chemical test that had shown three times as much fluorine in the skull as in the jaw bone, proving beyond doubt that the two were quite unconnected. Then Geiger counter tests, with all the animal remains recording a count of between 10 and 25, except three elephant teeth, which gave counts of 175, 203 and 355. Finally, a world-wide search that tore the whole thing to shreds by indicating Tunisia as the only source of fossil remains of elephants giving such high beta ray counts.

He lit another cigarette. 'That was in 1953-55,' he said. 'Over forty years after—too long a gap for the man who perpetrated the hoax to be identified.' The thin parchment skin of his face was crinkled in a smile. 'Extraordinary, isn't it? Picture him yourself, stealing off to Sussex one weekend with a pocketful of bones filched from some travelled family's private collection, then creeping out in the moonlight to bury them in a gravel pit where he knew workmen would discover them. And all those years, watching and saying nothing—just laughing to himself at such utter nonsense being taken seriously by the leading anthropologists and palæontologists of the day.'

The picture was so vivid, so detailed I couldn't help it: 'You would have been a student yourself when the bones were originally discovered.'

He looked at me with his head on one side like a bird. 'Yes, that's so.' He chuckled quietly to himself, then reached for his drink as though to drown his amusement. 'But what Pieter did wasn't done for a joke. He'd no sense of humour. None whatever.' He was frowning, his face suddenly serious. 'He was in deadly earnest. But unfortunately for him he was in Africa, out in the bush, not in a gravel pit in Sussex. There were no quarry men digging around in the cave-shelter where he buried his bones, so he had to dig them up himself. A youngster like that, rushing his fences . . .' He shook his head, no ghost of a smile. 'However well disposed you were, you couldn't help smelling a rat. And then, when he wouldn't let the evidence out of his hands, only photographs—well, they tore him to pieces, those that bothered. And now, of course, those books published in the Communist countries.' He sighed and gave a little shrug. 'A carbon-14 dating of 35,000 BP—that's something no anthropologist will readily accept for Cro-Magnon man. And from him of all people . . . they're not going to like it, not at all.'

'But they're scientists,' I said. 'Surely, if the evidence is overwhelming . . .'

'Where did those bones come from—did he tell you?'

'No. But he seemed pleased when I told him you felt he'd no right to keep the location to himself. He said they'd talk, they'd pass it on and soon everybody would know. Isn't that how things become established—the gradual accumulation of evidence?' And I began telling him again about the red dunes, how this had established in the old man's mind the low level of the Mediterranean during the Ice Age.

But he refused to accept that the dunes formed a vital link in the chain of evidence. 'I think you are confusing two things here. In my view, the essence of Pieter's genius is that he is willing to carry on an ethological—to use an American term—an ethological study, whilst at the same time developing in the field a new theory covering what to us has always been an evolutionary gap. If you had read his Journal . . . but then you probably wouldn't have understood it.' He sipped at his drink and turned to Sonia. 'I have spent most of today reading and thinking about a report of some very interesting psychological experiments carried out on rhesus monkeys—controlled experiments in captivity set against careful and protracted studies of these nearest-to-human primates in the world. And I have been comparing the conclusions this Harvard scientist arrives at with those reached by Pieter Van der Voort, not as a result of experimenting with monkeys, but achieved by taking a hard, detached look at himself. It's a fascinating study, starting with his childhood. His conclusion, basically, is that "normality" is only achieved within a social framework, that the loner represents the extremes, producing at one end of the spectrum the most debased of creatures, at the other end the most brilliant—the genius, the prophet, the great leader.' He chuckled quietly. 'The trouble is that Pieter cannot make up his mind into which category he falls.'

Sonia shook her head. 'I don't understand,' she said.

Nor did I. 'He went there to escape. It was the only place he knew where he could hide up and at the same time still be in contact with the evidence that supported his theory.'

But Gilmore shook his head. 'An experiment I would call it. These days we are so dazzled by our material progress—supersonic flight, nuclear physics, the moon landings, quasars, lasers, etc., etc.—we are apt to forget that our ancestors were quite remarkably advanced in other ways. You say that he was escaping into solitude. But remember, he had given way to his natural aggressive instincts—to the devil that is in all of us. And what if Christ were right—what if forty days and forty nights of lonely fasting and praying is the medically exact formula for inducing a state of self-hypnosis where environmental, even perhaps hereditary, instincts can be overcome? This I think was what he was trying to prove. Not an experiment with poor little captive monkeys, but an experiment with his own flesh, himself under the microscope, and then to have it interrupted. . . .' He hesitated, frowning. 'Lying in my bunk today I tried to put myself in his place, imagine how I would react when faced with a man like Holroyd seeking to take advantage of something I had discovered.' He shook his head. 'Not easy. He turned to Sonia again. 'You know he half killed a man in Russia—at a dig of his near Tashkent?'

She nodded. 'Yes. He told me. It was when he was ill, his mind rambling, and I wasn't sure.'

'Oh, it was real all right. He goes into it in great detail in his Journal. A Bulgarian. He tried to throttle him with his bare hands, a blind fury of rage after the fellow had stolen some artefacts from his tent. Fortunately his assistant was near at hand, otherwise he'd have killed the poor devil. A fit of uncontrollable violence like that . . .' He looked across at me. 'Now perhaps you understand why he was so disturbed, so mortified at his blind, instinctive attack on Cartwright.'

That night I dreamed I faced my father, both of us hell-bent on murder. Maybe it was the prawns we'd had for dinner. I was berthed in a pipe cot up for'ard amongst the sails, and woke in a muck sweat thinking I'd killed him. After that I dozed fitfully, feeling we were both of us doomed. Then suddenly it was four o'clock and Bert woke me with a cup of tea.

We were away at first light, motoring south in the wake of a big trading caique, the old canal banks straight lines of stone in a vast area of shallows. The flat marsh country, the grey dawn, depressed me and my mood was sombre. Ahead, on its hill, rose the massive bulk of Fort St George, and beyond it, the bare bleak island hills stood like early prints, rimming the open roadstead of Port Drepano.

The sun rose as we left the Canal, keeping between the three pairs of buoys that marked the dredged channel, and the towering heights of Levkas were touched with gold. The sea was glass, not a breath of wind. By seven-thirty we were abreast of Skropio, a steep little wooded island owned by a Greek millionaire, and half an hour later we entered Port Vathy, the houses sleeping in the morning sun and donkeys browsing at the water's edge. There was a small fishing boat selling the night's catch and near it a caique loaded with bright-coloured Turkish rugs. The Customs Officer greeted us in his own home, dressed in vest and trousers, not yet shaved, and when Bert had obtained permission to visit the inlets of Meganisi provided he finally cleared from Vathy, Florrie began to make enquiries about Holroyd.

'Holerod. Né, né.' The Greek official nodded vigorously and told her that the whole party had arrived the day before in a caique from limáni Levkas. They had enquired about a man who had been digging the year before in a cave beyond

Spartokori and he had taken them to see Zavelas. Would we like to talk to Zavelas who spoke English and knew everything that went on in Meganisi?

We found him on the waterfront, sitting at a table in the shade with the Pappas. He was a big, powerful man with a hooked nose and iron grey hair. The Greek Orthodox priest was younger, a very striking figure in his black habit, tall black hat, his dark beard combed and silky and his long hair drawn back to a little bun above the nape of the neck. I think it was the presence of the priest that made Florrie excuse herself and return to join Sonia on the boat.

Zavelas was a very different man to my garrulous friend at Preveza, quieter, more reserved. And very much tougher. He had gone to sea as a kid, tramps first, then whaling and sealing out of Gloucester, Mass. He had served in the U.S. navy during World War II, had been a lumberjack out west in the Rockies and had finished up as a cop in San Francisco. 'Fisherman's Wharf—you know it?'

'Yes,' I said. 'I did one voyage through the Panama Canal and up to S.F.'

He nodded, pleased. 'A good place. But plenty tough. I guess Port Vathy is quieter, eh?' He was smiling, his blue eyes staring at me very directly. Either he came of pure Greek stock or there was a touch of the Viking in his ancestry.

He was not the official headman, but his American background, particularly his police experience, set him apart from the rest of the inhabitants of the small island community. The police chief at Levkas was a personal friend of his—he mentioned this quite early on in the conversation, thus establishing his unique position. I got the impression that he and the Pappas virtually ran the place. Certainly the Customs official treated them both with deference.

Nobody had ordered coffee, but it came and I think it was on the house. I offered him a cigarette. 'English, eh? I guess we don't see many English cigarettes here in Port Vathy.' He took one. So did the priest and I left the packet on the table. 'Now, what's on your mind, fella?' He was suddenly a San Franciscan cop again, watching me closely as he lit his cigarette and began sipping noisily at his coffee. 'This guy—' he indicated the Customs officer—'says your name's Van der

Voort and you're in'erested in a man named Holerod who arrived yesterday.'

Holroyd had come in by caique at four-thirty in the afternoon, had left the other two members of his party to set up camp on the waste ground at the head of the inlet and had walked alone to Vatahori. He had got back to Port Vathy a little after nine and had then arranged with Vassilios, a local fisherman, to take them round to the west side of the island in the morning. 'Now, you tell me something.' His gaze fastened on Bert. 'Two days ago you slip a man ashore at Port Atheni without informing the Customs officer. Why?'

Bert was too astonished to say anything and Zavelas smiled, his eyes cold. 'You think we don't know what goes on in our own island?'

'I didn't think it mattered,' Bert said. 'He'd been here before——'

'Okay. No need to explain. We know all about Dr Van der Voort.' He turned to me. 'And you're his son. That right?'

'Yes,' I said. 'How did you know?'

'I have told you, Kapetán Constantinidi is an old buddy of mine. He is Chief of Police in Levkas.' And he added, 'You know Demetrios Kotiadis? Then I do not need to explain. We have been expecting you.' His blue eyes were staring at me. 'You wanna talk to the Doctor first or this Professor Holerod?'

'Holroyd,' I said.

He nodded, smiling. 'Like some more cawfee? No? Okay then, we go.' And he got to his feet.

Five minutes later we were chugging out of the inlet in the little boat he kept for fishing. 'The cave is in the Meganisi Channel facing Levkas. The Doctor took me there once, but there ain't nothing to see—just rocks and a big square hole in the ground he dug himself.' He was leaning forward, his head close to mine so that he could talk above the noise of the engine. 'He was camped there all on his own for about a month last year. Pappadimas took supplies out to him from Vatahori.'

'Why not from Vathy?' I asked. 'Or Port Spiglia? That's even nearer.' Vatahori was at the north-east corner of the island.

'I guess because the Doctor and Pappadimas are old friends.

When he first came to the island—that was before I got back from the States—he made Vatahori his base and hired Pappadimas and his boat to explore the whole of Meganisi, also some of the little islands like Kithro and Arkudi, parts of Levkas, too. I figured he must have been some sort of geologist. But then last winter Pappadimas showed me the collection of flints and bone fossils he'd left with him. Brought out a whole box full last year, and when he got cheesed off with digging around in that cave, he'd stay a few days with Pappadimas and his family, sitting for hours over that box of relics, making notes.' We had turned the corner of the inlet now and he was steering close in to the rocks. 'If he didn't have Doctor in front of his name, reckon I'd say he was a nut-case. But then I ain't had any sort of an education and all the long words he used—it was Greek to me.' And he laughed.

We were already opening up the entrance to Port Spiglia. It was a wild little inlet with the village of Spartokori perched high above a sheer rock cliff. The first cat's paws of the day breeze were just beginning to mark the flat surface of the water as we turned south into the Meganisi Channel. It was a narrow gut with a ridge of the Levkas mountains towering above us to starboard and a small island dead ahead, close in to the Meganisi side. 'That's Tiglia,' Zavelas said. 'The cave is just back of the shallows. And over there——' He pointed to the Levkas shore. 'You see that bay? It's called Dessimo. The Doctor was over there for a time last year.'

Inside of Tiglia Island the sea was a bright emerald green—shallows and a sand bottom. And as we opened the cove, we could see a boat drawn up close in to the rocks, the expedition's mess-tent a bright splash of blue. Zavelas leaned towards me again. 'First thing the Doctor did when your friend landed him at Vatahori was to get Pappadimas to bring him out here.'

'Did he leave him here?'

'No. They went back to Vatahori that night.'

'And yesterday?'

'Yesterday the Doctor is at Pappadimas's house. He is in Vatahori all day. But that don't mean he's still there today.'

He steered the boat into the shallows where the water was like crystal, the sand bottom very clear, and then he cut the engine. A short dark man wearing an old pair of khaki shorts, tufts of black hair showing above a dirty vest, waded out and caught our bows, drawing us in beside the other boat. 'This guy is Vassilios.' The fisherman nodded and smiled, a flash of even white teeth in a brown stubbled face. They talked for a moment and then Zavelas said, 'It's okay. The Doctor's not here. You wanna go up to the cave?'

The little beach was littered with gear, no sign of Holroyd and the others, and only the one tent pitched. 'Where is it?' I asked.

'Up there.' He pointed to a pinnacle of rock away to the right. 'Vassilios will show you.'

Bert stayed in the boat with Zavelas and I went up alone, following the fisherman. There was a faint track, and behind the pinnacle of rock, we came out on to a sloping platform looking south down the channel. There was an overhang here, and in the recess below it, a pit had been dug about two feet down at the outer end, but much deeper at the back. All three of them were there on their hands and knees scrabbling at the earth where rain had collapsed the edges of the dig, sifting the dry soil through their fingers. 'Here's another one,' Cartwright said. And the others peered over his shoulder as he rubbed the dirt from a shaped piece of stone. 'That's Solutrean surely?' He passed it to Holroyd who nodded. 'Definitely. Look at that willow-leaf point.'

They were so engrossed they didn't realize I was standing there, watching them. 'It's a pity we don't know the exact level from which it came,' Cartwright said.

Holroyd laid the piece of stone carefully down with several others on the edge of the pit. They were all sharp slivers of a very dark colour, almost black. 'The levels are probably disturbed anyway. We'll know more when we start to dig at the back. But it definitely has possibilities.' His tone was eager. 'Look at this arrow-head.' He had picked up one of the smaller slivers. 'Obsidian. And very advanced work—typical late palæolithic.' He held it in his hands, peering at it, fondling it almost. 'Beautiful! Beautiful work.'

Vassilios moved, dislodging a stone, and Holroyd looked up, saw me and scrambled to his feet. 'How did you get here?'

'Boat,' I said.

He nodded, waiting, Cartwright and Hans Winters, still

on their hands and knees, staring up at me. 'Has Dr Van der Voort given you permission to examine his dig?' I asked him.

He stepped out of the pit and stood facing me. 'To begin with, young man, I don't need his permission. I have authority from the General Direction of Antiquities to examine any cave-shelter in Greece.' He reached into his pocket and got out his pipe, a conscious effort to control himself. 'When did you arrive?'

'A few hours ago.'

'And you came straight here?'

I nodded.

'Then you haven't seen him yet?'

'No.'

'I saw him yesterday. He's in a cottage at Vatahori and I suggest you go and see him before you start asking me whether I have a right to examine this cave-shelter.'

'You mean he gave you permission?'

'He's in no fit state to lead an expedition and he knows it. Yes, he agreed that I take over.'

'I find it very difficult to believe that.'

His little eyes narrowed. 'He had no alternative.'

'And if this dig is important, who gets the credit?' I asked.

But he wouldn't give me a straight answer to that. 'If we did discover something important—' He was filling his pipe, frowning, his movements almost unconscious. 'Dr Van der Voort couldn't put it across.' His head thrust forward, suddenly belligerent. 'If you'd ever interested yourself in your father's affairs you'd know that. They wouldn't accept it from him. Nobody would.'

'But they will from you?'

'Yes, they will from me.' He lit his pipe, taking his time and looking at me over the flame. 'Anything else?' He tossed the match clear of the pit, waiting. And then he said, 'Well, there it is. Nothing for you to worry about—except perhaps your own affairs.' This last was said very pointedly, and then he turned back to the dig, leaving me to wonder whether he had seen that piece in the paper. Or perhaps Kotiadis had been checking up on me.

I wandered around for a moment, looking for the place where the old man had sat, crouching with that stone lamp in his hand. But the pictures Cassellis had taken showed open water. There was no vista of blue sea here, only the dark enclosed gut of the Meganisi Channel. This was a different site, and I went back to the boat, strangely disturbed by the knowledge that there was still another place Holroyd didn't know about.

That afternoon I went with Sonia to Vatahori. We didn't talk much, both of us wrapped in our own thoughts. It was about a two-mile walk from Port Vathy and it did us good, for it was a bright day with just enough breeze to keep us cool, and the island was very beautiful, full of wild flowers and a great sense of peace pervading.

'They say certain animals have a sense of beauty—places they constantly return to.' Sonia had stopped and was staring out across a green slope with olive trees and a glimpse of the sea beyond. 'Do you think our early ancestors appreciated beauty? This is so lovely.' Her voice was subdued as though the sheer perfection of land, sea and sky was a physical ache. 'I thought that olive grove was beautiful. But this . . .'

We stood for a moment, the sun warm on our backs. It was all so peaceful, only the murmur of the cicadas, the bleat of goats far off. I was very conscious of her then, the desire to touch her almost overwhelming, and the grass of the slope, the shade of the olives inviting. She turned abruptly and we went on, following the road until it turned the shoulder of the hill to give a view of Vatahori. The church and the school looked new, but beyond the cemetery and a dusty open space where the road ended, the old village sprawled over a hilltop like a dark stone rampart. The cottages were small and very old, the passages between no more than tracks of rubble or naked rock. Pappadimas owned one of the few two-storied modern houses, a little way out of the village on the stone track leading down to Port Atheni. His wife, with two brown-eyed children clinging to her skirt, took us round to the back where the old man sat at a table writing, with a glass of dark red wine beside him and the half-glasses he used for reading perched on the high beak of his nose. He did not hear us come, sitting hunched forward, totally absorbed, a dark, brooding look on his face.

'Dr Van der Voort!' Sonia ran forward, eager as a child, and as he saw her the brooding look was wiped away, his face lit up and there was a softness in his eyes I had never seen before. She kissed him, and when she straightened up, I saw that he was smiling. It was a quiet, gentle smile that transformed his whole expression so that suddenly he looked like the man I remembered.

Mrs Pappadimas brought two more glasses and a lemonade bottle full of wine. 'Krassi,' she said proudly. 'Kala.'

'Efharisto.' He was still smiling as he thanked her. 'It will probably send you to sleep,' he said, filling our glasses. 'They make it themselves.'

We were with him for about an hour, and most of that time he seemed unusually relaxed. No doubt this was partly due to Sonia's presence. His fondness for her was obvious. Also, he seemed to have come to terms with himself as though he no longer cared what happened. Yes, he had seen Holroyd. They had had a talk the previous evening. 'Of course, I don't want him to take over. But I can't stop him.' He seemed resigned. 'I'm tired, and anyway, I've other work to do. A lot of writing.'

I didn't understand it, all the fight gone out of him. Even when I told him about my visit to the cave-shelter, how Holroyd was already finding worked pieces of obsidian, it didn't seem to worry him. 'Did he comment at all?' And when I said they had agreed it was Solutrean, he nodded, smiling, as though he were actually pleased that they had got it right.

'There was an arrow-head,' I said, 'which Holroyd regarded as particularly beautiful work.'

'Was he able to date it?'

'He said it was very advanced work—late palæolithic.'

'He didn't use the word Cro-Magnon?'

'No.'

'Ah well, perhaps when they start to dig . . . they hadn't started, had they?'

'No. They'd only just arrived. They found it in some loose soil that had fallen from the side of the pit.'

'But they're going to dig?'

'Yes, at the back where Holroyd thought the layers would be undisturbed.'

'You should be there,' Sonia said.

But he shook his head.

'Just occasionally,' she said coaxingly. 'If you don't, then

161

Professor Holroyd will make use of it the way he made use of your book.'

'No,' he said. 'It's much better that the discovery should be announced by him. He can refer to it in the paper he's reading to the Pan-European Prehistoric Congress next month. They'll take it from him, whereas if it came from me . . .' Holroyd's words almost, and the note of resignation back in his voice. I had a sudden uneasy feeling that this was an act put on for our benefit. To hide his bitterness perhaps. And then Sonia mentioned that we had Dr Gilmore on board and he froze, a tense stillness as though the news came as a shock, instead of a pleasant surprise. 'You remember Dr Gilmore,' she said. 'You often spoke of him.'

He seemed to have difficulty finding his voice. 'What's Adrian doing here?'

'I cabled him,' she said.

'Why?' His voice was harsh. 'Why did you do that?'

'You were in trouble with the authorities, and then Professor Holroyd coming out . . . I thought Dr Gilmore——'

'How could he help?' He seemed strangely upset, as though shaken by some inner conflict. 'You shouldn't have involved him.'

'Well, he's here on the boat and he'd like to see you.'

'No.' For some extraordinary reason he seemed to shy away from the idea. 'I don't want to see him. I don't want to see anybody.'

She tried coaxing him, but it was no good. It was as though by opting out, by abandoning his work to Holroyd, he had withdrawn inside himself. Nothing would induce him to go down to Port Vathy. I offered to bring the boat round to Port Atheni, but it didn't make any difference. He seemed determined now to cut himself off completely from his own world. And to close the subject he asked me about my own plans.

I told him briefly, not explaining the purpose of my visit to Samos, and he said, 'Anatolia I know, all that Turkish coast. But the islands off . . . I don't think early man ever got to the Dodecanese.' And then he was questioning me about Bert again, asking about the boat and the diving equipment on board. The diving equipment seemed to fascinate him. 'A

162

spelaeologist, you say?' He was leaning back, his eyes half closed. 'And he's been exploring underwater cities.'

'Only two,' I said. 'One off the island of Andros, and a Roman port on the African coast. He's really more interested in old wrecks.'

'Have you done any diving yourself?'

'No.'

'A pity. I was thinking . . .' But then he seemed to lose track of what was in his mind, for he began talking about the Aegean and the successive waves of invasion from the east by primitive people worshipping the Earth Goddess. And then suddenly he was back to Bert again. 'He's a friend of yours?'

'I've chartered his boat, that's all.'

'He thinks a lot of you.'

I stared at him, wondering what he was after. 'Bert's a good fellow,' I said. 'And he took quite a risk bringing you here.'

He nodded. 'Yes. I appreciate that.' But I could see his mind was on something else.

'Why were you in such a hurry to come here?'

He stared at me, his eyes suddenly blank.

'You talked to the Barretts about having to get here before Holroyd, something urgent you had to do, and about some bones—bones you'd left here the previous year.'

'Did I?' His tone was vague—deliberately vague. And his face had a shut look. 'Oh yes,' he said. 'But that's all settled. I'm working on something else now.' And he added, 'When you come back. . . . You know where to find me now. Come and see me.'

'From Samos,' I said, 'I'll be sailing direct to Pantelleria.'

But he didn't seem to take that in. 'Maybe I'll have something to show you then.'

'What?' I asked. And when he didn't reply, I said, 'Are you referring to that lamp?' I don't know why I said that. It just seemed to come into my head.

'Lamp! What lamp?'

It was extraordinary. His whole face had changed, the brows drawn down and the lines back. A carved head on some great cathedral's gutter.

'The stone lamp you were holding,' I murmured, and his breath came in a hiss.

Sonia spoke then—quickly as though soothing a child. 'Paul saw it in a picture—some shots taken by that student of Dr Gilmore's, Cassellis.'

He leaned back, rubbing his hand over his face. 'Yes, of course. I remember now.'

'Where was it?' I asked. I would have pressed him for an answer, but Sonia reached out and gripped my hand, holding it tight with an urgent shake of her head. And instead of answering me, he said, 'So you're going to Pantelleria. I was there once. In 1964. No, '65. I can't remember.'

He passed his hand up over his brow. 'All lava. Black. A dreadful, volcanic place. And under the lava . . .' He was concentrating, almost struggling, it seemed, to keep his mind focused on what he was saying. 'Old places—middens . . . places where ancient man had lived before the island erupted.' He was speaking faster now, getting into his stride as he told how all vestige of man had been buried beneath an avalanche of molten rock. And then suddenly he was pressing me urgently to come back through the Corinth Canal and pick him up. 'By then perhaps I'll have broken through—I'll know the truth, I hope.' He looked at me, suddenly pleading. 'Come back for me. And if I'm here, then we'll go on to Pantelleria together.'

I didn't say anything, not relishing the thought of bringing the contents of looted Turkish graves out through Greece, and unaccountably my hands were trembling. His assumption that I would fit in with his plans . . .

'Paul.' He was staring at me urgently. 'I want you to promise. Come back. I may need you.'

But all I said was, 'I'll think about it.' He was sick. Sick in his mind, and it scared me. I finished my wine and got to my feet. 'I have to go now.'

He nodded, his eyes, deep-sunk in their sockets, watching me. 'You're like your mother,' he said. 'Ruth was like that. Physical courage, yes. But she couldn't face the turmoil that springs from the great well of man's loneliness.' He leaned a little forward. 'Do you believe in God?' The question took me by surprise. It made me feel uneasy. 'Well, do you?'

'I—I don't really know.'

'Do you never think about death and what happens afterwards?' He was smiling now, a little sadly. 'Well, never mind.

Go back to your boat and the nice uncomplicated life of the sea. But remember that half of you is me, and with that half you inherit the other side of man—Man the Seeker.' He chuckled to himself, but there was no mirth in the sound. 'Pray God it never leads you where it has led me.' He closed his eyes and leaned back. The brooding look had returned to his face and his mind was far away.

We left then, for he seemed suddenly exhausted. Or perhaps it was just that he wanted to be alone. Whatever it was, we were conscious of a mood of withdrawal. It didn't worry me, but Sonia felt it deeply, so that she was very quiet as we walked back through the village and down past the church. Above the slope of the hill with its olives she stopped suddenly, gazing out to the vista of sea beyond. 'You'll be sailing to Samos now, I suppose.'

'Yes,' I said.

'And from there you'll go straight to Pantelleria? You won't be coming back here?'

'No.'

She stood there, silent, looking lost and sad. I could feel her loneliness, and for the first time I understood her need, the desperate, driven search for the father she had never really known. Now she felt shut out. It was this realization, and perhaps the wine I had drunk, that made me say, 'Would you like to come with us?' The words were out before I'd given a thought to what I might be letting her in for.

'On a smuggling run?' Her pale eyebrows lifted and she smiled. 'That's nice of you, Paul. But no.' She shook her head. 'I must stay.' Her eyes were screwed up. I thought at first it was the sun, but then I saw the glint of tears as she turned quickly away. I caught her then, my arm round her, and suddenly she was leaning against me, sobbing her heart out.

'I'm sorry,' she breathed. 'And it's all so beautiful.' She didn't say what was beautiful. She was shaking uncontrollably. 'It's so bloody pointless, but I feel I must. He's all alone, and no money, nobody to make him feel he's wanted.' She had got her handkerchief out. 'I'll be all right in a moment.' And then she pushed away from me and stood very straight and stiff, facing me and not bothering to hide her tears. 'You did mean that, didn't you?'

'Yes.'

She stared at me a moment and then she smiled. It was like sunshine after rain, a smile that seemed to light up her whole face, so that for a moment she looked quite radiant. And then the sunshine vanished and she turned away, blowing her nose and searching in her bag for her compact. 'It wouldn't have worked, anyway.' She was in control of herself again now. 'Florrie wouldn't have liked it, and it's her boat.'

But when we got back on board, Florrie was much too concerned over the fact that Dr Gilmore wanted to stay with the ship to have worried about Sonia. 'He seems to think the whole voyage will be a downhill run like we had from Corfu. Bert's tried to explain to him what it's like when conditions are bad, but he doesn't seem to understand. Says he's too old to mind what happens to him now and he's enjoying himself. You must talk to him, Paul.'

Dr Gilmore was in the saloon, small, bird-like and very determined. 'My dear fellow, you must understand that I've never had a real holiday in my life. And you're going into the Aegean, something I've always dreamed of.' And he added, 'You needn't worry that I'll be a nuisance.'

'Florrie's afraid you'll be seasick and die on her.'

'That's very thoughtful of her.' His eyes glinted with laughter.

'Just practical,' I said, and tried to make him realize what it was like to be really seasick, how violent the movement could be when beating. 'You could be thrown out of your bunk, break your arm or your ribs.' But it was no use. He had made up his mind. What is more he had offered to pay Bert over and above the charter.

'I told you, I think, that I had had a piece of luck—financially. It was the football pools. Quite a long time ago now. I used to do them for fun, a change from teaching youngsters how man evolved from the Pliocene into the Pleistocene. It's rather funny really—a Reader in Anthropology landing a shared win in a football pool. I handed it all over to one of my least successful students who had gone into merchant banking and now it's quite a respectable sum. My pension, you see, doesn't really run to Mediterranean cruises, but I always promised myself that when I did retire I would use this money to do the travelling I had always wanted to do.'

It was hopeless to argue with him, and when I broke it to him that my father had withdrawn into himself and didn't want to see anybody, he accepted it without any sign of surprise. 'Well, that settles it,' he said finally. 'You'll have to take me with you.'

Florrie grumbled, of course. 'This is a sailing ship, not a boarding house.' But since we couldn't dump him ashore on Meganisi against his will, she had to accept the situation.

We sailed at first light the following morning, motoring round the north-west corner of the island and south through the Meganisi Channel to give Dr Gilmore a sight of the dig behind Tiglia Island. The three small orange sleeping-tents had blossomed on the beach beside the blue mess-tent. But there was no sign of life in the camp and the cave itself was obscured by the rock pinnacle, only the outer edge of the platform visible. Gilmore, still in his dressing gown, stood propped against the wheelhouse door, looking at it through the big ex-German U-boat binoculars until we were right out of the channel and had altered course for Atoko Island and the entrance to the Gulf of Patras. 'I don't understand it,' he said almost petulantly as he finally lowered the glasses. 'It's not like Pieter to give up so easily.'

'What else could he do?' I asked.

'He could fight.'

We should have known. We should have known, both of us, that that was just what he was doing. But now that I was at sea again I thought this was the end of my involvement with his affairs. My mind was on other things and it never occurred to me that the voyage would be no more than an interlude.

III: Interlude in the Aegean

IT WAS SONIA who gave us the first indication that Holroyd had dug up something of real significance. This was in a letter to Dr Gilmore, dated April 29, which we found waiting for us at the Port Captain's office at Pythagorion.

But that was later, after we had had nearly a month of the most perfect sailing, and by then I had almost forgotten about my father. The demands and routine of a boat at sea, particularly in enclosed waters like the Aegean, concentrate the mind to the exclusion of all but the immediate problems of navigation and seamanship. Add to this the world that daily opened before our gaze, a world of islands and little ports and coves where life had hardly changed since the days of Odysseus, and it is little wonder that I became so engrossed in it that for a time I was scarcely conscious even of my own predicament and was able to shut out of my mind the real object of the voyage.

Once through the Corinth Canal, we seemed to sail into the past. Athens and the Acropolis, then east down the gulf to Sounion. Here, amongst the salt-white columns of Poseidon's temple high on its promontory, we had our first glimpse of the islands, seeing them as the old Greek sailors saw them, milestones on the voyage to the Turkish coast. We said our own prayers to the god of sea and earthquake, and then we were slanting out in their wake, a full meltemi blowing from the north-east, the boat heeled, the sea hard and white, and Kithnos growing large over the bows. Tinos then and Mykonos, and Delos all to ourselves in the tiny cove of Fourni, with only just room to swing to our anchor, and Mount Cynthus, birthplace of Apollo, with its Sacred Way and the ruins of ancient cities falling to the sea, the fantastic beauty of the lionesses in moonlight. And then down through the 14-foot passage in half a gale to Naxos, the largest of the islands.

And apart from the ruins and the beauty of the villages, all newly whitewashed and spread across the high flanks of the islands like drifts of snow, and the long walks inland, there was always the sea. As the water got warmer, we were goggle fishing and Bert was diving. Even Dr Gilmore was swimming every day, and in the evenings he talked, endlessly and fascinatingly, about man's origins, about the Greeks and the people whose ruins we were seeing daily. He was a mine of information and I envied those who had had him for a tutor, he made it all so interesting.

But after Naxos, it was time to head east to the Dodecanese. And now Samos and the object of the voyage began to loom. As a result, I was keyed-up, already a little tense, when on the afternoon of May 5, we motored into the old harbour of Pythagorion, built by a tyrant named Polycrates some 2,500 years ago. Beyond the town, hillsides climbed in hunched shoulders rising to precipitous heights, the whole island lush with spring growth, the fresh green of fruit trees contrasting with the darker green of the pines that clothed the upper slopes. And away to starboard, where the lower eastern end of the island met the Turkish shore, was the narrow gut of the Straits, a lighthouse on a rocky islet showing as a white pin-point in the middle. I still did not know how I was to explain a night rendezvous with a Turkish fishing boat to the Barretts. It went against the grain deliberately to mislead them, and Dr Gilmore's presence aggravated the problem.

As we entered the kidney-shaped inner harbour the original limestone quays gleamed like polished ivory in the sun. We moored stern-on at the northern end to a bollard that was a stone column taken from Polycrates' old capital. Fishermen's nets, hung out to dry on the eastern harbour wall, made bright splashes of blue and purple and orange under the trees. With a feeling almost of reluctance I accompanied Bert to the Harbour Office to find the cable I expected waiting for me.

But instead of giving me time and date of rendezvous, it announced that 'my friends' had been delayed and advised continuing the cruise south to Rhodes. *Information and funds available Bank of Greece Rodos May 23.*

My first reaction was one of relief. But it only postponed the moment when I would either have to think up a convincing lie or else take Bert into my confidence.

'Good news I hope,' he said.

'It's from Borg,' I told him. 'Some Turkish friends of his. Wants us to meet them about the end of the month.'

He didn't like it. I knew he wouldn't, for the Arab-Israeli situation was worsening and it was with some difficulty I had persuaded him to sail east to the Turkish coast. But in this I had the support of Dr Gilmore, who had been reading up on the Dodecanese in the books he had bought in Athens and had developed an urgent, almost boyish enthusiasm to see as much as he could of the islands of Ancient Greece.

We talked it over at length that evening, and I think it was only the knowledge that I had money waiting for me in Rhodes that induced Bert to fall in with Borg's arrangements. We left two days later, and by then Gilmore had had an answer to a cable he had sent to a friend of his in Cambridge. It confirmed that there was a strong rumour that Holroyd would be making a sensational announcement when he delivered his paper at the Pan-European Prehistoric Congress on May 25.

Sonia's letter had not been at all specific. She was still at Port Vathy, living with a Greek family, and her information was based, not on visits to the dig, but on occasional meetings with her brother, and he was sworn to secrecy. All he would tell her was that two packages had been despatched by air to London for dating and that these would almost certainly 'throw new light on the relationship of Cro-Magnon and Mousterian man.' It was this which had caused Dr Gilmore to cable Cambridge, and when he had received the reply, he had written to his friend asking for a full report of Holroyd's paper to be sent to him at Rhodes. 'I cannot understand it,' he said to me the night before we left Samos. 'Pieter must have known the potentialities of that dig, and to leave it to Holroyd just when he'd reached the vital level . . . it doesn't make sense.'

But a force 6 south-westerly soon cleared his mind of such remote speculation. He wanted to visit the monastery of St John the Theologian, which crowns the island of Patmos like a colossal medieval castle, and we were beating into a steep breaking sea for twelve hours. He was not actually seasick, but he found it exhausting, even though he stayed in his bunk and the canvas lee-board was up.

With time to kill, we visited the islands of Leros, Kalimnos,

Pserimos and Kos. Gilmore wanted to see the ruins of the Ionian cities, particularly Budrom, which is ancient Halicarnassus where the tomb of King Mausolus was being excavated, but nothing would induce Bert to put into a Turkish port. 'It's not like Greece, you know. You're treated as though you're a bloody great cargo ship and you have to get clearance from the Harbour Master, Immigration, Customs, Health and Security Police. This happens at every port and it takes the better part of a day to get in and another day wasted getting out. It's hell!' Added to which, the news, picked up sporadically on the radio, was not good. Middle East tension increasing and the Russians reinforcing their fleet through the Dardanelles.

On May 23 we were in the little crater-like port of Panormittis on the island of Symi, being shown over the monastery and the twelfth-century church, with its columns taken from a much older pagan temple to Poseidon. And on May 24 we sailed into Mandraki, between the two arms of the harbour once straddled by the great bronze figure of the Colossus of Rhodes.

I was thinking of Kotiadis as I went ashore, feeling much more nervous in this big, crowded port, full of tourists, than I had been in the smaller islands. There was an airport here, and if he had checked up on me this would be the place they would pick me up. But the Port Captain's office showed no more interest in us than in any of the other boats along the quay, and at the Bank of Greece the banker's order was handed over and changed into drachmas without comment. They also had a cable for me, which I did not open until I was safely back on board: *Friends arriving Samos between June 10-12.* It was unsigned.

That meant we might have to spend three nights fooling about in the straits and what the hell did I tell Bert? 'Borg wants us to pick up his friends at Samos on June 10.'

But he had been having a drink with the skipper of a big schooner moored near us. Israeli planes had attacked Russian missile sites in the Canal Zone, and the schooner was pulling out in the morning. 'Cable him we'll pick them up at Athens.'

I took him ashore and filled him up with ouzo. But Florrie was more difficult to deal with. She sensed there was something odd. 'Why Samos?' she demanded. 'Why not here or at Athens, where there's a good air service?' She wanted to leave with the schooner in the morning.

But by now Dr Gilmore's mind had switched from Ancient Greece to Holroyd and the dig on Meganisi. He could not possibly leave, he said, until he had heard from his friend, Professor Stefan Reitmayer. That settled it, for Florrie regarded him as a very distinguished visitor, treating him with a strange mixture of awe and maternal affection. The schooner left without us and we stayed until the letter arrived two days later. It was just before lunch when Bert came in with it. We were all in the saloon having a drink, and I can remember now the eagerness with which Dr Gilmore slit it open, the expression of concentration on his face as he read it, the way he murmured, 'Good Heavens!' And when he had finished, he looked up, facing us, his expression grave. 'I am afraid I have to leave you and return to Cambridge. Congress have called for an investigation into Professor Holroyd's discoveries and I have been asked to give evidence.'

This letter is now in my possession. It is in two parts, and though it is a rather long letter and somewhat technical, the information in it is so important to an understanding of what happened later that I give it in full:

King's College,
Cambridge
May 25

Dear Adrian:

You asked me to let you have the fullest possible account of the paper Holroyd read to Congress this morning, also his answer to the questions you asked me to put to him publicly. I am writing this a few hours after the event, while everything is still clear in my mind, but I shall not post it until I can give you the reactions of the Organizing Committee of which, as you know, I am a member. They are by no means satisfied.

This was the second day of Congress and as Holroyd had let it be known that the subject of his paper was both sensational and controversial, we had allocated the first hour of the morning session to him. There was a certain air of excitement in the Great Hall as our chairman introduced him, for on entering to take our seats we had all passed the side table on which he had arranged a small collection of exhibits. There were the usual artefacts—but of obsidian. not flint, and they were in two groups, one being considerably more advanced than the other (which had similarities with the Levalloisian industries of North Africa and the Levant). There was also a display of fossil bones that included deer. But what caught and held the attention of all of us were fragments of three skulls neatly pieced together. One of them appeared to belong to Cro-Magnon man. The other two showed distinct traces of brow ridges and appeared to belong to Neanderthaloids. Both of these were somewhat blackened by fire, but the brain cases were almost complete, except that each had a fearful hole in the top of it, with splintering cracks running out in all directions. No question, both had been subjected to a terrific blow from a sharp-pointed weapon. One was instantly reminded of the baboon skulls Dart found in such profusion at Matapan and his assumption that *Australopithecus* had had a partiality for brains. The stage was thus set for Holroyd's sensational revelation.

Holroyd is, of course, at his best on the platform, and he can, I suppose, be forgiven a certain elation, knowing the sensation he was going to cause. However, I must admit to a feeling of hostility at the cocky way he walked to the lectern, the smug smile with which he surveyed his captive audience. Since I will be sending you a copy of the paper as soon as it is printed, I will confine myself here to the main points of his discovery and the conclusions he drew.

During the first ten minutes he confined himself to setting the scene—largely a description of the dig and its position on the island of Meganisi facing Levkas. He also outlined the object of the expedition. No mention was made of Van der Voort, either then or later. The geophysical nature of the site he described as Mesozoic limestone with a volcanic overlay. He then took us down through the dig, layer by layer, to demonstrate that, under the rock overhang at any rate water had not disturbed the orderly levels of man's occupation of the site. At about 10.30 he reached the major discovery—the skulls.

I should say at this point that his presentation of the facts was extraordinarily effective, that flat North Country accent of his giving it a down-to-earth quality that almost lulled one into accepting without query everything he said. The skulls had been found at a depth of about 12 feet below the present surface level of the shelter in association with obsidian weapons and animal bones. He showed us blow-ups of pictures he had taken of some of the weapons and I think you would have agreed that they could be categorized as belonging to a Levalloiso-Mousterian culture, though he used only the more general term Mousterian. He also showed us blow-ups of other artefacts that were undoubtedly of a later period, animal bones, too, all of them demonstrably Magdalenian. Yet the three skulls, both types of artefacts and the animal bones had all been found at the *same level*. What he was saying, in fact, was that a species of advanced Cro-Magnon type man had occupied the cave shelter contemporaneously with the more primitive Neanderthal type Mousterian man.

The last quarter of an hour was devoted entirely to the skulls, particularly the two with the brain cases broken open. Both these skulls were of the earlier, more ape-like Mousterian species of man, whilst the third was unquestionably of the much more highly developed Cro-Magnon type. The fact that they were found at the same level, together with artefacts of both species, is undoubtedly a serious blow to all those who subscribed to the view that *homo sapiens sapiens*, as exemplified by Cro-Magnon man, evolved from Mousterian man with the evolutionary impetus of the Würm Glaciation. But Holroyd claimed much more than that. Pointing to the holes in the two Mousterian skulls, he said, 'The theory that Mousterian man died out naturally because he could not compete against the new post-glacial species of man cannot now be supported. Here in my hands I hold the evidence—this poor, backward, ape-like creature was murdered. And not because he was hostile to the new species. He was murdered because Cro-Magnon man—hunter, artist, our own *homo sapiens sapiens* in embryo—was, like so many of our early ancestors, a cannibal. He ate the flesh of the earlier species he killed and he drove in the cranium with an obsidian hand-axe to get at the brain. And the marks of fire on these fragments of skull suggest that he cooked the head over a fire before scooping out the most delicate part of his meal.' And on this he sat down.

Pretty sensational stuff! The mystery of the decline of Mousterian man at the emergence of a true *hom sap* Cro-Magnon species solved and in a way that branded Cro-Magnon man as a murderer and a cannibal. There were questions, of course, but Holroyd dealt with them all most efficiently and convincingly. I left it until the very end to put your queries. It took him by surprise and for a moment he seemed at a loss. There was a long silence and I could sense the reaction of the hall to the mention of Van der Voort's name. There was hardly a person there who did not remember that extraordinary hoax.

Finally, Holroyd found his voice. He admitted that Dr Van der Voort had been associated with the expedition in its early stages and that he had done some preliminary work in Greece the previous year. 'I can assure you, however,' he added, 'that Dr Van der Voort had nothing whatsoever to do with this discovery. Indeed, at the time I unearthed the skulls he was ill and had severed all connection with the expedition.'

I then asked him whether it was true that his examination of the site had been due to information given him by Dr Van der Voort. He replied, 'No, sir. The information which led us to this particular site came from another source entirely—a Greek source.'

I was reluctant to call him a liar in public, but I have requested that the Committee meet briefly before tomorrow's session when I will lay your information before them.

May 26.

The Organizing Committee were greatly disturbed by the contents of your letter, which I read out to them at the meeting this morning. They felt that Holroyd's discovery, and the conclusions he had drawn from them, were of such vital significance that the questions raised in your letter must be investigated before Congress could publicly credit Holroyd with the discovery by publishing his paper in the form in which it was read. I could not of course substantiate the claims you made on Van der Voort's behalf, but inevitably a parallel was drawn with the case of Marais, also a South African. Moreover, as Grauers pointed out, the suggestion that Van der Voort was involved made it doubly important that Congress ascertain with absolute certainty that the skulls are what they purport to be before giving this discovery the stamp of their approval by publication of the paper.

In the end, it was decided to set up an investigating committee to look into the whole question and to report back as soon as possible. Grauers was appointed chairman and he has already requested Holroyd to submit all his evidence for examination. If I know Grauers, you can rest assured that he will be most Swedishly thorough, and also impartial. Naturally, he requires your personal attendance before the Committee. Can you fly back at once? It is very urgent, since Holroyd's reputation is at stake and Grauers insists that he be given the opportunity of cross-examining you on the information and charges made in your letter. We are trying to keep this 'within the family' at this stage, so please do not discuss it with anyone until you have appeared before the committee.

I am sorry to break your holiday in this way, but I am sure you will appreciate the necessity.

Yours ever,
Stefan

We saw Dr Gilmore off on an Olympic Airways flight that afternoon, and in the evening, the three of us alone in the saloon after an excellent meal ashore, I took the Barretts into my confidence and explained to them what Borg's cable really meant. To my surprise, Florrie accepted it as though smuggling were an everyday occurrence. Perhaps that was her Cypriot blood. It was Bert who was shocked. 'What did you expect, for heaven's sake?' she said. 'New engines and early-in-the-season charters don't come without strings attached. I knew all along it was something like this.' The odd thing was that she seemed actually excited at the prospect. Bert, more practical, wanted to know what would happen if a Turkish gun-boat caught us at the moment of transfer.

Fortunately, no Turkish gun-boat appeared. The night of June 10 was dark and within half an hour of our arriving on station, outside the little cove to the south of the straits where St Paul had once landed, a small boat arrived alongside. There were twenty-three packages, all quite small, in plastic bags and heavily padded. The transfer took less than ten minutes. By dawn we were past Samos, heading west along the rocky coast of Ikaria under full sail, the wind strong from the south—a sirocco.

The simplicity of the whole operation left us slightly deflated. Bert seemed the least affected, though I noticed he chose this moment to strip down the water circulation pump, which was worn and showing loss of pressure. Florrie was nearer to my own mood—a need to recreate artificially the excitement that was suddenly lacking. We started drinking shortly after eleven and by lunch time we were neither of us very sober. It was hot in the wheelhouse even with both doors open and for the first time she was wearing a bikini, her olive-brown flesh plump and smooth. I was stripped to the waist and I felt the warmth of her body against mine as she peered over my shoulder at the chart. 'How many miles to Pantelleria?'

'Almost seven hundred by the open sea route. Less if we take the Corinth Canal.'

Her hand touched me, ran gently down my backbone, exploring. 'And you want to go by the Canal?'

'Yes.'

'Bert thinks it's dangerous.' She giggled, excited by the thought of danger. 'I could persuade him.' Her hand slipped over my buttocks to my thighs, and I looked at her. Her lips were parted, smiling, her eyes inviting. If I hadn't been full of liquor I'd have held myself in check. A boat is too small a place in which to fool around with another man's wife. 'He's in the engine-room,' she said and her body was against mine, flesh to flesh, passion flaring. We were on automatic pilot, open sea ahead. What the hell! Her lips were soft and warm, the bikini a trifle. I took her on the floor of the wheelhouse with the black rock cliffs of the island where Icarus fell out of the sun trying his wings close to starboard, and Bert never knew.

And afterwards we were suddenly sober, strangely self-conscious of our nakedness. I didn't understand her, a nice husband like that and throwing herself at me like a whore. Dressed, we were like strangers—polite, almost formal, our bodies released from tension and the nerve vibration of excess energy.

'We'll go through the Canal,' she said, adjusting her bra. I felt like a gigolo being offered payment.

That night a strange thing happened. I came on watch at midnight, relieving Florrie, and it was very quiet as we slipped along at about four knots under sail. The sky was clear, diamond-studded with stars, the horizon a sharp line through the glasses. A satellite was wheeling like a comet across the edge of Orion's belt. For almost half an hour I had the company of dolphins, a whole school of them snorting and sighing all around me. Up for'ard I could see their shapes quite plainly, picked out by phosphorescence as they played in the bow wave. And then they disappeared as suddenly and as unexpectedly as they had arrived. Shortly after that I picked up the steaming lights of a vessel, bearing 345° and headed almost straight for us. The time was 02.40 and within minutes there were four other vessels, all approaching us fast from different points of the compass. Their steaming lights showed they were not fishing boats, and never in my sea-going experience having found myself in a situation like this, I called Bert.

'Destroyers,' he said. 'It's happened to me before. Not in the Aegean. Between Pylos and Malta. Have you sighted the carrier yet?' And having assured me that it would come up over the horizon 'like a bloody great gas flare' he turned over and went to sleep again.

It did just that about five minutes later, its topmast light coming up over the horizon on our port bow, a single red glow like an oil refinery flame. By then one of the destroyers was very close. A searchlight stabbed the night blindingly. It remained fixed on us for almost ten minutes and then was suddenly extinguished. When my eyes became accustomed to the darkness again, the carrier had crossed our bows and was to the north-west of us, not more than a mile away and looking like the slab-sided section of a sea wall.

'The Sixth Fleet,' Bert explained when he relieved me forty minutes later. And he added, 'Heading up for the Dardanelles like that, I'm surprised they let you inside the destroyer screen.' He was searching the horizon with the glasses. 'I'm glad we're getting out of this area.' He had a thoughtful look on his face as he put the glasses down. 'I wouldn't like to be here if the Americans and the Russians started a naval engagement. Times like this I can't help thinking we're all hell-bent on suicide, the whole effing human race.' He checked the wheel and the compass course, and then, just as I was going below, he said, 'Don't tell Florrie. She worries about her family. They're still in Cyprus.'

Two days later we passed through the Corinth Canal, and in the late afternoon of June 15 we arrived back at Port Vathy in the island of Meganisi.

IV: Man the Killer

I

WE ANCHORED off in four fathoms at the head of the inlet, the sun hidden by the western hills, and as we rowed ashore, the houses of Vathy glimmered honey-coloured in the evening light, their reflections mirrored in the still water. I could see Zavelas sitting at his usual place at the kaféneion and he beckoned to us. 'Kalispéra. You are back, eh?' It was difficult to know whether he was pleased or not, his face impassive. 'Good trip?'

'Yes,' I said. And Florrie added, 'The islands were beautiful.'

'I see them when I'm a kid. In caiques then. Not since.' A flicker of a smile showed in his eyes. 'Now it is cool and you like some cawfee, eh?' He waved aside Bert's mention of the Customs Officer. 'I send for him and you do your business here. Is more comfortable after you have been at sea.' He called to a boy playing in one of the boats and then clapped his hands for the proprietor.

Coffee and ouzo, the usual routine, and the ex-cop watching us, silent. There was something on his mind and it made me uneasy. Florrie felt it, too, for she was talking quickly, nervously, in a mixture of English and Greek.

'Why you come back?' Zavelas asked abruptly, the question directed at me.

Why had I come back? It was a question I had been asking myself. Curiosity, or was it something deeper, a premonition, some sixth sense warning me? Gilmore, when he had shown me Reitmayer's letter, had promised to let me know the result of the investigation. He knew the date we would be in Samos, but there had been no letter waiting for me at the Harbour Office there. 'Are they continuing work on the dig behind Tiglia?' I asked.

'Yes. But not Professor Holerod. He is in London. Only Mr Cartwright and the Dutch boy work there.'

'And my father—is he still at Vatahori?'

He shook his head. 'No. The Doctor is on Levkas. He has a small tent there and works alone.'

'In that bay you showed me—Dessimo?'

'No. It is somewhere else.'

'Where?'

'That's a secret between him and Cristos Pappadimas. But I can take you there if you want.' And he added, 'An' I guess the Doctor will be glad to see you. He's no money, and that's mighty hard on a poor Greek man like Pappadimas. He takes him what he can, and Miss Winters helps.'

'Is she still here?'

'In my house.'

I hadn't expected that and the thought of her so near brought back into my mind the picture I had of her, small, intense and slightly lost . . . it had been there all the voyage, the last sight of her standing on the quay at Vathy, a solitary figure waving us goodbye. The Customs Officer arrived, and whilst he dealt with Bert's transit-log, I sat there, drinking my ouzo and wondering about myself and the complexity of my motives as I exchanged small talk with Zavelas.

It was just after the Customs Officer left that a boat came in, passed close to *Coromandel* and then headed for the quay. I saw her head, pale tow against the dark-featured Greek at the outboard. She was searching the quay. I waved and she waved back, and then I was hurrying across to meet her. Florrie's eyes followed my movement; she knew how I felt—at least that's what she said afterwards, that she'd known all along I was in love with her. But I didn't know it myself then, only that the sight of her, so fresh-looking, so blonde and slim—alien corn amongst the Turk-dark Greeks—gave a sudden lift to my spirits.

'Paul.' Her face lit in a smile as she leapt like a cat from boat to quay. 'We saw you sailing in. From beyond Tiglia. I thought it was *Coromandel*. So we started straight back.' She was laughing, her face flushed, the words coming in a rush.

We talked for a moment, nothing in particular, talking for the sound of our voices, the sense of communication. The outboard coughed and died and the world broke in with Pappadimas tying the painter to a ring on the quay. 'Two days ago I had a cable.' She felt in the pocket of her anorak. 'From Dr Gilmore. I don't understand it.' She fished it out and handed it to me.

Urgent Vandervoort understands damage inflicted Holroyd's reputation. My letter Paul explains. Tell him on arrival possibility Holroyd returning Meganisi. Gilmore. It was dated June 14.

'Do you know what it means?'

'No,' I said.

'But the letter—he says he wrote to you.'

'I was expecting a letter from him at Samos.' And I told her about the investigation. 'Have you shown this cable to my father?'

'Yes' That's why I went out there with Cristos this afternoon '

'And what did he say?'

'Nothing. Just read it and handed it back to me. He didn't say a word.'

'Did he know what it was about?'

'I don't know. Yes, I think so. He must have done or he would have asked me about it. Instead, he just smiled.'

But I was wondering about the letter, what it had contained. 'You re staying with Zavelas?'

'Yes. I was at Vatahori till your father moved over to Levkas. Then I came here.'

'Zavelas knows something. I saw it as soon as he greeted us.'

'About Dr Van der Voort?'

'I don't know. Something. You don't know what it is?'

'No.'

'And you've no idea what this cable is about?'

'No. Except that Hans is puzzled. So is Alec. It's almost a month since Professor Holroyd left and they've been working on that dig all the time. They've found nothing. Nothing at all since they dug up those skulls. It's very odd.'

But I was still wondering what had happened to Gilmore's letter, how I could get hold of the facts with the least possible delay. Something must have come out at the investigation, something more than just a failure to give credit to another anthropologist for his earlier work on the site. I glanced at my watch. It was already well past six. 'If we took the boat now, how long would it take to get there—half an hour?'

'Three-quarters at least,' she said. 'It's at the south end of the Meganisi Channel.'

It would be getting dark by then. 'See if you can fix it with Pappadimas,' I said and went back to the kaféneion to tell the Barretts where I was going. We left at quarter to seven, and by the time we were in the Meganisi Channel the island of Tiglia was a dark bulk between shadowed walls of rock with the mess-tent a blue glow reflected in the shallows. Above us, the mountains of Levkas loomed black against the last of the sunset glow.

South of Tiglia, Pappadimas edged the boat close to the west side of the channel. The rocks were getting difficult to see, darkness closing in and the first stars showing above the dim outline of Meganisi. 'It's not far now,' Sonia said. Her voice sounded nervous. 'You won't find him very communicative. He lives in a world of his own. I'm afraid . . .' She hesitated, her voice barely audible above the noise of the outboard. 'It may be all in his imagination, you see. And yet he's convinced that if he could only get through the rock fall . . .' She was leaning so close to me that I could feel the breath of her sigh on my cheek. 'I don't know what to think. But I'm glad you're here. Perhaps he'll talk to you. So long as you're patient with him. He's very secretive about it. Hans came with me once, but he wouldn't speak to him, wouldn't show him anything. Said he was Professor Holroyd's stooge, accused him of coming to spy and practically threw him out. It was all very unpleasant and Hans had brought some stores, things he desperately needed.' The engine died as the bows nuzzled the rocks. 'Anyway, you'll see for yourself.'

We were in a narrow gut and Pappadimas came for'ard, hauling the boat along, both hands on the rock, until it grounded on a shelf of gritty sand. The water was very still, no sound at all. We got out and she took my hand, leading the way. There was a path of sorts, winding up between the rocks. It led to a steep slope and there was a musty smell of broom in the air. 'It's about another hundred feet up.' She let go of my hand. 'You'll find him camped under the overhang. I'll wait for you here.'

I hesitated, staring up at the dim outline of what appeared to be an enormous cavity scooped out of the cliff above. Then I went on alone, and where the overhang jutted black against the stars, the slope levelled off abruptly, and I stopped. The line of the cliff, the pale glimmer of open sea beyond. It struck a chord. The light was different, of course, but standing there, noting the configuration of sea and land, I had no doubt. This was where Cassellis had taken the pictures. I called to him then, stumbling among fallen rocks, but there was no answer and his tent when I found it was empty. It was a very small tent, the sort you have to crawl into on your hands and knees, and I stood there, wondering at his toughness, alone up here, living little better than the primitive men whose movements he was trying to trace.

The site was a good one, the sort of position that the ancient Greeks, with their eye for country, might have chosen for one of their temples. It looked down into the channel, and to the south I could just make out the flat expanse of the sea running out to Arkudi and the island of Ithaca. A solitary light, flashing red every three seconds, signposted the route to the Gulf of Patras. It was like standing on the bridge of a ship, for this natural platform was almost at the tip of a promontory formed by a spur of Mount Porro. There was no breath of air, no sound, everything very still. And then suddenly, from behind me, the clink of metal on rock, the clatter of stones.

I turned then, feeling my way deeper into the shadow of the overhang. Past a great rock fallen from the roof I saw the glimmer of a light. It came from beyond a mound of rubble, and when I had climbed to the top of it, I found myself looking down into a steeply-sloped cavern. I could see him then, a dark figure in silhouette. The light came from an old acetylene lamp and the single small jet of flame showed the cavern blocked by a fall. He was bending down, levering at the face of the fall with a crowbar, and he was so intent on what he was doing that he didn't hear the scattering of rubble as I scrambled down to the floor of the cave.

I was about ten yards from him then and I paused, curious at the care with which he was prising loose a lump of rock wedged against the cavern wall. He put the crowbar down and began tapping at it with a sharp-pointed hammer. It broke and then he was using the crowbar again, and when the rock finally fell away in pieces, he pulled a rag from his pocket, dusting the wall carefully. Then he put on his steel-rimmed half spectacles, picked up the lamp and peered at it closely, moving the lamp this way and that like a miner searching for traces of some precious metal in the face of the rock.

I was so fascinated I stood rooted to the spot, not moving, not saying anything. A strange guttural sound came from his throat, an exclamation of excitement, of satisfaction. And then some sixth sense seemed to warn him of my presence, for he turned suddenly, straightening up and facing me, the lamp held high. 'Who's that?' He reached for the crowbar, and I thought he was going to come at me with it, but instead he backed against the wall as though to conceal something.

'It's Paul,' I said, and I heard his breath escape in a long sigh. He took his glasses off then, leaning slightly forward, peering at me.

'What are you doing here? What do you want?' His voice was thick, a whisper I barely recognized. The beetling brows, the blue eyes lit by the lamp, wide and staring. Remembering that photograph, the hair prickled on my scalp, my nerves taut as I recalled what Gilmore had said: Loneliness, identification with the subject that had engrossed him for so many years.

I began talking to him then, explaining my presence, the words too fast. With an effort I forced myself to speak quietly, gently, the way you would talk to an animal defending its territory, and gradually he relaxed, became himself again.

'I thought for a moment . . .' He put the crowbar down and wiped the sweat from his face with the rag he had used to dust the wall behind him. Silence then, a silence that dragged, his breathing heavy, the only sound in the stillness of the cave. He was leaning against the wall, his lungs gasping air—an old man near the point of exhaustion.

He wiped his face again, recovering fast. He still had reserves of energy. 'Last time you were here, I said I might have something to show you.' His mood had changed, his personality too. He was smiling now and the smile transformed his face, lighting it with some inner excitement, so that he was suddenly like a child who has discovered something and cannot keep it to himself. 'Come here.'

He had turned and was holding the lamp to the wall, moving

it slowly back and forth as he had done when I stood watching him. 'Do you see anything?'

I had moved forward and was peering over his shoulder, wondering what I was supposed to see on the pale, grey surface of the rock.

'You don't see it?'

'I'm not a geologist,' I said, thinking it was something to do with the nature of the rock.

He sighed. 'You've got sharp eyes—you could always pick out a grey plover. . . . Now look——' And he began tracing a shape with his finger. 'Do you see it now?'

'What is it?' I asked, trying to understand.

'A rhinoceros,' he said. 'A woolly rhinoceros. See it? There's the back, the head, the horn. And there's what the French call *les macaronis*—the lines the cave artists drew to show the weapons entering the body, the moment of kill. The men who drew these animals were the witch doctors of their day and by picture-writing the kill, they gave their hunters confidence. Do you see it now?'

He was looking at me anxiously, expectantly, waiting to see my own excitement reinforce his own. 'Yes,' I said. 'Yes, I see it.' And for a moment I almost thought I did. But the rock wall was so marked by natural indentations, so scored by falls from the roof, that you could imagine almost any shape in the cracks and lines.

'It's not very clear,' he said, his voice mirroring his disappointment at my lack of enthusiasm. 'And the paint has gone. They scratched the outline first. Then painted the beast with ochre or charcoal, using a stick brush—sometimes blowing it on in the form of a dry powder. Here the paint is all gone. The effect of the air. But when I get deeper into the cave, beyond the rock fall . . .' He moved the light. 'Here's another.'

Again he traced an outline, but it was difficult to know whether it was real or whether he was imagining it, the way, when you're ill, you lie in bed seeing shapes in the cracks of the ceiling. 'And here——' He took me nearer the entrance. 'I discovered this last year. A pigmy elephant I think, but its so vague and indistinct I can't be sure about it. Do you know Malta? Ghar Dalam—a cave—there are the bones of small elephants there, and if the land-bridge existed . . .' He

187

straightened up. 'I thought it worth investigating, and now I'm certain. If I had somebody working with me . . .' He stared at me, his eyes fixed on my face, willing me, I thought, to offer to help him clear the rock fall. 'Nobody knows why I'm here, what I'm doing—not even Sonia.' He leaned towards me, his eyes boring into me. 'You're not to talk about it, you understand? You're not to breathe a word to anybody.'

'Of course not,' I said, wondering what it was all about. Skull fragments I could understand, bones and primitive weapons, but the scratches that he had shown me on the wall here . . . 'I came to see you about that cable from Gilmore.'

His head jerked up. 'Cable? What cable?'

'Sonia says she showed it to you.'

'I know nothing about it.' He was on the defensive, staring at me, his face expressionless.

I couldn't believe he had forgotten about it. But he was so locked up in himself. . . . 'Those skull fragments Holroyd found . . .'

'It's not my fault if he leapt to the wrong conclusions,' he said quickly.

'It was your dig,' I reminded him. 'You were working there last year.'

'Did he say it was my dig? Did he tell Congress that I discovered it?'

'No.'

'Then he's only himself to blame.' He was suddenly laughing, that strange, jeering sound, as though sharing a joke with himself.

I couldn't make up my mind whether he knew what had emerged at that investigation or not. But the thought was in my mind that he had known all along what would happen.

'Sonia showed you that cable,' I said, trying to pin him down. 'What did Gilmore mean when he referred to Holroyd's reputation being damaged?'

He didn't answer, but just stood there, staring at me, smiling secretly.

'You know he may be coming out here again.'

'Then tell him to keep away from here.' The big hands moved, clenched involuntarily, his hatred of the man naked and revealed. And then, his voice rising to some inner need for self-justification: 'I'm a South African. The English—they hate the South Africans. Always have.' He was reaching back to the Boer War and beyond, to the long rivalry of the Dutch and English, and he added, 'You're quarter Afrikaans yourself, whether you like it or not. I need you now.' The tone of his voice had fallen to an urgent whisper. 'I need your strength, Paul.' I thought he meant my physical strength to break through that rock fall. But then he went on: 'You're not contaminated by the touch of the thing, and I don't imagine you believe in ghosts. Maybe it's just my preoccupation with the past, but when I hold it in my hand—I feel something, a power—the power of evil, or so it seems to me. Something terrible.' He stared at me, his eyes gleaming in the dark. 'You don't understand? I'll show you.' He took me to his tent and bent down, reaching into it with his arms. 'Here you are. Hold this.'

It was heavy, a stone about the size of a man's head. The edges of it had been roughly shaped, the flat surface of it hollowed out in a shallow basin. 'What is it?' I asked.

'A lamp,' he said. 'A stone lamp.'

Of course—the lamp he had been holding when Cassellis took those pictures. 'Old?' I asked.

He nodded. 'Very old.'

I stood there, holding it in my hands, conscious that he was watching me intently, feeling that sense of evil again. 'No substance in the universe—' he was speaking very quietly—'not even rock, is inanimate. Absorbed into the fabric of that stone is the knowledge that I seek. It's like the walls of a house. It breathes the atmosphere of the past. Surely you've felt that in a house—the atmosphere left by those who have lived and died there?' And when I nodded, he said, 'But holding that stone, you don't feel anything, you've no sense of the past stirring in you?'

I didn't dare answer him, knowing that the horror building up inside me came, as it always had done, from him.

He mistook my silence for insensibility. 'Good!' he said. 'Now you understand why I need your help.'

But I didn't understand. I was confused, uncertain how to meet his need. 'I don't quite see . . .' But the sudden grip of his hand silenced me.

'I need you here. I need the companionship of somebody whose mind is closed to what I think I'm going to find. You don't comprehend the evil here. You don't think about the world you live in, your own species. You're just a normal, healthy human animal. That's why I need you. To keep me from thinking about my own species—the explosion of its populations, the massing in concrete jungles, the destructive assault upon the balance of nature which can only lead to nature's retaliation—a long, slow, terrible battle of disease, famine and war.' He let go of my arm, pushing his hand up through his hair and staring seaward as though looking beyond the dim line of the horizon into the distant past. 'This species of ours,' he said, speaking very slowly and clearly, 'is Mousterian man all over again. But whereas my knowledge of the steady debasement of Mousterian stock is founded solely on the deterioration of his artefacts, the case of modern man is quite different. Here the material progress is fantastic, his "artefacts" reaching out to the planets. It is the spiritual progress that has halted, even gone into reverse.'

He paused, breathing heavily, and his eyes slowly shifted from the horizon to my face. 'I once asked a great Swedish painter, a man who had travelled widely and who had lived, like I have, amongst peasant communities in many parts of the world, whether he thought we were a rogue species, and he looked at me, his blue eyes cold and full of dreadful certainty: "But of course," he said. And yet there's good as well as evil. I know that. The old Devil and the old God—Sade's doctrine and Christ's. And when I look at you I am reminded of Ruth. Your mother was artistic, cultured, the sweet goodness of mankind personified. And when I was with her my soul had no evil in it, none at all. So stay with me, Paul. For Christ's sake stay with me.' And he added, on a lighter note. 'My own mother was Irish, you know. Celt and Boer—it's like mixing the grape and the grain.' He reached for the lamp and I gave it to him, and he stood there for a moment, holding it in his hands, then he put it back in the tent.

'That man Barrett,' he said, straightening up, his voice suddenly practical. 'He's an underwater diver. And that's a chance I'll never get again if you could only talk him into it.'

'Into what?' I asked him.

'This cave.' He had turned and was looking back at the dark shadow below the overhang. 'It wasn't tunnelled out by the flow of an underground river. It's like Rouffignac, a sea cavern. In Rouffignac there are over a hundred *gravures* of mammoths. If I could get into the lower galleries here . . .'
He picked up his anorak and slipped it on, still talking, urgently, intently, about some theory he had that the whole great circle formed by the heights of Levkas, Meganisi, Kalomo and the mainland was the rim of a huge crater invaded by the sea after a volcanic explosion even more violent than that of Santorin. 'I never believed in Atlantis. The continent that disappeared beyond the Pillars of Hercules is nonsense—an error due to the story having emanated from Egypt. It was the Minoan civilization—"far to the west" from the Egyptian point of view —that was destroyed when Santorin was blown to pieces, their fleet sunk, their cities and their fertile plains drowned by huge tidal waves. And if the Santorin eruption could do that, why not here, with the level of the water altered, the old cave entrance drowned? Much further back, of course—ten thousand, maybe even fifteen thousand years ago.'
And he went on to talk of the geological formation, volcanic rock overlying limestone, and the Central Mediterranean fault, running up through Pantelleria, Etna, Vulcano, Stromboli, branching off to the Ionian Isles. 'Every year, in the hot weather, there are earth tremors here—in Levkas, Ithaca and Cephalonia in particular. Every so often there is an earthquake. Ithaca lost a thousand dead in 1953. They still talk of that earthquake on Meganisi. It did little damage there, but in Ithaca and Cephalonia whole towns and villages had to be rebuilt. When you get back to your boat, you look at the chart —you'll see it then, the great crater circle formed by Levkas, Meganisi and the mainland mountains.'
He led me to the edge of the platform, clear of the overhang, so that we could see the stars and the whole shadowy vista of sea and islands. 'Suppose I'm right,' he said, his hand gripping my arm. 'Then all to the south of us was dry land, all that area of sea we're looking at now was one vast plain full of game. Pygmy elephant, lynx and ibex, hippopotamus even. And then with the last Ice Age, reindeer and the woolly rhinoceros, to be replaced as the ice receded by bison, the first cattle, small

horses, a whole new breed of animals. And if this were part of a more general cataclysm, then perhaps this is the Flood—not rain, but inundation by the sea.' He laughed, excited now, his imagination running away with him. 'Picture it for yourself, this vast plain stretching away to what is now the Western Desert, a grazing ground for all the animals whose bones we have found in Africa. And amongst them, primitive man, standing erect, weapons in his hand—the jaw-bones of hyenas, deer-leg clubs, stones—hunting, killing, evolving all the time, and fascinated, like any child or ape today, by the holes in the rocks, the caves left by an earlier sea period. In those caves he searched for his first primitive god—a goddess, in fact—the Earth Goddess, to whom he owed his whole animate being. What more natural than that he should seek her in the bowels of the earth, offering propitiation, paying tribute to his wizard priests and in return having his next meal drawn on the rock canvas with his own weapons stuck in the beast's guts to ensure a successful hunt.'

The stillness of the night, the calm sea running away to the blink of that distant light, and the old man's voice conjuring a strange primeval world. Was it fantasy, the idea that this had all been land long, long ago? But listening to him, speaking, now that he had sea and land to point to, in a way that he had never done when I was a kid, vividly and with extraordinary intensity, it didn't seem to matter. To him, at any rate, it was real. Convinced himself, he came near to convincing me.

'Paul!' Sonia's voice, calling to me out of the darkness, broke the spell. 'I thought maybe you'd lost your way,' she said quickly, apologetically, conscious that she had broken in upon a moment of intimacy between us.

He saw us down to the boat, silent now, declining my offer of a night in comfort on board *Coromandel*. He was anxious to start work on that rock fall at first light, convinced he would break through at any moment to the gallery beyond. 'Don't forget,' he said. 'Ask Barrett if he'll do an underwater survey of the area.'

I nodded, sitting on the thwart and looking up at him as he stood balanced on a rock, a dark outline against the stars. 'That means anchoring here. What's the holding like?'

He hadn't thought of that. He didn't know what the bottom

was like or whether there was any current moving through the channel. 'It depends on the weather,' I said and started to tell him how exposed the boat would be. But at that moment Pappadimas started the outboard and the noise of it drowned my voice, beating back and forth between the rock planes that formed the sides of the channel.

Later that evening, sitting in the saloon with a drink in my hand, I found it quite impossible to convey to Bert the extraordinary sense of reality conjured by the old man's words. For that you needed to be standing on that promontory below the cave's overhang looking out across the flat plain of the sea, dim under the stars. But though to Bert the land-bridge theory was a lot of visionary nonsense, the cave was real enough, the prospect of discovering something of antiquity below the sea a lure, a challenge. 'If it weren't for those damned packages of Borg's. . . .' He was torn between the urge to make an interesting dive and the desire to clear for Pantelleria and get shot of his unwelcome cargo. In the event, we did neither, the weather deciding for us. We were up in the early hours laying out a kedge, and all next morning we rode to two anchors with a gale from the north-west driving a steep scend into the inlet.

That evening, with the weather moderating, a caique came in loaded with vegetables from Corfu, and when we went ashore after dark, Zavelas told us Holroyd had arrived. He also told us that the Russian fleet was reported to be patrolling south of Rhodes, that the Israelis had launched a series of Commando raids against missile emplacements on the west side of the Suez Canal and that Egypt was appealing to the Security Council. He had a little Japanese transistor set on the table in front of him. 'There is also a rumour that Turkey may mobilize. They are already concentrating more troops on the Anatolian coast opposite Cyprus and along the shores of the Black Sea.' The wind was dying now, the night quiet except for the radio, a woman's voice singing a Greek song.

Vassilios was bringing his boat into the quay. I waited, sipping my ouzo and watching for Holroyd. And when he came I got up and walked to meet him on the quay.

He stopped when he saw me, his head lowered like a bull on the defensive. He looked older, less cocky, a hunch to his shoulders. 'Well, young man?' He stood with his legs braced as though still feeling the movement of the sea, his head thrust forward. 'What do you want?'

'Where are you going?' I asked him. 'To your dig at Tiglia?'

'Where else?'

'I thought you might be going out to see my father.'

'Later. That'll come later.' And he added, his eyes narrowing so that the creases running back from the corners were very pronounced, 'You were in on it, were you? You knew what he was up to—wasting public money, making a fool of me. And with what object? Can you tell me that?' The anger was building up in him. 'Thought he'd get rid of me. Is that it? A clear field whilst he worked on the cave that really mattered. Well? Well, haven't you got anything to say?'

'I know nothing about it.'

'Well, if you won't talk I'll have to have it out with Van der Voort.'

'You leave him alone,' I said. I could see the old man now, his big hands opening and clenching. There'd be murder if Holroyd tried to interfere with him. 'Stick to Tiglia or go off and find some dig of your own. But don't cross the channel to where my father is working.'

'Why not?'

'Because he'll kill you if you do.'

I saw his eyes widen and he stood there, staring at me for a moment. And then without another word he went past me to the boat and Vassilios helped him in. The outboard roared and they slid away from the quay, out into the calm waters of the inlet, the light fading, everything still. I stood there, watching until they were out of sight, wondering what was going to happen. Then I turned to find Sonia standing a few yards away.

'He mustn't worry Dr Van der Voort,' she said in a small, tense voice. 'Did you tell him that?'

'Of course I did.' I was angry at her for stating the obvious, angry with myself for yielding to a compulsion I did not understand. And as I stood there, facing her, I was remembering the sense of something altogether evil I had felt up there alone with him the previous night.

She took my arm suddenly, her fingers gripping tight. 'What is it?' she asked. 'You're trembling.'

But I couldn't tell her what it was, for I didn't know myself.

'Do you remember those photographs Dr Gilmore brought with him to Amsterdam? The second one—he was holding something in his hand. A stone lamp, Gilmore said. D'you remember? What did they use a stone lamp for?'

'The ancients?'

'Yes, the ancients.' It was a strange, archaic word to use. 'Was there something special about a stone lamp?'

'No, of course not.' She said it briskly. 'They had to see and it was the only lamp they knew—a hollowed stone with animal fat and the wick floating in it. Isn't that what the Eskimos use?'

'Probably.'

She left me shortly afterwards and I rowed off to the boat. I needed a drink, a good stiff drink.

I was on my second Scotch when the Barretts came off in Zavelas's boat. They were very subdued. Even Florrie. They'd made up their minds. They wanted to clear for Pylos in the morning, and once through the channel, head direct for Pantelleria.

'Without going to Pylos to hand in our transit-log?'

'Yes,' Bert said. And his wife nodded. 'It's dangerous here.' They were thinking of the cargo we carried. I was thinking of Holroyd and my father.

'Zavelas is suspicious. I think he knows something.'

So they had felt it, too. 'Okay,' I said. All day, whilst we had been cooped up on board waiting for the weather to moderate, we had talked of little else, chewing it over with the intensity of people who have no means of getting away from each other. And now that they had finally made up their minds, I knew there was no shifting them. Like most easy-going men, Bert could be very obstinate once he had been forced to a decision.

'We can always plead stress of weather, an engine breakdown, something like that,' he said. 'The regulations allow for that, provided I post the transit-log back to the port of entry and give the reason for not clearing foreign.'

I nodded. We'd be in the clear then to come back if I could wring enough money out of Borg. 'So long as we stop in the Channel—I'd like to have a word with my father before we leave.'

'Of course. But I'm not making a dive.' And Florrie added,

'Zavelas warned us about that. If Bert dives, then they'd have to examine the boat to make certain he hadn't lifted some archaeological treasures off the bottom.' I knew that, but I had thought that in a little place like this . . . 'A pity,' I said, and left it at that. It was no use arguing with them.

We had supper then, and afterwards I took the dinghy and rowed ashore to say goodbye to Sonia. I still had some drachmas and I wanted to leave the money with her. It would be just enough to keep him going for a month or two the way he was living and I wasn't certain he'd take it from me.

It was very hot ashore, a preternatural stillness hanging over the little port. Zavelas was no longer at the kaféneion, but the proprietor sent his daughter with me to show me the house. She was about fourteen, a bright, dark-eyed girl shyly conscious of the fact that she was just emerging from the puppy-fat stage. Her short, white frock, immaculately laundered, gleamed in the dark. It was a breathless, suffocating night, no stars and the air hanging heavy. By the time we reached the house my shirt was sticking to my back. 'Spiti Zavelas,' she said, and with a quick smile and a swirl of her skirt she was gone, still looking as fresh as when we started.

Zavelas opened the door to me himself. 'Come in, fella.' And he showed me into a ground-floor room that was like a stage version of a Victorian parlour. 'So you're leaving in the morning, and now you want to see the Dutch girl, eh?' He was smiling, not quite a leer, but as near as dammit. 'Well, you're welcome.' He left me and I heard him calling to Sonia up the stairs.

There were lace antimacassars on the chairs, bric-à-brac everywhere, and the walls crowded with photographs—group pictures mainly, of cops and sailors and loggers. An English Parliament clock showed the time as nine forty-seven. I was still wondering where that had come from when the door opened behind me and I turned to find Sonia standing there. No puppy-fat on her and her face looking hot and strained. 'Mr Zavelas has told me. You're leaving in the morning.'

'Yes.' I began to explain the reason, but she cut me short: 'You could have stayed if you'd wanted to. You don't have to go with them.' I could almost hear her saying, *You're running out on him again.*

'I came to give you this,' I said quickly, getting out my wallet and explaining to her why it was better for her to have it. She took the dirty notes, counting them carefully. 'Eight hundred and seventy-five drachs,' she said.

It was a little over £12, not very much. 'I'm afraid it's all I've got left.'

'Never mind. It will help. And he's vegetarian—except for eggs and cheese. He eats a lot of eggs.' And she added, 'It's extraordinary the energy vegetarians have. Yet they're much gentler than meat-eaters.' She was just talking for the sake of talking, and she wanted to think of him as a kindly man. 'Are you a vegetarian?' I asked. She hadn't appeared to be when she was cooking for Cartwright and her brother at Despotiko, but I didn't really have any idea what she *liked* to eat.

'I think I might be—with a little encouragement. In Amsterdam I was. But it's so difficult, with other people.'

We might have gone on talking like that, keeping to neutral topics and avoiding personal contact, but at that moment the walls seemed to move, the ground swaying under my feet. It was the heat and the drink. That was my first thought, that all the liquor I had consumed that day had caught up with me. I could feel my body swaying, the room swimming before my eyes. And then, with a conscious effort, I seemed to have control of myself. The room was still again and I said, 'Vegetables are cheap in the islands here. At least he won't starve.' My voice sounded over-careful, the words thick and blurred. I must be drunk. Even in this cool, Victorian room, the air was stifling. I could feel the sweat on my forehead, my whole body clammy with the heat. 'I'll go now,' I said, remembering that time in Amsterdam when I'd flung her against the wall. 'I just came to give you those notes.' But she didn't seem to hear. She was standing very tense, her eyes wide, and there were beads of sweat on her forehead and on her short upper lip. 'What was that?' she breathed.

And then it came again, the room swimming, the ground moving under my feet. A piece of plaster fell from the ceiling, a puff of white dust on the lovingly polished case of the Parliament clock, and the clock itself shifting slightly before my eyes so that I thought it was going to fall. But then everything was still again and the clock remained there on the wall, oddly askew, and Sonia was close against me, my arm round her. We had come together instinctively, an involuntary movement, the two of us seeking comfort in each other. I could feel the warmth of her body. She was pressed close to me and my hand, touching her, feeling the warmth of her flesh beneath the thin fabric of her dress, discovered she was wearing nothing underneath it. She was as stark as if she were in her nightdress.

'That was an earthquake?' I murmured.

She shook her head. 'An earth tremor, I think they'd call it. We had one the other day. But not as bad.' She was still clinging to me and I put my hand under her chin and tilted her head back.

'Scared?'

She smiled. 'Not really. Surprised, that's all. It came as a shock.'

I kissed her then and for a moment we stood there, locked in each other's arms, unconscious of the risk we ran staying indoors, the world reduced to the two of us, the pounding of our blood louder than any movement of the earth. And then feet sounded heavy on the stairs and Zavelas called down to us: 'Van der Voort—Sonia! You get outside. Ghrighora! Quickly!'

He was there before us, with his wife and everybody else who lived in the street, standing in the middle of the road, very still and quiet, waiting anxiously. The air was oppressive, hot and humid. But nothing happened. 'Finished now, I think,' Zavelas said finally. 'A tremor. Nothing serious.' And he laughed, a little uncertainly. 'Not like San Francisco, eh? Guess if we were down at Fisherman's Wharf they'd all be reckoning it was the end of the world. That's a real big fault they're sitting on there. In Meganisi it's not so dangerous.'

His wife went back into the house, a big, broad, motherly soul already intent upon making certain that none of the things she treasured had been harmed. Through the open window we saw her in the room we had left, already working with brush and dustpan to sweep up the fall of plaster. 'It's the heat,' Zavelas said. 'When it's like this there is always a little danger. But usually later in the year.' He looked at me and his manner changed, a cop again, responsible to authority for the security of the island which was his home. 'It is reported to Levkas that you leave for Pylos. I guess they would like the Doctor to go with you. We will know for sure in the morning, but I would advise you to arrange it.'

'I don't think he'd agree to that,' I said.

He stared at me, the blue eyes hard. 'I'm warning you. That's all.' And then he shrugged. 'None of my business, you understand.' His voice was kindly, almost paternal, and he patted me on the shoulder with his big hairy paw. 'But I think it's better he goes with you. Okay?'

'They can't force him,' Sonia said in a small, tight voice.

'They can do anything they damn well like. You know that, Sonia.' And Zavelas added, 'I think maybe Kotiadis come here in the morning.' And with that he left us and went back into the house.

Sonia walked with me down to the quay and we didn't talk. Something had happened to us, and we knew it, so that we were both of us absorbed in trying to sort ourselves out. 'I'll see him in the morning,' I said as I got into the dinghy. 'We'll stop in the channel on the way out.'

'If Pappadimas is here, I'll come out there,' she said. 'Anyway, I'll be on the quay to wave you off.' And she added quickly, 'I think Zavelas is right. I think he should go with you.'

The thought was in my mind, too—but not because of the authorities. 'I'll have a talk with him.'

She nodded, looking very solemn. 'He's interested in Pantelleria. That might help.'

'He's also obsessed by that damn cave of his.' I hadn't much hope that he'd agree. 'Goodnight.' And I pushed away from the quay without touching her, feeling she was a million miles away, the old man between us again.

'Goodnight, Paul.'

She turned, not looking back, and I started to row out to the boat.

We were up at six-thirty the following morning, for in a boat the size of *Coromandel* there is always a lot to be done in preparation for a long sea passage and we had the kedge to recover. By eight, Bert was away in the dinghy to see the Customs official, leaving me to get the sails ready for hoisting whilst Florrie cleared the breakfast things and stowed everything below. It was a perfect day for the start of a voyage, clear and bright with the wind back in the north-west—very light, but since this was the prevailing wind direction along the coast we could expect it to increase during the day. By eight-thirty everything was ready, only the main anchor to bring in, and we were waiting for Bert.

It was almost nine before he put off from the quay, and as he sculled the dinghy alongside I could see by his face that something was wrong. 'You've been a long time,' Florrie said as he tossed the painter to me.

He nodded, sitting there in the dinghy, looking up at me. 'I had to wait while they phoned through to Levkas for instructions.' He reached up, gripping the bulwarks, and hauled himself on board. 'They're being difficult,' he said. 'It's that bloody man Kotiadis. He's at police headquarters in Levkas. We can sail, but on one condition—that we take Dr Van der Voort with us.' He was staring at me. 'You'd better fix it, otherwise God knows what will happen.' He was angry. Angry because he was scared. 'I've a good mind to throw those packages overboard, right here in the harbour, and by Christ I'll do it if you don't get us out of here.'

'I can't very well shanghai him,' I said. 'What happens if he say No?'

'Then they'll impound the boat, maybe arrest the three of us. That's what your copper friend implied.' He turned on his wife then. 'You thought that escapade off the Turkish coast just a bit of fun. It was easy. I grant you that. A piece of cake. But they've got all our movements taped, every port we've been in and the dates. And they've a pretty good idea what we were up to in the Samos Straits that night.'

'How do you know?' she asked, on the defensive.

'Zavelas. I had about a quarter of an hour, with him hinting at all sorts of things—even the possibility that we might have an agent stowed away on board. Maybe it's just an excuse. I don't know. It doesn't matter, anyway. They know enough to justify any action they care to take, and they want to get shot of Van der Voort.'

'But why?' I asked. 'He's doing no harm, working quietly away. . . .'

'It's the international situation. Kotiadis is still convinced that he's some sort of an agent.' And he added, 'I don't care how you do it, but get him on board and let's get out of here. I'm not having my boat impounded, for you or anyone else— it's all Florrie and I have got. If you don't get him on board, then I'll come ashore and do it myself.' He was near to tears, he was so upset, the words pouring out of him.

'Okay,' I said. 'If that's what you want, we'll fetch the anchor now and go round and pick him up.' My hands were trembling at the thought, but there was nothing else for it. I could see it from the Greek point of view, the Middle East flaring and themselves on the edge of the volcano. They had a right to get rid of anybody they didn't trust. 'You've got clearance for Italy, have you? Or do they still want us to go to Pylos for clearance?'

'I don't know,' he said. 'The Customs official is coming round with us in Zavelas's boat. He's keeping the transit-log until they've seen Dr Van der Voort on board, and Kotiadis is coming from Levkas in a coastal patrol boat. I think we're going to be escorted outside territorial waters.'

I pulled the dinghy astern and made the painter fast to a cleat aft. Then we got the anchor up and jilled around, the engine just ticking over. We didn't talk. There was nothing else to be said. Zavelas came down to the quay and got into his boat. The Customs official joined him and they put off, arrowing a wake into the inlet, the outboard noisy in the quiet of the port. Sonia stood close by a bollard, a small, still figure. She didn't wave and we got under way, the three of us subdued and silent.

Half an hour later we were in the Meganisi Channel, the water glass-calm and no breeze at all under the sheltering heights of Levkas. The depth at the southern end was sixty-five fathoms, too deep to anchor, and Bert steered close in to the rocks on the Levkas side, holding her there whilst I hauled the dinghy alongside and jumped into it. Florrie passed the oars to me, and as I pulled away she called out: 'Paul. There's a boat in there. I can just see the outboard.'

I leaned on the oars, letting the dinghy drift whilst I turned to look. High above me I could see the overhang, the great scooped-out hollow in the near-vertical hillside pale in the sunlight. I couldn't see the boat, only the shape of the rocks

that marked the gut where Sonia and I had landed. I had a
sudden premonition, a feeling I had arrived too late, and I bent
to the oars, pulling hard for the shore. It was barely twenty
yards, and in a moment I had opened up the gut and there was
Vassilios in his dirty singlet dozing in his boat. 'Where's
Professor Holroyd?' I called to him.

He turned and stared at me uncomprehendingly, moving aft
to catch the dinghy's bows. 'Professor Holroyd—*poó ine*?'
He pointed above us towards the overhang, now hidden by
the rocks, and I scrambled past him, the boats rocking violently
as I leapt for the shore. Christ Almighty! The bloody fool! I'd
warned him. The track zig-zagged up through the rocks and I
clambered up it, moving fast, praying to God that I wasn't
too late. The low beat of *Coromandel*'s engine drummed against
the cliff, and to the north I could hear the waspish sound of
Zavelas's outboard coming down the channel. It was hot and
the blood pounded in my head as I clawed my way up.

And then a voice said, 'You're too late.'

I stopped then, looking up to see Holroyd standing poised
on a rock above me, wearing a pair of red bathing trunks and a
white shirt.

'How do you mean?' The words came in a gasp and I stood
there, panting, wondering what the hell he'd been up to.
'What's happened? What have you done?'

'Done?' He seemed puzzled. 'Nothing,' he said. 'Nothing I
could do. He's gone.'

I didn't get it for a moment. But he wasn't hurt. He hadn't
been in a fight. That was all that mattered and a feeling of
relief flooded through me. I climbed the last few feet and
joined him where he stood on the slope below the platform.
'You stay here,' I said. 'I want to talk to him alone.'

'Well, go ahead. Maybe you know where he is.' And he
stood aside to let me pass.

I had started up the slope, but then I paused. Something in
his voice, his choice of words. . . . I stared at him, but I couldn't
see the expression of his eyes. He was wearing dark glasses, his
head bare, and from where I stood now he was a slightly
ridiculous figure, the shirt hiding his bathing trunks so that he
looked as though he were wearing a mini-skirt. 'He'll be in the
cave,' I said.

But he shook his head. 'I've tried there.'

'Beyond the rubble? It goes in about ten yards.'

'I've been right to the end,' he said.

'And he's not in his tent?'

'No. And I searched everywhere.'

'Then probably he's at Vatahori.'

'Vassilios says not. He saw Pappadimas this morning.' He thrust his head forward. 'If you ask me, he's abandoned his dig and cleared out.' And he added angrily, 'But I'm not falling for it this time.'

'I don't believe it,' I said. 'He's just avoiding you. That's all.' It seemed the most sensible thing for him to do.

'Maybe,' he said, but I could see he wasn't convinced. 'You go and have a look for yourself. I'll go on down to the boat and wait for you there.'

I left him then and climbed the slope to the platform below the overhang. I hadn't been there in daylight before and I stood for a moment staggered by the view. The island of Arkudi was almost due south, a massive pile seared brown by the sun, with the flat plain of the sea all round it, its surface rippled by the breeze. And beyond Arkudi, Ithaca and Cephalonia, merged into one great mountainous mass half-hidden in a haze of heat. To the west, beyond the long scorpion tail of Meganisi, more islands and the mainland mountains rearing misty heights. I could hear the old man's voice talking as though in a dream of the hunting lands of early man, and again I felt the strange atmosphere of the place. Even in daylight, in the full blaze of the sun, it had an eeriness, a sense of evil. Or was that just my imagination?

I shrugged it off and turned to the tent. It was still there and when I peered inside the first thing I saw was the stone lamp. He wouldn't have gone without that, surely? There was his camera, too, and his notebooks, and the sleeping-bag was neatly spread as though it hadn't been slept in that night. I called his name then, but there was no answer except the sound of my voice echoing back from the cliff above. And when I had clambered to the top of the rubble, I could see at a glance that he wasn't in the cave. It was in dark shadow, of course, but I could see right to the rock fall and there was no way through.

I went back to the platform then and searched about for

some way by which he could have climbed to the heights above or made his way to the end of the promontory. But the cliff was almost sheer, the great scooped-out hollow in it sealing the platform off entirely. There was no possible way of leaving the place except by the path up which I had climbed. And here, at the south end of the channel, it was a long swim across to Meganisi. To get away he would have to have had a boat.

Zavelas and the Customs official had arrived by the time I got down to the gut again and Holroyd was talking to them. 'God knows,' I heard him say, and Zavelas nodded: 'We will see Pappadimas, but first we must wait for Kotiadis.' He saw me and his eyebrows lifted. 'You don't find him, eh? Then you must go back to your boat and tell your skipper he is to stay here. I guess Kotiadis won't be long now.'

'We can't anchor here,' I said. 'It's too deep.'

He conferred with the Customs official. 'Okay,' he said. 'Then you must go back to Vathy and wait there. You cannot leave without your transit-log. You understand?'

I could hear the chug of *Coromandel*'s diesel very close, and once I had manoeuvred the dinghy out of the gut, I had only a few yards to row. Seeing me come off alone Bert knew something was wrong and his face, behind the glass windshield, looked sullen and angry as he backed out into mid-Channel and cut the engine. 'Well, what's happened? Where is he?' And when I told him, he shouted at me, 'Then find him, for Christ's sake. The bloody old fool!' And he rounded on Florrie. 'Why the hell did you persuade me to come back this way? If we'd gone direct to Pantelleria——'

'Paul had to come.'

'Why? Why did he have to come this way?' And he added, his words coming wildly, 'Paul wants this. Paul wants that. And this daft old man buggering up the whole trip.'

'You're behaving like a child,' she said stiffly.

'So I'm like a child, am I? Well, I'll tell you this—if we lose the boat, I'm through. I'll leave you and go back to the Persian Gulf. Make some real dough before I'm too old.'

'You're too old now,' she said. 'You'll always be too old.' And she turned and went below, leaving him with a shocked look on his face.

'Christ!' he breathed. 'I should have left that bitch years ago.

All the things I've done to keep her happy. . . .' His face had crumpled, a sad, tired face on the verge of tears. 'To hell with her! You, too—to hell with you both!' And he went into the wheelhouse, standing there, staring at the chart, anything to drive out the loneliness that was in him.

He was a failure and he knew it, and I was sorry for him. 'I'm going ashore again now,' I said.

He nodded, not saying anything, not looking at me, a shut look on his face. God! I thought. Loneliness must be a terrible thing, the loneliness of a marriage gone wrong. And I had contributed to it. Without thinking I had thrust them over the edge of neutrality into open hostility. I felt guilty. But there was nothing I could do about it. If it hadn't been me, it would have been somebody else. Probably had been. Probably she'd thrown herself at other men.

I got back into the dinghy then and rowed towards the Levkas shore, leaving *Coromandel* drifting, with him standing there alone in the wheelhouse, not caring any longer. There was only Vassilios in the gut now. The others had gone up to the cave. He helped me ashore, and when I reached the platform I found them clustered around the tent, the old man's notebooks lying on the ground and Holroyd standing with the stone lamp in his hand. 'Do you know what this is?' he asked me and there was an undercurrent of excitement in his voice.

'Yes,' I said.

'Where did he get it?' He was looking at me intently, holding the thing in his two hands carefully as though it were some fragile pice of glass. 'Brought it with him, I suppose—like those skull fragments.'

'I don't think so.'

'No?' He sounded doubtful. 'I've seen stone lamps like these in the museum at Les Eyzies and at the Grotte de la Mouthe.' He turned it in his hands, looking down at it with extraordinary intensity, like a connoisseur examining some precious antique. 'Are you sure he didn't bring it with him?'

'Why are you so interested?' I asked.

He stared at it a moment longer, and then he put it down on the ground, carefully, and with obvious reluctance. 'Do you know what it was used for?' he asked.

'To light their cave-shelters, I imagine.'

He nodded. 'But in the Vézère—at de la Mouthe and in some of the other caves—their cave artists used these lamps to light their work. That's how they painted in the dark recesses of their cave temples.' He had turned and was staring towards the shadowed hollow of the overhang. 'We'll go up there, shall we, and have another look?'

'There's nothing there,' I said. 'Just the cave blocked by a rock fall.'

He was looking at me, trying to read a motive behind my words. 'Winters tells me Dr Van der Voort was working night and day to clear it. Why?'

I shrugged, not wishing to excite his interest further. There was the sound of an outboard in the channel, a small boat headed for the gut. I could see Sonia in the bows so it must be Pappadimas.

'I'll be up at the cave,' Holroyd said, and he started up the slope, his white shirt flapping round his legs.

'It don't make sense to me,' Zavelas said, 'leaving his camera and his notes.' He bent down and picked up one of the notebooks. 'Know what language this is?' he asked, handing it to me. I opened it to see the familiar spidery writing, but no meaning to the words. 'It sure ain't English.'

'No,' I said, sensing his uneasiness. As an ex-policeman he was intrigued by the mystery of my father's disappearance, but overlying that was his political responsibilities and the note-books worried him. They worried me, too, for I knew they weren't written in Afrikaans.

He glanced at his watch and then at the channel. The white of a bow wave showed beyond the northern tip of Meganisi.

'Kotiadis?' I asked.

He nodded. 'I think so.' He sounded relieved, anxious to hand the problem over to higher authority.

Sonia's reaction to the news, which she had heard from Vassilios, was one of absolute disbelief that my father's disappearance was deliberate. 'Something's happened—an accident. He would never have left this place till he had got through that rock fall. You know that, Paul. You said last night that he was obsessed by the need to break through it. How could you possibly think he would abandon it?' She was breathless from her hurried climb, her voice coming in quick gasps. 'Have you searched the rocks?' And she added, 'I sent Pappadimas to search the channel, just in case.'

I did my best to calm her. He'd disappeared once before. Why not again? With Holroyd in the vicinity I thought anything was possible. As for an accidental fall, he was as sure-footed as a goat. But she didn't believe me. 'You say Professor Holroyd was already here when you arrived. Have you thought what might have happened when he met Dr Van der Voort? Suppose . . .' she stared at me, her meaning obvious.

'Then we'd have found his body floating in the water.'

'Not if he was unconscious. And Professor Holroyd may have been here before—during the night.' It was what she wanted to believe—anything, even murder, rather than face the alternative that the old man's mind had given way.

'Holroyd's surprise at finding him gone was genuine,' I said.

But she wouldn't accept that. 'Something terrible has happened. I feel it. I feel it here.' And she banged her hand against her firm little breasts. And then quite suddenly she turned on me as though I were to blame. 'You don't want to believe me, do you? You leave me money for him, and you think that's that. You don't want to be involved in any trouble.' The way she said it reminded me of Florrie hitting out at her husband and it made me suddenly mean.

'You tell me I'm running out on him once more, and by Christ I'll give you a hiding you won't forget.'

'You said it, I didn't,' she flashed.

Zavelas put his big hand on my shoulder. 'I think we go up to the cave now.'

Holroyd was down at the far end, close by the rock fall, brushing at the wall with his handkerchief. He had a torch in his hand and he moved it back and forth the way my father had done. 'Do you see?' he cried, turning to us as we crowded the entrance of the cave. He didn't bother to conceal his excitement. 'Look!' And he began to trace it for us with his finger. It was the rhinoceros the old man had traced for me— the rump, the tail, the two hind legs. 'Some sort of animal,' he said. 'Do you see it?'

'Yes, I see it,' Sonia said and her voice seemed to mirror his own excitement.

'That lamp,' Holroyd went on, addressing himself to me. 'Now we know what it was used for and that he found it here.'

But all I could think of was the rhinoceros. *Some sort of animal.* Holroyd didn't know what it was—couldn't know, for the forelegs, all the head, were hidden by the rock fall. Or was this another outline? Had the old man found more animals etched deeper in the cave? 'Give me the torch,' I said and grabbed it from him, peering along the wall. But there was the elephant, a few feet nearer the entrance and coated thick with a new layer of dust. I heard Sonia's voice behind me exclaim, 'Lieve help! Surely that's an animal. I can see the dome of its head.' She caught hold of my arm. 'It's what I told you—he'd never have left this place of his own accord.'

I brushed her hand away and turned the torch on the cave end, on to the fall itself. The rocks were pale-coloured, sharp-edged, but that didn't prove anything. A new fall would look no different from the old fall opened up. But he'd a crowbar here and his geological hammer. The beam of the torch revealed no sign of any tools, and when I directed it above our heads it showed the roof, badly cracked and faulted. 'Epikin-dynos—sighá!' Zavelas exclaimed. 'Is dangerous.'

'It must have been that earth tremor,' I said, and I swung the beam of the torch back to the lines marking the rump of the rhinoceros. 'Two nights ago he showed me the whole outline. He had just cleared it—the head, the horn, the whole animal. Now look at it, and he was working here all day yesterday.' I turned to Holroyd. 'Better collect Cartwright and Hans and start digging. Can you get some of your own people down here?' I asked Zavelas.

He nodded, quick to grasp my meaning, but not moving. 'No hurry now,' he said gently, and, with the two first fingers and thumb of his right hand together, he touched his forehead from right to left in the Orthodox manner. I saw Sonia's face very white in the beam of the torch. She didn't say anything. She knew as well as I did that Zavelas was right—the old man couldn't possibly have survived under the weight of that fall.

'I'm sorry,' Holroyd said, and to give him his due I think he meant it. Probably this was something anthropologists feared, an occupational hazard. 'I'll move camp up here and we'll start work right away.' His eyes strayed towards the rhinoceros and I knew the incentive to dig was not the recovery of my father's body. His gaze shifted to the roof, squinting up at the cracks as though assessing the danger, measuring it against the scientific potentials. 'We'll be back here with all our gear in about an hour.' And he walked quickly out towards the bright gleam of sunlight beyond the rubble.

Zavelas patted my arm. 'We all have to go some time, fella. And that way it is quick.' The sympathy in his voice was real. But then he said, 'Now I go and tell Kotiadis.' And I knew he was relieved, the old man's death solving a problem that had worried him.

I followed him out of the cave, Sonia's hand in mine, her fingers clasping tight. I didn't look at her. I knew if I did she'd burst into tears. 'He's right,' she whispered as we came down off the rubble into the hot sun. 'It must have been very quick.' There was a catch in her voice as she added, 'He wouldn't have liked to linger. Better go whilst he was still driving towards something he believed in.'

I could feel her nails in the palm of my hand. 'You and I,' I said. 'We should have been switched at birth. You'd have understood him.'

'He'd still have wanted a son.' Her voice sounded infinitely sad.

We were halfway across the platform then and I saw Kotiadis down by the tent. He came to meet us, still wearing the same light grey suit, his face impassive behind his dark glasses. He ignored Zavelas's greeting, walked right past him and thrust one of the notebooks at me. 'You see this before?'

I nodded, surprised at the violence in his voice.

'Is written in Russian. Connaisez-vous? What for is he writing in Russian, eh?' His voice was literally trembling, so intense was his feeling at this discovery.

It didn't matter to him that the writer of those notes was dead. He didn't believe it, anyway, convinced that my father had disappeared 'for convenience' as he put it. As for the suggestion that the notes were written in Russian for reasons of scientific security, he simply ignored it, firing questions at me in a steady stream—about the old man, about where he had been and where we were planning to go. I suppose he was under pressure, his superiors and the Middle East tension, but I wasn't in the mood to make allowances. To me he was a stupid, bloody-minded bastard, a typical bureaucrat, and I told him so.

'You are under arrest,' he shouted at me. 'All of you.' He pointed up the channel. 'You go with the boat to Vathy now. Then I take you to police headquarters at Levkas.'

Anger exploded in me then, exploded into violence, my hands reaching out to grip him by the collar and shake some sense into him. Sonia called to me and I hesitated, and in that moment my arms were seized and pinned to my side in a great bear-hug, Zavelas talking over my shoulder, fast and urgent in Greek. Unable to move, I let the torrent of words pour over me. They were both of them shouting now, the violence of their altercation drumming at the rocks, so that it sounded as though they were having a furious row. Then suddenly it was all over and Kotiadis was smiling, holding out his hand to me. 'Pardon,' he said. 'I did not understand. Please to accept my sympathies.' Zavelas released me then and Kotiadis added, 'Now we must recover Dr Van der Voort's body.' The way he said it, the watchful, wary look in his eyes, I knew the future depended on that—the finding of my father's body.

Sonia's hand touched mine, a gesture of understanding, of sympathy, but I shook her off. I didn't want sympathy. I just wanted the clock turned back, the years in Amsterdam again. Atonement for my own callousness. I felt unutterably depressed. Not so much at the old man's death, but because of the wasted years.

It was in this mood that I took Kotiadis up to the cave and began clearing the loose debris of the new fall, Sonia working beside me, both of us for our own individual reasons endeavouring to lose ourselves in the hard physical work of shifting rock. Holroyd returned, bringing Cartwright, Hans and Vassilios with him. They had tools and a pressure lamp, but no wheelbarrow, so that everything still had to be taken out to the rubble pile by hand. It was hard, back-breaking work, fine rock dust hanging in clouds, clogging our nostrils.

By one-thirty the whole outline of the rhinoceros was clear on the wall again and we had progressed to the point where the cave was almost as deep as when I had surprised my father working in it late that night. We broke for lunch then, Sonia having come back with Florrie and a great pile of sandwiches they had cut on board. Apparently Bert had located a shelf of rock and the boat was moored bows-on to the shore with an anchor out astern. 'He's planning a dive this afternoon.' Florrie was looking tired and strained.

'Well, tell him to be careful,' I said, conscious still of the atmosphere of this place and not wanting another tragedy.

She gave me a wan smile. 'You don't have to worry about Bert when it comes to diving. It's something he's really good at.'

I knew that. I'd watched him dive in the harbour at Patmos. And then later, under his instructions, I'd gone down myself in shallow water off Leros. I wouldn't have done that if I hadn't had complete confidence in him. But to start diving now. . . . 'It would be more help if he came ashore and gave us a hand.'

'He's not thinking of helping you,' she said. 'It's just to take his mind off things.'

It was shortly after the lunch break that Hans uncovered the end of the crowbar. We felt we were near then, but time passed as we worked more carefully at the face and we found nothing. It was all broken rock and the roof unsafe, the ceiling fractured so that you could pull great chunks of limestone away with your hands. Zavelas had brought three men from Spiglia and by evening we were in a distance of about eight yards. For the last hour Kotiadis had stood watching us. It was not difficult to guess what he was thinking.

We packed it in at sunset and, apart from the crowbar, all we had found was the old man's watch and a tin filled with carbide. They were not more than a foot apart. It would seem that, after refilling his acetylene lamp and lighting it, he had laid the carbide tin down and then, perhaps because he knew he had some hard, jarring work ahead of him with the crowbar, he had removed his watch from his wrist and put it down beside the tin. The watch was a write-off, of course, the face and works completely shattered. It had a stainless steel case and the leather strap was almost black with sweat. Sonia said he had bought it in Russia, but marks on the case showed that it was Swiss-made.

The only man who was satisfied that night was Holroyd. What looked like the head of a deer superimposed on the rump of some larger animal had been uncovered, and on the opposite wall the vague outline of a very complex drawing was just beginning to emerge. He was impatient for the morning when Zavelas had promised to bring more men and also at least one wheelbarrow. With a wheelbarrow the work would go much faster and he was sure that they would break through into an undamaged gallery beyond the fall.

Bert, too, was not unhappy. He had started diving shortly after three in the afternoon and had worked his way steadily along the underwater face of the Levkas shore below the cave. He described it as 'very broken, with deep crevices between what looked something like the flying buttresses supporting a medieval cathedral.' He had explored every one of those crevices, some of them over 50 metres in depth and most of them very narrow. In only one case had he failed to reach the end. This was more a cave than a fissure, the curved sides suggesting that it had been worn by water over a very long period. About 30 metres in, it had been partially blocked by a fallen slab. There was a gap, but it was small. He had gone in about 2 metres with his aqualung scraping rock all the time.

'I was running short of air by then,' he said. 'Also I'd only got a small hand torch, so I backed out. I'll have another go at it tomorrow.' He wasn't sure whether that was the end of the cave or whether it opened out further in. 'There wasn't much light, you see. If I could anchor over it and take down a spot-light . . . it's a bit tricky like, 'cos if it don't open up you've got to back all the way out.'

Back at Vathy he was still talking about it. The row with his wife, the harsh words said, seemed wiped from his mind. And for her part, Florrie seemed to take it for granted that nothing had changed. Sonia was on board with us and when I told her what had happened between them earlier, all she said was, 'What did you expect? Only a fool would go into marriage with her eyes shut to the sort of man she was tying herself to for life, and Florrie isn't a fool.' She was looking at me very directly as though to say 'and nor am I.'

She had supper with us and then I rowed her ashore. She sat in the stern, her face a pale oval in the starlight, and she didn't speak until we were close in to the quay. 'Bert seems very excited about that hole he's found.'

'It's a challenge,' I said. 'An object for doing something he likes doing.'

'Yes, but he seemed to think if he could get through he'll find the cave continuing.'

'With pictures of animals painted in brilliant colours, I suppose.' That was what the old man had hoped and the cave was Holroyd's now.

She caught the note of bitterness in my voice, for she said gently, 'Surely to prove him right—wouldn't that be something worth while?'

'Not my department,' I said, thinking of Holroyd starting at crack of dawn, intent on breaking through to the cave beyond. 'I'll get his body out and then I'll go.' And I added, without conscious thought, 'There's something about that place, a voodoo, something—I don't like it.'

The bows touched and she sat there for a moment, staring at me, silent. Then she jumped for the quay, and with a quick goodnight she was gone like a shadow into the night. I leaned on the oars, wondering what the hell she expected of me. The old man was dead, and though his death might mean more to her than it did to me, she surely couldn't be childish enough to think that I could carry on where he had left off.

When I got back to the boat, Bert was on deck to take the painter. 'Can you give me a hand at the workbench?' he said. 'I'm rigging a battery-operated spotlight. It'll be better than trailing a long cable, but I need help with the water-proofing.'

I suppose you could call it a displacement activity. Give a man like Bert a technical problem and he lost himself in it completely, everything else forgotten. It took us just over two hours to fix and test that spot, and all the time he was talking about how he'd get through the crevice if he found the cave opening out beyond it.

Afterwards we tuned in to Radio Athens and listened to the English news broadcast. Florrie had gone to bed and we were alone in the wheelhouse, a drink in our hands and the announcer telling of gun duels across the Suez Canal, air strikes and Cairo in an uproar of militant demonstration. The Security Council of the United Nations was meeting in the morning. 'Florrie used to get tracts from an outfit called the British

Israelites,' Bert said as he switched the radio off. 'That was when we were in Great Yarmouth. Bloody queer stuff, too; prophecies based on the pyramids and the Bible, that sort of thing. Didn't go for it myself, but one thing I remember— they were convinced Armageddon would start in the Middle East.' He raised his drink, his battered face creased in a smile. 'It's times like this I'm glad I'm just a simple bloke with a boat of my own and things to occupy my mind. Give me a cave to explore or a bit of engineering to do and I don't give a damn whether the human race is hell-bent on self-destruction or not. There's so much in the world, why the hell aren't we content with what we've got? We go to the moon. Space platforms next. And yet we can't sort out a little matter like the Jews and the Arabs living together. And right here beneath our keel a whole underwater world, virtually unexplored, full of marvels and so bloody beautiful. Makes you sick, don't it?'

That was the longest speech I had heard him make in the two months I had been with him. 'Well, to hell with the human race!' He grinned and downed his drink. We went to bed then. Tomorrow they would dig out my father's body, and then I'd have to bury it again and we'd sail for Pantelleria. I lay in my bunk, sleepless, thinking about the future, and about Sonia. A new dimension. I'd never had to think about anybody but myself before.

2

WE WERE UP at seven next morning, and after tea and a cigarette, began winching in the anchor chain. A boat put out from the quay, and by the time we had got the anchor stowed, Zavelas was alongside with Kotiadis. 'You do not mind if I come with you?' He climbed on board, smiling politely. The patrol boat had returned to Levkas and he was taking no chances.

The day was overcast, hot and very humid, the sea a sheet of glass. Bert and I took it in turns to go below for breakfast. Kotiadis had coffee, nothing else, and he didn't talk much, his eyes watching us warily. By eight forty-five we were in the Meganisi Channel, and as I wolfed my bacon and eggs, I wondered what he'd do if we continued straight through it, heading for the open sea. He came on deck with me as the engine slowed and we coasted in to the shore below the brown gash of the overhang. A boat lay in the gut, nobody in it and no sign of life on the rocks above. 'They are working in the cave,' Kotiadis said. 'Today we discover the truth.'

I turned on him angrily. 'You won't be satisfied till you see his body, will you?'

He looked at me, his eyes hooded against the cloud-glare. 'No. The evidence of my own eyes—that is important in my business.'

Bert was manoeuvring close in, positioning *Coromandel* over the shelf to the south of the gut. I dropped the kedge over the stern and then, after taking the bow warp ashore in the dinghy and making it fast to the rock it had been looped over the previous day, Kotiadis and I hauled her in close while Bert paid out astern. When everything was fast, *Coromandel* was lying as before, bows-on to the shore with lines out fore and aft. Moored in this way, she was broadside to the direction of the channel and this had a bearing on what happened later.

'Don't be too long,' Bert said as I got into the dinghy with Kotiadis. 'Conditions are ideal and it may not last.' His mind was set on the dive he had planned. It was a tricky one and Florrie had very sensibly insisted that he wait till I was back on board.

'I'll be right back,' I told him. 'They're not likely to have discovered anything yet.'

But I was wrong there. The three of them had been working since first light, and when we reached the cave, Holroyd met us, stripped to the waist, his pale, almost hairless torso glistening with sweat. 'I think we're almost there.' He said it flatly, but there was a gleam of excitement in his eyes as he set the rock fragments he was carrying down on the pile, examining them almost automatically before going back into the darkness of the cave.

Kotiadis was not interested in prehistoric caves and he had clearly mistaken the gleam in the Professor's eyes. 'You have found Dr Van der Voort's body?'

Holroyd turned and stared at him. Then he laughed, an extraordinary, almost macabre sound. 'There is no body,' he said. And I realized that the man was under extreme nervous tension, the laugh a sort of release. 'Come on in. I'll show you.'

Cartwright and Winters stopped work as we reached the fall. They had progressed another two yards or more since dawn. 'Look at this.' Holroyd picked up the pressure lamp, which had been placed to illuminate the face of the fall, and held it up. 'See the way the roof rises at that point? Didn't notice it yesterday—too intent on clearing the rubble.'

'I did point it out,' Cartwright said diffidently.

'But without drawing the obvious conclusion.' Holroyd turned to Kotiadis. 'You want to know what happened to Van der Voort. The answer is there. You can see the line of the old fall, and there, where the roof lifts up, all this section —that's the new cave-in.'

Kotiadis lit a cigarette, the flame of his lighter illuminating his face, hard and uncomprehending. 'I do not understand. Where is Dr Van der Voort?'

Holroyd swung the lamp close to the rock fall. 'In there,' he said. And he added, 'Show them, Alec.'

Cartwright reached up, the crowbar in his hand, inserting the point of it into a dark gap they had opened up near the roof. The crowbar went in without meeting any resistance. 'Another hour,' Holroyd said, 'and we'll be through the rock fall, into the gallery beyond.'

'And you think Dr Van der Voort is there?' Kotiadis asked. 'Where else could he be?'

But Kotiadis was not convinced. 'Why does he not call out?'

Holroyd shrugged. 'There are several possibilities. This is a sea cave. It may go in a long way. There may be other galleries, galleries on different levels even. Or we may find there has been another fall further in. As I see it, Van der Voort broke through the old fall some time during the twenty-four hours between this young man seeing him and my arrival here yesterday morning. There was that earth tremor, you remember. That would account for the new fall, and if he were in there, exploring the galleries at the time, then he would have been trapped.'

'If he is trapped, then he must wish to get out,' Kotiadis said, his cigarette glowing in the half-darkness. 'Sound in a tunnel is very loud.' He moved to where Cartwright stood, standing on tiptoe, his face close to the crowbar. 'Dr Van der Voort!' he shouted. And then again, listening intently after each call. 'You see. He does not answer.'

'As I say, there may be another fall. He may be injured, or possibly suffering from lack of air. He may be unconscious, even dead.' The way Holroyd said it I thought he hoped it would be the latter.

These buggers talking, arguing about it. 'We're wasting time,' I said, and seizing hold of the crowbar, I began to attack the remnants of the fall. No need now to carry the rubble out. I just prised the rocks loose and thrust them behind me, working with a desperate, frenzied speed. If he were injured, or lying in a coma, half-asphyxiated, the sooner we got to him the better. The others responded to my urgency, even Kotiadis. The rocks and rubble flew, dust hanging in a choking cloud.

I had started at the point where Cartwright had thrust the crowbar through, hoping for a quick breakthrough. But the roof here was so badly fragmented that as fast as I cleared the rubble supporting it, fresh falls occurred. It meant prising all loose material out until I reached more solid rock, and this took time. In fact, it was about half an hour before I had opened up a safe gap into which I could work my head and shoulders. With the torch I had brought with me held out at arm's length, I could just see through the dust an open gallery beyond, and at the extreme limit of the torch's beam the cave seemed to narrow. But whether it was the end of it or another fall I could not be sure. I stayed wedged in the gap for a while, calling out to him, but there was no answer, and in the end I crawled back and Hans took my place.

The dust was very thick now, for Zavelas had arrived with Sonia and three extra men who were already at work trundling the rubble out in a wheelbarrow. 'What could you see?' Holroyd asked. 'Is the gallery clear?'

'For about twenty yards.' I was feeling exhausted, my shirt sticking to me, heavy with rock dust. 'After that I'm not sure. Maybe another fall.'

'And no sign of Dr Van der Voort?' Kotiadis's voice was barely audible against the noise of rubble being shifted, his figure a dim outline in the dust-hazed cavern.

I shook my head. 'None.' I felt defeated, drained.

A hand touched mine, Sonia's head in outline against the glow of light from the entrance. 'Come outside for a moment. You're wet through.' She had sensed my mood. 'The fresh air will do you good.'

But there was no fresh air, only heat and a heavy, louring atmosphere, a sultry world, the clouds hanging low, a blanket of humidity. 'What do you think has happened to him?'

'How the hell do I know?' He was either dead, or else he had gone deeper into the cave. 'He may be shut in behind another rock fall.' It was the best one could hope. 'Why didn't the old fool wait till I returned? He must have known it was dangerous.'

'He wouldn't think of that. Like my brother and Alec—Professor Holroyd, too—they don't think of danger when they feel themselves to be on the threshold of an important discovery.'

'No, I suppose not.' I was thinking that Holroyd didn't care whether the old man was alive or dead. All he was interested in was the cave. And Kotiadis—all he wanted was a body to satisfy his superiors that the dangerous agent of his Communist-obsessed imagination was accounted for. 'I'm going back now,' I said. I wanted to be there when they broke through into the gallery beyond.

But it was another half hour before they had opened up a gap large enough and safe enough for a man to crawl in. Cartwright was at the face then so that he was the first through, calling to us that he could see the end of the cave. 'Nobody here, I'm afraid.' His voice came to us as a resonant whisper running through the rock.

Holroyd had shouldered his way through the Greeks and had his head and shoulders in the gap. 'Have a look at the walls, Alec.' His voice was muffled, his broad buttocks almost filling the gap, and the distant whisper answered that there were traces of *gravures*, another rhinoceros, more reindeer.

By then I was on the rubble of the fall, right behind Holroyd, tugging at his shirt-tails. 'To hell with your bloody scratchings,' I shouted. 'Either go on in or let me pass.'

I could feel him hesitating. The gap was barely wide enough for his bulky body. But then his legs moved and he began to crawl through. I followed him, the rubble loose and jagged against my chest. Dust clouded the beam of my torch as we slithered down the rubble on the far side. And then we were on the packed dirt floor of the cave and could stand upright. Ahead of us the roof slanted down until it met the floor about thirty paces from us. No sign of Cartwright. And then Holroyd moved and the beam of my torch showed the side tunnel, a black, gaping hole. 'Are you there, Alec?' Holroyd's voice boomed in the confines of the cavern. A whisper answered us from the bowels of the earth: 'Down here. There's a sort of chute. A blow-hole I think. But go carefully. It slopes down quite steeply.'

I went in then, Holroyd following, both of us bent almost double. The angle of descent was about twenty degrees, the floor brown dirt, packed hard, walls and roof smooth, hollowed out by water. And then suddenly I could see the end, the roof coming down, the floor falling away into black shadow. I crawled past Cartwright on my hands and knees, and where the tunnel fell away, I lay prone, probing down with my torch. It certainly looked like a blow-hole, the rock walls smoothed by the pressure of air and water and almost circular in shape, like a pipe angling down very steeply. I couldn't see the end of it because it curved away to the left.

Holroyd crawled up alongside me, his breathing heavy in the still air of the tunnel. 'We'll need a rope to get down there.'

'Yes,' I said, knowing that my father hadn't a rope. It wouldn't be difficult to get down the pipe, breaking your descent with your back against one wall, your feet braced against the other. But to climb back up again would be impossible. I was trying to reconstruct in my mind what had happened.

I heard the rattle of matches in a box and Holroyd struck one, a sudden, blinding flare, and then the flame burning steady without a flicker of movement. 'No air current.'

'It probably finishes below sea level.' If Bert were right about that cave, then this was probably the vent for the air pressure caused by storm waves in the channel.

'He must have been desperate to go down there.'

And Cartwright's voice behind us said, 'He had no alternative.'

That was true, if he had wanted to escape. But I knew that

what had driven him to explore that blow-hole was his obsession with the scratched drawings of early man, his hope of finding cave paintings. He would have gone down it whilst the light of his acetylene lamp was still bright. He would be in darkness now.

'Van der Voort!' Holroyd had inched himself forward, his hands cupped to his mouth. 'Dr Van der Voort!' The North Country accent boomed in the shaft. We listened intently for the faintest sound. But there was no answer, not the smallest whisper of a reply. 'It sounds deep.'

'We're still at least a hundred and fifty feet above sea level,' I said.

'Aye. Just what I was thinking. And if it's water down there, then I'm afraid there's not much hope.' He had moved back and was turning himself round. Facing Cartwright, he said, 'I suppose that light nylon of ours is with the Land-Rover?'

'We've plenty of rope on board,' I told him.

'Then the sooner we have it, the sooner we'll know what's down there.' He was already moving back up the tunnel.

Daylight and the sight of sea and sky was a welcome relief after the claustrophobic confines of that cave. Sonia came with me back to the boat, her last hopes pinned to Bert's dive. He was waiting for us, pacing impatiently up and down the deck. 'Have you found him?' And when I shook my head, he said, 'Then what the hell have you been up to all this time? I warned you conditions might not stay like this.'

'Well, they have,' I snapped; no breath of air and the boat riding to her reflection, as still as if she were moored in a dock. 'We want about fifty fathoms of rope, that's all. I'll take it to them and then I'll be right back.' And I explained what it was for.

'So you think he's still alive?'

'I know he is,' Sonia's voice was intensely determined.

'There's a chance,' I said, and we looked out the rope. It was under the life jackets in a deck locker, sixty fathoms coiled on a light wooden drum, and I rowed across with it while Sonia stayed to help Bert get started on his dive. Hans had come down to the gut to collect the rope. I handed it to him and backed the dinghy out, and as soon as he saw me coming back Bert climbed over the side on to the ladder. He looked big and ungainly with his flippers and the cylinder on his back, his stomach bulging where the belt carrying the weights caused the flesh to sag. He wasn't wearing his wet suit for fear of snagging it on the rocks. I saw him slip his mask down over his eyes, settle the mouthpiece in place, and then Florrie passed him the spot, and with a wave in my direction, he flipped backwards to disappear under the oil-flat surface of the sea. Before I was halfway back to *Coromandel* the line of his bubbles passed me headed for the shore.

Sonia took the painter, and as I swung my leg over the low bulwarks Florrie came out of the wheelhouse. 'Bert said to tell you the engine's all set to go if you need it.'

I looked at her. 'Why should I?'

'I don't know.' Her face looked worried, lines of strain showing at the corners of the eyes. 'He's been in a state about this dive all morning. It was the waiting, I think—when you didn't come back for so long. It made him nervous.'

I looked up at the sky and south to the open sea, a weather check that was so automatic, so routine that I was barely conscious of it. I was thinking of the blow-hole, the rock pipe twisting into the bowels of the earth with one of them slithering down it, the rope taut around his waist, and of Bert, deep underwater, following the beam of his spotlight into the cave's darkness. One of them should be able to produce the answer. An hour at most and we should know for certain.

I went into the wheelhouse and got the glasses. From our mooring the platform below the overhang was just visible. If they found him, they'd try to hail me from there. There was nobody visible at the moment. Sweat dripped into my eyes. The heat was heavier than ever. I wiped my face, envying Bert in the cool depths. 'Would you like some coffee?' Florrie asked.

I shook my head.

'It's iced. I've had it in the fridge since breakfast.'

Iced coffee! I nodded. 'Please.'

'I'll get it.' Sonia left us quickly.

Florrie caught my eye. 'She needs to keep herself occupied.' And she added, quietly, 'So do I. But there's nothing to be done, is there? Just wait.'

'He's a bloody good diver,' I said.

She nodded.

'Then what are you worrying about?'

She gave an exaggerated shrug. 'It's the heat, I suppose. If we were in Malta I'd say it was sirocco weather.'

The hot wind from the Sahara sucking up humidity as it crossed the sea. I nodded and raised the glasses. I had seen a movement on the platform. It was Kotiadis, pacing up and down, smoking a cigarette. Zavelas appeared and they talked together for a moment, standing with their faces turned towards me. Then Kotiadis nodded and they came on to the rock path, descending quickly towards the gut. A few minutes later Zavelas's boat shot out into the channel, the hornet noise of its outboard fading rapidly in the thick air as it headed north.

Sonia arrived with the coffee. It was ice-cold, black and sweet, and we drank it waiting in the sultry heat of the open deck. Florrie glanced at her watch as she put her glass down. 'He's been gone a long time.'

'How long?' She always kept a check on the time he was down.

'Twelve and a quarter minutes.'

'Stop fussing, you old hen,' I said. It was extraordinary how possessive she was. She could call him a failure, spit in his face, cuckold him even, but she couldn't do without him—couldn't bear him out of her sight.

'I'm not an old hen.' She was smiling, warmth in her eyes, a fondness. 'A young one, perhaps.' She giggled. And then, suddenly serious again, 'Bert's a cautious type. You can't have failed to notice that.' An impish gleam in her eyes now. 'Not like you. He likes to weigh things up, mull over every problem. Most things he thinks over so long somebody else has to make up his mind for him. But not when he's diving. He doesn't think under water; he just reacts. He's reckless as hell.' There was a note of pride in her voice and I glanced at Sonia, wondering if she would behave with such extraordinary inconsistency.

'He's got just over an hour of diving time in that tank, and that's not allowing for the time he might be above water exploring inside the cave.'

She nodded. 'I know all that. But I still worry.'

Time passed slowly, the three of us sitting around on the foredeck, no sun, the air thick, and its thickness plucking at our nerves. Nobody hailed us from the area of the overhang. There was nobody on the platform and no news. Bert had started his dive at 11.17. Before half an hour was up, Florrie was looking uneasily at her watch. By midday she was voicing her anxiety. I was getting worried, too, wishing I had insisted on going down the blow-hole myself, anything rather than sit here doing nothing.

'He's only three minutes' air left.' Florrie's voice was taut.

Once again I reminded her that inside the cave he probably wouldn't need his aqualung. But I knew it didn t satisfy her. She was standing up now, leaning against the wheelhouse, the spare diving watch clumsy on her slender wrist as she stared at the sweep hand ticking off the seconds, occasionally stealing a quick glance at the rocks. 'Paul. I think you should go and see what's happened.'

'He wanted me here on board.'

'I know that, but he's been a long time. Too long.' Her voice was urgent, the dark eyes suddenly pleading. 'You've been down twice with him. You know how to do it.'

'I think so.' By then some of her anxiety had rubbed off on me. 'I'll get the gear up, anyway,' I said reluctantly.

It was whilst I was below in the workshop that I felt the slight movement, *Coromandel* coming alive, rocking gently at her moorings. And then, when I was coming up with the spare diving equipment, Sonia's voice called to me. 'There's somebody on the rocks, hailing us.' I dumped the cylinder on the wheelhouse floor and seized the glasses. It was Vassilios. He was pointing towards the open sea. And then he was leaping down the rocks.

I turned, moving quickly to the port side. A dark line showed in the sticky haze, and beyond it, towards Ithaca, the sea white with broken water. My reaction was immediate, instinctive. I reached for the engine switch, turned it on, and then pressed the starter button. The big diesel thudded into life.

'No! No, Paul!' Florrie was screaming at me. 'You can't leave him.' But then the black line reached us and the wind hit, a wild howl in the rigging. The ship heeled. A wave caught us and she lifted at the bow like a horse rearing and snubbed on the warp with a jar that nearly knocked me off my feet. I dived out of the wheelhouse, fighting the sloping deck and the weight of the wind to throw off the bow warp. Florrie was there before me. 'Mind your hands!' Released, the warp took charge, smoking as the turns whipped across the cleat, the wood charring.

White water on the shelf now and all along the shore rocks, and the boat swinging stern-on to the wind. But still too close. Much too close. The noise of the sea and the rocks, a great cacophony of sound like the roar of rapids made that clear. 'I'll let go aft,' I shouted at Florrie. 'You take the helm. Head for the centre of the channel.' I saw her eyes wide, her mouth agape, and then, thank God, she headed for the wheelhouse. Sonia was already crouched over the anchor warp when I reached the stern. 'It's jammed,' she shouted.

I thrust her hands away, not gently. The nylon line was stretched so taut it looked no thicker than a piece of heavy string. 'Have to cut it,' I shouted in her ear and ran for the diver's knife that was amongst the gear I had lugged into the wheelhouse. Just the sharp edge of it on the stretched nylon and it stranded and zinged away over the stern like a broken violin string. And *Coromandel*, released, went roaring up the channel with the wind. Florrie tried to bring her round, but the waves, beating back from the Meganisi shore, knocked her head off, and the wind held her. I tried myself, but it was no good. And anyway it didn't matter. Even if we could have got her round, we could never have stayed there, stemming the storm, for the whole channel was rapidly becoming a maelstrom as the waves, piling in against the narrowing rock walls, were flung back to meet in chaos in the middle. I piled on power and ran for the north end of the island, where the down-draughts blattered at us, the whole ship shivering; but here at least the sea was flat, close under the lee of the cliffs.

By the time we were anchored in Port Vathy, Florrie was in a state of shock, moments of hysteria alternating with long periods in which she just sat, keening quietly to herself, her eyes staring into space. She was convinced Bert was dead, and having seen the mill-race running through the channel, I didn't rate his chances of survival very high, particularly as the wind didn't start to ease for a good four hours. By nightfall it had gone completely, everything still and the sky clear.

But long before that I had weighed anchor and tucked the

ship in under the cliffs west of Spiglia, within sight of the channel, waiting for the sea to moderate. Shortly after 17.00 hours I poked our bows round the corner. There was still a steep sea running, but with the wind taking off it was lessening rapidly. As we came abreast of Tiglia a boat put out from the shallows behind the island—Vassilios waving to us frantically.

Florrie grabbed the glasses. 'He's pointing back to the cove. It's Bert. I'm sure it's Bert.' She was laughing, almost crying, as I swung the wheel to port. I caught Sonia's eye, both of us wondering how she'd take it if we found him dead there on the beach. Broadside to the waves the boat rolled wildly, and then we came under the lee of Tiglia and Vassilios was alongside, shouting excitedly, a flood of Greek lost in the din of the engine.

'*Livas*,' Sonia said. 'He keeps on repeating the word *livas*. I don't understand what he means.'

Vassilios was scrambling on board. Florrie, crouched by the bulwarks, bulky in her scarlet oilskins, took the painter. He said something to her and then ran for'ard, barefoot on the spray-wet deck. 'It's Bert,' she called, her face white. 'He'll guide you in and handle the anchor.' And she disappeared aft to make fast the painter.

He took us close in to the island and let go the anchor in a patch of still water, the echo-sounder showing barely three feet under our keel, pale sand and the rocks of the island towering above our mast. Bert's aqualung cylinder lay on the sloping sand of the cove; his flippers, too—a lonely, tragic pile of gear.

Vassilios came aft as Florrie brought his boat alongside. He spoke to her, quickly, urgently, and her face cleared. 'He's all right.' She sat down suddenly on the rail capping, half laughing, half crying, relief flooding through her. 'Wounded, he says. I think his arm is broken. But he's alive.' And she added, 'He was caught inside the cave by the *livas*. He swam all the way across the channel—under water with a broken arm. Isn't that wonderful!' She was a bundle of emotion, pride and excitement shining in her eyes.

Vassilios had made him as comfortable as he could in the lee of some rocks at the back of the cove. When we reached him, the excitement had gone from Florrie's eyes, in its place love and a great tenderness. She was like a mother with him then as we carried him down to the boat and ferried him across to *Coromandel*.

He was in considerable pain, the bone of his left forearm broken between wrist and elbow and showing white through the raw, bruised flesh. He'd lost a lot of blood and his face was pallid under the dark suntan. But he was conscious and whilst I got the morphine ampoule out of the medicine chest, he gritted his teeth and made an effort to tell me what had happened to him down there in that flooded cave.

He had arrived off the crevice entrance at 11.21. Depth 38 feet. The spotlight showed the crevice continuing, no block, and it seemed to widen out about five or six yards in. He described the entrance for me in detail, so that I could find it again, he said. The gap below the fallen slab was barely two feet high, and after scraping his cylinder and nearly ripping his air pipe on a snag, he had turned on his side. About two yards in he had been forced to turn into the normal position, and a little further in, the rock cleared from above him and he was able to use his flippers. A few more yards and the spot showed the walls receding on either side. He appeared to have entered a big cavern. The depth gauge showed 36 feet. Following a bearing of 240°, which was roughly the direction in which the entrance had run, he swam across the cave and was brought up by a solid wall of rock on the far side. The distance across he reckoned at about 20-25 yards. With no sign of any continuing tunnel, he had then circled the walls, maintaining a depth of between 35 and 40 feet.

'I thought I'd see what the height of it was then,' he said, holding his right arm out so that I could roll his sleeve back to make the injection. 'I hit the roof about fifteen to twenty feet up and that's when I found the continuing gallery, a gaping hole slanting up quite steeply.' He sucked in his breath as I jabbed the needle into his flesh none too skilfully. 'Then I was out into another sort of expansion chamber, the water obscured by sediment and my gauge reading virtually nil. In fact, my head came out of the water almost immediately. It was quite a big cavern, shaped like a lozenge, with continuing galleries at each end and a hole in the roof, quite a small hole with a rope hanging down from it.'

'Was that the bottom end of the blow-hole?'

He nodded. 'Looked like the rope we lent them—nylon, you see, and the same size, the end of it trailing in the water.'

'Did you call to them?'

'Yes, but I didn't get any answer. And there was nobody in the cave that I could see, which didn't surprise me—you could come down the rope easily enough, but getting back up again would have been bloody near impossible.'

'Too high?'

'No, it wasn't that. About ten or twelve feet, that's all. But the blow-hole was sloping, so that the rope lay flush against a smooth lip of rock. You'd never get your fingers round it, not with the whole weight of your body dragging on the rope.'

'They could have knotted it at intervals; or simply tied it round their body and been hauled up.'

'Well, they hadn't done either.' He said it irritably, his voice a little weaker. 'But there was somebody down there.'

'Who was it? Did you see him?'

'No, I didn't see anybody.'

'Then how do you know somebody was there?'

'I just felt it. The way you sense when there's a shark around. A sort of presence.'

The morphine was taking effect much quicker than I had expected, his eyes drooping, his voice tailing off. 'And then the spotlight, you see. I'd swum to the western end. At that end the floor of the cave rose out of the water in a dark curve like the back of a whale. Very slimy. But I managed to climb out and up to the ledge leading to the gallery. It was low. Sloping up in a curve. I put the spot down and got the cylinder off my back. I was unfastening my belt. I didn't want weights or flippers hampering me as I clambered around in that gallery. And then the spotlight shifted. I grabbed at it and the beam swung wildly as my flippers slid from under me. That's when I fell. I fell about six feet—into darkness.' He was drowsy now, his voice fading. 'No spotlight. It had gone. I swear it had been switched off.' His words were slurring, his head beginning to loll.

'Somebody took it—is that what you mean?'

He nodded vaguely. 'You don't believe me. . . .'

227

'You hit your head. Everything went black.' It was the only possible explanation.

'Of course. Knocked out. And then the surge.' His head dropped. 'Scared me. That's what scared me. And the body.'

'What body?'

'In the water . . . something . . . it touched me.'

'My father? Was it my father?'

'Don't know. Dark, you see, and the surge and this bloody arm.' His voice trailed off. 'No light. I was a long time—getting the cylinder back on—then feeling my way—remembering . . .' His eyes closed.

Florrie's hand touched his brow, smoothing out the grooved lines. 'He's out of pain, now?' I nodded and went back up to the wheelhouse and started the engine. We got the anchor up and then I backed her out of the shallows and turned her bows to the north.

'Where are you making for?' Sonia asked. 'Levkas? There's sure to be a doctor at Levkas.'

'No, Vathy,' I said. 'I want a word with Kotiadis.' Bert could have imagined it. He'd been scared and half dazed with pain. But somebody had to be informed. 'He'll tell us where to find a doctor.'

Vassilios joined us in the wheelhouse. The same dirty T-vest, the same frayed khaki shorts. I was at the wheel, thinking of the old man. A body, Bert had said. But he could have imagined it. And the spotlight? Had he imagined that, too? It could have slipped. But some instinct told me that it hadn't slipped, that the presence he had sensed was real. I set the engine controls to maximum revs. It was a lurid evening, shafts of sunlight slanting on the water, the underbellies of the clouds black and louring, and my mind darkened by the fear of tragedy.

At Vathy, Kotiadis promised to see Holroyd himself as soon as conditions made it possible for him to get down the channel. Meantime, he advised us to call in at Skropio on our way to Levkas in the hope of finding a doctor there. This was fortunate, for among the guests on that millionaire's island we found an eminent Athens surgeon. He not only set Bert's broken arm, but insisted that he and Florrie stay at the villa till he had recovered from the shock and the mild concussion.

'You'd better take *Coromandel*,' Florrie said. 'I'm sure Bert would agree.' I would have taken it anyway. I think she knew that. This was after she had come back for the clothes they needed, the varnished launch alongside and a car waiting for her on the jetty. There followed a long list of instructions about the food on board and the need to turn off the gas to the galley stove, and then she was in the launch and with a quick wave she was whisked away towards the pine-dark loom of the island.

The time was 21.34 by the wheelhouse clock, and ten minutes later we had the anchor up and were motoring out of the little natural harbour, the resin scent of the pines following us until we were into the open water of Port Drepano.

It was the first time we had had the ship to ourselves. Such an opportunity for two people in love, and all we did was hold each other's hand and peer into the night, watching for Elia light on the north-east corner of Meganisi, which would enable us to clear the shoals between Skropio and Port Vathy. And at Vathy . . . if the news were good, then we could relax here on board, the ship to ourselves, nobody else. And suddenly I was thinking of Florrie.

But Sonia wasn't like Florrie. She wasn't like any girl I'd had before. And even while I was imagining how it would be, I knew that when it did happen, it would somehow be entirely different.

'If there's no news . . .' her fingers tightened on mine. 'You'll try to get in underwater—the dive Bert did?'

Our minds had been on entirely different tracks. 'There's the rope,' I said. 'They should have got him out by now.'

But some intuitive sense seemed to warn her it wouldn't be as simple as that. She wanted to know how much practice I had had, how expert I was. I didn't tell her I'd only had two dives under Bert's instructions. The deepest I'd gone was twenty feet and that in the crystal clear water of the Aegean. 'Bert had bad luck, that's all,' I said. No point in two of us being scared.

It was almost midnight when we finally reached Port Vathy, the village in darkness, not a light to be seen anywhere. As soon as the anchor was down, we went ashore in the dinghy. Zavelas had seen us coming in and he met us on the quay. His face was grave. Part of the roof of the main cave had collapsed.

Vassilios had just brought the news. 'He says it could take two days, maybe more, to clear the fall, and they will need timber to support the roof.' It had collapsed at the point where we had broken through the earlier fall.

'Anybody hurt?' I asked.

'Vassilios didn't say, so I guess not.' He glanced at Sonia. 'Your brother's okay. He was out in the open with the ánghlos constructing a ladder of rope.'

'Which ánghlos?' I asked. 'Cartwright?'

'Né—Cartwright.'

'What about Holroyd?'

'Professor Holerod is missing. Also a Greek man from Spiglia—Thomasis.'

'You mean they're trapped the other side of the fall?'

'I guess so. But no worry. Kotiadis is there and in the morning we will take timber over to support the roof. Also a caique leaves here for Levkas an hour ago with instructions for the patrol boat to come here with more timber.' A hairy hand gripped my arm. 'Don't you worry. Two days and we have them out. Okay? That's not too much. Just time to decide if there is a God or not, eh?' And he patted my shoulder, smiling gently. 'Tomorrow we load timber and begin to dig. Maybe we're inside in one day. And there is a friend of yours arrived by caique tonight—the old guy who is with you when you first come.'

'Dr Gilmore?'

'Yeah, that's him. He's gone to sleep with the Pappas at his house.'

'Is he all right?' Sonia asked.

'Sure, he's okay. I guess he's tougher than he looks. Two days in a caique—that's a long time for a man his age.' And he added, 'You go and see him in the morning. I tell him what happens, but I think he is too tired to understand. He kept shaking his head and saying the Professor and Dr Van der Voort should not be together. It seemed to worry him that Professor Holerod was trapped inside the cave with the Doctor.'

It worried me, too, and Sonia's face was a white mask in the darkness. But at least she hadn't heard Bert's rambling reference to a body.

We arranged that the baulks of timber to shore up the roof would be ferried out to *Coromandel* first thing in the morning, and then Zavelas went off to his house. Sonia went with him, leaving me to pull back to *Coromandel* on my own. It wasn't at all what I had planned.

I made the dinghy fast to the cleat aft and then relieved myself by the light of the stars. The night was soft and very still, the water brilliantly phosphorescent. It was the first time I had had the ship to myself, and when I went below the saloon seemed strangely empty. Complete and utter silence enveloped me. I poured myself a brandy and sat for a moment thinking about the cave with its unstable roof, Holroyd and the Greek marooned in the dark by that new fall.

A faint buzzing invaded the silence. Leaning my head back I could hear it vibrating in the hull, gradually getting louder. An outboard.

I went up on deck. The sound came from the entrance to the inlet. And soon I could make out the dim, dark shape of the boat. It passed quite close, Vassilios bringing Kotiadis back. But though I hailed them, they held on for the quay, my voice drowned in the ugly band-saw noise of the engine. I went down into the workshop then and looked over Bert's diving equipment, noting that there were still two cylinders full, mentally checking over the routine.

It was almost one o'clock before I got to bed. It had been a long, exhausting day, and I was tired, too tired perhaps, for in spite of the brandy, my mind kept going over all the details, particularly the details of Bert's dive.

I was woken shortly after six-thirty by the bump of a boat alongside and the sound of Greek voices. The first baulk of timber had been dumped on deck by the time I had my shorts on and had reached the wheelhouse. It was a glorious day, the sun already warm and a slight haze shimmering on the water. The timber was rough, the Greeks none too gentle, and by the time I had seen to the stowing of it, Zavelas was alongside with Dr Gilmore.

He didn't look tired at all. Bright as a button, I thought, as I helped him aboard, while Sonia held the boat steady. 'I haven't kept you waiting, I hope.' He shook my hand, formal and dapper in his grey suit and panama hat. 'A beautiful morning.' He stood smiling and gazing round him. 'It's so nice to be on the water again. London was very hot—a heat wave. But I had a day at Wimbledon—some very good tennis, a superb men's four.' Sonia passed me his suitcase and a hand-grip. 'Book presents,' he said. 'That's why it's so heavy. I managed to get an excellent treatise on submarine archaeology for Mr Barrett. Do you think he'll like that?'

'I'm sure he will,' I murmured.

'Good, good. And there's a book by Holroyd. I thought it would interest you. Also a typescript of the paper he read. Most revealing.' And then, almost without pausing for breath, 'And I'm sorry to hear about Mr Barrett. Poor fellow. I was so looking forward to seeing him again. Is he in much pain?'

'He'll be all right,' I said.

Sonia swung her leg over the bulwark. 'Dr Gilmore. I think we should leave now.'

'Yes, yes, of course, my dear.' He smiled at me, that same quick, bird-like glance. 'I talk too much and you're in a hurry, naturally. But it is so nice seeing you again.'

She took him below and I started the engine, while the two Greeks, who had been stowing the timber, dealt with the anchor. Zavelas took them off, and as I headed up the inlet, Sonia poked her head up the saloon companionway. 'Paul. Have you had any breakfast?'

'It'll wait,' I told her. I wasn't all that hungry.

'No it won't, Not if you have to make that dive.' She was tense, excited, and it showed in her eyes. 'Coffee and eggs? I know there are eggs on board. I got them for Florrie myself —fresh laid and about the size of ping-pong balls.'

Soon the smell of coffee began to drift up from below. And then Gilmore came up into the wheelhouse, looking a little incongruous in pale seersucker trousers and a blue shirt decorated with crimson sea horses. 'I hope my rather strange apparel doesn't put you off your course.'

'Very suitable,' I said.

He smiled, a little self-consciously. 'One of my students—a very distinguished professor now—insisted on taking my wardrobe in hand. It was really quite fun—I think he enjoyed it.' He was silent for a moment, gazing at the bulk of Levkas straight ahead, his eyes crinkled at the glare. 'Now, I want to talk to you about your father and this man Holroyd. There may not be time after we get to the cave, so I'd better tell you briefly now.' He perched himself on the flap-seat at the side of the wheelhouse.

Quickly he ran over the situation as he had found it on his return to Cambridge. Holroyd had been entirely co-operative, submitting his specimens to the test called for by the committee, with only one proviso, that he was present throughout and that the bones and artefacts were never out of his sight. This the committee had regarded as reasonable, since he was not only being accused of pilfering another man's work, but also of faking the basis of his paper.

Gilmore had reached Cambridge on June 1, only two days before the decisive meeting of the committee. By then all the tests had been completed, and the results known. Without exception they had proved satisfactory. He gave me a short summary of the results, covering chronometric and relative dating, with reference to the geological structure in which they had been found, and finally the carbon-14 method. 'This last gave a date for all three skull fragments of around 27,000 years ago, and the teeth and bones were of the same period. They'd even passed the fluorine test, so that when I arrived, fellow members of the committee greeted me with a certain coolness, in some cases outright hostility. They were all, of course, considerably younger than I was, a fact that Holroyd had used to advantage, the implication being that my ideas were ante-diluvian and the doubts I had expressed about his discovery and theory due to senility.'

Sonia appeared with a tray, wafted into the wheelhouse by the smell of coffee. 'You might have waited. I want to hear it, too.' She poured the coffee, while he repeated what he had just told me. 'Well, if Professor Holroyd regards you as senile, he'll get a shock when he sees you in that shirt.'

'It wasn't just Holroyd. It was most of the Committee.' He was smiling, his arms folded, and so pleased he seemed to be hugging himself. 'Even Stefan thought I had gone too far. And Grauers made it clear that he doubted whether I had any evidence whatsoever to support my attack on such a dis-tinguished member of the academic world.'

We were off Spiglia then and Sonia took the wheel, while I

sat on the starboard flap-seat eating my breakfast and listening, fascinated, to Gilmore's account of the scene as the Investigating Committee gathered in the lecture room at Trinity College. Including Holroyd and himself, there were eight men and one woman present. The proceedings were not expected to take long, a mere formality to clear Holroyd's name. The specimens were laid out on the table before him.

'I must tell you,' Gilmore said, 'that his statement that the skull fragments had been found by himself and the two other members of the expedition, and that their discovery was not in any way connected with Pieter Van der Voort had been accepted, and for reasons that will become self-evident I did not challenge this.

'The proceedings were opened by Professor Grauers, a short statement of the reasons for forming an investigating committee. He then called upon me to reiterate the charges. "Or you may wish to withdraw them, in view of the rigorous tests which have been made?" I said I did not wish to withdraw anything, except the first charge of taking credit for another man's work. I then put the question to Holroyd again, asking him point-blank—had the discovery of the skull fragments been connected in any way with Dr Van der Voort? "The answer to that is No," he said, directing his reply, not to me, but to the Committee—Grauers, in particular. I suppose any man as politically astute as Holroyd learns to be a consummate liar. He said it categorically, and then, still facing the Committee and speaking in that bluff, honest, North Country voice of his, he said, "Van der Voort had been working in the area the previous year. This I have never tried to conceal from you, gentlemen. Owing to the circumstances, which you already know about, I had no opportunity of discussing it with him. As I have said before, the information which led me to the site was from a Greek source. He may have visited the site. In fact, I believe now that he did. But he failed entirely to recognize it for what it was. Instead—and this I learned subsequently—he concentrated on quite another site, not on the island of Meganisi, but in a bay known as Dessimo on Levkas".'

Gilmore smiled. 'A half truth, you see. So much more convincing. And they believed him. But to make it absolutely clear, I asked him whether, in that case, he took full responsi-

234

bility for the authenticity of the specimens. He was looking at me then, and I thought I saw a mounting flicker of doubt in his eyes. But by then he had committed himself too deeply. "Of course." And that was it. I had him then, provided I had guessed Pieter's intentions correctly'.

He paused, his eyes searching the wheelhouse. 'You haven't got a cigarette, have you?'

I found one for him and lit it. 'Silly of me, but I never carry them now. They're supposed to be bad for me.' He drew on it gratefully, holding it as usual between finger and thumb as though he had never smoked before in his life. 'Now, where was I?'

'Dr Van der Voort's intentions,' Sonia said. 'I don't quite understand. He couldn't have intended anything.'

'Oh, but he did, my dear. This was his revenge. He planned it, every move.' He was smiling gently to himself, as though enjoying some private joke, and his eyes were far away, back in that lecture room at Trinity. 'You remember I told you both about the Piltdown skull, how it had fooled everybody for years. And I also told you how Pieter had been caught faking the evidence. Piltdown had always had a fatal fascination for him. Now, unless my reading of human nature—his in particular—was quite inaccurate, he had done it again. But this time, he had rigged it so that the man who had made use of his work before, and was doing so again, would take the rap. At least, that was the supposition I was relying on when I reiterated my charges and accused Holroyd to his face of planting the skull fragments in that dig to substantiate a theory he had borrowed from another man.'

'But I don't see——' Sonia had turned to him, fascinated, her eyes bright. 'How could you be certain? How could you prove it?'

She was too excited to concentrate and I took the wheel from her, for we were close in under the cliffs, making the turn into the Meganisi Channel. Behind me I heard Gilmore say, 'That was what they wanted to know, all of them hostile. And I wasn't sure I could prove it. I was playing a hunch, nothing more. I had been just two days in the country and the experts had been working on those specimens for almost a week. With the whole Committee against me, even Stefan

Reitmayer, I wasn't going to play my hand until I had seen theirs. Everything depended, you see, on their not having used a Geiger-counter. I didn't think they had. Too simple for them. And anyway, too obvious. A man of Holroyd's standing, if he was salting a dig with fake specimens, wouldn't slip up on a thing that had bust the Piltdown hoax wide open. However, they had done a fluorine test. But in the main, Holroyd's case rested on the carbon-14 tests, which had given a similar dating for all his specimens. The Committee were prepared to accept this as conclusive evidence.'

'But it was, surely,' Sonia said. 'If they were all of the same date——'

'They could still be from different sites.'

'You mean Dr Van der Voort had deliberately collected together the fragments from different sites? I can't believe it. To be certain they'd stand up to tests, they'd all have had to be carbon-dated.'

'Precisely.' Gilmore was smiling happily.

'But he had no facilities for testing—either out here or in Amsterdam.' She stared at him. 'You mean they were from Russia?'

'Of course. All of them. Approximately the same date—27,000 BP. All with about the same fluorine content. And the site in which he buried them was right, too. But there had to be something, otherwise there was no point in his doing it. There had to be some simple way in which Holroyd could be discredited, and I was relying on my hunch that he would use Piltdown as his model.'

He paused, still smiling, almost hugging himself with enjoyment. 'They were sitting there, all of them looking at me, and I was thinking what an old fool I was, risking my own reputation for the sake of a man I'd only seen once since he'd been a student. There's no quarter in the academic world and to attack a man as influential as Holroyd was tantamount to suicide. I got up and went to the door, not saying a word. They probably thought I was walking out, defeated.' He gave a little chuckle and tossed the end of his cigarette out through the wheelhouse door into the sea. 'At least, that's what it looked like when I came back into the room with the young technician and the equipment I had borrowed from Geology.

They were all talking, and then suddenly they stopped and stared at me, and a sort of stunned silence gripped the room.'

I had cut down the revs and now he stood up so that he could see down the channel. 'That island must be Tiglia. That was the site of the dig. I remember now.' He reached absent-mindedly for the packet of cigarettes that I had left lying on the shelf above the instrument panel. 'If I'd gone ashore that day, I might have been the one to discover those skull fragments.'

'But you wouldn't have claimed it as your own discovery,' I said.

'No. And I suppose that's the difference.'

'But what happened?' Sonia demanded. 'You haven't told us what happened.'

He smiled. 'You want it all spelled out for you. Well, just what I'd expected. We didn't have to go beyond the skull fragments. The Cro-Magnon skull gave one count, the two Neanderthal-type skulls quite a different count. There was no argument. There couldn't be with the Geiger-counter clicking away, proving beyond any doubt that the two types of skull could not have come from the same dig. Of course, Holroyd started to try and bluster it out. But they were all sitting there, staring at him, dumbfounded at first, then accusingly, and the words just stuck in his throat. Finally he got to his feet and walked out, leaving the skulls lying there on the table. In a way, that was more damning than anything—his sudden complete lack of interest in them.'

'Has there been any public announcement?' I asked.

'No, no, my dear fellow, of course not. The Press were never in on it, and officially it will all be hushed up. But no doubt it will leak out. There's a lot of talk already. Though Holroyd hasn't yet resigned from any of the committees and other bodies he serves on, it will be the finish of him. Unless . . .' He paused to light the cigarette he had taken.

'Unless what?' I asked, for he was staring out through the windshield, his mind apparently on something else.

'He's a very clever talker, very convincing. A political, rather than an academic animal, and not to be underrated on that account. If he were to come up now with something spectacular——' He looked at me quickly, a darting glance. 'Last night—that ex-policeman—he said there was a rhinoceros drawn on the wall of this cave and that Holroyd was very excited about it.'

'There's a reindeer too,' Sonia said. 'And what looks like an elephant—just scratch marks, very faint.'

'And these *gravures* were discovered by Pieter Van der Voort, not by Holroyd?'

'Yes,' I said. And I told him how I had found my father working on the rock fall that night, his desperate urgency to break through into the cave beyond.

He nodded. 'It's what I suspected, that he was on to something of real importance. That's why I hurried out here, as soon as I knew Holroyd had left for Greece. I was afraid . . . He hesitated, staring at me, strangely agitated. 'However, this is an accident. An earth tremor, they tell me.' He shook his head. 'Something nobody could have foreseen. Nevertheless, if Pieter is dead, then Holroyd can reasonably claim . . .' He gave a little shrug. 'Well, we'll just have to hope for the best.'

We were past Tiglia then, the rock gut opening up and a boat lying there, the scar of the overhang just visible. I pointed it out to him and he shaded his eyes against the glare, staring at it, his interest quickening: 'A perfect site, very typical— provided, of course . . .' He moved to the wheelhouse door, looking back over the port quarter at the site on Meganisi below the rock pinnacle. 'Two of them, and both natural observation posts. Tell me, did your father say anything about the sea-level here—what it would have been like twenty thousand years ago?' And when I explained that all to the south of us, as far as the African shore, he believed to have been one vast plain, with Meganisi the western flank of a volcano, he nodded his head vigorously.

'You think that's possible?' I asked.

He smiled. 'Anything is possible. But proof—that's another matter. We know so little.' He was staring at the Meganisi shore. 'A volcano, you say.' His eyes gleamed, bird-like in the sun.

'He thought it might have erupted—a bigger eruption than Santorin.'

He nodded, gazing ahead to the distant shape of Ithaca. 'Fantastic! And the skull fragments, those bones he sent for dating—thirty thousand years ago at least.' And then, speaking quietly, as though to himself: 'Even as far back as that man knew how to knap or flake the hardest substances to produce sharp-cutting instruments—flint, for instance, and chert. And in volcanic regions, the brittle, black, glass-like substance we call obsidian. It's the oldest and most basic of all industries and a very good case has been made out recently for these primitive industrial centres—these city communities, you might call them, founded on the presence of a workable raw material—being the precursor of husbandry. It has put the whole conception of city centres much further back in time.' He had apparently a theory of his own that the cave artists were a product of these first city communities, a means of encouraging the hunters on whom they depended for bartering their products, and that it was the superior organization developed by Cro-Magnon Man that had destroyed the Neanderthals.

'A little far-fetched, perhaps,' he murmured. 'But something I would like to have discussed with Pieter, particularly if he has discovered the work of cave artists so close to an area that could have been rich in obsidian.' He shook his head, smiling to himself. 'All of scientific research into prehistory is a sort of jig-saw puzzle. Fitting facts to theories until the sum of all the facts establishes without doubt a complete and irrefutable picture.'

A small boat was moving out of the gut, coming towards us now. It was Vassilios, and Hans was in the bow, his blond hair immediately recognizable. He came aboard, while Vassilios took the bow warp out.

We off-loaded the timber by throwing it into the water, where Vassilios secured it with a rope for towing ashore. And while he helped me get it overboard, Hans told me what had happened inside the cave the previous day. With the borrowed rope tied around his waist, he had descended the blow-hole until he had reached the point where it entered the cavern in which Bert had surfaced. He confirmed that this cave was lozenge-shaped and that galleries entered it from either end; also that it seemed to be influenced by tidal variations or surge, since the walls and slopes of exposed rock were damp-looking and black with slime. After calling repeatedly without receiving any reply, he had untied the rope from about his waist and climbed back up the blow-hole to report to Holroyd.

I asked him whether he had left the end of the rope hanging down into the water and he said he had. Cartwright had wanted to go down then, but Holroyd had ruled that there was no point until they had some means by which they could be certain of climbing out of the cave after they had lowered themselves into it. Finally, it was decided to construct some sort of a rope ladder, and he and Cartwright had climbed back through the gap opened in the rock fall to do this. Holroyd had stayed on inside the cave to examine the walls for *gravures* and make rough drawings.

'Presumably he had a torch with him?'

'Yes. And the Greek stayed there to hold it for him.'

'What about the rope? Was the upper end secured to anything?'

'The crowbar. We had it wedged across the upper end of the blow-hole.'

I then asked him if he could remember the exact time of the roof collapse.

'Yes,' he said. 'As soon as I was told what had happened, I looked at my watch. I thought the time might be important. The fall occurred just before 11.30.'

'And how long since you had left Holroyd?'

'Oh, about a quarter of an hour, twenty minutes—something like that.'

Which meant that if Holroyd's urge to examine the cave was so great that he was willing to go down the rope on his own, he could have been into the lower galleries about the time Bert was starting to work his way into the underwater entrance.

Vassilios was waiting and Hans climbed down into the boat, Sonia calling to him to be careful. He grinned, mouthing a reply against the scream of the labouring outboard. Slowly the raft of timbers drew away from the side. There was nothing now to hold me back and I was suddenly trembling as I stood there by the bulwarks, staring at the beauty of that sun-bright scene, the mountains falling to the narrow channel, the shallows by Tiglia bright emerald against the sea's deep blue, and white clouds hanging like puffs of smoke over the mainland heights. A fish broke the surface, a gleam of silver gone in a flash, and up by Spiglia a lone cottage poked a white face

240

round a brown shoulder of rock. And above me the sun god riding high. All that beauty, and my mind six fathoms deep in the dark bowels of a sea-filled cave.

'Does that mean Holroyd has access to the gallery Pieter is in?' I turned to find Gilmore close behind me, peering at me with an intent bird-like expression. 'Is that what he meant?'

I thrust my hands behind me, forcing my mind to concentrate. 'He has access to where I think my father is. But that doesn't mean he's availed himself of it. Anyway, my father may be dead.'

Gilmore nodded. 'And that, of course, we won't know until they've cleared this roof fall and got Holroyd out. Unless, of course . . .' He hesitated, watching me speculatively, and I knew he was thinking of the underwater entrance. 'How long will they take, do you think, to get through the fall?'

'Zavelas said maybe tomorrow.'

Sonia was staring at me, her eyes wide, indignant with disbelief. 'You're not going to wait till then, surely. He's been down there three days already.'

'No, of course not. Only . . .' But I stopped there. I couldn't tell her about the body, and Bert could have imagined it. 'Give me a hand with the gear,' I said, but she had already turned into the wheelhouse to get it.

Gilmore had followed her, but in a moment he popped out again, smiling, a book in his hand. 'A present for you.' He held it out to me. *Homo Sapiens—Asia or Africa?* by Professor W. R. Holroyd. I stared at it, thinking the old boy had chosen one hell of a moment to present me with a book on anthropology by Holroyd. 'The book can wait,' he said as I took it from him. 'But I would like you to read what I have written on the flyleaf. Sonia has told me about this dive, that you hope to get into the cave by an underwater passage. If you succeed, I fear you may find yourself involved in tragedy.'

I stared at him, wondering what he meant. But he didn't say anything further and I opened the book. On the blank page at the beginning he had written: *For Paul Van der Voort: This book, which was published eighteen months ago, would appear to be largely based on your father's writings—the theory propounded in his unpublished work balanced against the arguments he used in* The Asian Origins of Homo Sapiens, *the second of his two books published in Russia and other Communist countries*. He had signed it—*Adrian Gilmore*.

'I'm afraid he may know about that book.'

'Yes,' I said, glancing idly through it. 'Yes, I think he does.' A piece of paper fell out, fluttering to the deck. I stooped and retrieved it, a brief cutting from a newspaper headed *Search for Embassy Official's Killer Switched to Continent*. D.T. Mar 28 had been pencilled against it. 'Dear me,' he said as I read it. 'I'm sorry. I quite forgot about that.'

I looked at him. 'You knew it referred to me?'

'Van der Voort is not a very common name—not in England, anyway.'

'But this is from the *Daily Telegraph* presumably, of March 28. It wasn't something you happened on by accident.'

'No. No, I'm afraid I was curious—I asked a young friend of mine to check the newspaper files for me.'

'I see.' I put the cutting back between the pages and closed the book. So Interpol had been informed. That meant that Kotiadis knew, had known probably since we had left for Samos, certainly since our return to Meganisi. Zavelas, too, I thought, remembering how he had watched me that first evening. 'Well, if I make a balls of this dive . . .' I laughed, an attempt to dispel the tension. 'Solve a lot of problems, wouldn't it?' But it wasn't Kotiadis that worried me, or any information about my background that had been passed on to Interpol. It was the dive I was scared of—the dive and what I might find down there. Trembling, I reached for the jacket of the wet suit Sonia was holding out to me and struggled into it. By the time I had zipped it up she had dumped the cylinder on the deck beside me. It was heavy, 72 cubic feet of air compressed to 2250 p.s.i., and the stem indicator showed that it was full. It should last me an hour if I controlled my rate of breathing —if I didn't panic in that cave entrance and start sucking in air like a locomotive. I held out my hand for the demand valve and she handed it to me, watching as I screwed it on and checked that it was working properly. Then she helped hoist the tank on to my back, passing the straps over my shoulders as I settled the weight and secured it in position. Watch, depth meter, diving knife, torch and mask; finally, the heavy lead-weighted belt. I was all set then, the mask pushed up on my forehead, the gum pad in my mouth. I cracked the valve and heard the air hiss as I drew a shallow, tentative breath. It was okay. Everything was okay. Except for my heart, which was thumping nervously as I thought about that cave.

Slowly I waddled backwards to the ladder. The whole outfit seemed to weigh a ton as I manœuvred myself outboard, wishing to God Bert was there, if not to dive with me, at least to give me moral support. Again I tested the air supply, checked the stem indicator. Tank full. Air coming easily. I started down the ladder. 'Good luck!' Sonia was wearing a bright artificial smile. I didn't say anything, thinking of all the women down through time who had seen men off into danger with that same bright smile. I pulled the mask down over my face, down over my eyes and nose, my teeth grinding on the gum pad teats as I began to breathe through the mouthpiece. I had no confidence, only a feeling of fear. And I was still afraid when I hit the water.

3

I HAD GONE IN backwards, both hands holding the mask to my face, the way Bert had taught me, the masts and their two faces whirling against the sky to vanish abruptly as the sea closed over my head. Then I turned over on to my belly in a froth of bubbles, hanging there in the water, blind and weightless now and sinking slowly as I exhaled, the beating of my heart seeming unnaturally loud. The froth of bubbles drifted away and the bottom leaped into vision, clear in the glass pane of the mask and looking nearer than the 18 fathoms in which we had anchored. It was rock and sand, with weed waving, and I was alone. Nobody else in all that wet world. The shape of the boat, etched in shadow, moved lazily with the weed, and the kedge warp was a pale line looping down to the anchor, which lay on its side like some forgotten toy.

I was still trembling, my heart pounding loud in my water-logged ears. Not because of the aqualung, the unfamiliarity of dependence on compressed air—I was already breathing gently and regularly. It was the dim buttressed shape of the under-water shore at the extreme edge of visibility, the knowledge that I had to penetrate into the interior of the rock, squeezing through a narrow hole into flooded galleries that had already nearly cost an experienced diver his life. The fear of that had been with me all night, had been building up throughout the morning.

I lay face downwards, my head back, staring ahead through the sunlit flecks that hung suspended like dust in the water to the dark wall that edged the shelf, trying to stop the trembling, to key my nerves to action. My left hand came out, an involuntary flipper movement to hold myself on an even keel, looking white and very close, the diving watch staring at me, the dial enormous against my wrist.

It was the sight of that watch that got me started. The movable dial had to be set. That was the first thing—the time check. I twisted the bevelled edge until the zero mark was on the minute hand. The time was 09.47. In theory the cylinder on my back contained at least 60 minutes of air, but only if I were careful and controlled my breathing the way an experienced diver would. That was what I was doing now, the periodic hiss of the demand valve as I took in short, shallow breaths, followed by the blatter of bubbles behind my head as I breathed out. But would I be so in command of my breathing inside that cave? I thought I had better work on the basis of minimum duration—30 minutes. That meant being out of the cave by 10.17. And something else I had to remember, not to hold my breath if I came up in a hurry. That way you could rupture your lungs as the pressure lessened and the compressed air in the lungs expanded.

I was still looking at the dial of my watch, magnified by the water, and the sight of the second hand sweeping slowly round the dial made me realize that time was passing and every minute spent hanging around was a minute of underwater time wasted. My reaction to that was immediate, a sort of reflex. I jack-knifed, diving down and heading for the shore, arms trailing at my side, my legs scissoring so that the flippers did the work and bubbles trailing away behind me as I exhaled to make depth.

A school of small-fry changed from dingy grey to a glitter of silver as they skittered away from me to reform like soldiers on parade beyond my reach, all facing me, motionless, watchful. A rock grew large in a sea of grass, a starfish flattened against it and somebody's discarded sandal lying forlorn and alien in this world of water. And everything about me silent, so that the hiss of air as I cracked the demand valve to breathe in was unnaturally loud. And every time I exhaled the rush of bubbles past my head sounded like the burbling wake of an outboard motor.

The silence and the loneliness pressed on my nerves and at that rock I turned to stare back. I could just see *Coromandel*'s hull, a dark whale shape bulging from the ceiling of my wet world. The depth meter on my right wrist showed 32 feet. Everything was deadened as the pressure built up on my eardrums. With thumb and forefinger pressed into the hollows of the mask, pinching my nose, I blew my ears clear. Instantly the noise of my breathing, the pops and crackles, the hiss of the demand valve, were preternaturally loud.

Reassured by the dim outline of the boat, I turned and flipper-trudged to the underwater cliffs, gliding weightless along great fissured rocks. Like flying buttresses, Bert had said. But it was the dark, gaping mouths of the fissures that held my gaze. I was thinking of octopuses and groupers big as sharks, my imagination filling the black cavities with all the monsters of the deep.

It was the loneliness, of course. In my two previous dives I had been following Bert. Not only had he been there to instruct me, to give me confidence, but he had kept ahead of me so that I had had him always in my field of vision, a fellow human being who was both nurse and companion. Now I had nobody, and I had to penetrate the deepest of those yawning fissures, negotiate a hanging slab of rock, and then find my way up through flooded caves and blow-holes.

I looked at my watch. Four and a half minutes gone already. I should have come in on a bearing, but I had forgotten the diving compass. I wasted time trudging north and had to turn back when I failed to find the fissure Bert had described in such detail. I reached it at 09.58 and hung there, motionless, off the black gut between two buttresses of rock. It was like the entrance to an ancient tomb, or the adit shaft of a drowned mine.

Through my mind flashed the things Bert had told me—the

sense of something lurking, his spotlight disappearing, the touch of a body on the surface water of that cavern. Imagination? And then I was thinking of the old man, locked up alone inside those cliffs for more than three days. That was enough in itself to drive a man mad—even a sane man with no knowledge of the prehistory of the place, the world these caves had known before a blasting of the earth's crust had brought the sea flooding in.

Thinking of the old man had one good effect, it overlaid my fear of lurking sea creatures with a deeper, more personal fear. I unhooked the torch from my belt, hung it by its strap to my wrist, and then, with a quick movement of my flippers, plunged head-first into the blackness of the gut. The rock walls closed in, the water skylight above my head a dull, greenish glimmer, but enough to dim the light of my torch.

The depth gauge read 38 feet.

And then the water sky disappeared. I was in black darkness, rock all round and the fallen slab blocking my path. The gap was a long gash barely two feet high, an ugly mouth with sea anemones lurking and the movement of nameless things in crevices and cracks. I could hear my heart pounding, and the hiss of the demand valve, the burp of my bubbles, were loud in the confines, resonant like the movements of some monstrous stomach.

I turned on my side and squirmed my way in, the torch thrust out ahead, my shoulders scraping rock. The cylinder on my back bumped with an unearthly bang. Bubbles of exhalation clouded my vision. Queer sounds dinned in my ears, that stomach coming with me, noisier and more monstrous in the confines.

And then my arm thrust clear, and with a final heave, I was through, back into the vertical narrowness of the fissure, so that I had to flip over on to my belly to still the clanging din of metal scraping rock. The torch showed the walls a paler colour. Limestone by the look of it, which meant that I was already inside the volcanic overlay. Also, they were smooth as glass, a calcareous coating the significance of which I did not appreciate at the time.

More curious than afraid now, I straightened my body into a near-standing position, the tips of my flippers just touching the floor. With my arms stretched up I could touch the roof. It was smooth and curved in an arch. Either it had been fashioned by man, or it had been worn that way by water—the sea or some underground river.

A dozen yards or so farther in the walls fell back abruptly on either side. I had entered the first cavern. Here I did not have to waste time searching for the outlet. I simply breathed in and so lifted myself to the roof, and in a moment I had located the blow-hole Bert had talked about.

I switched the torch beam to my watch and was astonished to find it was only 10.04. It had taken me just six minutes to negotiate the entrance. It had seemed an age. The depth gauge read 23 feet.

I was suddenly full of confidence then. The blow-hole was more like a rising gallery, but even so it would only be a moment or two before I surfaced in the upper cavern where Bert had seen the rope hanging. And it was in that moment that I nearly drowned. I suppose I had knocked my mask scraping through the fissure. At any rate, there was water in it, and suddenly it was over my nose and I panicked. I forgot that it was my mouth I was breathing through, that the nose didn't matter. Desperate, I held my breath, stationary, alone, only the torch beam stabbing at impenetrable darkness. And then I tried to suck in air through my nostrils, got sea water instead and tore at the mask, driving with my flippers for the surface. But there was no surface, only rock. A rock prison like a huge tombstone holding me in a watery grave. It was the thought that this was a grave that brought me to my senses, made me remember the drill for clearing a mask that Bert had taught me, sitting on bright sunlit sand in six feet of water. Lean the head back, hold the top of the mask against the forehead, tilting it, and blow through the nose. I did it, my head hard up against the rock ceiling, emptying my lungs in one despairing snort. Bubbles poured past my face, my head no longer bumping rock as I began to sink; with absolute concentration I forced myself to breathe in through my mouth. The hiss of air as I cracked the demand valve, the feel of life in my lungs again —and miraculously my mask was clear. I felt suddenly drained, utterly exhausted, and yet at the same time wondrously exhilarated as though I had surmounted some great obstacle.

Feeling more confident than at any time during the dive, I re-located the entrance to the blow-hole and flippered my way into it, head first. It was circular in shape and about four feet across at the entrance. Inside, it proved very irregular. There were places where it narrowed to little more than a pipe, others where it widened out into expansion chambers, and the angle of the slope, as well as its direction, varied considerably. Also the walls, though smooth, were not glazed like the entrance cave below.

All this was observed more or less automatically, my mind being concentrated on what I would find when I broke surface in the upper cave. Thus it was that, when the beam of my torch showed me a man's legs, I was slow to react.

I had just paused in one of the expansion chambers to glance at my depth gauge. It now read ten feet and I remember thinking that I was already over halfway up the blow-hole. The walls closed in again as I entered a particularly narrow section, and it was then that the beam of the torch showed him swimming away from me.

At least, that was my first thought, seeing in the dim light of my torch the soles of his feet, the white of legs disappearing into the red of swimming trunks. And for a moment I accepted it, noting that, as I checked, he seemed to swim away up the tunnel, his legs trailing off into the miasma of sediment-saturated water through which the torch beam could not penetrate. And because I could swim and breathe in that tunnel it didn't shock me the way it should have done to find another man down there.

I suppose the truth is that my nerves were so concentrated upon what I was doing that my reactions to anything extraneous were uncommonly slow. I went on after him, the tunnel rising more steeply, and round the bend, where it was wider, I saw him lying like a log broadside to me, white shirt clinging to a white body overblown by the optic enlargement of the water.

No flippers. No cylinders. No belt, no mask, and the legs and arms bent as though in movement, but quite still.

It was Holroyd.

That was when I reacted, when my heart turned over and my stomach suddenly became a void, wanting to evacuate itself. I knew now what I had been swimming through that hung suspended like miasma in the still water.

He was dead, of course. He couldn't possibly be alive, lying so still in the water without a mask, his eyes staring straight at me, unnaturally enlarged. He looked like a very learned frog, an albino, pop-eyed, ready-to-croak frog. Indeed, at that moment a bubble of air, or gas rather, detached itself from him and went sailing away up the final slope of the tunnel to burst with a noise like a distant gunshot at the surface.

And when I had watched that bubble break and knew I was at the threshold of the upper cavern, my gaze returned to something that had puzzled me. Holroyd's right hand was gripped around a metal object that shone dully in the beam of my torch. I paddled nearer and reached out. The fingers were crooked, stiff as hooks in their state of rigor, and yet when I caught hold of the object it lifted clear of his hand. Instantly the corpse drifted up the last few feet of the tunnel to break surface, gently, silently, in the cavern.

I was left holding in my hand the heavy spotlight that Bert claimed had been whipped away from him by some unseen presence.

I did not at that moment draw any conclusions from the fact that the stiffened fingers were not actually gripped round the torch handle. My mind simply recorded it, too shocked by the discovery of his body to think of anything else as I followed it upwards and broke surface myself in the cavern.

There is something instinctively revolting about being in a confined space of water with the corpse of a drowned man. I played the beam of my torch over the cavern, saw that it was as Bert had described it—the lozenge shape with gallery entrances yawning at either end, the rope hanging down from the gaping hole in the roof, the ledges of darkened rock—and then I had propelled myself to the side and was hauling myself up out of the water. The rock was blackened with slime and very slippery, indicating some sort of tidal or surge movement of the water level inside the cavern.

Just clear of the water, I pushed the mask back off my face, removed the mouthpiece and lay there panting. The atmosphere was warm, the air I sucked into my lungs heavy and humid. Stretched out on a sloping slab of rock, I reached up and got a fingertip on the ledge above me. The belt and cylinders were heavy after the weightlessness I had experienced during the dive. The time was 10.09. I had been 22 minutes under water—22 minutes of diving time gone. I had to remember that.

Somehow I got out on to the ledge and slithered forward on my stomach until at last I was above the tidemark, safe on dry rock. Here I relieved myself of the weight of the belt and shucked myself out of the straps that held the cylinder to my back. I had been making for the entrance of what I believed to be the western gallery, and after removing my flippers, I climbed the last few feet to the mouth of it. Only then did I put my gear down, on the flat of the gallery floor where there was no chance of anything slipping down the sloping ledges of rock into the water.

Standing there, my head almost touching the gallery roof, I tried Bert's spot, pressing the rubber we had so carefully taped over the switch. The bulb glowed dully and then faded, the battery exhausted. There had been hours of light in that new battery when Bert had started his dive. I put the spot down with the rest of my things and turned the beam of my diving torch on to the hole in the roof of the cavern where the rope hung forlornly, a pale umbilical cord, its end falling to the black pool of water. The surface of the pool was still now, flat like a floor of glass, except for Holroyd's body floating there, motionless, the white shirt clinging like an attenuated shroud. And beyond the body, dark rocks climbing to the gaping arch of the gallery's continuation on the far side.

No sound—the whole cavern gripped in utter silence; a grave-like stillness. Only my own breathing for company, the thud of my heart. I was remembering what Bert had said. Was there a 'presence' here? He had said he had sensed it the way you sense a shark lurking. But that might have been the hypersensitiveness of a man alone in an underwater cave.

The spotlight's faded bulb was a reminder that my own torch had a limited life and I switched it off to save the battery. Instantly, I was enveloped in darkness so black that I felt as though my eyes had suddenly become sightless. How the hell had Bert managed to grope his way out with no torch and under water? I was shivering, but not with cold, the jacket of the wet suit clinging snugly to my body. I was thinking of Holroyd. Had he been alive, here in this cave, when Bert climbed out to where I stood now? Was it Holroyd's presence he had sensed?

I sat down abruptly, still shivering, and tried to think it out. Holroyd had come down that rope, and the rope's end trailed in the water. But he couldn't have drowned there, not with rock ledges all round. And the spotlight. Was it his hand that had reached out from the dark to grab that source of light? But then I remembered how his fingers had been crooked so loosely over the handle and a sudden chill invaded my stomach.

Of course, if he had slipped, as Bert had slipped, his grip could easily have been loosened as he fell. But if he'd taken the torch, then he must have been alive when Bert entered the cave. Alive, he would surely have spoken to him, made his presence known. And Bert had talked of a body—the cold touch of a body as he had sunk through the water towards the blow-hole tunnel.

Afraid suddenly of the dark thoughts in my mind, I switched on my torch again and instantly the beam of it flooded the pool with light. Quickly I scrambled to my feet, stepping forward, intent on reaching Holroyd's body. I had to examine it. That was my one thought. I had to find out for myself the cause of death. Nothing else would drive out the dreadful thought that was then at the back of my mind. But moving forward, quickly like that, my feet on the slime instead of hard rock, I only just saved myself from the sort of fall that had knocked Bert out and broken his arm.

Panting with fright, I recovered myself, turning and stepping back into the yawning archway of the gallery behind me. And then I saw it. The beam of my torch was on the gallery wall and the etched shape of a mammoth stared me in the face. The high-domed head, the great curve of the tusks—it seemed to be charging towards me along the pale rock wall. And behind it was another, etched more deeply, the lines of the drawing sharp and black, and it too was possessed of an extraordinary sense of movement.

I stood there, rooted to the spot, panic mounting with the sense of remembered evil. Then, slowly, I began to advance into the gallery, Holroyd forgotten, my imagination running riot. My thoughts had taken a frightening turn. And as I moved forward, I saw mammoth after mammoth, the torch beam shadowing the deep-cut lines, so that the shapes of the beasts stood out very clear, with hard scratched lines running into their bodies. And there were other drawings, scratch marks that were geometrical, like a hut, a rhinoceros super-imposed on the slanting rump of a mammoth, the suggestion of a fish, or perhaps a lizard. And then, suddenly, there was colour.

It was on the roof, where it sloped upwards—a great band of red. I didn't see it as a shape, not until I was right underneath it. Then suddenly I saw it, a large-horned bull sprawled lengthways along the run of the gallery roof, a beast in full flight, and falling, forelegs stiffened, head thrown back, the eyes staring, wild with fear. The realism of it was fantastic, the painting enormous—so enormous that I wondered how the artist, using the bulges of the rock for belly and rump, had been able to keep the perspective of the whole in mind.

I swung the beam of my torch away from that monstrous death-throe painting, probing the continuation of the gallery, and where the roof rose, the gallery opened out into a cavern, and it was all red. That was the overwhelming impression—a cave the colour of dried blood. But as I moved slowly into it the colouring separated into individual paintings—bulls and bison, some reindeer, a lynx, three ibex close together and a bunch of tiny horses galloping over a cliff.

The torch trembled in my hand, the beam fastening on a bull, vertical on the wall. Again the head was reared back, the forefeet braced, the whole animal ochre red, caught and held in the moment of its fall to death. I was appalled. Standing in the centre of that cavern, which was about fifty by thirty feet, I played my torch on the walls and roof, and one by one the red beasts dying leaped to life as the beam touched them. The whole cave was a charnel house, a portrait gallery of hunted animals, and all so life-like, so animated, so full of the dreadful certainty of death.

A short gallery led to another, bigger cave. I moved into it in a daze. The roof was lower, the smooth silt floor humped in strange pits, and the witch doctor artists had filled every inch of their rock canvas. Bulls and deers and bison, ochre-painted the colour of stale blood, and at the far end my father sitting, his back propped against the wall and his eyes staring like blue stones into the beam of my torch. I thought he was dead. But then his mouth opened, and the breath of a question came from him, sibilant in the stillness—'Who are you?'

'Paul,' I said, my voice barely recognizable, so gripped was I by my dreadful surroundings.

'Paul?' He seemed not to understand, his appearance wild, his voice dazed.

I shifted the torch in my hand, directing the beam of it on to my face.

He recognized me then. 'So it's you!' His words sounded like a sigh of relief and I saw his limbs move, an awkward attempt to rise to his feet. His face was grey with stubble, the eyes deep-sunk and staring. 'Give me that torch.' His voice was hoarse, a harsh whisper desperate with urgency.

I didn't move. There were questions that had to be answered, and I stood there, rooted to the spot, my mouth dry, my tongue mute. There was an atmosphere about that place—something old, very old, that touched a chord, a deep subconscious instinct. And as though he read my thoughts, he said, 'You are in the presence of the Earth Goddess. Man's oldest god. And this—' His thin hand moved—'This is her temple. Move the beam of your torch to the right—over there. Those bison— they're being driven over a cliff. Superb!' he breathed. 'And I've been here in the dark, unable to see since . . .' He checked himself. 'How long is it? How long have I been down here?'

'Almost three days,' I said.

'And only a few hours—of light—to see what I had found. All those years, searching. . . .' He was trembling, his voice on the edge of tears. And then he moved, sheer willpower pushing him up till he stood erect, the rock wall supporting him and his limbs shaking under him. His head—ascetic, skull-like with age and exhaustion—was outlined against the red flanks of a charging bull. 'The torch,' he whispered, the urgency back in his voice, his hand held out—begging for the light.

I passed it to him then, and he snatched it from my hand in his eagerness to see what he'd been living with in darkness— his fantastic discovery. Slowly he swung the beam, illuminating that butcher's cavern with its great beasts tumbling into traps, driven over cliffs, or caught in the moment of death with the weapons of the hunters scoring their flanks. 'Look!' he breathed, the beam steadying on the red shape of a bison painted on the roof. 'See how the cave artist used the bulge of that rock to emphasize the weight of the head, the massive power of the shoulders.' The torch trembled in his hand, the croak of his voice almost breathless with wonder. 'I haven't seen anything like this since I was in Font de Gaume. I was just a youngster then, and I had left the Dordogne before they discovered Lascaux. I've seen photographs, of course, but that's not the same.'

By then I had got a grip on myself, was thinking of Bert, and Holroyd's body in the pool out there beyond the further cavern. 'What happened after the rock fall trapped you?' I took hold of his arm. It was thin and hard, all bone under my hand as I pressed him for an answer. But he was still intent upon the beam of the torch, lost in a world of his own as he feasted his eyes on the paintings. It was only when I asked him how he'd found them that I got any sensible reaction.

'By accident,' he said, his eyes following the beam as it illuminated a gory mêlée of animals superimposed one upon another. 'I'd only matches. And not many of those—no other light. But that's how I saw it first—this temple to Man the Killer.' He said those words as though they carried a personal message. 'Look!' See how the charcoal has been used to express the terror in that reindeer's eyes—marvellous!'

I slid my hand down his arm and took hold of the torch. 'I have to save the battery,' I said. But he didn't seem to understand. He was beyond practicalities, entirely rapt at the wonder of his find, and he tightened his grip on the torch so that I had to wrench it from him. It wasn't difficult. There was no strength left in him.

'Give it to me.' He was suddenly like a child, pleading. 'You don't realize what it means—all the hours sitting here—waiting, praying for a light to see them by.'

'Sit down.' My hand was on his shoulder, urging him. And then I switched off the torch and in the dark he cried out as though I'd hurt him physically. Then suddenly he sank to the floor of the cave, exhausted.

'Now,' I said, sitting down beside him, my back against the

wall. 'Tell me what happened. You were through the old rock fall, exploring the upper cave, when that earth tremor brought the roof down. What happened then?'

The darkness was total, and in the darkness I could hear his breathing, a rasping sound, very laboured.

'Did you have your acetylene lamp with you?'

'Of course.'

'And you'd found the blow-hole?'

'Yes. I was in there, examining the walls, when it happened —the ground trembling and the crash of rock falling.'

In the blackness, without the distraction of the cave paintings, he began to talk. And once he had started, it was like a dam breaking, the whole story of his discovery pouring out of him.

He had gone back up to the cave-shelter to examine the rock fall, and realizing there was no way out, that he was trapped with little chance of being rescued, he had explored the only alternative, going down the blow-hole until at last he reached the end of it. Then, with his back braced against the wall of it, he had peered down, leaning perilously over the gap and holding his lamp at the full stretch of his arm. He had seen the glint of water, the vague shape of the rock ledges and the shadowed entrance to a gallery beyond. 'I was afraid at first.' His voice breathed at me out of the darkness, a croaking whisper, tired and faint. 'It seemed a desperate step, to let myself fall into the water, the lamp extinguished—no light, nothing but darkness.'

He had tried to climb back up the slope of the blow-hole, but it was too steep and his muscles were tired. And then gradually the acetylene flame of his lamp had weakened. Finally he had worked his way back down to the end of the blow-hole. There he had managed to slip the box of matches he carried into the empty wallet in his hip pocket, and as the flame of his lamp dwindled to nothing, he had let himself fall. 'I had no alternative. I was at the end of my strength.' He paused, breathing heavily, re-living in the darkness his experience. 'It was easier than I had expected. The water was cool, refreshing. And when I'd hauled myself out and recovered from the shock, I felt my way into the gallery and worked along it with my arms stretched wide, touching the walls, and when the walls fell away, I knew I had entered some sort of cave. That was when I struck my first match.'

He was excited then, his words coming faster: 'Can you imagine, Paul—how I felt? The sudden realization. All those paintings. And nobody to share my discovery, no means of telling the world what I had found.' He laughed then, that same hard jeering laugh that I remembered and hated. But this time he was laughing at himself, at the irony of it. 'All my life—seeking. And now suddenly I had stumbled by chance on what I had been searching for. I struck match after match. I was crazed with excitement.' He paused. Then added slowly, 'In the end there were no more matches. I was in darkness, complete darkness, standing like a fool in the greatest art gallery in the world and I couldn't see it.' He sighed, a dreadful, tearing sigh. 'Well, that's how it was. That's how I stumbled on the work of Levkas Man.' He repeated those words slowly— Levkas Man. 'That's the name I have given to him. Sitting here in the dark I've had time to think—about this cave and about what it means. I've no doubts now. My theory was right. A land-bridge did exist. And now I must start at the other end —at Pantelleria. If something similar exists on Pantelleria. . . . Give me that torch again.' His hand clawed at my arm. 'I've been in the dark so long. How long have I been here, did you say? Three days?'

'About that.'

'Seventy-two hours.'

'But not all in darkness,' I said. 'You had a spotlight, didn't you?'

'Yes. For a few hours. It was magnificent—very bright. But then it faded.'

'Bert could have helped you. He was an expert diver. He could have got you out.' I was angry, angry at his stupidity. 'Why did you do it? If you'd only spoken to him. . . .'

'So it was Barrett. I didn't know.' His voice sounded suddenly tired. 'If he'd spoken to me, explained who he was. I thought——'

'How could he?' I cut in. 'You damn near killed him. He's suffering from concussion and a broken arm.'

'I'm sorry. It was that torch of his. I had to see.'

'He was lucky to get out alive.'

His hand was on my arm again. 'You don't understand. You can't imagine. To be alone—in the dark—unable to see these paintings. All my life——'

'To hell with your life, and your scientific searchings! We're talking about people now. Live people. A man called Barrett.' And I added harshly, 'There's Holroyd, too. He's dead now. But he was alive when he came down that rope.'

There was silence then, a ghastly stillness, no sound of breathing even. It was as though the shock of my words had rendered him speechless.

'What happened to him?'

Silence.

'He was dead when you hooked the spotlight on to his fingers. He'd been dead some time.'

'The battery was just about exhausted then,' he murmured, as though that constituted some sort of an explanation.

'Was that why you took Bert's spot—for fear he'd see what you'd done?'

He sighed. 'You don't know what it's like to be in total darkness, and then to watch his glow-worm figure climbing down out of that hole in the cave roof.'

'You knew who it was, then?'

'Of course.' His voice sounded remote, infinitely sad. And then, as though Holroyd's death was of no real importance, he said, 'When I began my Journal, I was endeavouring to strike a balance between the good and the evil that was inside me, to find out whether there was any hope for our species —what sort of a being Man really was. Well, now I know.' There was a pause, and then he said, 'Do you remember that night you came to me, up above in the entrance to the cave-shelter, I said this place was evil?'

'It was outside,' I said. 'Under the stars, and you were holding that stone lamp in your hand.'

'Yes. I could feel it in the stone of that lamp. And all the time I have been alone here in the dark, that sense and know-ledge of evil has burned itself into me. Man is a killer, and he carries the seed of his own destruction in him. Switch the torch on again, just for a moment—so that you can see what I'm talking about.'

I did so and his skull-like head leaped out of the dark at me, its beetling brows, its deep lines and the mane of white hair standing up from the dome of his forehead. He was leaning back, his head against the wall, pressed against the red belly of that bull. His eyes stared past me as I swept the beam of the torch over the cave. 'Now, just the two of us—seeing it for the first time. There have been bears here—those pits in the floor are their hibernating beds. But no humans. We are back twenty thousand years at least and in all that time man hasn't changed.'

'You killed him? Is that what you're saying?'

He stared at me, frowning. 'Haven't you understood a word I've been saying? I'm talking about my Journal—about my attempt to define the nature of Man.'

'And I'm talking about Holroyd,' I said, trying to pin him down. 'I have to know what happened.'

'Why? What possible interest is it to you?' And he added slowly, staring up at the bison pawing the roof, 'He shouldn't have come here. You shouldn't have let him.' And he added wearily, 'He could have climbed back up that rope.'

'He was trapped, trying to rescue you.'

But my words didn't register. 'Instinctive defence of territory,' he murmured. 'It's in all of us, and it goes very deep.' He gave a dry cough. 'You didn't bring any water with you, I suppose?'

'No. Nor any food.'

'The food doesn't matter. But I'm dry—very dry. It makes it difficult to talk.' He leaned forward, his eyes fastening on mine. 'All my life has been a struggle. Always seeking after truth. Nothing else has ever mattered to me—not since your mother was killed. There was a moment when I thought I could live life differently, through you. But I failed in that, and afterwards I resumed my restless seeking.' He reached out suddenly, grabbing hold of my hand, his fingers hard and dry, his voice urgent. 'When we get out of here—we'll go on together, eh? Promise me, boy.' His grip was weak, his hand trembling. 'You're bound for Pantelleria, isn't that right? We'll start there—on Pantelleria. Then we'll complete the chain of evidence—irrefutable proof. They'll have to recognize me then. They'll have to accept my theory.'

It was fascinating, almost terrifying, his sheer egotism. He

258

seemed to be living in a world of his own, divorced from other people. 'All the time we've been talking,' I said, 'there are men up above us working at that rock fall, trying to get through to you.'

His eyes widened, suddenly blazing. 'Then stop them.'

'They're trying to reach you.'

'I don't want them here. This——' His hand moved, indicating the cave—'This is something between us alone. Just the two of us. Nobody else. Tell them I'm dead, anything—but keep them out of here. I'm not going to have anybody else——'

'They're also looking for Holroyd,' I said.

'Then tell them you've seen him and that they needn't bother any more.'

I shook my head. 'There's still the Greek. There was a Greek with him.'

He was suddenly very still, his body sagging. 'Who's up there—Cartwright?'

'Cartwright and Hans Winters, about half a dozen men from Vathy. Zavelas, too, and Kotiadis.' He didn't say anything after that and I got to my feet. 'If they don't get through that fall by tonight, I'll have to try and get you out underwater.'

'No.' He said it emphatically, a total rejection of the possibility that made me turn and look at him. His eyes were closed and there was a stillness about him, a resignation. I had a feeling then that he had accepted the inevitability of death and that his closed eyes were a conscious rejection of sight, preparation for the darkness that would close in on him again when I had left. This feeling was so strong that for a moment I felt completely numb. It was strange, the two of us so distant all these years and yet the sense of closeness, of communication without words.

'You can't stay here,' I heard myself murmur.

He didn't say anything for a moment, his body shuddering. 'I'm not afraid of death.' It was a declaration. His eyes opened and he stared about him with extraordinary intensity, as though trying to fix the painted walls of his prison firmly on the retina of his brain. And then suddenly he put his hands up to his face, covering his eyes, and his body shook with a strange sobbing sound.

'I'll go now,' I said awkwardly.

'Yes, go—quickly. And remember, when you sail from Levkas, there'll be nobody alive but yourself who has seen the work of these cave artists. It will be your secret—and mine. Do you understand?'

I was staring at him, appalled.

'Do you understand, Paul?'

'Yes. Yes, I think so.'

He reached up and seized hold of my hand again. 'If I'm right—and I am right—the trail of Levkas Man leads on through the Sicilian offshore islands of Levanzo and Marettimo to Pantelleria and the coast of Africa—Tunisia probably, maybe Djerba.' The grip on my hand tightened convulsively. 'Paul! Promise me. Promise me that you'll go on. That you'll follow the trail, prove me right.'

'I've no qualifications. And anyway . . .'

'You don't need qualifications. All you need is conviction and the driving urgency that it gives you. Experts will always follow a dedicated, determined man. Look at Schliemann—an amateur. He believed in Homer. And as a result, he discovered Troy, Mycenae, Knossos. You could be the same. Building on my reputation and on the manuscripts I have left with Sonia. Promise me.' He was staring up into my face, the grip of his fingers suddenly like iron.

I didn't know what to say. That I'd no money? That his world was too remote? That, anyway, Cartwright would break through that rock fall to discover Holroyd's body and the painted cave that he so desperately wanted to preserve for himself as a total secret? 'I'm going now,' I said finally.

The grip on my hand slowly relaxed until his arm dropped slackly, and he sat there, his back against the wall, his body bowed. He seemed suddenly to have shrunk, the collapse of his spirit deflating him physically. I left him then, feeling sick at heart, hating the place and the evil that lurked there, glad when the paintings were behind me. I didn't look back as I entered the gallery of the mammoths. I didn't want to see his loneliness, the crumpled dejection of his body squatting there below the red belly of that bull.

I came out into the cave beyond with its pool of black sea water. And there was Holroyd's body still floating, a reminder that something had been done here that could not be undone. The atmosphere of evil breathed down my neck, emanating from the painted caves. Alone, I had difficulty getting the heavy cylinder on to my back. I did it in a sitting position, and as I struggled to my feet, the torch shone on a half-segment of stone. I recognized it instantly—another of those Stone Age lamps. I should have realized the significance of it, lying there broken on the rock floor, but my mind was on other things and it didn't connect. All I knew, as I slung the lead belt round my waist and pulled the mask down over my face, was that its presence added to my sense of evil. I was in such a hurry then that I almost forgot to check the state of my air. Nervously my fingers felt for the stem indicator, relieved to find that the cylinder was still almost half full.

I entered the water with only one thing in my mind, to get the hell out of that place as quickly as possible. But then, when I was in the water, my fears left me. The practical side of me seemed to take command. Almost without thinking I swam over to the rope, drew the diver's knife from the sheath strapped to my calf, and cut the end of it where it trailed in the water. I tied a bowline, and then, making a noose, slipped it over Holroyd's arm. That was when I saw the wound in his head, the white of bone jagged around a grey pulp. His skull had been cracked like the shell of an egg. I trod water for a moment, staring at that wound half-concealed by the dark hair waving like weed in the water, understanding now what the old man had been talking about, his total rejection of rescue. Understanding, too, the broken segment of that stone lamp.

I felt suddenly very cold, cold in my guts, and I turned quickly and dived for the blow-hole, trailing the corpse behind me like a dog on a lead. What I had started to do instinctively, a sort of tidying-up operation, now became a matter of urgency, for I couldn't leave it there in the pool to stare the first rescuer in the face. But it was only when I came out through the roof into the lower cavern, the hiss of the demand valve in my ears and the blatter of my bubbled exhalations disappearing into the hole behind me, that I paused to consider what I was going to do with it.

If I took it out into the channel it would be discovered almost at once, and then the questions would start. The alternative was to conceal it in a crevice, but that meant weighting it with a rock, and the only means I had of fastening a rock to it was with the rope. I hung there in the cave, the body ballooning above me, ghostly at the end of its umbilical nylon cord. Tie a rock to it and if it were discovered, then it would be obvious that his death had not been a natural one. The bubbles of my breathing warned me that I could not stay there indefinitely. I glanced at the watch on my wrist. It was 11.12— almost an hour and a half since I had left the boat. And I had forgotten to check the time when I had entered the water in the cavern above.

I dived then to where daylight showed as a pale glimmer below the fallen slab. My torch showed a crevice above the slab. I pulled on the rope, got hold of the stiff cold body and pushed it in, trudging energetically with my flippers. I left him there, taking the rope end with me, and wriggled through under the slab into the open water of the Meganisi Channel.

I can still remember the growing brightness of the sunlight as I slanted upwards, going out past the rock with the sandal on it, across a plain of sea grass until I could see the underwater shape of *Coromandel*, a dark whale-shadow bulging below the surface of the sea, which was like the back of a mirror, flecked with a myriad dust-motes iridescent in the sun. And as I broke through it and saw the boat with its masts against the blue sky, it was like coming out of a nightmare.

I reached the ladder, clambering awkwardly out, no longer weightless, cylinder and belt dragging at me. And then Sonia's face, as I pushed the mask up blinking in the sun, and Gilmore behind her, the red sea horses bright as blood. 'Are you all right, Paul? What happened? You've been so long.' Her voice was remote, a muffled sound, my ears clogged.

'I'm okay,' I mumbled, collapsing on the hot deck, where I lay in a pool of water, my lungs gasping for air. I felt utterly drained, tired beyond belief. Her hands were on my shoulders, working at the straps. She was bending over me, and when she had freed me of the weight of the cylinder, she groped under my body to find the quick release clasp of the belt and slipped the lead weight from my waist.

I sat up then, feeling dazed—the sunshine, the sky, the smell of the land and the mountains towering brown; but it was like a picture postcard, something unreal. The reality was in my mind, the memory of that cave with my father talking and Holroyd's body floating in the still, dark pool.

'What happened? Did you find him?' Sonia, still bending over me, her face drained, her eyes large. 'Are you all right?'

'Yes, I'm all right.' My voice sounded disembodied, remote.

'What happened then?'

'Nothing.'

'You've been gone over an hour and a half. What did you find?'

'Nothing, I tell you.' I got to my feet, standing there shivering in the sunlight.

'But . . .' She was staring at me, searching my face, probing for the truth I dare not tell her. 'You found him? You must have found him.'

I started to push past her, but she gripped my arm. 'Please——' She was clinging to me and I flung her off.

'Leave me alone,' I said.

'Tell me, Paul. Please tell me what you found.' And then she added on a conciliatory note, 'You're shivering. I'll get you a towel.'

'I'll get it myself.'

I was at the wheelhouse door, her hands clutching at me. 'What happened, for God's sake?'

I looked down at her, seeing her pale face, frightened and bewildered, and wondering whether to tell her. But this wasn't something I could share with anybody else, not even her. And Dr Gilmore there, listening, alert and curious. 'It's up to the others now.' I got clear of her then and went below, where I peeled off the jacket of the wet suit and towelled myself down, standing naked in the saloon, my mind going over and over everything I'd seen, the things he'd said. And when I was dry, I wrapped the towel round me and went over to the drink cupboard. I thought a cognac would steady me, help me to see things in perspective. I poured myself a stiff one and drank it neat, feeling the fire in it reach down into my guts. But it needed more than that to deaden the memory of what had happened. I poured myself another, drinking it slowly this time and trying to think. And then Dr Gilmore came in.

He sat himself down facing me, still alert and curious, but

not saying anything. He just sat there watching me, waiting until I was ready. And gradually I realized I would have to tell him.

He had shifted his position, was leaning slightly forward. 'Holroyd's dead, is he?' And when I didn't answer, he added, 'That's why you're drinking—why you were so abrupt with Sonia.'

I nodded. 'Yes, he's dead,' I said.

'And Pieter?'

'He's very weak—exhausted. He says he's not afraid of death. He wants to be left there.'

After that he got it out of me, bit by bit—the cave, the body, the whole story of that fifteen minutes or so I had spent with him. And when it was done and I had told him everything, he sat there, silent and sad-looking, not commenting, not condemning, just quietly thinking it out whilst I had another cognac. And then footsteps on the companionway and Sonia standing there.

'Well?' She looked from one to the other of us, searching our faces. 'All this time I've been waiting up there, not knowing . . .' Her voice trailed off as she stared at Gilmore.

'Bill Holroyd is dead.'

'But Dr Van der Voort?' She didn't care about Holroyd. His death meant nothing to her. Wide-eyed, her gaze switched from Gilmore to me. 'Did you find him?'

'Yes.'

'Then why didn't you tell me? To leave me in doubt . . .' She stopped there, conscious suddenly of the atmosphere, the sadness in Gilmore's eyes, the lack of any sense of relief that I'd found him. 'He's dead—is that what you mean?'

I didn't say anything. What could I say? I finished my drink, staring down at the empty glass, her eyes fixed on me, feeling a coldness in my stomach, seeing him still, propped against that wall, against the red belly of that bull.

'Tell me,' she said. 'For God's sake tell me. I'm not a child.'

Her gaze had shifted to Gilmore and there was a long silence. And then finally the old man said, 'I think, my dear, you have to face the fact that they're both dead.'

I felt a sense of relief then. The decision I had been groping for confirmed and taken out of my hands. But she was too determined a person to accept it without knowing the details. 'But how—what happened?' She was facing me again, white-faced. 'Why didn't you tell me? Something happened while you were down there.'

'Nothing happened,' I said.

'Then what are you hiding from me? Why didn't you go straight ashore?'

'Ashore?' I was confused now; the strain and the effect of the cognac. I thought she had guessed that Gilmore was lying. 'Why should I go ashore?'

'To tell them, of course. To tell Hans he needn't risk his life any more. . . .'

'You tell him,' I said, and reached for the bottle.

Her eyes widened, two angry spots of colour showing in her cheeks. 'You're drunk.'

I nodded. 'That's right. You expect me to stay sober after a dive like that?' The neck of the bottle was rattling on the rim of the glass.

She frowned. 'It's not the dive that's scared you.'

'No?' I couldn't stand it any more, this persistent probing. 'I'm too tired to argue,' I said. 'I'm going to my bunk.' And I went past her, walking carefully, the glass in my hand. Let Gilmore sort it out, tell her what he liked. I got to my cabin and sat on the bunk for a moment, drinking slowly, wondering what they'd do when they got through that rock fall. But my mind was comfortingly dulled, and when I'd finished my drink, I crawled naked on to my bunk. I didn't care any more. I didn't care what they did. I didn't care what they thought. I didn't even care if the wind got up and the ship broke adrift. I closed my eyes and sank into oblivion. Somebody else could deal with the whole damned mess.

V: Legacy of Violence

RED BEASTS sprawled across my vision, their eyes staring, and a great hand was on my shoulder, restraining me, as the broken face fell back screaming, and I opened my eyes to see the face of Kotiadis, dark and stubbled, hanging above me. 'You will get up please and come to the salon.' My mouth was dry, my eyes unfocused. 'What is it?' I murmured. 'What do you want?' My mind was still half lost in the dream world from which he had woken me.

'In the salon please—at once.' His voice was harsh and urgent. I could hear voices, the bump of a boat alongside.

'Okay.' I rubbed my eyes, feeling like death. I'd no clothes on and the cabin was hot, my body bathed in sweat. Veins of light swam across the deck beams above my head, the shimmering reflection of sun on water coming in through the single porthole. 'What's happened? Have they got through the rock fall?'

'No. Not any more.'

'Well, what the hell is it then?'

'All foreign yachts are to leave Greece immediately.'

I swung my legs off the bunk and sat up. 'Why? What's happened?'

'It is the order of the Government.'

'Yes, but why?'

'I explain when you are dressed. You are to proceed now to Levkas.' He left me then.

The time was 15.18. I pumped the wash basin full of water, sluicing it over my face and body, and then, feeling a little better, I slipped on a pair of shorts and went through into the saloon. Kotiadis was standing talking to Zavelas and two officers, Sonia and Gilmore sitting silent on the far side. The place seemed overcrowded, the air acrid with the smell of Greek tobacco, and the atmosphere was tense. A sudden silence fell as I entered. 'What's going on?' I asked Gilmore.

'The patrol boat from Levkas,' he said. 'They arrived about ten minutes ago.' He seemed to have shrunk and his voice sounded tired. 'They say there is going to be a war.'

'I do not say that,' Kotiadis exploded. 'We prepare. That is all. And it is for your own safety.' He turned to me. 'You will take this boat immediately to Levkas for examination.'

I looked at him warily, wondering what it was all about. 'And if I refuse?'

'Then you are under arrest and Kapetán Constantanidi will put men on board to take her there.' He indicated one of the officers. 'This is Kapetán Constantanidi.' The police chief was a small, fierce little man, with a smile full of gold teeth. 'But at the moment he has many other things to attend to, so it is better you do not refuse.'

'What about Miss Winters and Dr Gilmore?'

'They want us to go with the patrol boat,' Sonia said, her face white, her eyes dark-ringed. 'They've abandoned the search and we're to leave Greece immediately.'

'I tell you again it is for your own safety,' Kotiadis repeated. 'There are already some Russian ships in Leros. Our government is negotiating but ...' He gave a Gallic shrug. 'All foreign nationals are to leave Greece.'

'We heard it on the wireless,' Dr Gilmore said quietly. 'The Russians are requesting the use of bases in the Dodecanese. The Turks are involved too, of course, and the situation is not at all healthy.'

I stood there feeling numb and unable to grasp all the implications. Man the Killer! I could hear the old man's voice—a rogue species carrying within itself the seeds of its own destruction. And Bert, nice, simple, uncomplicated Bert, talking about Armageddon starting in the Middle East. 'They know Holroyd is dead,' Gilmore said. 'They're presuming your father is, too.' His eyes, staring at me, seemed to convey a private message.

I didn't say anything, afraid to commit myself. Kotiadis and the police chief were watching me. And Sonia, sitting there, white-faced and still. 'How do they know ...' I hesitated. 'About Holroyd?'

He turned to Zavelas and the ex-cop moved his big bulk

nearer to me, explaining how they had broken through the fall about the time I had surfaced from my dive. It was a small hole and Thomasis had spoken to them from the other side. That was when they learned that Holroyd was dead. 'After the fall, when Professor Holerod don't return, Thomasis go down the small tunnel to search for him. His torch is not good, but he can see water below and the Professor's body floating in it.' Zavelas could not say how it happened. 'I guess his hands slipped on the rope as he went down, or maybe he don't find a way to get out of the water.' He shrugged. 'Anyhow, he'd drowned down there.'

'And—my father?' The words came slowly, little more than a whisper.

He shook his head. 'Thomasis don't see anyone else. He says he called out many times, but there was no answer, so I guess he's dead, too. I'm sorry.' He glanced at Kotiadis. 'A strange man, but we in Meganisi liked him.'

I stood there, hardly breathing, my hands trembling, while Zavelas explained how they'd widened the gap and got the Greek out, and then there had been another cave-in.

'And what about Cartwright?' I asked. 'Where is he now?'

'Back at the camp by Tiglia, packing his gear.'

I turned to Gilmore. But he was staring at the floor, the Greek cigarette he had been smoking sending up an unheeded spiral of smoke from the ash-tray beside him. He wasn't going to help me. And Sonia staring at me wild-eyed.

The police chief said something in Greek, looking pointedly at his watch. Kotiadis nodded. 'Well, what you decide? Constantanidi says he has many important things requiring his attention at Levkas and in the islands. Do you take the boat to Levkas or not?'

'Paul, you can't . . .' The words seemed wrung out of her, checked by the touch of Gilmore's hand on hers.

She knew. That was all I could think of in that moment. She'd got it out of him, and now there they sat, the two of them, both knowing the old man was still alive, both staring at me, waiting. And the terrible thing was, I knew what I was going to do. I just hadn't the guts to put it into words.

Sonia rose to her feet, coming to me slowly as though walking in her sleep, her eyes moist. 'Do something,' she hissed. 'For Christ's sake do something. You can't just leave him there.'

'Why not?' I said harshly. 'It's what he wanted—to be left there in that bloody charnel house of a cave.'

'But you're his son.'

'You think you know him better than I do? You weren't down there with him. You don't understand——' I laughed the way he'd laughed, that jeering sound. *You don't understand.* How many times had she said that to me? 'There's no point,' I muttered. And Zavelas behind me said, 'Is too dangerous, that cave. And I guess we can expect mobilization any time now.'

'Hans and Alec,' she said, her eyes fixed on my face. 'They'd try. You've only got to tell them——' Zavelas's big hand reached out and patted her arm. 'Like this guy says, there's no point—just to bring his body out of one hole in the ground to bury it in another.'

'Who said anything about a body? Dr Van der Voort is alive.'

His hand dropped, his blue eyes staring. 'How can you say that? You don't know.'

'But he does,' she said fiercely. And when Zavelas shook his head, bewildered, she cried out in a high-pitched hysterical voice, 'Ask him. Ask him whether his father is alive.' Gilmore had risen. His hand was on her arm. She shook it off. 'He was in that cave this morning, diving with an aqualung. Ask him.'

Zavelas turned to me. The room was silent. They were all watching. 'Is that right? Is the Doctor alive?'

'No,' I said. I heard the hiss of her breath, saw the appalled blaze in her eyes and knew that Gilmore hadn't told her the whole of it. My hands clenched and my voice was hard and angry as I told Kotiadis I'd like a word with my friends alone. 'Then they can go and I'll take the boat up to Levkas for you.'

He nodded, said something to Constantanidi, and then the two officers left. 'He is putting men on your ship to clear the bow line and lift the anchor. You have perhaps two or three minutes, then you will please start the engine.'

He left us then and Zavelas followed him. But at the foot of the companionway he paused, his big bulk filling the gap. 'This country is not like America or England, you know. We are a small peoples with many difficulties, many enemies. I guess you know that. But remember, we are also very obstinate. If necessary we shall fight. Holerod is dead, and even if the Doctor were alive, you don't have a hope in hell of saving him now. I'm sorry.' He stared at us a moment and then he heaved himself up the companionway.

We were alone then and I turned to Gilmore. 'You should have told her.'

He nodded, his head moving slowly without any of his usual alertness, his eyes sad. 'But my dear fellow . . .' He reached for his cigarette, puffed at it briefly and then stubbed it out. 'Yes, I suppose so. But it's not so easy. Miss Winters—Sonia is very fond of him and . . .' He shook his head unhappily.

'All right,' I said angrily. 'If you won't tell her, I'll have to.' She had been staring at me all the time, her breath coming in quick pants, her small breasts moving against the thin nylon of her shirt. Footsteps pounded on the deck, orders in Greek coming to us from above. Bluntly I told her the facts, how I'd found Holroyd, drowned in that cave, his head split open, probably by that Stone Age lamp, and the old man sitting there, alone, knowing it was the end, that for him there was no way out. But she didn't believe me. She didn't want to believe me. 'It was an accident,' she breathed. 'He fell—from the rope. . . .'

'Into a pool of water,' I said. 'Water doesn't give a man a gash in the head.'

'He might have slipped. Bert slipped and broke an arm. Or perhaps a piece of rock from the roof . . .' She was beginning to cry. She knew there was no way round it, that what I'd told her was the truth. Suddenly she wasn't fighting it any more. 'So you'll just leave him there.'

'He was very weak,' I said quietly.

'To die—alone—in the dark?' She was sobbing wildly. 'How can you be so cruel—your own father? And his discovery, that cave. . . .'

'It was what he wanted.' More orders and the sound of feet moving aft. 'I have to go and start the engine now. They're about to heave the anchor in.'

She didn't say anything. There was nothing to say, anyway. 'You'd better get your things.'

She nodded dumbly. Gilmore followed her. 'I'm so sorry,' he murmured ineffectually. 'So terribly sorry.'

I went up to the wheelhouse and pressed the starter button. The deep throb of the diesel filled the ship with sound, the deck planking drumming at my feet. The patrol boat had been standing by to cast off. Kotiadis stepped back on board as the anchor came up. 'Constantanidi is going first to Spiglia so I come with you.'

Behind me a voice said, 'Paul. What happens to you now?'

I turned. She was dry-eyed, looking more of a waif than ever, with one of Gilmore's suitcases in her hand and a pile of her own things over the other arm.

'If there's a war, then I'll be all right. It's in times of war they need people like me, isn't it?'

She didn't comment. Instead, she said, 'I don't see why we have to go in the patrol boat.'

Gilmore had appeared, carrying his other case. 'I tried to talk them out of it, but I expect they have their reasons.'

The anchor was on deck, the two boats drifting. Kotiadis looked at her. 'Are you ready, Miss Winters?'

She nodded and then turned to me. 'Is there nothing——?'

I shook my head. 'He was very near the end, anyway. It's better like this.'

I don't know whether she believed me or not. I'm not even certain she understood. She stared at me a moment, standing very still, biting her lip, her eyes luminous with tears. But whether for him, or for what might have been between us, I will never know, for she got control of herself and went past me, moving towards the rail in a daze. Kotiadis took the suit-case and helped her over on to the patrol boat. Gilmore followed. 'We'll see you in Levkas, I expect.'

I nodded. But I thought that very doubtful. The Greek sailors cast off and the patrol boat gathered way, heading north up the channel, a froth of white water at her stern. Sonia had not once looked back. I pushed the gear lever into forward, swung the wheel over and brought *Coromandel* round on to the line of the patrol boat's wake. I saw the flick of a lighter reflected in the glass of the windshield. Kotiadis was in the wheelhouse now, standing behind me, the smell of his cigarette rank in the hot air. Neither of us spoke, and abreast of the

272

southern end of Tiglia I left the wheel and went out on to the starboard deck. Hans and Cartwright were busy dismantling the mess-tent, Vassilios loading his boat. The orange sleeping-tents were already struck. They didn't look up as we steamed past the southern opening to the cove, the water there a flat sheet of brilliant green, the rocks above pulsating in the heat.

I had set the engine revs fairly low, so that we were doing no more than four knots. The time by the wheelhouse clock was 16.10. Just over four hours before it was dark. I pushed past Kotiadis to the chart table and measured off the distance to Levkas port. It was exactly 11 miles—$8\frac{1}{2}$ to the entrance of the canal. Back at the wheel I steadied her on a course of 35°, which would take us just to the east of Skropio Island, and engaged the automatic pilot. 'Can I get you anything?' I asked. 'A drink, some coffee?'

'Thank you—coffee.' His heavy-lidded eyes were screwed up against the sun-glare, the cigarette dangling from his lips. He was still wearing his jacket and I wondered whether that meant he was armed.

Down in the galley, I lit the gas ring and put the coffee percolator on. There was tinned ham in the fridge and I cut myself some sandwiches. By the time I had finished them, the coffee was made and I took it up to the wheelhouse. Skropio's wooded slopes stood like a dark hat floating above the milk calm of the water. Not a ripple anywhere and the boat thudding along as though we were on rails. 'Black or white?' I asked him.

'Black.'

He watched me as I poured it and I wondered whether he knew I was dangerous.

'Sugar?'

'Thank you.'

I handed him the cup and he took it with his left hand, his eyes on me all the time, his right hand free.

I pulled the flap-seat down and sat on it. The coffee was scalding hot and the sweat trickled down my body. 'Well, what happens now?' I said. 'When we get to Levkas.'

'You will be sent on to England.'

'I'm from Holland, not England.'

'You have an English passport.'

'Am I under arrest?'

He didn't say anything.

'If you're at war, then you don't have to take any notice of Interpol.'

'We are not at war. And the English are important to us.'

'The man I killed was a Communist. You hate Communists. Doesn't that make any difference?'

He shrugged. 'I have my instructions.'

'And the boat?'

'It will be searched. Probably impounded.'

'Why?'

His eyes flicked open. 'You ask me why? You are in Pythagorion on June 10. You leave that night. Our information is that you were in the Samos Straits and that you have a rendezvous with a Turkish fishing boat. Correct?'

I finished my coffee, the two of us watching each other. 'Yes, quite correct,' I said.

'Then explain, please.'

'A smuggling job.'

I gave him some more coffee, and then, as we closed Skropio Island and motored close in along the shore, I told him the whole story, and by the time I had finished, Skropio was astern of us, and we were passing another wooded island, Sparti, our bows headed slightly east of north and the sun beginning to fall towards the dark rim of the Levkas mountains. Visibility had improved, and beyond the open roadstead of Port Drepano, I could just see the buoys marking the dredged channel into the canal. Four miles to go. One hour at our present speed. 'You mentioned Byron to me once. . . .' And for the next quarter of an hour I used every argument I could think of to persuade him that I could be of some service to his country if I were at liberty. After all, in the event of war they would need ships' officers. But it was no good. He had his instructions. 'If it had not been for the accident to Dr Van der Voort, you would have been deported when you arrived back in Meganisi.'

We were off Mara Point then, close in to the Levkas shore, and I was relieved to see the patrol boat coming up astern. It passed within two or three cables of us doing about 12 knots. It would be in Levkas inside of half an hour. I looked at the clock. It was now 17.21 and the sun was already behind the towering bulk of the mountains. In forty minutes we should be in the dredged channel, with shallows all round us and darkness only two hours off. 'Time for a drink,' I said. 'Whisky or cognac? I'm afraid there's no ouzo.'

'Cognac, thank you. But from the bottle, eh? 'And he smiled at me thinly. He was taking no chances, and when I came back up to the wheelhouse, I let him pour it himself. Then I asked him whether he'd any idea what we'd been smuggling out of Turkey.

'You told me—antiquities from old tombs.'

'Would you like to see them?'

'When we get to Levkas.'

'There are twenty-three packages. When we get to Levkas, will you ring Leonodipoulos for me?' If they were museum pieces, I thought perhaps I could do a deal. But he only laughed. 'They are Turkish. Leonodipoulos is only interested in Greek antiquities.'

There was nothing for it then, and I sat there drinking my cognac, watching the cat's paws of an evening zephyr slip beneath our bows. The sky deepened in colour. The channel buoys grew larger beneath the solid bulk of Ayios Giorgios fort. And all the time Kotiadis stood there, leaning against the back wall of the wheelhouse, the glass in his hand, but hardly drinking. Astern of us, the sea was empty, not a sign of any other vessel right back to the dark shape of Skropio and the outline of Meganisi.

We entered the dredged channel at 18.06, chugging slowly between the first two buoys, the water suddenly a muddy brown on either side. To starboard was the small island of Volio, the fort above it on its hill, but all ahead of us it was a flat Dutch landscape. I was at the wheel now, a big trading caique coming south. We met her just after we had passed the second pair of buoys, the channel narrow and the ripple of her bow waves breaking where the shallows on either side were only six feet deep. The entrance to the canal proper was marked by the final pair of buoys and there was a red-roofed hut to port, on the extreme edge of the saltings, where cattle grazed in the shadow of the steeply rising hills beyond.

I reached back to the chart table, picked up Chart 1609, folded it to the large scale plan of the canal and propped it in front of the wheel. Just over a quarter of a mile beyond the entrance a green-flashing buoy marked the fairway, where the channel made a slight dog-leg to the west and was crossed by the curving line of an older canal. And, just before it, there was an unlit buoy marking shallows with a depth of only one foot to starboard. This was the spot I chose, and as we slipped between the last pair of buoys, I took the glasses down from their hook and searched the whole line of the canal ahead. I could see the fairway buoy quite distinctly, with the mound of Paleo Khalia to the right of it, and beyond was a great sheet of shallow water stretching all the way to limáni Levkas, and not a sign of a mast, no caique to pull us off before it got dark.

In the last stretch before the buoy, there was a line of stones to port and the low island of solid ground to starboard was topped by the crumbling remains of a small redoubt. I looked round at Kotiadis. He had put his glass down and had just taken out his packet of cigarettes. I set a course of north-west on the automatic pilot, a course that would take us diagonally across the canal and into the shallows on our port side. His lighter flicked as we came to the end of the flat little island. The canal was eighteen yards wide, the unlit buoy less than a hundred yards ahead, and the saltings falling back, the shallows opening out. The moment had come, and I engaged the automatic pilot. 'Quick!' I shouted. 'Grab it!' and I flung myself out of the wheelhouse door, running aft along the deck. Kotiadis followed me. 'What is it?' he asked as he joined me.

'The jib preventor,' I said, leaning over the stern. 'It must have shaken loose.'

He didn't know anything about boats and for a moment he stood there, watching the wake for a non-existent piece oı equipment. And then he suddenly remembered that we were in the canal and nobody at the wheel. He turned, and in that moment we grounded, right opposite the unlit buoy. There was no sudden jolt, just a slow coming to a halt and the white of our wake turning to a useless churning of muddy water.

He stared at me. 'Cretin!' But that was all he said. No doubt he had his suspicions, but he didn't voice them, and after an ineffectual attempt to get off under power, he was fully occupied helping me to get the dinghy over the side and a kedge run out astern. It all took time, and because the nylon warp was fixed direct to the anchor, with no intermediary length of chain to weight the stock down, it did not dig in as the strain came on it, but ploughed through the mud bottom. Clouds hung over the mainland hills and for a brief period they were rimmed with pink, while the clear sky overhead turned to a cold duck's egg green and the darkening mass of the Levkas heights changed from purple to black.

By the time we had made three attempts to winch ourselves clear, it was dark enough to see the lights of the port two miles away, with the red and green lights of the channel buoys to the south and the fairway buoy winking green, its flashes so close you felt you could reach out and touch it. 'It's no good,' I said. 'We'll have to wait for a caique to tow us off in the morning.' He followed me down into the saloon and I gave him another cognac. And since we were there for the night, I repeated my suggestion that he might like to have a look at what we'd smuggled out of Turkey. I was curious myself, and I hoped that, with his interest in Greek antiquities, they would prove exciting enough to tempt him.

The first package I brought up from the bilges was one of the smallest and proved to contain a short necklace of thin gold beaten into the form of tiny shells. I saw his eyes gleam as he handled it, but when I said he could have it if he'd give me the opportunity of getting clear of Greek waters, he put it down as though it were too hot to hold. 'And what do I say to Constantanidi?' He smiled and shook his head. 'Tomorrow when we are in Levkas, the Customs take charge of this.'

'On behalf of the government,' I said. 'You won't get it.'

'No. But I have my job.' He was still staring at it. 'Oréo,' he murmured softly. 'Is very beautiful.'

'Then take it,' I said. 'Whilst you have the chance.'

But he shook his head again. 'It is of no importance to me. And if there is war—what good is it then?'

I was watching his face, sitting across the table from him, my nerves tense. 'Okay.' I got to my feet. 'Then I'll throw it overboard. And all the rest of the packages.' And I picked it up and turned towards the companionway.

'No.' He had risen, too. 'It is all the property of the Greek Government.'

'Balls!' I said. 'It belongs to a man called Borg, who's a crook anyway.' I tossed the necklace on to the table in front of him and then I went for'ard, to where I had pulled up part of the cabin sole, and brought up two more packages, putting them on the table in front of him. 'You open those, while I get the rest.' I could hear him removing the polythene covering as I went for'ard again. When I came back into the saloon, he was carefully unwrapping a drinking-cup of the same beaten gold from its cocoon of cotton wool. His eyes were bright, the cigarette in his mouth burning unheeded, and as he pulled the last of the cotton wool away and the goblet-shaped cup lay gleaming, he picked it up in both his hands. That was when I hit him—in the belly first, and then a short jab to the jaw. He sagged, his eyes wide and surprised, his long face looking longer and blood welling where his lip was cut.

He slumped across the table and I pushed him back on to the settee berth. He sprawled there slackly, and he hadn't got a gun. I fetched a morphine ampoule from the medicine chest and injected him in the arm the way I had injected Bert, and then I went on deck for some rope. He was still out when I returned. I put a clove hitch round his wrists and ankles, tied the rope round his waist and then slipped the little gold necklace into his pocket. At least it would be something.

After that there was a lot to do and I worked fast, coiling the long nylon anchor line into the dinghy and rowing with it across to the unlit buoy. It was night now, the sky studded with stars, the water black. I tied the end of the line to the eye on top of the buoy and hauled myself back to the boat. I tried winching her off without the engine first. I was scared of getting the line wrapped round the prop. But she wouldn't come. Even with the engine astern on full revs she didn't budge, and I stood there, sweating, the deck pounding under the soles of my feet and the line to the buoy stretched so taut it was like a thread. I thought for a moment I'd have to lighten her by pumping fresh water over the side, but then, suddenly, the flashing light of the fairway buoy was swinging towards the bows and I slammed the gear lever into neutral, running aft and hauling in the slack as she drifted stern-on towards the buoy. Then I snubbed the line on a cleat, made fast and left her to ride there by the stern while I dealt with Kotiadis.

He was heavier than I thought, and I had trouble lowering him into the dinghy. It seemed a long row to the low island with the redoubt, and the mud and the slimy stones of the bank made it difficult to get him ashore. I slipped the rope free of him and left him there, rowing wearily for the buoy. And then I found the knot had been drawn so tight I couldn't undo it. I seemed to be struggling with it for hours, the sweat dying cold on my body and my knees trembling with exhaustion. But at last I managed to free it and then it was only a matter of a few yards to the stern of the boat.

I clambered back on board, made the dinghy fast and stood for a moment in the wheelhouse, alone at last and trembling. The quickest way to clear Greek territorial waters was to head up the Canal past the port of Levkas and out by the northern entrance. West from there it was all open sea. But the Canal was unlit, and though I had been down it once in daylight, I didn't dare risk it, and there was always the chance, with an emergency on, that they would be checking all boats. Reluctantly I turned *Coromandel*'s bows south and headed for the double line of red and green lights that marked the dredged channel.

It was 21.38 when I passed between the last set of lights. I was shivering by then and I switched to automatic pilot and went below to put on shirt and trousers and a sweater. Until that moment I had been too concerned with getting rid of Kotiadis to think about what I should do when I had the boat to myself. I went back up to the wheelhouse and got out Chart 203. Going south round the island of Levkas meant passing back through the Meganisi Channel. It was 12 miles to the point where we had been anchored and I had made that dive, another 10 miles to Cape Dukato, the south-western tip of Levkas. Say three hours if I could maintain maximum speed of 8 knots in unlit waters. And then I was measuring off the distance to Cape Aterra, the north-westernmost point of Cephalonia. From the Meganisi Channel, it was 23 miles on a course of 225°. I could be there by 02.30 with almost two hours of darkness to spare, and I should then be that much further on my way to Africa.

I checked the course and went below to get myself a meal. By the time I had finished it, Point Kephali was astern and I could just see the eight-second double flash of the light on Meganisi's Elia Point fine on the port bow. I made some coffee then, put it in a flask and took it up to the wheelhouse. And after that I had no time for anything but navigation, for there was no moon, only starlight, and I was dependent on exact courses to clear the islands and shoals to the north of the Meganisi Channel. Shortly after 22.00 navigation lights passed me steaming north and I wondered whether Kotiadis would be conscious enough by the time that caique entered the canal to attract its attention. By then I could see the dark outline of Sparti through the glasses, and a quarter of an hour later I was passing Skropio, thinking of the Barretts, wondering how they would feel if they knew their beloved boat was thundering past them, out of their lives.

But I couldn't help it. I couldn't help any of the things that had happened. It was all part of the pattern that had started way back in the house in Amsterdam. I could only bless them that they had a boat with fuel tanks that gave a range of over 3,000 miles, and those tanks three-quarters full. And then I was into the Meganisi Channel, the bulk of Tiglia just visible and the sound of the engine beating back from the rocks on either side. I was thinking of the old man then, our two lives meeting for the last time in the dreadful interior of that cave—the red bull and Holroyd's body floating up through that blow-hole. My hands were shaking, the palms wet with sweat, and I prayed. Prayed that he had died quietly, that he was at peace now.

I couldn't see the gut where Pappadimas had landed me, or the overhang. The steep slopes rising to Mount Porro were one dark mass. But I saw the end of the promontory, the open sea beyond, and with a feeling of relief I turned on to 225° and switched to automatic. I thought he was lucky in a way. Lucky to have found what he had been searching for and to die there in the certainty that he was right, his theory proved at least to his own satisfaction.

I was drinking coffee then, smoking a cigarette, my hands still trembling. He was dead, and I was still alive—his violence, his restlessness, still living in me. At dawn I should be alone, with nothing between me and the Libyan coast but 300 miles of open sea. I could turn west then, to the Messina Straits—

North Africa or Spain. Or I could turn south. I thought I'd turn south, and then east along the Libyan coast—Beirut probably. If he were right—if we were going to destroy ourselves—better to be at the centre of it than die on the periphery by remote control.

I switched on the radio, but all I could get was music and the voices of men talking in languages I did not understand. The night had become very dark, no stars now and my world reduced to the dim-lit area of the wheelhouse. Shortly after midnight I picked up Guiscard light on the north end of Cephalonia. In two hours I should be clear of Greek waters—free and on my own. I felt the blood stirring in my veins, and I left the boat to steer herself while I got myself a drink.

Down below, in the saloon, the golden gleam of the goblet Kotiadis had been fondling caught my eye. I remembered a cardboard box Florrie had discarded. I got it from her cabin, a blue box with the name of a boutique—Asteris—and underneath: *Souvenir of Rodos*. It had contained a mug she had bought for the boat and I packed the goblet into it, bedding the priceless piece of beaten gold in cotton wool. Somewhere, some time, I would post it to them—a souvenir of the voyage. And then I sat there, smoking a cigarette and smiling to myself, amused at the thought of Bert telling somebody else what a kind, generous man Borg was.

Later, much later, the dawn broke, spilling pink across the sky. I was on deck then, tired and bleary-eyed with lack of sleep, watching as the last of Greece faded away astern, the mountains of Cephalonia a dark cloud-capped rampart low on the horizon. The sea was flat calm, no breath of wind touching the surface, and there was no ship anywhere in sight. I watched as the clouds were edged with gold and the sun rose above them, a great burning orb, and then I swung the wheel over and turned the bows to the south.

AUTHOR'S NOTE

UNLIKE most of my novels, *Levkas Man* is not the result of any one particular journey. It has, in fact, been gradually taking shape in my mind over the years, and during that time a number of quite unrelated experiences have contributed to its growth. The first of these occurred more than a decade ago when F. T. Smith, then my editor at Collins, in a mood of great excitement, talked to me for over an hour about the astonishing discoveries made by a Dr Leakey in Africa. From that moment I became fascinated by the search for the origins of our species.

In 1963 my father died and the sad experience of going through his home and dealing with the relics of a lifetime was one that I felt many people must have suffered. That same year my wife and I had sailed our boat down to Malta with the object of exploring the Eastern Mediterranean. Two years later, knowing of my interest in early man and that we were planning to sail in the Ionian Islands off the west coast of Greece, Alfred Knopf, my American publisher, sent me a cutting from the *Christian Science Monitor* about a cave-shelter discovered by a Cambridge palæontologist, E. S. Higgs, not far from the Greek-Albanian border. We visited this cave-shelter and saw his team at work on it. We also dropped our anchor in all the ports and coves of Levkas and the neighbouring islands, and in 1967 explored the volcanic area of the Central Mediterranean fault—the Lipari and Pontine islands, including Vulcano and Stromboli, and south from Sicily to that extraordinary laval heap, Pantelleria.

But I think the most dramatic of all the experiences that have contributed to the atmosphere of the book was a visit we paid in 1968-69 to the Dordogne and Vézère cave-shelters in France, and here I have to acknowledge my debt to the French authorities for permitting us to examine the cave paintings at Lascaux; the cave remains officially closed, except for scientific study. Here I was very fortunate in having Jacques Marsal as my guide. It was he who discovered the cave paintings with three young companions in 1940.

This, then, is the raw material out of which, over the years, *Levkas Man* has gradually grown. The theories upon which it is based are academic, and here I would like to acknowledge the kindly and constructive help I received from Eric S. Wood. For the purposes of my story I have taken some liberties with geology and with the placing of the various cave-shelters; none with the settings, all of which I have personally explored. The red dunes do exist; they were shown to me by E. S. Higgs.

HAMMOND INNES

Kersey—1970

ACKNOWLEDGEMENTS

The author has quoted from the following works: Raymond Dart: *Adventures with the Missing Link* (Hamish Hamilton); Kenneth Oakley: *Frameworks for Dating Fossil Man* (Weidenfeld and Nicolson); W. J. Turner: lines from 'The Caves of Auvergne', which appears in *Modern Poets*, ed. J. C. Squire (Martin Secker). The author is also indebted to many other source books, including of course Robert Ardrey's *African Genesis*.

CORFU

Despotiko (cave shelter)

Jannina

Ayios Giorgios
The Red Dunes

PAXOS

Arta

Nikopolis

Amvrakikos
Gulf

Preveza

Levkas

LEVKAS

MEGANISI

ARKUDI

ATOKO

Missolonghi Navpaktos

ITHACA

Cape Aterra

CEPHALONIA

Gulf of Patras

The Narrows

Patras

ZANTE

Katakolon

Vasse

Navarino Bay

Pylos

Methoni